W9-CMA-139

Praise for Zoë Sharp and her Charlie Fox thrillers!

"Sharp is part of a very small group of writers who actually talks the talk and walks the walk. She really knows this stuff and so when she writes, it feels more real than most non-fiction books. Sharp deserves a genre all her own. . . . [If] you are just discovering Zoe Sharp, then you are in for a real treat."
—Jon Jordan, *Crimespree Magazine*

"As action-packed and streamlined as the Suzuki the main character, a self-defense expert, rides. Zoë Sharp has an apt last name. She delivers yet another sleek, sharp thriller."
—David Morrell, best-selling author of *First Blood* and *The Shimmer*

"Charlotte (Charlie) Fox is one of the most vivid and engaging heroines ever to swagger onto the pages of a book. Where Charlie goes, thrills follow, and in *Killer Instinct*, Zoë Sharp keeps them coming hard and fast."
—Tess Gerritsen, best-selling author of *Ice Cold*

"If you're looking for an author who can deliver high-octane thrills every time and a character who is NOT to be messed with, you've found them. Zoë Sharp and Charlie Fox *both* kick ass."
—Mark Billingham, best-selling author of *Death Message*

"Anyone with a brain wants Charlie Fox for the girl next door. Funny, compassionate, and with moves that can—and do—kill, Charlie is the indelible creation of the remarkable Zoë Sharp. A kick-ass great read, *Killer Instinct* debuts Charlie in a tale of greed and lust that will keep you riveted from page one."
—Gayle Lynds, best-selling author of *The Book of Spies*

"Charlie Fox is tough, compassionate, and kicks ass to protect others— how could anyone not love her? Zoë Sharp is a master at writing thoughtful action thrillers, and *Killer Instinct* is no exception. Read it!"
—Meg Gardiner, Edgar Award-winning author of *The Liar's Lullaby*

"If you only know Charlie Fox from *First Drop*, *Second Shot*, and *Third Strike*, you don't know Charlie. What you've got in your hands is a rare and special treat. It's like finding some lost Jack Reacher novel or a couple of non-alphabet Kinsey Milhones that nobody knew existed. Don't let anyone tear it from your hands without drawing their blood. These early Zoë Sharp books haven't been a secret, but they've been harder-to-get than Charlie Fox in your bed. Think of these as the early years of Charlie Fox—she's lethal and relentless, but still raw from the military experience that made her the kick-ass, take-no-prisoners bodyguard that she's become. But there's more going on in these books than breakneck action and adventure. Charlie has heart, maybe too much for a woman in her profession . . . and it's that caring, that humanity, that makes her much more than a killer babe on a motorbike. These books are your chance to discover Charlie Fox as she discovers herself, her strengths and her weaknesses, and sustains the scars to her body and soul that make her such a unique and compelling character."

—Lee Goldberg, award-winning author of the *Monk* mysteries

By Zoë Sharp

Charlie Fox thrillers

KILLER INSTINCT

Zoë Sharp

Busted Flush Press
Houston 2010

Killer Instinct
A Busted Flush Press paperback original.

Originally published in 2001 by Piatkus (UK).
This edition, Busted Flush Press, 2010

Cover design: Lisa Novak
Cover photo: City scene © iStockphoto / Anna Dudko
Cover photo: Motorcycle © iStockphoto / Scott Hirko

ISBN: 978-1-935415-13-8
First Busted Flush Press paperback printing, May 2010

BUSTED FLUSH
PRESS

P.O. Box 540594
Houston, TX 77254-0594
www.bustedflushpress.com

Acknowledgements

First of all, I have to thank those people who patiently let me pick their brains; especially PC Michael Wilkinson for his inside information on police procedure; James for filling me in on what really happens behind club doors; Ian 'this won't hurt' Cottam and Lee Watkin for teaching me the basics of self-defence; Colin and Jane Greenhalgh for their extensive bar experience; and remedial therapist Wendy Seabrook. Any mistakes are strictly by my own introduction.

A few people trawled through the initial drafts and pointed out the major plot-holes. My grateful thanks for this dedication go to Peter Doleman, Claire Duplock, Sarah Harrison, Tim Winfield, and all the members of the Lune Valley Writers' Group, particularly Clive Hopwood, whose criticisms were the most painful, but the most accurate. You were all brilliant.

The biggest 'thank you's of all belong to my husband, Andy, who has suffered with me all the way; to Derek and Jill for encouraging me to write in the first place; to the staff at Piatkus Books who first gave me a chance; to my gracious copyeditor Sarah Abel; to David Thompson at Busted Flush Press, who has taken Charlie under his wing, and Lisa Novak who came up with the eye-catching new covers. And, of course, to my agent, Jane Gregory, and all the team at Gregory & Company.

Lastly my grateful thanks to the inimitable Lee Child, for being such a big supporter of my work and all-round nice guy.

Foreword
by Lee Child

I WAS ON tour in the UK in the spring of 2002, for my sixth novel, and at the end of one of the events a woman came up to me and told me she loved my books, which is always a wonderful thing to hear. I responded happily—believe me, no forced politeness is ever required on such occasions—and then she said, "But Zoë Sharp is better."

Naturally I asked, "Are you Zoë's mom?"

She denied any family connection, and I filed the name away, because at heart I'm a reader, not a writer, and if a well-read fan offers a recommendation, I take it seriously. I write only one book a year, after all, but I read hundreds, and life is too short for bad books. Rushing from place to place on tour didn't give me time to go shopping, but fortunately free books are a currency in the publishing trade, so I had my publicist call Zoë's publicist, and within a day a copy of *Killer Instinct* was biked over to my next stop, and I read it in short order.

And was very impressed.

Triply impressed, actually. Firstly, because apart from anything else, this was a debut novel, and there was nothing shy or tentative about it, and it waded straight in and tackled—secondly and thirdly—two huge challenges. Some things are just very, very difficult to do, because of the weight of cultural heritage and tradition and the limits set by others' prior failures—but Zoë had gone right ahead and done them very successfully. (Full disclosure: Obviously I had never met Zoë at that point; knowing her as I now do, if I see her tackling a challenge, I get the body bag ready—for the challenge.)

The first challenge she beat was the difficulty of creating a truly convincing tough-girl protagonist. It shouldn't be difficult, but it is. (Don't get me—or Zoë—started on the legacy left by two centuries of sexism in our culture.) But Charlie Fox came across as real, true, and authentic. She wasn't like anyone I knew—which to me is the point of thrillers: I don't want to read about people like the ones I know—but she was someone I would want to know, and she felt like she could show up around the next corner. She wasn't over-explained; her backstory was sketchy . . . above all, she didn't seem invented. She just was.

The second challenge Zoë beat was to make an obscure and provincial place—in this case Lancaster, in North West England—seem convincingly dangerous. None of us has a problem believing New York City or Chicago or L.A. are jungles, but almost no writers can make a smaller location tough without a few winces and a lot of suspension of disbelief along the way. But Zoë did. As it happened, I knew Lancaster fairly well—I lived near it for seven years—and she wrote it like I felt it.

So, two big challenges easily defeated in a debut novel. Triply impressive. The next day I asked my publicist to call for Zoë's second book, which was just out. I read it—and it was just as good. I have been a big fan ever since.

Lee Child was fired and on the dole when he hatched a harebrained scheme to write a bestselling novel, thus saving his family from ruin. Killing Floor *went on to win worldwide acclaim. The hero of his series, Jack Reacher, besides being fictional, is a kind-hearted soul who allows Lee lots of spare time for reading, listening to music, and the Yankees. Visit Lee online at www.leechild.com.*

One

I SUPPOSE I ought to state for the record that I don't make a habit of frequenting places like the New Adelphi Club, which is where this whole sorry mess began. Maybe if I'd run true to form and avoided the place, things might have turned out differently.

The New Adelphi was a nightclub that had risen phoenix-like from the ashes of the old Adelphi, a crumbling Victorian seaside hotel on the promenade in Morecambe. It had a slightly faded air of decayed gentility about it, like an ageing bit-part film actress, hiding her propensity for the gin bottle under paste jewellery and heavy make-up.

I should have seen the changes coming, of course. Over the last eight months the Adelphi has had 'under new management' written all over it. The first inkling of a revolution had been a line of skips along the front wall of the car park. The next, a sheepish visit from Gary Bignold, the assistant manager, to tell me that I no longer had use of one of the upstairs function rooms for my Tuesday night class.

'Sorry, Charlie,' he'd said awkwardly as he'd broken the news. 'We've got a new boss man and he's sweeping clean. He's decided that making a few quid every week so you can teach a load of frumpy housewives how to slap down flashers in the park just doesn't fit in with his game plan.'

I teach women's self-defence, have done for four years now. I use gymnasiums in local schools, indoor badminton courts in leisure centres, and even the converted ballroom of a country house that's now a women's refuge. Finding a replacement venue for this class wasn't going to be impossible, but it wasn't going to be a piece of cake either. I thought regretfully of the lost revenue, and shrugged.

'Don't knock it 'til you've tried it,' I said. He'd caught up with me in the car park, near the skips. I was packing my jogging pants and trainers into the tank bag of my RGV 250 Suzuki for the ride home to Lancaster, only five miles or so away.

Gary hovered from one foot to the other until I'd double-zipped the bag and clipped it down. 'So what's happening to the old place then?' I asked, tucking my scarf round the neck of my leather jacket. 'They going to pull it down and build yet more luxury flats that nobody wants?'

'Nah, this new bloke, he's dead switched on,' Gary said, relieved enough to be chatty. 'He's going to turn this old dump into a nightclub. I've seen the plans. It's going to be absolutely excellent. Couple of bars, split-level dance floors, bit of food. The business. You'll have to come. Opening night. I'll get you in free, no trouble.'

I raised an eyebrow and he looked hurt at my scepticism. 'I will,' he repeated. 'I'm going to run the bars for him. It's all been agreed.'

I didn't say anything as I swung my leg over the bike and kicked it into life. Gary sometimes lets his enthusiasm run away with him. He looks too wide-eyed to ever be put in charge of anything more than asking the next person in line if they want fries with that.

I gave him a cheery wave as I circled out of the car park, ignoring his shouted assurance that he'd give me a call when they were about to re-launch.

It's a good job I wasn't holding my breath.

The New Adelphi Club opened about six months afterwards, just after Christmas. In record time if the murmurs in the building trade are to be believed. It seemed Gary had been right about the new boss being a mover and shaker.

At night the neon on the outside of the building lights up low cloud with an eerie violet glow and is visible from halfway across Morecambe Bay. It's become quite a local landmark.

I learned from the local paper that Gary did, indeed, become the bar manager for the new enterprise, but he never called to offer me those free tickets. I must admit I hadn't really expected him to.

It came as quite a surprise to myself, then, that I ended up at the place only a month or so after it opened.

That was my friend, Clare's fault, not mine. She'd dropped it on me over the phone a few days before. 'There's this karaoke competition on at that new club in Morecambe this Saturday,' she'd said, out of the blue. 'I fancied giving it a whirl, but Jacob won't go, so will you come along and lend some moral support?'

I hesitated. Clare's a mate. I've known her and her feller, Jacob, ever since I first moved to Lancaster, but I thought such a request was stretching a friendship too far. 'I didn't know you were into that sort of thing,' I said cautiously, playing for time.

She laughed. 'Well, Jacob says I haven't much of a voice. He says my strangled mewlings make the nocturnal warbling of our elderly tomcat sound like Pavarotti, but I reckon he's just too much of an old fogey to want to go to a nightclub.'

I vaguely heard rude mutterings by someone at the same end of the line as Clare, and she laughed again. Jacob must be in his early fifties, his dark wavy hair streaked through with grey, but he's one of those men who oozes sexual attraction. Always laughing behind eyes the colour of expensive plain chocolate, and just as tempting. If he could reproduce that kind of chemistry in a lab he'd be a millionaire.

Clare is twenty-five years his junior, more my own age. Tall, slender, she has endless legs and a metabolism that means she can binge peanut butter straight out of the jar without putting on an ounce. I recognised years ago that food was not going to be one of my indulgences in life if I wanted to stay in a size twelve.

I envied Clare the ability not to gain weight more than I envied her her looks, which were stunning. She had long straight hair to go with the legs, golden blonde without bottled assistance, and a sense of style I guess you just have to be born with.

She also rode a ten-year-old Ducati 851 Strada motorcycle like a demon and had the distinction of once having outrun a bike copper through the local Scarthwaite bends at well over a hundred. He'd pulled her over out of curiosity and his chin had bounced off his toecaps when she'd taken off her helmet. Where anyone else would have had their licence taken away for three months, she didn't even get a producer.

'So, Charlie, what do you say?' Clare prompted now. 'I don't really want to go by myself,' she admitted.

I heard Jacob in the background again, loudly this time. 'You're not going alone until they've caught that bloody rapist!'

'Yeah, that too,' Clare said. 'You've heard about that, I suppose?'

I agreed that I had. It was a vicious attack that had only happened a few weeks previously. I'm not the morbid type, but I took a professional interest in the crime. Enough to keep tabs on the progress—or lack of it—in the news reports.

When you make your living teaching people, mainly women, how to avoid potentially ending up in the same situation, you tend to notice anything that affects business. When new pupils turn up at my classes with a sudden burning desire to learn how to reduce a large, hairy would-be mugger to a jellied heap on the pavement, you tend to ask what sparked off their interest. You don't come out of it looking too good if you haven't heard all about the latest stabbing, rape, or murder. Particularly if it took place on your own doorstep.

In this case, the victim was just turned eighteen, walking home along a gloomy footpath near the River Lune late one Thursday night and not smart enough to take a taxi. When she'd regained consciousness two days later she was only able to give a hazy description of her attacker.

He'd raped her with a knife held at her throat, then beat her savagely around the head. The police announced piously that it was a miracle she wasn't dead. As it was, the doctors predicted that she was going to need months of physio, speech therapy, and counselling. The surgeons had managed, after a fashion, to save her right eye.

Lancaster may have its share of violence, but it's still not the kind of town where things like that happen on a regular basis. The local paper was having a field day with tabloid-style headlines it never normally got to air. Public figures expressed their outrage. Worried citizens wrote to their MP.

Prominent policemen promised early results. It was a brutal and senseless attack, their spokesman said. The culprit must have been covered in his victim's blood. He must have been spotted arriving or leaving along the busy main road which shadows the river. He must have got home in a dishevelled and excited state. He would, they prophesied, soon be under lock and key.

As it was, several weeks had now gone past. Nothing happened. Appeals were made on the television and would-be witnesses obligingly came forward by the dozen. Unfortunately, none of them had anything of real value to tell. It appeared that the only witness of any sort was a derelict wino called Jimmy.

Jimmy thought he might have seen a car, and he even thought it might have been on that evening, but through the fog of his perpetual alcoholic stupor, he couldn't quite recall the registration number. Or the model. Or the colour.

There was an air of fear in the city that you could almost reach out and touch. I'd noticed it in my students, seen it on the street. Even over the distortion of the telephone system I could hear it now in Clare's voice—and in Jacob's, too.

I sighed.

'OK,' I said. 'I'll come with you. Just don't expect me to sing!'

Which was how, a few days later, I came to be waiting for Clare in the car park of the New Adelphi Club, twiddling my thumbs and rapidly having second thoughts about the whole exercise.

It was partly because the noise level belting out of the place was so high I feared permanent hearing damage if I ventured any closer. The bass could be physically felt across the other side of the tarmac. I could well imagine that at closer proximity the high frequency would qualify as an offensive weapon.

In the ten minutes or so since I'd parked up and sat, watching people arrive and go in, I'd come to the conclusion that I was probably ten years too old to be there, which made most of the clientele too young to buy cigarettes, never mind alcohol. Also, in a clean pair of black jeans, an almost-ironed shirt, and my least tatty leather jacket, I was wearing way too many clothes.

Despite the chill of the evening—it was February, after all—the boys were all wearing tight little vests that showed off how many hours they'd spent down the gym, or untucked luridly coloured shirts that tried to hide the fact they didn't know where the gym was. The girls looked like they'd come out in their night-dresses. God, I felt old.

A new set of lights swept into the car park, and Jacob's rusty old cream Range Rover pulled up next to where I'd parked the bike. Clare waved through the window as she killed the motor and hopped down out of the driver's seat.

'Hi,' I said. I nodded to the car. 'I thought for a moment Jacob had changed his mind about coming.'

'Oh no,' she replied with a little grimace. 'He drew the line at just lending me the car.'

I eyed the skimpy little frock Clare was nearly wearing as I dumped my helmet on the Range Rover's back seat. 'The way you're dressed I won't ask why you didn't come on the bike.'

She looked down at herself with a wry smile. 'It would have been cold, wouldn't it?' she agreed, then nudged my arm. 'Come on, Charlie, lighten up.'

'Lighten up? You'll be beating them off with a shitty stick looking like that and I'm the one Jacob's relying on to get you home in one piece,' I grouched. In view of her glam appearance I tried to do something with my untidy mop of pale reddish blonde hair, but it spent too much of its time stuffed under an Arai bike helmet to pretend to have a style now.

She grinned at me again. 'Don't worry, if we walk in holding hands they'll all just assume we're gay.'

'Yeah,' I said sourly, 'and I don't have to ask which one of us they'll think is butch.'

Clare locked the Range Rover's door and linked her arm through mine. 'Well,' she said, a smile dimpling her lovely face, 'we should both be safe then, hm?'

To start with, we nearly didn't get into the New Adelphi Club at all. Gary's new boss man had employed some very useful-looking door staff. Two big guys I didn't recognise, which came as a bit of a surprise really, when I think about it. I thought I knew all the local hardcases.

Clare didn't have a problem. They waved her through staring at her legs so hard that afterwards I doubt they would have been able to pick her face out of a line-up.

I didn't merit such appreciation. I just got an arm like a steel girder across my path as one of them grabbed hold of the front of my jacket.

'Oi, can't you read?' he demanded. He jerked his head to the six-inch square sign half-hidden behind him on the wall, which was headed 'Dress Code'. 'No leather jackets and no denims!' he stated, stabbing a finger at the appropriate lines. God knows what he would have done if he'd known about the Swiss Army knife I always kept as an emergency tool kit in my jacket pocket.

I looked down at the meaty fist screwing up the leather. He had gold sovereign rings on three out of four fingers and a blurred blue tattoo disappearing up his wrist into the sleeve of his dinner jacket. It reappeared again over the top of his shirt collar, an indecipherable squiggle just to one side of the knot of his clip-on bow tie.

I couldn't help getting the feeling that if Clare and I had been dressed the other way round, she probably would have still walked straight in, but now wasn't the time to lose my rag. I always have the greatest respect for someone whose pain threshold allows a tattooist to stick so many needles into their neck.

'How about you let go of me and we'll start this again?' I said, keeping my voice reasonable.

'How about you just fuck off and come back when you're properly dressed?' he sneered, shoving me backwards half a step.

'How about you learn to pick up your teeth with broken fingers?' I shot back. He was pissing me off big time, and this was not professional behaviour. He was muscle and menace, not the right material for working the door. They should have kept him in a cage somewhere until they needed real trouble sorting out. I didn't think I qualified for the strong-arm tactics straight off.

'Hey, what's going on? You causing problems already, Charlie?'

We both turned, which is not easy when you've got someone practically lifting your feet off the floor.

It was Gary. He was wearing a white dinner jacket to distinguish himself from the underlings, and trying to look like Humphrey Bogart in *Casablanca*. I don't think he quite pulled it off.

'It's all right, Len,' he said. 'Charlie Fox is OK. I know her. What's the problem?'

The doorman slowly, and with great reluctance, uncurled his fingers from my jacket and put me down. 'She's not properly dressed,' he muttered, a bully caught in the act by one of the teachers. He didn't quite shuffle his feet, but he came pretty close to it.

Gary gave me a studied glance. 'That's about as properly dressed as she gets,' he said, flashing a quick smile. 'I think we can bend the rules about the jeans just this once, but the boss man's in tonight so you'll have to lose the jacket,' he told me apologetically. 'I'll check it for you.'

I shrugged out of my jacket and let him hand it over to the cloakroom staff. Len stood and glared at me like a lion that hasn't made a kill for weeks and who's just been whipped back from a freshly slaughtered antelope.

The other doorman was also dressed in a dinner suit, and sporting that comedy blend of joined beard and moustache that just circled his mouth. The rest of his head was shaved smooth of hair. Both of them were wearing walkie-talkies with clip-on mics and earpieces. Curly wires disappeared under their jacket collars.

The bald doorman had been leaning against the wall during the whole exchange. His only energy expenditure was to chew gum. He made no moves to get involved on either side. Now he grinned at me slyly as Clare and I passed through into the bowels of the club. It made my scalp itch.

'You'll have to tell me what you think of the place now it's been re-done,' Gary yelled down my ear over the thunderous beat of the music.

The narrow entrance way had opened out into the club proper. It had changed so much since I'd last been inside the old Adelphi that if it hadn't been for the unaltered façade I'd have thought they'd pulled the whole place down and started again.

We'd come out on what was now the first level, overlooking the basement dance floor. I looked up and saw the cellars weren't the only thing that had become open plan. The ceilings of the next two floors up had been partially dismantled, revealing bars and more dance floors. I didn't want to be impressed, but I couldn't help it.

Clare and I fought our way through the crush to one of the bars on the next level up where Gary gave us both a drink on the house. The full extent of his generosity became apparent when I looked at the prices, even though Clare just had a glass of dry white wine and I stuck to mineral water.

'So, when's the karaoke start?' Clare asked him, leaning close so he could hear her over the din.

'Oh you're going to have a bash at that are you?' he said, preening under the attention. Like most fellers he had to look up slightly to make straight eye contact with Clare. Particularly when she was wearing four-inch heels. 'That's terrific,' he told her. 'To be honest, it's been a bit slow to take off. The girl who's won it the last three Saturdays in a row isn't much cop, but she's got enthusiasm. The crowd seem to like her.'

He offered to take us up to the smaller dance floor where the contest was taking place and introduce Clare to the DJ who was in charge of it. 'Dave Clemmens is a scream,' he said. 'Just tell him what you want to sing and he'll look after you. No trouble.'

We followed him deeper into the club, up a winding spiral staircase. Out of habit I checked out the nearest exits as we went. Dave the DJ held court at one side of the raised stage area on the other side of the floor. Gary guided Clare across with his hand resting lightly on the small of her back. I was deemed strong enough to make my own way there unaided.

Dave was another of those blokes who obviously spent more time admiring himself in the mirrors down at the gym than he did slouched in front of the TV at home. He'd worked hard on the vanity muscle groups, emphasising his biceps and pecs.

As Gary introduced us to him, his eyes flickered from Clare's face down her body to her legs and back again, with a slow smile forming on his lips as he offered her his hand.

'Delighted, Clare,' he said, holding on to her fingers slightly longer than was necessary. Clare gave him the sunny smile of someone who's used to eliciting such a response from men.

The stare he treated me to was less driven by lust, more by curiosity. I could see him playing mix and match with the relationship between the two of us. Frankly, I didn't much care what combination he finally came up with.

He soon switched his attention back and started asking a few questions about Clare's background. Had she sung before? Had she entered a competition like this before? She answered them all easily enough, leaning forward to talk to him. 'So where are you from, Clare?' Dave asked now, scribbling notes on a pad balanced in front of him. His other hand worked the controls of the deck with the sureness of long familiarity.

'I live near Caton village, just the other side of Lancaster,' she said.

'Uh-huh, and what's your phone number?' It was tagged so neatly onto the back of the other questions that Clare nearly fell for it, opening her mouth to speak, then closing it again quickly. She shook her head with a smile and wagged her finger at him.

'Ah well,' he said, 'you can't blame me for trying.' He checked the list on his pad. 'You'll be up last, but there's only eight tonight, so don't stray too far. If your friend wants to stay about here she'll get the best view.' He put just enough emphasis on the word friend to give it a whole host of meanings.

I smiled sweetly at him and said nothing.

He shrugged, reaching for his microphone. 'OK, ladies and gents, this is what you've been waiting for! Another chance to hear the least-talented people in the area step up to the mic and make arse-holes of themselves!'

I was surprised at the intro and didn't try to hide it. Dave grinned at my reaction.

'OK, first up, as always is the reigning champion from last week. Where is she? There she is, can't carry a tune in a bucket, but what she lacks in being musical, she makes up for in volume and guts. Step up to the mic, Susie Hollins!'

Despite this remarkable lead-in, the girl who scrambled up onto the stage was flushed with excitement rather than anger. She was pretty in a conventional sort of way, medium height, blonde streaks running through naturally dark hair, and a blouse that went see-through enough under the artificial lights to show the generous cut of her bra.

There was something vaguely familiar about her that I couldn't place. Funny how you can never recognise someone out of context. I frowned while I dredged through my memory files, but came up empty.

Now, Susie stood fiddling with the microphone and primly adjusted her micro-length skirt as Dave gave his spiel about her.

'You all know Susie. She works behind the meat counter at our local supermarket, and she can weigh out my sausages any time! She's here tonight as usual with Tony—give us a wave, Tone—there he is! Got your own groupie, haven't you, Sue? Mind you, with a voice like this, she needs all the help she can get. Give it up now, ladies and gents, for Susie Hollins!'

Susie launched straight into her number with plenty of gusto, but Dave was right. She did need a watertight container to carry the tune. She didn't have the range to hit the high notes, or the breath control for the phrasing of the song.

Still, you had to hand it to her, she was up there giving it her all, and the crowd were cheering her on. Or maybe they were just trying to drown out the sound of her voice.

One thing was for certain, though. Susie Hollins may have been no great shakes as a karaoke singer, but I didn't think that was reason enough for anyone to want to kill her.

Two

SUSIE FINISHED HER song, bright-eyed and breathless. Dave shook his head at the reception she got, including a very possessive kiss from Tony. He'd elbowed his way to the front of the crowd while she'd been doing her bit. The way he dived on her mouth the moment she hopped off the stage was like a brand.

Tony was short and stocky, with eyebrows that met in the middle over the bridge of his nose. He looked thick as a brick. He was also well on the way to being plastered, and as he pushed his way up to speak to Dave, I carefully stepped back and gave him room.

'We'll be at the bar when you need us,' he told Dave arrogantly, one arm draped round Susie's shoulders.

Dave replied with a quick gesture of fingers to forehead that could almost have been taken as a salute. Judging by the wink he gave me, it was more likely to have meant 'dickhead'. Tony didn't seem to notice. He steered Susie away and they swaggered across the dance floor.

The contestants that followed demonstrated clearly why Susie had won so often and so easily. In the kingdom of the blind, she was definitely the one with the monocular vision.

Seventh up was a spotty teenager who clearly thought he was a star in the making. 'There you go, ladies and gents,' Dave commented as he left the stage, 'perfect boy band material if ever I saw it—can't sing and can't dance, but I wouldn't be surprised if he had a recording contract before the night is out.'

There was general laughter and he paused to nod to Clare. She smiled nervously, clutched quickly at my hand, and was up on the stage. There were a few whistles of appreciation which Dave waved into silence.

'Yeah, yeah, I know, but settle down, boys. This is Clare Elliot, and it's her first time up here on karaoke night at the New Adelphi Club, so go easy on her, OK?' There were raucous shouts at that and Dave grinned at them. 'Clare's an accounts secretary for the local paper, lives in Caton, and—sorry to disappoint you, boys—but she's already spoken for.' He looked at me as he said that. I held his gaze levelly and gave it back to him without additions or subtractions.

'So, here she is, and even if she turns out to be as tone-deaf as the rest of you lot, at least you can put your fingers in your ears and enjoy looking at her. Give it up now for Clare Elliot!'

As the cheers died down I realised that I'd no idea what song Clare had chosen. It took me a couple of beats of the introduction before I recognised 'Cry Me A River'. Clare paused a fraction to gather herself, then closed her eyes and started to sing.

Life's a bitch, isn't it? Not only had Clare been front of the line when looks and brains were handed out, but she'd been right up there in the queue for vocals as well.

The familiar words of the song came out clear and powerful, raising the hairs on the back of my neck. To begin with there was a stunned silence. By the time Clare reached the first chorus it was obvious she was far and away the best there.

I felt someone jostle my arm and glanced sideways to find Tony had returned from the bar, dragging a disgruntled-looking Susie with him. He didn't look any more attractive when he was gawping, and her prettiness had disappeared in the face of jealous spite.

'She's a ringer,' Susie swore. 'That bitch is no amateur. They've brought her in just to stop me winning again!' Her voice had that slight slur of someone who's approached the evening's drinking not as the designated driver.

Tony wasn't so good at expressing himself in words, but he managed a couple of things of an earthy nature that only succeeded in making him sound more ignorant than he had before. Susie stood fuming visibly for another half verse, then resorted to violence.

As she launched herself at the stage, Clare stopped singing and gave a squeak of fright. Susie tried to snatch the mic out of her hand. I looked round for security, but there was no sign of anyone near. Even Gary was long gone.

When Clare had asked me for moral support, I didn't think this was quite what she had in mind. I had already started to move when Susie backhanded Clare across the face. Oh shit.

The stage was a couple of feet above the dance floor, which gave her an advantage of superior height. I evened up the odds by bringing Susie back down to my level. I simply grasped hold of one leg, swung her round off her feet, and let go.

She had no idea how to break a fall and she landed, hard, on her backside a couple of metres from the stage, showing her underwear to the world. A space in the club goers appeared magically around her. Everyone backed away to the edges of the floor. It was clear I was going to get an audience rather than any assistance.

I stepped between the two women with my hands spread to placate. 'Come on now, Susie, don't make trouble,' I said. 'Just leave her alone.' I had to give her a chance to back down, otherwise if I damaged her I was going to be neck-deep in trouble.

Susie cursed as she scrambled to her feet. She was quite a bit taller than I was, and she had me easily in weight. My only advantage was complete sobriety and the sort of blacklist of dirty tricks that I definitely don't teach to my pupils.

She came at me again. I stood my ground until she was half a stride away, then ducked under her reaching claws, grabbed, and gave a good twist with some leverage in just the right place. Susie ended up right back where she started. Well, maybe she landed a little harder this time.

She wasn't short of guts, I'll give her that. As fast as she could get back up she was charging me again, like an enraged Spanish bull. I felt like a matador as I fended her off. I noted with mild interest that she travelled further face down, sliding along the polished dance floor on her lavish bosom.

I had time then to look round for back-up, which seemed to be a damned long time coming, in my opinion. I made sure the fourth time Susie went down, she went down more solidly, and stayed down for longer.

She had no special fighting skills, had lost her temper, and was too close to being drunk to work out a decent strategy of attack. I was working round a fairly basic series of aikido throws, using her size and speed against her, but I was getting pretty bored with the game.

This time when she regained an upright position it had finally penetrated that she had to be more careful. She clenched her fist and tried to throw a good old-fashioned right. She couldn't have given me any more warning of the punch if she'd sent me faxed confirmation.

I blocked her easily enough, and caught hold of her arm, circling her wrist to dig in deep with my fingers and thumb on the underside. She bellowed and froze like her muscles had gone into spasm.

I was suddenly aware that I had something of a tiger by the tail. As long as I kept hold of her I was OK. The pain you can inflict using Kyusho-Jitsu pressure point techniques is more than enough to render an opponent immobile. But unless I was prepared to actually knock her out, things were going to get very interesting when I let go.

There was also the possibility that sooner or later Tony was going to come out of his stupor long enough to wade in. I didn't want to have to hold on to Susie, and deck her amorous boyfriend at the same time. Not without either giving or receiving some serious injury. Damn it.

The problem was solved for me by a big man who pushed his way through the crowd. I noticed the way people deferred to him, and stood my ground. Our gaze met over Susie's loudly swearing form and his brow quirked upwards.

He stopped a pace away and took in the scene, not rushing into anything. He was wearing black trousers, expensive enough to drape well as he moved, and a black silk shirt without a collar. His eyes were so pale a colour as to be almost translucent.

'You seem to have everything pretty much under control, but would you like me to take this off your hands?' he enquired politely, inclining his head slightly as he spoke so that it was almost a bow.

'What?' I said, then glanced down as if noticing Susie for the first time. 'Oh, *this?* Well, that would be kind of you,' I smiled, adding with an edge, 'seeing as the security in this place seems to be worse than useless.'

He paused a moment, the merest hint of a smile tugging at the corner of his mouth, then took hold of the back of Susie's neck hard enough to whiten his knuckles, professionally yanking her free arm round and halfway up her back. I relinquished control with some relief.

'Don't go away, I'd like to talk to you,' the man said to me, adding cheerfully to his captive, 'Come on, lady, time to go!' He strode off the dance floor propelling Susie vigorously ahead of him.

I turned back to the stage. Clare was standing with her hands over her face, sobbing.

Tony was glaring furiously. He started forwards as soon as Susie and the man disappeared. I backed off rapidly, but he swept straight past me, muttering, 'The stupid, dozy *bitch*!'

Dave suddenly seemed to recover his powers of speech. 'Hey Tony, looks like Susie really goes for the caveman approach,' he called after him.

Tony spun round, eyes blazing. 'And you can shut up an' all, you dickless little shit!' he yelled at him. 'It's all a bloody fix, anyway!' and he stormed off.

'Oh excuse me! What's the matter, love, haven't you been milked yet?' Dave returned, and laughed. After a brief hesitation, the crowd joined in, but they were laughing to cover their own uneasiness. There was no humour there.

I went and gave Clare a hand down from the stage, finding her trembling. I cut dead Dave's solicitous remark and led her upstairs to one of the quieter bars. I left her at a corner table while I went away and came back with a non-diet soft drink.

'Here, drink this,' I said. 'It's only lemonade, but you need the sugar.'

She took the proffered glass with a shaky smile. 'I thought it was supposed to be brandy for shock?' she managed.

'Yeah, well. For one thing I can't afford brandy in here, and for another I don't think Jacob would appreciate me letting you get nicked for drink driving in his motor on the way home.'

We sat for a few moments in silence while she emptied the glass and set it down. She touched a hand to her face gingerly.

'You're going to have a hell of a black eye in the morning, but the skin isn't broken,' I told her. 'Some decent make-up should cover up the worst of the damage.'

'Thanks,' she said ruefully. Even bruised she still looked glamorous, like someone out of one of those made-for-TV movies about marital abuse.

'How do you do it, Charlie?' she asked suddenly, taking me by surprise.

'Do what?'

'One minute there was this loony grabbing at me, the next she was on her nose on the floor. Every time she came at you, you just knocked her straight back down again. She just came at me so fast I panicked, but you made it look easy. Maybe I should enrol in one of your classes. I could do with knowing how to throw the bad guys lightly over one shoulder.'

'That's only a very small part of what self-defence is all about, Clare, and you know it,' I said hurriedly. 'You are far more likely to be injured if you stand and fight. The best idea is to learn to spot trouble at a distance and then get well out of the way.'

'Yeah,' she said with some asperity, 'like you've just done, you mean?'

I sighed and said nothing. I'd broken my own rules with Susie, and it didn't sit well with me. Once you decide that you have no choice but to fight someone, you have to go in hard and fast and finish it quickly.

If she'd had any sort of training—and any sort of wits about her—I would have had big problems just by messing about with her the way I had done. I'd given her more than enough time to get the measure of me. Time to realise that she had to look past the surface illusion.

To most opponents I don't seem like much of a threat. I just look ordinary. Nondescript shaggy hair, average height, medium build. Most of the time I don't set out with a confrontational stance; that's almost as bad as appearing weak. If you go looking for a fight, you'll probably find one, and you shouldn't be surprised about it if you do.

I view self-defence like wearing an expensive watch. You don't keep flashing it about trying to impress people. Instead, you keep it up your sleeve, but in the back of your mind you have the confidence of knowing that you have the exact time whenever you need it. I felt I'd been waving my timepiece under Susie's nose, and it ruffled me.

'Hey, Charlie! I can't leave you alone for five minutes before you're getting into trouble again, can I?'

I twisted in my seat as Gary approached and sat down. He grinned at me, then noticed Clare's face.

'Oh Christ, I didn't realise that little cow had actually managed to land one on you,' he said. 'From what Dave's just told me I thought Charlie had got to her before she had a chance. Are you OK?'

Clare drummed up a brave smile and nodded. She aroused this immediate, instinctive desire in the male of the species to protect and pamper. I wondered if she was even aware that she was doing it.

'Look,' Gary said, 'I'm really sorry about what happened tonight. I hope you won't let it spoil your view of the club. Things like that just don't happen here very often.'

'Come off it, Gary,' I snorted. 'You've got real security problems, and you know it. This place is a rabbit warren. Oh, you've got plenty of cameras dotted around the place, but it's no use having that kind of surveillance if either nobody's watching the screens, or they just don't react to what they see.

'When it comes to keeping a lid on any trouble you're way understaffed. You haven't even got a man on every floor, and the guys on the door are so hyped up on testosterone they're more likely to start a fight than stop one. If Susie had been packing a knife she could have had Clare cold and melted away into the crowd before your lads got their act together enough to get their fingers out of their arses.'

From up on my high horse I'd ignored the way Gary's eyes had started to bulge when I'd launched into my speech. The reason soon became apparent.

'You seem to have a pretty low opinion of my club, Miss Fox,' said a deep voice from behind me. I didn't have to turn round to recognise the man in black who'd disposed of Susie for me. Oh shit. Ah well, attack to defend.

'There you go,' I said to Gary, without breaking stride. 'This is exactly my point. You've even got the boss man reduced to playing chucker-out. Now is that the best use of his time?'

I heard the man chuckle as he moved into my line of sight, sitting down at the same table. It was starting to get crowded. Gary fidgeted nervously, like he didn't know whether to stay or go.

'You have a certain style, Miss Fox,' the man said. He offered me a well-manicured hand, adorned with a signet ring. Fire flashed from the whole carat diamond set into the gold. 'My name is Marc Quinn.' His grip was firm, but light. Obviously Marc was sure enough of himself not to feel the need to clasp hands like he was trying to crush a billiard ball. 'I'm delighted to meet you properly, in slightly more conducive circumstances,' he added.

'Me too,' I said. I introduced Clare and Marc made a gracious apology. He assured her that Susie was currently cooling her heels in the gutter outside, then strangely switched his attention back to me. Those pale eyes were disturbingly intense.

'It's a few weeks since I was last here and I don't get round each of my clubs as often as I'd like,' he remarked. 'Have you been to the New Adelphi before?'

I laughed. 'Oh come on,' I said. 'You must be able to think of something better than the old "do you come here often?" line!'

He allowed himself a tight smile. 'If that's what I'd meant, then yes I probably could,' he returned coolly. 'I was merely trying to find out if you'd noticed these problems with my club security over a period of time, or picked up on it all this evening.'

I took a mental step back. 'This is my first time at your club,' I said, making my tone as businesslike as his own. It would probably be my last, I didn't add.

'In that case, you're very astute, Miss Fox,' he said. That incline of his head again, regal. He had his hair cut by a stylist, not a barber, but at least they hadn't managed to make him look like a football player.

'I reckon we need someone like Charlie working here, Mr Quinn,' Gary put in eagerly, only to be silenced by a barbed glance from Marc.

'It might not be quite up Miss Fox's street to throw out drunken troublemakers in a nightclub,' he pointed out dryly.

'It should be. She teaches self-defence. Used to hold a class here before the place was altered. Isn't that right, Charlie?'

I agreed that it was and could see Marc reassessing.

'Really? I thought you handled yourself pretty well back there,' he said. 'Ever done any of this kind of work before?'

'The odd time or two, nothing heavy,' I said. Just keeping the druggies out of the ladies' loo on disco night at a local pub. I'd learned some illuminating new swear words and a respectful caution when it came to dealing with fired up girls who had long fingernails.

He sat back in his chair, considering. As he moved the silk shirt flowed like liquid. It would have cost me a week's money.

'I'll be frank with you, Charlie,' he said, coming to a decision. 'We do seem to be having trouble recruiting staff here. I try to use people I've worked with before, but getting them to stay in this area is proving difficult, to say the least. The ones I am getting simply aren't the right calibre. I came up yesterday to personally take care of two people I suspected were stealing from me.' He made it sound like they were now reinforcing concrete in a motorway bridge support somewhere.

'Stealing from you?'

'That's correct. A hand in the till, some computer equipment, wine from the restaurant.' Out of the corner of my eye I saw Gary's Adam's apple give a convulsive jerk at that. Marc went on without a flicker. 'When they started getting blatant about it I decided the time had come to let them go. Now I find that the safety of the customers is compromised, and I have to act quickly. Would you be interested in meeting with me to discuss a possible part-time job here? Just Saturday evenings for now, Fridays later if it works out?'

'OK,' I said. I couldn't see the harm in talking to the man further, whatever the final outcome. I didn't kid myself that the money wouldn't come in useful. Besides, he intrigued me.

He reached into the single front pocket of his shirt and pulled out a business card with a designer look to it. There was a handwritten phone number on the reverse, local, by the first three digits, and a mobile. 'That's where I can be reached for the next week or so. Call me—and don't leave it too long.'

That slow smile again. He stood up, shook Clare's hand and mine, then got in one last shot at Gary. 'By the way, when it says no denims in the dress code, it means it. If you work for me, you don't break my rules—not for anyone,' he said, and walked away across the bar.

Gary waited until he was out of earshot, then let his breath out in a gush of relief. 'Wow, Charlie, he must have really taken a shine to you.'

'Hm.' I looked at the card he'd left with me again, and stuffed it into the back pocket of my offending jeans. If I'd any idea of the trouble it was going to cause, I'd have borrowed Gary's lighter and set fire to the damn thing instead.

Three

I SLEPT IN until eight the next morning, but made up for it by working out before breakfast. I was inspired to take up weight training again when I moved into my current flat, which was once a gym. It stands on the increasingly fashionable St George's Quay—rented, I might add—overlooking the River Lune.

When it had been a gym, it had never been a frilly sort of a place. Apparently the only women who used to go there were the owner's girlfriend, and a strapping wench who went in for Miss Great Britain competitions. It was a place for people seriously interested in building their bodies, not posing in a leotard.

When I moved in all the previous owner had done was to haul out the fixed weight machines and benches. The walls are still peeling whitewash, except the one still covered full length in mirrors. The light bulbs and the floorboards are bare. I'd taken down the posters of oiled muscular men and women demonstrating the visible benefits of vitamin supplements, ripped out the urinals in the gents' changing room and put in some old kitchen units I bought cheap from the second-hand furniture place two doors along.

The rest stayed more or less as it was. What was the office now houses my bed, and the main gym area has become my living room. I'd even hung my punchbag on the hook in the ceiling that had been put there for that purpose anyway. It swung elegantly in a corner, lending a certain sophisticated something to the place.

People usually comment admiringly about the size of the flat, and how lucky I am to live there. They don't notice the creeping damp patches, or the collection of buckets for when the wind is driving the rain under the roof slates from just the right angle.

I pay a pittance in rent, but with no written agreement. I knew full well when I moved in that the whole building was under sentence, and the landlord could chuck me out at any moment. Still, having viewed an increasingly depressing range of rat-infested bedsits when I first came to Lancaster, I figured that on the whole, it was worth the risk.

When I'd had enough of the weights I dropped them in a corner and headed for the shower, stripping off my jogging pants and T-shirt as I went.

While the roomy gents' changing room has since become my kitchen, the smaller ladies' room I use as a bathroom. I'm the only person I know with no bath but three showers. It still has the sign of a muscular female in a typical body builder's pose on the door. The only way you can tell the sex is that she has a bikini top stretched round her rippling upper torso. I leave her there to encourage me not to go over the top with the training.

Afterwards, I dressed in jeans and an old shirt. Breakfast was toasted crusts, because I'd already eaten the rest of the bread and forgotten to get a new loaf. I dumped my toast plate in the sink and scooped the jogging pants into the washbag when I was done. Living on my own I have to be strict about being tidy, otherwise I'd never be able to see the floor.

On a reflex I refilled the filter coffee machine and switched it on. Before long the whole place was filled with the heavy wafting scent of own-blend Java from the tea and coffee merchant in town.

I emptied the kitchen rubbish bin, a tricky operation because I never get round to doing it until it's way overflowing, and struggled down the stairs to dump a weighty black bin bag out on the pavement. They come first thing on a Monday morning and I always forget until I actually hear the council truck grinding its way along the quay, by which time I've usually missed them.

I was just making sure the top of the bag was secure to prevent it being raided by the swat team that is the local semi-stray cat population, when I heard the heavy rumbling of a big diesel. I looked up to see the local mobile video man, Terry Rothwell, pulling his big Mercedes van into a parking space on the other side of the road.

Everyone round here knows Terry. He'll never go down in the history books as a great thinker, but his heart's in the right place. I met him not long after I moved in, through his business partner, Paul.

Paul runs a video shop in Abraham Heights, just back from the quay, and rides an old, but pristine black Kawasaki GPZ900R.

It often works out that way. If you have a bike, everyone you seem to meet has one too. I think nearly all my friends in Lancaster have some connection or other to motorcycling.

When I first arrived here, Paul and Terry were great. Helped me sort out the wiring and even found me a second-hand video player at right money. I may not own any carpets, but you've got to get your priorities right when it comes to life's luxuries. In my case it was hi-fi, microwave, video—probably in that order.

Even if you don't hire out movies you can't miss Terry's van. It's green. Not a nice subdued British Racing, more Kawasaki Racing. A bilious shade of lime, bordering on fluorescent. On the side, in big pink letters, are the words, 'The Big Green Video Machine'. I asked him once whose idea the nauseous colour scheme was. He proudly accepted full responsibility. 'You may not like it,' he said, 'but you sure as Hell can't ignore it.' I had to agree he had a point, there.

Terry himself is a pretty noticeable character. He's about six-foot four and rather rotund with rubbery features that make him look more like a caricature of somebody else than a person in his own right. His hair is also receding and he will insist on growing the remainder long and brushing it forwards to cover the inadequacies. Windy days make him comically nervous.

He seems to do well out of the video game, though. The van was only two years old and when he's off duty I've seen him driving round in a two-door Merc coupé with a private plate on it. Somebody once told me Terry thought driving a prestige car would help him pull the birds. No offence to the guy, but a crash diet, plastic surgery and a decent hairstyle would probably work better.

By the time he'd eased his bulk out of the van I'd crossed over to meet him. 'I'm glad you're in,' he said. 'I've got that new Keanu Reeves film in we were talking about.'

He unlocked the side door and slid it back. Inside are racks of the latest films. I leant against the door aperture while he scribbled in his book, scouring the shelves with my head on one side to read the titles. He has so many films I want to watch that I always come away with a crick in my neck.

'You're in a good mood,' I observed, climbing in.

'Well, I've had a very useful morning so far,' he said, shutting the book and giving me a satisfied smile. 'Been round chasing a bad debt.'

'Successfully, obviously.'

'Oh yeah, the guy didn't have the cash on him, but I don't think I've done too badly out of it. He gave me this instead, look,' he said, and leant over into the front of the van to retrieve something from the passenger seat. I averted my eyes from the buttock cleavage that suddenly appeared at the back of his jeans. When he straightened up he was holding a rectangular object, about the size of a telephone directory. He flipped the lid open to reveal the neat screen and keyboard of a portable computer. It looked like a toy in his huge hands. 'Well then,' Terry said proudly, 'what d'you think of that?'

'Neat,' I said, trying not to sound too nonplussed. I can't get over the uneasy thought that computers are something I really ought to get into and understand, but I just can't raise the enthusiasm. 'Where on earth did you pick this up?'

'Ah-ha! Like I said, I've been debt collecting. A customer who hadn't paid his video hire bill. Bloke from that new club in Morecambe, as a matter of fact.'

It took me a moment before his words sank in. Then I suddenly remembered Marc's comment from the night before. *A hand in the till, some computer equipment, wine from the restaurant* . . .

'Terry,' I said. 'Are you sure it's legit?' Something in my voice bothered him and I watched a myriad of expressions register across his rubber-like features.

'What?' he demanded, suddenly looking from me to the computer as though it had abruptly burst into flames. He scratched worriedly at his armpit. 'Well, yeah,' he said, sounding anything but positive. He turned the computer over as if it might have 'stolen' written on the underside. 'Come on, what gives, Charlie?'

I explained about my conversation with Marc. 'It just seems a bit of a big coincidence, that's all,' I said. 'I don't know how much they cost, these lap-tops, but they won't be cheap. If they came by it by legal means, someone must have borrowed a barrow-load of videos at a few quid a time to owe you enough to do a straight swap.'

Terry smirked. 'Ah, I wasn't born yesterday,' he said, 'I've been offered enough hooky gear in my time to be able to smell it.' He tapped the side of his nose to indicate it was very hush, hush. 'But there's videos and then, there's videos.'

I said, *oh yes*, in what I hoped was a knowing sort of way, and left it at that, but Terry wasn't to be deflected. He put the computer down. After a quick look round in a shifty manner guaranteed to make any casual observer sit up and take notice, he lifted up a false panel above the cab of the van, whipped out a video and handed it to me.

It wasn't in one of his usual cases, which are the same squint-inducing colour scheme as the van. This was in a very plain, rather cheap-looking wrapper. I forget the title now, but it was wincingly corny. I knew instantly that the film inside would contain a warbling sound track, repetitive dialogue, no plot to speak of and lots of writhing bodies filmed from angles that were gynaecological in their intensity.

I've seen one or two and they make me feel deeply uncomfortable. The dead look in the performers' eyes—I can't bring myself to call them actors—disturbs me. I can never believe that the people involved are doing that sort of thing from choice. They all look doped up to the eyeballs in any case. I pulled a face and handed the video back.

'It doesn't take long to build up a big bill when you're hiring two or three of these a week,' he said and named a price that made my eyebrows rise of their own accord.

'That's for *renting* them? For that money I'd want shares in the film company.' I was intrigued despite my distaste. 'What's so special about them, or don't I want to know.'

Terry grinned and opened the box. The video inside had the title repeated on an otherwise plain label. 'There you are,' he said. 'No certificate. This little lot are hot off the boat from Spain and Amsterdam and they didn't come via the official board of censors. You wouldn't believe what's on half of 'em, sadomasochism stuff, animals and all sorts—but I draw the line at kids,' he said quickly, with the air of someone adopting a high moral tone. 'If anyone gets caught with one, they didn't get it from me, that's for sure. They could throw away the key just for what I've got in the van at the moment.' He jerked a thumb at the false floor.

'So some guy hired out enough of these that he gave you a lap-top computer in payment?' I said again. I still found it hard to believe.

Terry nodded, grinning. 'He's got a week to come up with the money, otherwise this goes straight into the small ads,' he said. 'Although, actually, I might keep it. I've never had one of these before.' He picked up the portable again, fiddling around until he found the on/off button.

The little computer whined into life, making buzzing and clicking noises like an electronic budgie. He stared for a few moments at the screen, which was tilted away from me, jabbing a couple of buttons, his brows drawn down. 'The cheating bugger,' he said.

'What's up?'

'It's asking me for the password. He never mentioned anything about passwords. Bloody hell.'

'Can't you go back and ask whoever it was you got it from what the right password is?' I said, peering over his shoulder.

'We didn't exactly part on good terms,' Terry admitted. 'In fact, he probably did this on purpose. Bugger.'

I sighed. For someone who's obviously pretty successful in business, he can be very naive sometimes. He stood there looking at the little computer like a kid who's just had his new toy broken in the school playground by the class bully. I swear I saw his bottom lip quiver. Mind you, the way parts of his fleshy face tended to wobble out of sync with the rest of him when he moved quickly, it was difficult to tell.

A sudden thought seemed to occur to him. 'Hey, are you still mates with that computer bloke up at the Uni?' He raised his eyebrows hopefully.

I sighed again. No way did I want to help Terry get into a possibly nicked computer, given to him by some bloke in payment for illegal porn videos, but Terry's been a bit of a mate and I just couldn't stand the thought of the hurt look if I said no. Besides, I probably owed him a favour or two.

'OK,' I said. 'I haven't seen Sam for ages, but I'll ask him if he could try and get round it for you, if you like?'

Terry looked relieved. He switched off the computer and folded the lid shut again. 'Would you?' he said. 'That'd be great. Tell you what, shall I leave it with you? If you can get your mate to have a play with it, I could pick it up later on in the week sometime.'

I agreed and he handed the machine across. It wasn't much bigger than a ream of A4 paper, and looked so innocuous. We hopped back out onto the street. He swung the Merc's side door shut and climbed into the cab. 'I'll see you right for videos,' he called as he started the engine. I stuck the computer under my arm and walked back up the stairs to the flat.

WHEN I GOT up the next morning the lap-top was where I'd left it on the coffee table. I worked round it for most of the morning, but eventually I couldn't put it off any longer.

I looked up the number of the university and dialled. After a short delay, they put me through to the right department. I asked whoever picked up for Sam, and the receiver was plonked down on a desktop. I heard someone calling, then cowboy-booted footsteps.

'Yeah?' His voice sounded bored. It was nearly lunchtime.

'Hi Sam, it's Charlie.'

'Oh, right!' he said, suddenly perking up. 'Great to hear from you. When are we going out for another razz?'

I'd met Sam out one day in the Trough of Bowland. When the roads are quiet the Trough is fantastic biking country. In the summer I tend to go out there early in the morning when you can just get stuck into those long sweeping bends.

I was doing that at about six-thirty one Sunday morning when an old green 750cc Norton Commando appeared out of nowhere and proceeded to trample all over me. I gave chase, but I just haven't got the faith, or the courage, to hammer fully committed into blind corners and crests.

After a few miles he pulled in to a lay-by where there was a little burger caravan and I followed. The look on his face when I took my helmet off would have been worth a photograph. We had a brew, got to the point of exchanging phone numbers and met up regularly after that for a quick blast.

When Sam started suggesting we met up in the evenings, however, and without the bikes, I began to back off. He's a sweet bloke, but a touch on the sensitive side for my taste. Chaotic dark hair framing the long face of a Chaucer knight, with expressive dark eyes that follow you round the room like one of those Greenpeace posters against seal clubbing.

I suppose I knew he'd take things further if I gave him a sign, but I also knew the sparks were all on his side. I didn't think it was fair to let him believe anything might come of it, and I hadn't spoken to him for a few months.

Now, I explained about Terry's password-protected machine and asked if he thought there was anything he could suggest. I don't know exactly what it is that Sam does with computers, but he seems to be a bit of a whizz kid.

'Yeah, no problem,' he said. 'I'll see what I can do. Most of these lap-tops aren't that difficult to get into. What's the make and model?'

I grabbed the computer and read off all the identifying marks I could find. 'Shall I bring it round?' I asked.

'Er, well, you're just down on the quay, aren't you? Why don't I pop round to you tonight, about eight-thirty?' he said, adding quickly. 'If that's OK, of course. I just thought it would save you carting it about strapped to the back of that bloody Jap rice-burner of yours.'

'At least my bike only burns oil, it doesn't dump most of it on the road,' I said. 'Half eight is fine. I'll see you later.'

'Yeah, great. I'll look forward to it,' he said.

I put the phone down wondering if I'd done the right thing.

IN THE AFTERNOON I packed my work-out clothes into my rucksack, climbed onto the Suzuki, and headed across town to the refuge.

I've been holding self-defence at the Shelseley Lodge Women's Refuge for the last couple of years. On paper, I suppose it doesn't make much financial sense to do so, but actually the arrangement suits us both quite well.

I teach there three times a week. The classes are open to all, and often people mix and match which days they attend, depending on their schedule. The residents of the Lodge are free to join in any time.

My regular students pay me their tuition fees direct, but Shelseley take the class fees themselves for their own people, if they charged them at all. Still, I didn't have to fork out for use of the venue, so I couldn't begrudge them my labours. Not for the work they were doing.

Shelseley Lodge had been turned into a women's refuge some time in the early seventies by the late mother of the present owner. Old Mrs Shelseley had used premature widowhood as the perfect opportunity to take in single mothers and battered wives as fast as she could make up camp beds for them. And if deserted husbands turned up in the middle of the night to kick up a fuss, she'd even been known to appear, a terrifying apparition with a shotgun and curlers, to show them the error of their ways. I'd never met her, but I thought she sounded wonderful.

I very much doubt that the new Mrs Shelseley knew one end of a shotgun from the other, but she was just as effective at shifting unwanted visitors. Ailsa had arrived temporarily at the Lodge as a trainee solicitor to offer advice to the residents on matters of divorce and child support.

She'd taken a fancy to the place in general—and the owner's son, Tristram in particular—and had stayed put. Although she's since given up the law and retrained as a counsellor, she can still spout enough legalise to put the fear of God into marauding men when the need arises.

I reached the entrance to the Lodge and turned the bike between a pair of red brick gateposts. The driveway was short and claimed to be gravel, but every summer the dandelions staged another covert incursion and I think they were finally winning the battle.

As always, there was a motley collection of cars sprawled in front of the impressive Victorian house. Where space was tight someone had even driven one of them onto the lawn, leaving gouges in the sodden grass like a mistreated billiard table.

I slid the bike into a gap near one of the elegantly proportioned bay-fronted windows, and killed the motor, pulling off my helmet. Into the quiet that followed came the raucous squeal of children at war. Somewhere upstairs, a baby cried relentlessly.

The front door stood open as usual beneath a fanlight made from delicately-coloured glass in leaded panes. The matching panels in the door itself had long since fallen victim to one set of angry fists or another, and now consisted of reinforced safety glass. My boots echoed on the faded black and white tiles as I walked down the hallway, calling a hello as I went.

Ailsa stuck her head out of what was supposed to be their private sitting room and beckoned me through. When I went in I found Tris squeezed into a corner, trying to read a book on William Blake. Nearly all the other available chairs were taken up by a bedraggled-looking woman with bruised eyes and four young children.

'Hi Charlie,' Ailsa said brightly, subsiding her generous frame onto a seat, her loose Indian cotton dress billowing around her for a moment like a collapsing big top. 'Won't be a moment. We're just trying to sort out these forms from the Social. Be a dear, Tristram, and put the kettle on.'

Out of his wife's line of sight, Tris sighed, carefully inserted a bookmark as he rose, and disappeared into the narrow kitchen. When I couldn't stand the scruffy round-eyed stares of the kids any longer, I went to join him.

Tris was standing at the sink, staring out into the garden at the lines of terry nappies, flapping like pennants. He was absently trying to dry a teapot with a towel that was too wet to make any difference.

'D'you want a hand?'

'Hm?' He took a moment to bring his mind back on track. 'Oh, yes please, Charlie. Sorry, miles away there.'

Ailsa had cut his hair again, I noticed. It looked like she'd done it with blunt nail scissors, by candlelight. There was a chunk missing over one ear, and half his fringe stood straight up in the air. Ailsa had all the hairdressing aptitude of a bottle-nosed dolphin, but Tris was too good natured to complain.

Left to his own devices he would have favoured something more in the romantic poet style but, he once explained to me with a weary smile, the proliferation of unwashed small children about the place made headlice a very real concern, and a short haircut a necessity.

He was still wearing his working uniform of a short-sleeved white tunic over black trousers, and he smelled of lavender, and orange blossom. When what had once been the drawing room hasn't been commandeered as an overflow bedroom, Tris uses it for aromatherapy massage.

The kettle on the hob began to scream and I lifted it off the heat with a slightly scorched oven glove. Between us we managed to load a tray with all the required equipment for tea and were manoeuvring our way back into the sitting room when the door into the hall swung open again.

A small boy in a football jersey shoved his head through the gap. ''Scuse me, Aunty Ailsa,' he said, a vision of angelic politeness, 'but the filth's here.'

Ailsa smiled at him, taking the news of the arrival of the police without undue surprise. For one reason or another, they were regular visitors at Shelseley.

'OK love,' she said to him. 'You'd better show them in. Oh, hello Tommy,' she went on when the first of two uniformed constables edged into the room, taking off their hats.

The young officer she'd addressed manfully stifled a blush at her familiarity, and tried to ignore a derisive glance from his colleague. The other man was the older of the two, though that wasn't saying much. Neither of them looked old enough to drive. Wasn't that supposed to be another sign that advanced age was creeping up on me? My God, I wasn't expecting that when I'd only just hit my quarter-century.

'Now then,' Ailsa said briskly, 'what can we do for you this time, Tommy?'

From his expression, Tommy's dearest wish was that she'd stop calling him Tommy, but he decided to let it pass. It was his mate who spoke up instead.

'Actually, Mrs Shelseley, it isn't you we wanted to speak to today. It's Miss Fox.'

I'd been halfway through pouring a cup of tea, and the guilty start I gave at the mention of my own name sent a splatter of hot brown liquid over the table top. I glanced up quickly while Ailsa rescued her forms from the flood and sent Tris for a cloth.

I helped mop up, glad of the pause so I could rack my brains to try and come up with a suitable reason why the police were after me. The first thought that popped up was that it might be something to do with the hooky lap-top Terry had given me.

'Yes, that's me,' I said. 'Why, what's the problem?'

Tommy's mate ignored the question. 'Is there anywhere we can talk in private, Miss?' he asked.

Tris offered use of the drawing room and led us through, frowning. The room was huge. Clean and bright, with his massage couch set up in the centre and a stack of clean dark green towels on a rattan sofa to the side. Tris hastily shifted the towels so we had space to sit down, and left, still looking pensive.

'So, what's the problem?' I said again when I was alone with the policemen.

Tommy's mate ignored my question a second time. He was really starting to become quite tiresome. Instead, he posed an unexpected one of his own. 'Were you at the New Adelphi Club in Morecambe on Saturday evening?'

'Yes,' I said, feeling suddenly cold. I sank down onto the sofa Tris had cleared, and clamped my hands together in my lap.

Even as a kid I've always been more afraid of getting into trouble than of getting hurt. I frantically tried to think back over the weekend's events. I knew, logically, they couldn't possibly be here because of Terry's computer, and I couldn't find anything else that would call for two coppers to be tracking me down at work and giving me the third degree. 'What's this all about?'

I'm always wary of the police. You ride a motorcycle and it tends to colour your view of the boys in blue. Still, I suppose it was a nice change to be greeted by a uniform whose opening gambit wasn't, 'Are you *aware* of the national speed limit, madam?' Maybe, in this case, it would have been preferable.

I looked from one to the other. Tommy sat down at the other end of the sofa and tried a reassuring smile, but the other one paced round the room, poking along the bottles of Tris's essential oils and making little snorting noises to himself as he read the labels. 'Look at this lot, Tom,' he said. 'Frankincense, chamomile, ylang-ylang.' He picked one of the bottles off the shelf, turned it in his hand. 'Sandalwood. What's that for, then?'

I dredged through my memory for Tris's explanations. I knew sandalwood was calming, a sedative and an aphrodisiac, but I wasn't going to tell him that. It also had antiseptic properties, and was good for dry skin. 'Acne,' I said shortly.

He was still young enough for the terrors of rampant spots to be too close for comfort. He put the bottle back on the shelf quickly.

'Look,' I said, 'I very much doubt you two are here for a guided tour of aromatherapy oils, so why don't we just cut to the chase?'

They glanced at each other and the younger one, Tommy, pulled out his pocket book. 'According to reports we've received, you had a bit of an altercation with a woman at the New Adelphi Club on Saturday night. A Miss Susie Hollins?'

So that was it. 'Altercation isn't quite the word I'd use to describe it.'

'And what word would you use, exactly?'

I didn't like the tone, it was too quiet, too tactfully noncommittal.

I sighed again. 'She clouted a friend of mine,' I said. 'All I did was hold her off until the management arrived. She started it, as any one of a number of witnesses should be able to tell you. If she's telling you I jumped her, she's lying through her teeth. Is that why you're here? Is that what she's saying?' I looked from one to the other, seeking confirmation, but they were giving nothing away.

'Oh, she's not saying anything, Miss Fox,' the older policeman said.

That chill again. 'Why? What's happened?'

'I'm afraid Miss Hollins is dead,' he said. It was obviously the most thrilling bit of news he'd had to impart since he left police training college. He was trying hard to put the right subdued note into his voice. 'Her body was discovered yesterday morning.'

I stared at them blankly. Susie was dead? 'How?'

Tommy gave me an old-fashioned look which said I should know better than to ask, and consulted his notebook again. 'Obviously we can't discuss details, but I can tell you we're now involved in a murder enquiry,' he allowed. 'We understand you were one of the last people to see her alive, so we need to know all of what you can remember about Saturday night.'

I told them everything then, of course I did. About rescuing Clare from Susie's attack, about Marc Quinn stepping in to deal with her. 'He told us he'd thrown her out of the club, and I didn't see her again for the rest of the evening,' I finished.

'And her boyfriend, this Tony, you said he seemed pretty upset with her?' the younger one asked.

'Highly pissed off, but he didn't leave when Susie did. I don't know when she was killed, but I saw him again a couple of times later on. Once about half an hour after she'd been chucked out. He was consoling himself by chatting up a red-head in the lower bar. When

Clare and I left at about quarter to midnight the pair of them were staggering into a taxi, giving each other a pretty good impression of mouth-to-mouth resuscitation. It was a private hire cab, I think, a blue Cavalier. I didn't notice which firm, sorry.'

'That's OK, we can check with the club. They would have had to call it from there.' He made scribbled notes, then backtracked to the previous page. 'So, you said Mr Quinn threw Miss Hollins out and then came to speak to you? How long was he with you?'

I frowned, considering. 'He was there about ten minutes or so. Then he disappeared and I didn't see him again until just after Dave had done his final set. That's when they presented Clare with her karaoke prize. We left shortly after that.'

'That would be Dave Clemmens, who was the DJ in charge of the karaoke, right?'

I nodded.

'And what about you? Where did you go when you left the New Adelphi Club?'

'Can I prove my whereabouts, you mean?' I demanded. 'Why, do you think I killed her?' I held his gaze levelly.

'No, Miss Fox,' he said, with a grim smile. 'I don't.'

I didn't understand exactly what he meant by that until later, after the police had gone, when I heard the regional report on the afternoon news. They didn't name her, of course, but I don't think there was more than one murder of a young woman in the area for them to go at.

Details were sketchy, but the reason I wasn't on the suspect list was immediately obvious. I just wasn't equipped for it. In addition to having her throat half cut and being beaten to death, Susie Hollins had been repeatedly and viciously raped.

Four

CLARE RANG ME later that evening. The police had been to see her, too, and she was as stunned as I was by the whole thing. I let her talk it through without major interruptions. To let her equilibrium right itself.

'I can't help feeling guilty,' she finished, illogically. 'I mean, it was sort of because of me that Susie got chucked out, and if she hadn't . . .' Her voice tailed off uncertainly.

'Oh Clare, don't even think about that,' I told her. 'Susie made her own choices. She just made some bad ones. Getting thrown out of the club was her fault, not yours. You didn't provoke her. And she could have just got herself a cab home.'

'I know, you're right,' she said, sounding forlorn. 'I just feel really bad about it.' She paused, sighing. 'I'm glad you were there, though.'

'That's OK,' I said. I was standing leaning against one of the deep set windows in the flat, watching the lights of the traffic on the other side of the river, streaming across Greyhound Bridge towards Morecambe. The movement was soothing, hypnotic in its droning regularity.

I took another swig from a bottle of cloudy wheat beer I'd found as a pleasant surprise lurking in the salad drawer at the bottom of the fridge. 'So, how's the black eye?'

'Oh, don't. Jacob's been giving me stick about that ever since, but it covers up all right. One of the boys on the crime desk wanted to interview me about my little fracas with Susie as a side story for the next issue, by the way,' she added with an audible grimace. 'He not only wanted to get Photographic to take pictures of me without make-up, but said he'd get the art department to touch it up and make it look like a really worthwhile bruise. Cheeky bastards. I told them you were the one they should be talking to.'

I spat most of the mouthful of beer I'd been about to swallow back into the bottle. 'Oh no,' I said, spluttering. 'I can just see the way they'd write the story and I can quite do without that kind of publicity, thank you very much!'

'Oh come on, Charlie, it might give business a boost. After all, there should be hordes of women who want to learn self-defence after this. You'll be turning them away in their hundreds.'

The laughter in her voice was infectious and I couldn't help a smile, but kept my voice sober. 'Oh yeah? All some tacky story in the local paper will do is throw down a challenge to all the punky kids in the area. Remember that boy last year?'

He'd been fourteen or so, cocky, sneering. He'd walked into one of my introductory classes unexpectedly armed with a small pocket knife. I hadn't moved quite fast enough and I still had the scar, a pale three-inch line across my ribcage that didn't tan well in the summer.

'Oh,' Clare said, suddenly becoming serious. 'Yes, I do. Sorry, Charlie, I wasn't thinking.' She was sounding subdued again.

'Don't worry about it. And don't dwell on this whole thing, either. It sounds heartless to say it, but people do stupid things every day and get away with it. Susie was just plain unlucky.'

How many times did I teach my students how to avoid making themselves easy targets? Don't walk home alone at night. Don't take short cuts. It seemed so obvious to me that I found myself unsympathetic towards anyone who didn't follow the simple rules. Some people seemed almost to have a death-wish.

Rape is one of those life-changing experiences that you never entirely recover from, you never really get over. You put it behind you, and you try to move on, but it will always be there, colouring your thoughts and actions. Like a big mental and emotional scar.

If it's touched you personally, you look at other people taking risks with a sense of anger, as though they're belittling your own experience. Like a cancer victim watching people casually smoking. If I could have done anything to avoid having been attacked, I would have done it.

'I don't care how stupid she was. Nobody deserves to die that way,' Clare said now, with a touch of belligerence. 'What he did to her—it just makes me feel sick to my stomach.'

'They must have told you more than they told me, then,' I observed. 'The police wouldn't do more than say it was a murder enquiry.'

'I talked to the girl on the crime desk at work,' Clare admitted. Although she was only in accounts, Clare's always seemed to be very pally with most of the editorial staff at the paper. 'She knows all the gen, but they're not allowed to publish half of it. The police want to hold back as much as possible to try and trap the killer. They don't want a copy cat, either, which doesn't really bear thinking about.' I could almost hear her delicate shudder.

'Can you find out some more of the details for me?' I asked. I'd already had twenty questions from Ailsa. My pupils were bound to talk about the Susie Hollins murder, too. Bound to ask me if I really thought my theories could help them to avoid meeting a similar fate. Until I knew what had happened to Susie, I couldn't answer that. Students get very nervous at unanswered questions. She hesitated.

'Clare,' I said dryly, 'I'm hardly likely to go to print in the rival freesheet with it, now am I?'

'OK, I'll ask,' she said, 'but I can't guarantee she'll tell me more than she has already.'

She agreed to give me a call later on in the week and invited me round for a meal the following weekend. I rang off with a feeling of unease that I couldn't shift. And although Jacob makes curries that strip the enamel off your teeth, it had nothing to do with the prospect of his cooking, either.

THE SENSE OF foreboding still hadn't gone by the time Sam arrived. He turned up so exactly on the dot of eight-thirty that he must have been waiting outside the door, one finger hovering above the doorbell, eyes on his watch.

I answered the door to be met by a big smile and a waft of expensive aftershave. I always find that strange on someone who obviously doesn't own a razor. The lower half of Sam's face is covered by a straggly anarchist's beard. He sauntered in, the only way you can walk when you're wearing cowboy boots, in a pair of black Wranglers and a bike jacket. 'Hi,' he said, dumping his battered AGV helmet on a chair and shaking a box of computer disks at me. 'Lead me to your computer.'

'Hi Sam, I've put it on the desk. Help yourself.' I offered coffee and went to see to the machine, which was down to the last nutty dregs in the bottom of the pot. I like coffee that way, but it's the sort of thing other people tend to tip into plant pots when they think I'm not looking. That can be a real pain when you consider I don't have any pot plants.

I gave up and flicked on the kettle. When I came back Sam had opened up the lap-top and was pondering the message on the screen. He'd put on a pair of wire-rimmed glasses for close work and his long eyelashes brushed against the lenses. Most women would kill for them.

'We need a password. I don't suppose we know anything about the guy who owned this, do we?' he asked. I shook my head. I wasn't about to tell Sam that the only thing I knew about the previous owner was that he was a weirdo. 'Pity. People usually use something obvious like their date of birth, or their dog's name as a password.'

'Fido?' I suggested.

Sam rolled his eyes. 'In this case, it has to be something with seven letters,' he said.

'How about if you spell it, P-h-i-d-e-a-u?' I got a dark look. The kettle clicked off and I retreated to pour water on the instant coffee.

'I've tried a few obvious ones, like "let-me-in", but I think we'll try a more lateral approach,' Sam said when I returned. He linked his hands together and cracked his fingers out straight in front of him. It made me wince.

He picked out a disk, switched the machine off and slid it into the drive slot before switching back on again, holding down a number of keys as he did so. The lap-top whirred and hummed again, then presented him with an 'A' and a flashing block at the top left hand corner of the screen.

'Way to go,' I said, impressed.

'Thank you for your adoration, but we're not there yet,' Sam said, darting me a quick grin over his shoulder. 'That's just logged me on to the floppy disk drive.' His hands flew over the keys with the sureness of a touch-typist. He had long slender fingers, spoilt only by the fact that he bit his nails. 'I have a little program here that will keep bombarding it with seven-letter words until we hit the right one. All I have to do now is let it get to work.'

He leant back in his chair, looking smug and reaching for his coffee cup. We talked about something and nothing while his program ran, making the little computer buzz and hum to itself. Sam might have sounded confident, but I noticed he kept one eye on the screen all the time.

'Thanks for taking so much trouble over this,' I said.

He waved a negligent hand. 'No sweat. Besides, this is kiddies' stuff, really.'

'I'm sorry if the challenge isn't up to your usual standard. What do you normally do for laughs—hack your way into the Bank of England?' I said in a sarky voice.

He grinned in such a way that I realised he probably did.

'So, where did you get it, this password program?' I asked.

'All my own work,' he admitted modestly.

'You ought to market it.'

He snorted into his cup as he took another slug of coffee. 'Yeah, and the profits might just pay enough to keep me one step ahead of the serious fraud squad. Think about it, Charlie, if you need to get into a password-protected computer without the password, you're not exactly on the level, now are you?'

I raised my eyebrows, but was saved from having to think of a reply by the computer itself, which had stopped making noises and was displaying a single seven-letter word on the screen.

'Ah-ha, here we are. Bacchus,' Sam read. 'Bacchus? Mean anything to you?'

I trawled through my mental vocabulary and shook my head. 'Not a thing.'

'OK, pick a new seven-letter word and I'll over-write it.'

'Pervert,' I said immediately, almost without thinking. He raised his eyebrows, but typed it in anyway. 'OK, now let's see just what he's got on here that he didn't want us to see. Hm, that's odd.'

'What?' I asked.

'There's nothing here to protect,' Sam said. 'Of course, he could just have been trying to make life awkward for your pal.'

'What are all those?' There seemed to be a list of files available.

'They're just the system files, the ones that tell this lump of plastic that it's a computer to start off with,' he explained. 'I meant there are no actual data files on here. He must have wiped them all off before he handed the machine over.'

'That's a pity,' I said. It could either mean that the guy was perfectly legit, and just didn't want Terry reading his private correspondence, or it could mean that he didn't want anyone to be able to prove the machine had originally belonged to someone else— the New Adelphi Club, for instance.

'Of course,' Sam said slowly, 'it just so happens that I can probably retrieve whatever it is that *was* on there.' I realised by his smug expression that he'd been playing me along, waiting to see my reaction.

'Go on,' I said.

'I've got a utilities program that can un-delete files. I can even retrieve data off floppy disks that have been re-formatted.'

This didn't mean too much to me, but it was obviously an impressive feat. I looked impressed. I was about to thank him for his trouble, but it was clear he loved the challenge of this sort of thing, so I just said, 'I just hope when you've done all this there's something interesting on the damn machine to read.'

He drained his coffee cup and stood up. 'If you're not busy I'll nip round tomorrow after work and we'll see what we can come up with,' he suggested with studied casualness.

'I'm teaching tomorrow evening, and I've got an interview for a new job some time this week,' I improvised quickly, 'but Wednesday would be OK.' I didn't like the light that had come on in his eyes and I really didn't want the guy getting ideas about me. I like Sam, don't get me wrong, but I just didn't want to lose him as a friend by having to turn him down on a more intimate level.

'What's the new job?' he asked now. 'You starting another class up?'

I shook my head. 'I broke a fight up at that new nightclub in Morecambe, the New Adelphi, and the boss offered me a job on the doors.'

Sam stared. 'Don't take it,' he said bluntly.

I cast him a speaking look. One that said there's a line here, Sam, don't cross it.

He flushed. 'Sorry, I know it's none of my business, but you'd be a fool to get into that game, Charlie. A few of the lads from the Uni are into it, and it's shit money for the amount of abuse you have to take. The cops never believe your story over a punter.'

I bridled a little at being called a fool. As far as I'm concerned Sam doesn't have the right to make judgements on what I do with my life. Things like that have a tendency to make me stubborn. And that's when the trouble starts. Sam must have known he was pushing his luck because he changed the subject and, soon after that, he left.

After he'd gone I dug out my old school dictionary and looked up Bacchus. It was only an abbreviated pocket version and it didn't list either Bacchus or Adelphi. Not much help there, then.

With a sigh I put the dictionary down and moved into the kitchen. I put together a rough and ready tea from the freezer. I really must remember to go shopping. I ate listening to the hi-fi and planned an unexciting evening involving a paperback novel and an early night.

IT WASN'T UNTIL the following day, when I was gathering clothes together for a darks' wash, and checking through the pockets, that I found Marc Quinn's business card. It was still in the back pocket of the jeans I'd been wearing to the New Adelphi Club.

On impulse, I tried both the numbers. The land line turned out to be the most expensive hotel in the area. Marc wasn't in, so I left my name and number, but no message, with the frighteningly efficient receptionist. I tried his mobile next, but that was switched off. I left a brief message on the answering service, then promptly forgot all about it.

I spent an uneventful day, the calm before the storm. I did the washing, made an initial stab at the ironing. I had a trip round the covered market in the middle of town and stocked up on real vegetables rather than tinned or frozen substitutes. I even finally got round to buying some fresh bread.

In the early evening I went and taught my class at the university leisure centre how to escape from a front stranglehold. I was back in the flat by eight. I must only have been home around half an hour when the phone rang.

I hesitated a moment before picking up the receiver. I suppose I'm just naturally cautious, but a year or so ago I picked up a fascinating gadget that alters the tone of your voice, making it deeper, more like a man's. It was specially made for women who live alone, for fending off obscene calls. I flicked it on and reached for the receiver. 'Hello?'

'Good evening, may I speak to Charlie?' A man's voice, the accent neutral. Initially I failed to place where I'd heard it before, but the interesting way he curled my name round didn't incline me to hang up.

'Hang on, I'll get her,' I said. 'Who is it?'

'My name is Marc Quinn. She does know me.'

I pressed the secrecy button on the phone and switched off the device. It gave me a moment to think. I hadn't been prepared for him to call so soon.

'Hi, Marc,' I said, speaking undisguised. 'I just called you earlier to arrange that appointment you mentioned. I didn't think you'd to get back to me so quickly.'

'Ah, well, when there's something I want, I don't like to wait,' he murmured seductively.

I pulled a face. 'In that case, remind me not to have sex with you,' I said waspishly.

He laughed out loud at that. 'Touché,' he said with a wry note in his voice. 'Not very good at accepting flattery, are you, Charlie?'

'When that's all it is, no, I'm not,' I agreed flatly.

'Hm, you need the practice, then. So, how soon are you going to come and see me?'

I reached over to the desk and retrieved my diary. It was more of a play for time. I already pretty much knew when my classes were during the week. He suggested a time for the following afternoon at the club. It seemed ironic that the excuse I'd made to Sam was solidifying into reality, even if it was a day late.

I have to admit, I liked listening to Marc's voice. Concealed in the background was the faintest trace of a regional accent. He had obviously worked hard to eradicate it, but on the phone it seemed more noticeable than it had face to face. I tried and failed to place it.

'Until tomorrow, then,' he said as we wound up our conversation, and the line disconnected.

I looked at the dead receiver before I put it down. 'I hope you know what you're doing, Fox,' I said, but I wasn't giving myself any answers. I guess I was just obstinate that way.

Five

THE NEW ADELPHI Club looked different in daylight. Seedier, somehow. Less inviting. It was certainly quieter than it had been that Saturday, though, which had to be a bonus.

I parked up the bike at the front of the car park. I noticed with approval that security cameras had been installed overlooking the parking area, although I couldn't remember whether they'd been there before. I made sure the Suzuki was covered by one of them.

Even so, I stuck my roller-chain round the rear wheel and swinging arm, just to make sure. The insurance premiums I pay on the bike, considering it's coming up for seven years old, are stratospheric. I don't want them going into low earth orbit because of a theft claim.

The main entrance was locked up tight when I arrived. There didn't seem to be a doorbell, and hammering on the door itself produced no signs of life. After a few minutes I gave up and wandered round towards the rear of the building.

The back entrance was where the old kitchens had once been and nothing much had changed. Where the front of the Adelphi had been grand and sweeping, the back was a hotchpotch of styles. Hasty additions built for function rather than form. It was interesting to see that Marc hadn't bothered spending his valuable money on tidying things up back there.

The old kitchen door was propped open with a broken breeze block, and a Transit van was pulled up close to it. As I approached Gary came out, carrying a crate of bottles, which he dumped into the back of the van. He was dressed in a T-shirt and jeans, and looked much more at home in them than he had in his penguin suit of the weekend.

'Nice to see somebody working,' I said by way of a greeting.

He spun round with a start. 'Christ, Charlie, you frightened me to death!' he cried. 'What are you doing here?'

'Well, it was your idea, actually,' I told him. 'I'm here to see Marc about a security job. You suggested it.'

Gary was pale and sweaty. I think his idea of physical exercise is lifting the arm holding the remote control for the TV. 'Marc's coming here this afternoon?' he demanded now. I nodded. 'Oh hell, we're way behind today. I was supposed to have all this lot swapped over this morning. Give us a hand, will you?'

Which is how I came to be lugging bottle crates between the numerous bars and the back of the van. I quickly came to understand Gary's breathless and perspiring state. I stripped off my leather jacket and dumped my helmet on a chair, but I couldn't do much about my leather jeans. By the time I'd made half a dozen trips myself I was in pretty much the same state as he was.

'How often do you have to do this?' I gasped as I reached the van with yet another crate of empties.

'Too often,' he grinned back, wheezing.

I picked up one of the bottles from the latest batch. It was vodka, I think, with nearly an inch of liquid remaining in the bottom. 'Hey, you got a glass on you? There's still some left in this one.'

'Very funny,' he said, retrieving the bottle and ramming it back into the crate. 'The bar optics don't always pick up the last dregs, and it's not worth the hassle of taking them down and pouring them by hand. Not with the amount of spirits we go through here in a week.'

He hopped out and slammed the van doors shut behind him. As we walked back through into the club he caught my arm. 'Listen, Charlie, do me a favour and don't mention this to Marc, will you?' he said suddenly. 'Like I say, I was supposed to have all this done this morning, and the boss can get really funny if you don't do things by the book.'

'No problem,' I said. 'My lips are sealed.'

I collected my jacket and lid, and he led me back through to the main lower dance floor. Without the heavy musical overlay, milling bodies, and the clever lighting effects, the decor just looked tacky, overblown. The smell of last night's cigarettes hung on the air like a leaking gas main.

I perched on a bar stool and watched Gary work. His movements were quick, economic, as he worked his way along the line, fixing new bottles upside down onto the optics to replace the ones he'd taken away. I like watching anyone with such manual dexterity. Plasterers and pastry chefs fascinate me.

There was the sound of locks being worked and a heavy door opening on the split-level above us. It threw a shaft of natural light into the club that had been missing before. I looked up and watched three shadows growing larger as they advanced.

'Look, I better finish off upstairs,' Gary said hastily. 'I'll see you later, Charlie.' And he scurried off.

The shadows finally took solid form on the gallery above the dance floor where Clare and I had had our first view of the revamped club. It was Marc, flanked by the two doormen who'd been working that night; the bearded one, and my old mate, Len.

'Charlie? You're early,' Marc said when he caught sight of me.

I glanced at my watch. 'No, actually I believe *you're* late,' I said calmly.

I saw Marc's head come up at that, surprise tinged with a trace of anger. Well, tough. The job would be useful, but I didn't *need* it. No way did I want to be scuttering around like Gary, afraid of treading on the boss man's toes.

Even from that distance, I saw Len's big hands instinctively curl round the top rail of the balustrade. You didn't have to be a psychologist to work out he'd rather have them round my neck. What's your problem, sonny? I made a mental note to be careful around him.

The trio moved down the stairs to my level and Marc came across to shake hands. 'Regardless of the timing, I'm glad you're here,' he said. 'I believe you've already met Len and Angelo.'

We nodded to each other. Angelo didn't look like he belonged to his name, but I wasn't about to point that out. Today they were both in their civvies, black bomber jackets and trousers, and vaguely police-issue rubber-soled boots.

Angelo was shorter in stature, but just as broad as Len. At first glance, he looked mildly less psychotic than his partner, but that wasn't saying much. They took up station a respectful distance from their boss.

Marc offered me a drink as he waved me to one of the tables. I asked for coffee. 'Of course. There's a filter machine in the office. In fact, I'll have one, too,' Marc said. 'Len, would you mind?' I glanced up and was surprised to see that the big man moved instantly to fulfil the request. No sullen hesitations at being asked to play waitress. Marc obviously commanded respect as well as obedience.

'So, Charlie, how do you come to know so much about security?' Marc asked now, sitting back in his chair to study me, head tilted to one side. He was wearing a dark suit that he hadn't bought on his local high street, over a hand-stitched shirt that even someone with my limited sartorial knowledge could tell was Italian, and damned expensive.

'I picked it up, here and there,' I said cautiously. I wasn't about to tell him about the rather specialised training I'd been through. It felt as though it was all a long time ago, in another life.

Before you can attack a building, they'd taught me, you have to know how to secure it. Points of entry, minimum number of personnel, and their most effective positioning. The New Adelphi had too many twists and turns, too many dark corners. It would not have been my first choice of somewhere to try and make a stand. It was too perfect for an ambush.

'Here and *where* would that be?' Marc pressed now.

'Army, mainly,' I said and watched his eyebrow lift.

Behind him Angelo made a succinct and uncomplimentary remark about the Women's Royal Army Corps. I turned my head to meet his eyes without flinching, but then, I'd heard them all before, and worse. Much worse. Angelo stared back at me as he put a match to the end of a cigarette, challenging.

Marc backed him down with a single look, then turned back to me. 'How long were you in?'

I knew to the day, but I shrugged. 'Long enough,' I said.

'Why did you leave?'

'I was asked to go,' I said, forestalling any further questions on that tack by adding, 'It's personal, and I'm not prepared to talk about it.'

He heard the finality that flattened my voice, and those pale eyes searched my face for clues. I didn't give him any.

'So after you were *asked to go*,' he went on, putting emphasis on the last three words, 'what have you done since?'

'I've done a bit of keep fit and aerobics training, a bit of personal training at the local gym, but mostly I teach self-defence to women.'

Len reappeared at this point. He obviously had more domestic graces than I'd given him credit for, because he neatly placed two plain white cups in front of us. Individual portions of cream and sugar were balanced with the spoon on the saucer of each. I was impressed.

Len ignored my murmur of thanks, but Marc's nod of approval seemed to keep him happy. He retreated to a bar stool next to Angelo, holding station a discreet distance away.

'Textbook theories are all very well,' Marc said, stirring the cream into his coffee, 'but unfortunately the sort of opponent you'd have to deal with in a nightclub has probably never come any closer to martial arts than watching a Bruce Lee film. They have an unpleasant habit of not playing by the rules, don't they Len?' he called.

Len came to his feet again and moved back across the dance floor with a nasty swagger, flexing his fingers by his sides. He was grinning in a way that made sweat break out on my palms. 'Martial arts, eh?' he said. 'Load of bollocks. Go on, then, how about you try having a go at me?'

Ah shit, I thought. Just what I need. I glanced back at Marc, but his face was shuttered, withdrawn. It was clear this was a test, and I was on my own to prove I could pass it.

I slid a fairly big smile onto my face and forced myself to stay sitting down. I didn't want to put forward any form of provocation. If I stood up now, took up any sort of stance, or appeared to be taking him seriously, things were going to get way out of hand.

I knew little about the sort of ability Len had. I had to guess from his behaviour the other night that he'd started—and finished—more than his share of brawls. If he'd been working club doors for any length of time he was going to know at least as many dirty tricks as I did, and probably more. He was also maybe twice my weight, and a good six inches taller.

I was further handicapped by being dressed in bike leathers and boots, which would cut down my speed. Plus the fact I had no real desire to hurt him. That is not a good way to go into a potential scrap.

It's one of the things I stress hardest when I'm teaching my classes. By the time events reach the stage where you have to stand and fight, you have to be fully prepared to put everything you've got into it and not hold anything back. You might only get one chance.

Most important of all now, was the fact that I didn't want *him* to damage *me*.

Most people would have taken his expansive stomach as their first objective, but he looked like he was packing too much muscle. That left me with the smaller, harder to hit targets—ears, eyes, nose, throat and groin. These required less strength, but more accuracy and speed.

I've found from experience that even the most slow-witted of men have pretty good reactions when you go for their wedding tackle. Often out of all proportion to the value of the equipment.

While I didn't think for a moment that Len would go so far as to beat me to a bloody pulp right there on the dance floor, if I didn't come up with something pretty quickly, it was probably going to hurt. Lateral thinking was called for.

I rubbed my hands together and glanced around me. 'So, do we fight here or shall we go outside?' I said briskly, looking expectant. 'Only, I'd hate to bleed on the furniture, seeing as the cleaners have obviously been round already today.'

I glanced at his face and saw the faintest flicker of surprise. 'Eh?' he said.

'Well,' I went on, looking doubtfully around me at the floor space available. 'I suppose we could have a go here, but if we're going to do the thing properly, there's not much room. I'd hate to crack my skull on the table leg when I fall over. Not on top of you already having broken my nose,' I added cheerfully. 'God, they'll be mopping bits of me out of here for weeks. I hope your cleaners aren't squeamish, Marc?'

Len was looking less sure of himself. I pressed the advantage, such as it was, for all I was worth. 'Are you left or right handed? I only ask because I've been having a bit of trouble with a tooth on this side,' I said, gesturing to my mouth. 'If you're going to clout me hard enough to knock a few teeth out, do you think you could make it on the right, about up here? It might just sort it out.'

Len's hands had stopped clenching at his sides. He was starting to grin, which was not a pretty sight in itself. Thank Christ for that.

I got to my feet, dragged my chair a little way from the table, and stood on it. I purposely didn't stand up straight, so that it only lifted me slightly higher than my opponent. 'That's better,' I said. 'Now I can reach.' I put my hands up in the classic mock-fisticuffs position. 'OK, guy, whenever you're ready!'

That did it. He threw his head back and laughed out loud. Then he turned and strutted to his bar stool. 'See,' he said to Angelo, 'I told you it was a load of bollocks.'

I climbed down from my chair slowly and moved it back, feeling drained. You don't realise how much adrenaline you've been pumping round your body until suddenly you don't need it any more. My legs were wobbling so much I had to sit down. When I looked up Marc was watching me carefully. 'Nice act,' he said quietly, with a cynical smile. 'So, is this martial arts thing a waste of time, then?'

I shrugged. 'I don't know,' I said tiredly. 'I don't teach martial arts. I teach self-defence.'

'And what's the difference?'

'Self-defence,' I said slowly, looking him straight in the eye, 'is all about getting out of dangerous situations without getting hurt.'

The smile faded gradually and he looked rueful. He nodded, understanding. 'Like that?' he asked, inclining his head in Len's direction.

'Yeah,' I said, finding a smile of my own. 'Just like that. I've just defended myself. The fact I didn't have to resort to violence to do it is just my good fortune.'

Marc looked thoughtful as he drained his coffee cup. He came to his feet. 'I'm not sure whether your peculiar brand of diplomacy won't be lost on most of my customers, but I think I'd like to see you try it out,' he said, as he buttoned his beautifully tailored jacket. 'You can start on Saturday.'

WHEN I LEFT the New Adelphi Club I just had time to call in at the supermarket before I was due at Shelseley Lodge. I was getting low on the essentials like toothpaste and washing up liquid and I couldn't put it off any longer. I went via the nearest petrol station. The Suzuki's a thirsty little sod unless you take it really easy, and I was running on fumes.

I suppose I'd enjoy shopping more if I had a car, or a big touring bike with hefty panniers. As it is I have to watch the size and shape of what I buy as much as the content. If it's a choice between dried packet peas or the tinned variety, I go for the packet just because it's easier to carry.

I usually go round with two baskets, because I know that's roughly what will fit in my tank bag and rucksack. When they're full, I have to stop, although there are occasions when I've ridden home with a box of cornflakes stuffed down the front of my jacket. Or had to eat some surplus item standing in the car park, purely because there was no way of carrying it. Such are the routine problems of everyday biking life.

I started riding a motorbike while I was in the army, mainly I suppose just to annoy my parents. Not that joining up hadn't done so enough already. Still, when you've been nothing but a big disappointment to them from the word go, you may as well go the whole hog.

My parents are typical upper middle class. Nice big detached Georgian house in the country, Volvo estate and Jaguar saloon on the gravel driveway. My mother even has the obligatory brace of Labradors and owns a pair of those green Wellington boots with the buckles on the side.

My father is a doctor—a surgeon. I failed to live up to his expectations from a very early age. I should have been the first-born of twins, a girl and a boy, but by some freak of fortune I came into the world alive and my twin reached it dead.

I think things began to go downhill as soon as the midwife turned to him and said, 'Well congratulations, sir, at least you have a daughter.' He went off to cancel my brother's place at Gordonstoun and his interest in me was never really revived.

The cool and logical mind that makes him so good at his profession is carried over to his personal life. He and my mother must have had sex at least once—I'm an only child—but conjuring up the image of it defies my imaginative powers.

He never even flickered when I told him I was joining up. He asked in a detached manner where I was expected to do my training, and to please let my mother know in advance when I was coming home on leave, so she could get my room ready. Then he went back to his newspaper as if the subject was of no further interest to him.

My mother was horrified, but more, I suspect, for the social implications than anything else. A son in the army is one thing, although unless it's one of the more up-market regiments it doesn't hold quite the same kudos that it used to. A daughter in the WRAC is quite another thing. She even took me off to one side and asked me if I was gay.

I think it was about my third or fourth leave that I turned up on the first motorbike I bought after passing my test, a second-hand Yamaha 350cc Powervalve.

It provoked the strongest reaction from my father yet. He took me off into his study, sat me down, and handed me pages of case notes. They were all of people he'd dealt with who'd received injuries in motorcycle accidents. It was gory stuff, made all the more gory for being written in such a detached, clinical manner.

Case after case, they made me shiver. Eventually I looked up and demanded to know if my father thought this would put me off motorcycling. 'I know the risks and I'm careful,' I said defiantly.

'I'm sure you are, Charlotte,' he replied. 'I have no intention of trying to influence your decisions one way or the other. The only thing I ask is that you ride with the correct protective clothing.' Just when I thought he was showing signs of affection, he added, 'It makes reconstructive work so much easier.'

In the end, though, it wasn't my fondness for motorbikes that curtailed my army career. I wonder if my parents would have found it easier to forgive me if it had been.

Or for me to forgive them.

By the time I came out of the supermarket, the light had gone and it was threatening to rain. The wind was a lazy one—it went straight through you because it couldn't be bothered to make a detour.

I rode quickly through the dwindling daylight to the Lodge and slotted the bike into a space at the edge of the gravel, near the overgrown tangle of rhododendron bushes. Lights were blazing from every window as I walked through the front door.

I called out as usual as I hit the hallway, but no one answered. I poked my head round the door into Tris and Ailsa's sitting room, but that was empty too.

Moving more cautiously now, I walked through the ground floor of the house, under ornate plaster mouldings muffled by years of magnolia emulsion. Where were they all?

The only logic place to look for the entire household was the ballroom, and that's where I headed now. It sounds grander than it is. At some point early in her opulent marriage, old Mrs Shelseley had commissioned an extension on the back of the Lodge specifically for parties. The structure the architects had devised was around forty feet square, elegantly proportioned, with a line of French windows down one side leading out into the gardens. A row of dusty chandeliers hung from the high ceiling.

Apart from children's birthdays, and at Christmas, the room was mostly idle now, although I understand that events there used to be the height of the local social calendar. Tris still calls it the ballroom, with hazy childhood memories of a more glorious age. Ailsa just calls it a bugger to heat. I used it for my classes and for that it was perfect. It even had a proper sprung wooden dance floor.

As I came in I found just about everyone gathered round where Ailsa was urgently speaking to them. Half the people present turned to glance at me, then shifted their attention back to Ailsa.

'Look, I'm sure it's just a coincidence,' she said. 'The police would have said if there was any reason to be concerned, surely? There's nothing to worry about. Please.'

She was trying to be reassuring, but there was a note of strain in her voice that belied her soothing words. Like Tris, Ailsa wore her hair short, making her head seem too small for her body. She wore large silver hoops in her pierced ears, that caught the light and jingled slightly as she spoke.

Whatever the discussion had been, my arrival seemed to mark its closure. The women dispersed, muttering, clutching children who were unnaturally quiet and well-behaved. It was probably that which unnerved me the most.

'Ailsa?' I said, moving forwards. 'What's the matter?'

'Oh hello, Charlie love,' she said. She sank onto an elderly brocade chair, shoulders slumped, looking more tired than I'd ever seen her. 'Some of the girls are a bit bothered by this Susie Hollins thing, that's all.'

I must have looked a little baffled. Attacks on women happen, as most of the residents could testify first hand. It still didn't quite explain the council of war. Ailsa saw my expression and gave a heavy sigh.

'They were both here,' she said reluctantly.

'What do you mean, both here? Who was?' But even as I asked the question, I knew. It came to me with a sense of creeping awareness that as soon as Susie Hollins had climbed onto the stage at the New Adelphi Club, I'd known that I'd seen her before.

'Susie and the other girl,' Ailsa confirmed. 'In fact, Susie was only here a month or so ago. That boyfriend of hers, Tony, has a hair-trigger temper and a jealous streak, which is not a good combination at the best of times. He'd convinced himself that she was seeing someone else, apparently, and beat her up. She spent about three days here, I think, swearing long and loud that she was finished with him for good. Then he came round grovelling and back she went.' Her lips twisted into a bitter smile. 'Like a lamb to the slaughter.'

She suddenly seemed to realise the macabre aptness of the expression. Her mouth formed a soundless *oh*, and her eyes began to fill.

Tris patted her shoulder, looking awkward. 'Come on, love,' he murmured. He was trying to be bracing, but there was a note of panic there that only men get when faced with a woman about to cry.

Ailsa gave him a wan smile, sniffed, and made a determined effort to pull herself together. 'I'm all right,' she said. 'Really. I must get on, there's so much to do. I just don't know what to say to them to convince them they're over-reacting, that's all.' She got to her feet, moving as far as the doorway before she paused. 'Two of the girls have left already, you know,' she said. 'Just packed their bags and went. They never even said goodbye.'

'It's their loss, Ailsa,' I said. 'You put your heart and soul into this place. They won't find anywhere better.'

She nodded jerkily a couple of times, grateful for the support and still trying to hold back the tears. 'I know, it's just—' she trailed off, then finished with feeling, 'Oh, bloody men!' and stamped away down the corridor.

I turned to find Tris standing where she'd left him, looking downcast.

'I wouldn't take it personally,' I told him.

He sighed. 'I stopped doing that a long time ago,' he said. 'Otherwise I would have thrown myself off a cliff by now.'

Six

THE CLASS I taught late that afternoon was packed, mainly with Lodge residents. It seemed that just about all the women at Shelseley had suddenly decided that self-defence was a subject they could no longer afford to ignore.

I had planned to teach them how to escape from a pinned-down potential rape situation on the ground, and had dragged out the heavy crashmats ready, but at the last minute I changed my mind. Something told me that particular lesson would have been a little too emotive right now. I went through wrist locks instead, and came away vaguely regretting that I'd chickened out.

Afterwards, I stuck my head round Tris and Ailsa's door to find Ailsa alone, poring over what looked like books of accounts. She invited me in for a cup of chamomile tea. I accepted more to be sociable than because I especially like the stuff.

'It was busier than I was expecting,' I said as she poured the straw-coloured liquid from a chipped Wedgwood teapot.

'Well, love, I suppose I can't say I'm surprised,' she said, but her eyes had drifted back to the books in front of her. Distracted, she brushed a hand through her spiky hair.

I put my head on one side and regarded her. 'What happens if they all leave?' I asked quietly.

Her hand stilled, then dropped. 'We struggle,' she said briefly, closed the book and sighed. 'When old Mrs Shelseley died she left us some money to maintain the house for as long as it remains a refuge, but we had to re-roof the entire place about four years ago, and that ate up most of the capital. We get grant money, and some charity funding, but the bulk of it comes from social services, and to be honest, Charlie, that's what pays the bills. We can't afford to lose them.'

She looked about to say more, but a commotion had kicked up in the hallway outside, and Ailsa paused as she worked out if it was serious enough to warrant her intervention. Years of experience had tuned her senses to the point where she could instantly recognise the difference between the screams of a playfully violent children's game, and those which greeted the unexpected arrival of a drunken ex-husband and father.

It was soon clear that this was neither. After only a moment's hesitation, Ailsa was on her feet and moving for the doorway with the sort of speed you wouldn't expect from a woman of her size. Slower in mind, if not in body, I was half a stride behind.

We weren't alone in recognising an emergency in progress. Doors were opening all along the hallway, and up on the landing as well. There were already half a dozen women in the hall itself, clustered round a dark-haired girl in her late teens or early twenties. She was slumped on her knees by the bottom of the stairs, clutching at the ornate newel post like a drowning swimmer, and wailing.

'Oh God,' Ailsa muttered. She hurried forwards and bent close to the girl. 'Nina, love, what is it? What's happened?'

The girl turned her face in the direction of the voice, but her eyes had that thousand-yard stare of deep shock.

'O-outside,' she managed at last. She swallowed a couple of times, her throat working convulsively. 'There w-was a man. Outside.'

Ailsa threw me a single pleading look over her shoulder. I gave her a slight nod, knowing immediately what she was asking of me. This wasn't the time to argue, and besides, the girl, Nina, had started to shudder and shake. I thought there was more than a fair chance she was going to throw up, which didn't make me eager to hang around here.

I stepped round both of them, heading for the open doorway, and the darkness beyond it. The group melted back to let me through. Nobody offered to walk with me, but then, I hadn't really expected them to.

I went down the stone steps and moved quickly to the side of the house. I stood there for a minute or so, out of the sweep of light flooding from the un-curtained windows, waiting for my eyes to adjust, and my nerves to steady.

The pause gave me chance to listen for the sounds of movement, but there was nothing apart from the rattle of wind across bare branches, the hum of traffic from the main road, and the jump of my own heart.

I was mildly surprised to find that I wasn't scared, though. Not that mind-numbing fear that freezes your blood. Instead, I could feel my senses dilating, my instincts reaching out into the night. Rather than dulling my responses, apprehension was serving to give me a sharper edge.

I had no doubts that if the girl said she'd seen a man lurking out here, she was probably right. His intentions might be sinister, but I was determined that I was not afraid of him, whoever he was.

I'd been down that road once before, and had returned coated with the bitter grime of pain and experience. I had so nearly not come back at all. It was interesting to know some good had come of the journey.

I eased myself away from the wall and tried to walk quietly across the gravel, which was an impossibility even in bare feet, never mind in the heavy-soled bike boots I'd changed into after the class. Every few strides I had to pause to clear the echo of my own footsteps from my ears.

I spent a quarter-hour moving as silently as I could through the area surrounding the drive. I wasn't stupid enough to force my way deep into the undergrowth. It would have been asking for trouble.

Even so, I found no trace of an intruder. Nothing.

By the time I got back into the hallway, the crowd had mostly disbanded. One or two of the hardier ones were lurking on the stairs. They asked me if I'd spotted anyone, and took my negative answer with sceptical smiles. Whether that was because they doubted there was anyone to find, or because they thought I was just trying to allay their fears, I couldn't be sure.

I found Ailsa back in the sitting room, squeezed onto the sofa with her arm round Nina, who still seemed as distraught as she had been when I'd gone out. Tris had appeared by this time, and was perched on a chair on the other side of the room, hollow-eyed and anxious.

Ailsa glanced up at me sharply when I came in, but I shook my head. She looked relieved.

I moved round into Nina's line of sight, and crouched in front of her. 'Whoever he was, Nina,' I said, speaking carefully, 'he's gone now. You're OK.'

Nina had her arms folded round her body, and was rocking gently back and forth. 'It's my fault,' she mumbled. 'It's all my fault.'

Uncomprehending for a moment, I caught Ailsa's sorrowful glance, and I understood then why Nina was at the refuge. She'd been raped.

I remembered Ailsa telling me a few details when the girl had first arrived. She'd been raped by a friend of the family, and when she'd told her parents, their first reaction had been of disbelief, and denial. Betrayed, Nina had run, ending up at Shelseley.

I put my hands on her shoulders. 'Nina, listen to me,' I said, my voice sharp enough to cut through the layers. 'It's not your fault. Nothing that has happened to you is your fault. Don't let it destroy you, or he's won. Do you hear me? Is that what you want? To give up?' I ignored Ailsa's murmur of protest and plunged on. 'Come out fighting, Nina, come back stronger. Stop giving him this power over you, otherwise you'll never be rid of him.'

She twisted weakly in my grasp. 'You don't know what it's like,' she moaned.

'Oh yes I do, Nina,' I said, and my voice was grim enough to register. 'Trust me, I know exactly what it's like.'

There were certain similarities. I'd also known the men who had raped me, all four of them. *Donalson, Hackett, Morton, and Clay.* The names ran through my mind like a mantra. They'd been on the same military training course and while they hadn't exactly been my friends, I was supposed to have been able to trust them with my life.

I still don't know why they picked me. There were only two other girls on the same course, so I suppose that cut down the odds a little. I spent months afterwards wondering what weakness in me they'd recognised. What had marked me out as a victim.

Eventually, I'd realised that I was not special, nor fatally flawed. I'd simply been in the wrong place at the wrong time. Sometimes, it's easier to believe in fate. That the story lines of our lives are already written, you just follow the script. But maybe I just didn't want to believe that my whole reason for being was to be raped and beaten by a group of drunken squaddies.

People told me I'd been lucky to survive, but it took me a long time before I could begin to view that state of affairs with any sense of happiness. Fear had evolved very slowly into anger. A desire followed first to learn self-defence, and then to teach what I'd learned to others. It gave me back control of my own existence.

I stood up, letting go of Nina's arms, and watched the top of her bowed head. She'd stopped caring much about her appearance since the attack, never wearing make-up and letting her hair grow unstyled. It hung lankly around her face, so fine that her ears stood out through it. Her shoulders were rounded. I don't think I'd ever seen anyone look more utterly defeated.

Ailsa made 'leave now' motions with her eyes. I nodded silently, and headed for the door, picking up my helmet and rucksack as I went. Tris got up to show me out.

'Don't you think you were a little hard on her?' he said quietly, once the living room door was closed behind us.

I shrugged my way into my rucksack. 'She's had months of hand-holding and sympathy,' I said. 'She's physically recovered, the memory's fading. What she needs now is pushing until she starts to push back. She needs to face what she's been through and deal with it, not bury it under layers of cotton wool and hope it all goes away.'

Tris considered that for a moment. 'Not everyone responds the way you expect to that kind of stimuli,' he pointed out gently. 'Not everybody has the strength of character to cope.'

'They have to,' I said, glancing at him as I turned to go. 'What else is there?'

Despite my words, I looked around me carefully as I walked down the steps again and across the gravel to the bike. The screen of rhododendron bushes looked quiet, but to be truthful, for all I could see through it, it might as well have been one-way glass. I jammed my helmet on, feeling suddenly vulnerable as it cut down my peripheral vision.

The Suzuki started up first kick. For once I didn't linger to let the motor warm up fully, paddling it backwards out of its space and moving quickly towards the road.

All the while, I could just feel a set of eyes on my back. It might be paranoia, but I couldn't seem to shake it.

I rode straight home, taking the shortest route. On the way I passed Terry's video van parked up on his round. You couldn't fail to recognise that revolting colour-scheme, even in the dark.

When I reached the flat I had just enough time to hurriedly tidy my usual debris before Sam was due to arrive. As I passed the answering machine I noticed that the message light was blinking and I hit the rewind button.

It was Clare. 'Hi, Charlie. I've got the details on that, er—story you were after. I can't give them to you over the phone, but if you want to call round, I'll let you know what I've managed to find out.' Her voice sounded strangely solemn as she added, 'I hope you've got a strong stomach.'

I almost rang her there and then, but a glance at the clock told me there wasn't time. As it was, Sam rang the bell just after six, armed again with a box of computer disks and a big grin.

He was wearing his usual scruffy bike jacket and battered AGV lid, together with dusty black trousers and trainers. He had a long college scarf wrapped round his neck to keep out the wind, but no gloves and his fingers were white from the cold. I don't know how he stands it.

He presented exactly the sort of image that people like my parents hate so much about motorcycling. The fact that Sam has a very good degree in something to do with computers and could probably be earning a fortune as a programmer instead of tinkering at the Uni has nothing to do with it. A lout in a suit with a sharp haircut would get their vote every time. Even if, when you asked him a difficult question, someone else had to push his chest in and out.

Sam unfolded the lap-top on the coffee table and his fingers started dancing over the keyboard. I put the coffee on and left him to it. I had to admire his concentration. By the time the coffee had filtered and stopped making blocked drain noises, he was still tapping away. He barely turned his head when the mug went down beside him, just murmured his thanks and carried right on.

I was in the kitchen, staring moodily out of the skylight and thinking about Nina when Sam gave a sudden whoop of triumph. I moved back through to find him sitting back and taking a swig of his coffee, looking pleased with himself again. The Cheshire cat would have been a manic depressive by comparison. 'OK, we're in,' he said. 'What am I looking for?'

'Some clue as to the original owner of the machine,' I said.

Sam put his mug down and scanned the list of files that had appeared on the screen. 'Of course, some of these are incomplete, but I should be able to find something,' he said.

'Great.' I hesitated, fought briefly with myself, then gave in. 'Have you eaten? I was going to chuck some pasta together if you fancy it? Nothing outstanding.'

'Terrific!' Sam said. 'I didn't know you could cook.'

'You shouldn't make rash statements like that until you've tasted it,' I warned and headed back to the kitchen. I dug out the dried tagliatelle, a tin of plum tomatoes, garlic, chilli, and the secret ingredient, a Hot Pepperami sausage. Not exactly *cordon bleu*, but then, I wasn't out to wow him with my cooking.

I threw the ingredients together quickly. It was my usual stand-by and I could do it in my sleep. I set the kettle boiling for the pasta and went back to see how Sam was getting on.

'I hope you don't mind breathing garlic fumes all over everyone at work tomorrow,' I said.

He looked up blankly. 'Hm?'

I shook my head. 'Never mind. How're you doing?'

'Well, not as well as I'd hoped,' he admitted. 'The most I seem to be able to get is some of the file names, but the contents might as well be Swahili for all the sense I can make of them. Look.'

He opened a file at random. All I saw was a string of smiley faces and the sort of squiggles that could have belonged to some complex algebra problem. He shut the file down again and tried another, with the same result.

'Here are the file names, if they mean anything to you—delivery dates, stock, distribution, contacts. It just looks like it's been used for standard accounts stuff. I assume they copied everything before they passed the computer on to your mate, otherwise somebody's going to have quite a bit of explaining to do to the tax man.'

'And there's no way of finding out anything else?'

He rummaged in the disk box he'd brought with him. 'Well, if it's a very simple file I might have something here that would work, but it's a bit of a long shot,' he said doubtfully.

I heard the kettle click off and went back to the kitchen to pour the boiled water into a pan with the pasta. I stuck it on the hob and returned to the lounge.

By the time I got there Sam seemed to be having more success. 'Here's what's in the delivery dates file, but it's not a lot,' he said. 'Some of the data at the top of the screen is just totally corrupted. There's not much hope of getting anything out of that. Then we've just got a string of numbers. They could be dates, but it's not much to go on.'

I sighed, disappointed. 'OK, Sam, thanks for trying anyway,' I said.

'No problem,' he replied, but didn't sound as though he meant it.

He was still frowning when I left him to go and see to the food. When I came back with two plates Sam had shut the computer down, in disgust presumably, and had left it on the desk. He was sitting on the sofa, chin in his hands, and looking deep in thought.

It didn't affect his appetite, though. He wolfed down the pasta making all the right appreciative noises. He ate with his fork turned round, scooping food onto it and into his mouth. My mother would have fainted at the sight.

Still, at least he was well trained enough to clear the plates away afterwards without being asked. He hadn't progressed past the stacking them in the washing-up bowl stage, but you can't have everything.

It was just after eight-thirty when he left. As soon as he'd gone I rang Terry. I tried his mobile number first. It was switched on and he picked up straight away. I told him we'd managed to get into the computer, and what Sam had found on it. It sounded pretty lame when I laid it out for him, but Terry seemed pleased.

'That's terrific! That should be just enough to worry the bastard!' he said, sounding devious. 'Do me a favour and hang onto it for me for a few days, would you? I'll come and pick it up over the weekend. Cheers for that though, Charlie, you're an absolute doll!'

'Oh great,' I muttered as he rang off. 'Now I'm inflatable.'

Seven

ALMOST AS SOON as I put the phone down, it started ringing. I picked it up half-anticipating that it might be Terry again.

Even though I'd been thinking about her earlier, I certainly wasn't expecting it to be my mother on the other end of the line.

'Charlotte,' she said. She was trying for friendly warmth, but unease pitched her cultured voice a tad too high. I even thought I could hear the faint rustle of a nervously twisted string of pearls.

For a moment I almost panicked as I opened my mouth and nothing happened. No sounds emerged. I shut it again quickly.

'Charlotte?' she said again, a question this time, sharper. 'Charlotte, are you still there?'

I cleared my throat. This time it worked. 'Yes, I'm still here,' I said neutrally. 'What do you *want*, Mother?'

She didn't ring so often now. Just after I got kicked out of the army and the fuss had started to abate, her attempts then to build a bridge between us had been more earnest, and more frequent. She'd written long letters that I pointedly returned to sender. She'd even driven over to see me a few times.

Now she'd fallen back on the telephone, and even that method of communication had become sporadic. She'd become slowly discouraged by my stubborn lack of cooperation, my refusal to acknowledge that the stance she'd taken had any basis in validity.

I don't know what irritated more. That in some ways she seemed to be giving up on her only child so easily, or that she doggedly persisted. Even with the constantly increasing timescale, I was dismayed to find that talking to her still actually hurt. A physical pain I hadn't been prepared for.

There was a mildly offended pause before she replied, swallowing my snotty behaviour, pouring oil, as she always did. 'I don't want anything, darling,' she said soothingly. 'I just wondered how you are, that's all. We haven't heard from you in a while, and I just thought—'

'Mother, you haven't heard *from* me for several years,' I interrupted, stony. 'Why would I suddenly either want to get in touch with you now, or want you to get in touch with me?'

Another hesitation, like a fractured satellite link. 'Well,' she stumbled. It was uncharacteristic, and unlike her. She valued her poise as much as she valued her classically understated wardrobe and her middle-aged Tory-politician's-wife hairstyle. 'I just thought there might be something you needed, or—'

'There's nothing I need from you,' I said, appalled by the waver I let slip through unmasked. I closed my eyes with the effort of stopping back the tears. It was suddenly vital that I didn't let her know she could still get to me. 'There's nothing I want that you can give me,' I went on, colder now, in control. 'Unless there's something wrong, or either of you are ill, please stop calling me, or I'll have my number changed.'

I thought I heard a soft gasp at the deliberate cruelty. 'Oh, *Charlotte*,' she said, letting her distress through for the first time.

'Goodbye, Mother,' I said, and put the receiver down.

For what seemed like a long moment I sat and stared stupidly at the dead telephone. Parents are supposed to love their children regardless, aren't they? Overlook their faults, forgive their sins. And most of all they're supposed to trust and support them in times of trouble. Not back away. I could understand Nina running for shelter when she'd failed to get the loyalty she'd anticipated from her own parents.

After all, it's not in the Good Parenting Handbook that they're allowed the luxury of letting their distaste show all too clearly, however sordid the predicament in which their offspring find themselves. That's not in the rules.

I thought of Nina again. Oh yes, I knew exactly what it was like. To have your parents frowning at you, with doubt behind their eyes. I think that was the worst thing. That they'd believe I'd willingly taken part in what my attackers were claiming was practically an orgy.

The court martial of Donalson, Hackett, Morton, and Clay had been a shambles. Faced with the prospect of helping convict their mates, vital witnesses on the same squad miraculously developed myopia, or amnesia, or both.

Even one of the girls who was supposed to speak up for me seemed suddenly unwilling to stick her neck out. Either by accident or careful design, it began to look as though I was totally to blame for the 'incident', as they politely termed it.

The end result was that the four accused were let off, and I was unceremoniously chucked out. That should have been the end of it. Sometimes, I wished to God I'd left it there. That way, my mother would never have had the chance to express her doubts about my innocence so publicly.

I sat there, fighting the emotions that crashed over me in waves. Anger was followed by a bitterness I could taste in the back of my throat, and a fierce determination not to forgive my mother, however Christian it might make me feel.

Much as it gives me no satisfaction to admit it, a good dollop of self-pity was in there somewhere, too. I thought I'd stopped feeling sorry for myself. It was disappointing to discover that all it took to bring it all back was something as trivial as an unexpected phone call.

It took me a while to shake myself out of it, to get back to the more pressing problems at hand.

Partly to make sure the phone was engaged if my mother tried to call me back, and partly so I wasn't upset if she didn't bother, I rang Clare. I forced my mind back to the message she'd left on the answering machine. '*I hope you've got a strong stomach,*' she'd said. Did I really want to know what she'd found out?

I dialled the number anyway. I had another class to teach the day after tomorrow at the refuge, an open one this time, and I just knew I was going to get asked awkward questions about Susie. I needed to know, even if I didn't really want to hear.

I shivered abruptly, as though someone had walked over my grave. Maybe that incident at Shelseley, and now that brief contact with my mother, had just made me more jumpy than usual.

Jacob answered the phone just when I was about to hang up. He told me Clare was in the bath. 'Come round if you like,' he offered generously. 'It might persuade her to get out of the water before she turns into a completely wizened old prune. I'm going out in half an hour in any case, so you two can have a girlie chat.'

My vision of a quiet night in evaporated. I sighed as I picked up the bike keys and my leather jacket. With a sense of foreboding, I headed for the door.

I HAVE TO admit that I approached the subject matter for my next class at Shelseley two days later with a new wariness. I'd spent a couple of hours round at Jacob and Clare's place. When I'd left I had a much clearer idea of what had happened to Susie Hollins, and a sickness in my soul.

Susie might have been stupid, and petty, and quick to temper, but as Clare had said, nobody deserved to die that way. The picture that emerged from the police reports the paper had obtained was not a pretty one.

Susie had either gone willingly with her attacker, meaning it might have been someone she knew, or she'd been too frightened by his threats to put up much of an initial struggle. He'd taken her out to a secluded spot, not far away, and there he'd had his fun . . .

Now I faced my class with a new passion. We were in the ballroom, as usual. The light had gone early, dimming until only blackness was visible through the French windows, and all detail of the garden had disappeared from view. Years ago, the ornamental wall sconces had been augmented by a haphazard array of fluoro tubes. They added significantly to the overall light level, but did nothing for the ambience.

It was a largish group, a dozen or so, ranging in age from late teens to late forties. They listened to me gravely. After the earlier rape, and now Susie's murder, I knew I had their full attention.

'Attacks and sexual assaults on women,' I told them, 'are rarely carried out in the place where first contact takes place. 'We'll call this first location point A, and the second one B. A is where he picks you up, grabs you, and B is where the actual assault takes place.

'Point B is his choice, his territory,' I added. 'If you allow yourself to be immobilised and taken there, you will be on his ground. You will not only be at a major psychological disadvantage, but the risk to you *doubles*. You must do whatever you can to avoid being taken to point B.'

I glanced round their serious faces. I didn't have to elaborate further than that.

'Supposing he's got a knife?' one woman asked. Joy was in her late twenties, skinny to the point of gauntness, but with a very pretty face if you went for the emaciated look, and red hair cut in a bob. She was a relative newcomer, but keen, often turning up at several classes in a week.

I gazed at her levelly. 'Run away,' I said.

There was a smattering of laughter at that, but it died away when I didn't join in.

'I'm serious,' I continued. 'Choosing to stand there and fight someone who's got a knife is lunacy. Trust me on this. Unless you're cornered, you turn and you run like hell. That's your best option by far.'

'Yes, but supposing he's in trainers and you're in high heels,' Joy persisted. 'You're not going to get very far, are you?'

'True,' I allowed. 'OK, I know it isn't always possible to run, which is why we're going to cover knife defences in this class.' I went over to my rucksack and pulled out the fake plastic daggers I used just for this purpose.

I told the class to pair up and handed the daggers round. There was an odd number, and it was Joy who ended up with me. She looked nervous at the prospect. I grinned to reassure her as I handed her the dagger.

'OK, to start off with, let's look at what to do if he's got the knife at your throat.' I positioned us so that she had a hold of the front of my sweatshirt with her left hand, the knife held against the side of my neck with her right. 'Come on, Joy, take a firm grip,' I instructed. 'Remember, you're trying to kill me here.'

Whoever had killed Susie had got a firm grip on her, all right. A death grip. He'd jammed the knife so hard against her throat that the blade had peeled back the skin, slicing into flesh and muscle, opening up the blood vessels so her strength and her will to fight drizzled away. Had he enjoyed then violating her slowly weakening body? Had it given him an added thrill?

I swallowed as I buttoned down tight on the thought. I showed the class how to twist suddenly away from the weapon, dropping away and down to the side, then striking at the hand that held it. By wrenching the wrist back on itself, you could turn the tables, taking control of the knife hand and using their own blade to shear at the arm that still held you captive.

It was a fairly simple movement, and repetition made it surer. I went through it again a few times, then let them all practise for five minutes or so. 'Remember,' I said, 'go for the arm that's holding you. Don't be tempted to stab them anywhere else. You're not out for vengeance here, you're just effecting your escape.'

'If it came down to it, could you actually do it?' Joy asked now, and there was an edge to her question. 'Could you actually kill a man who was attacking you?'

I paused, giving it some serious thought. I noticed the rest of the class had hesitated, stopped to listen.

'It depends what you mean,' I said at last. 'If you're asking have I got the ability to do so, then I suppose yes, I have. I know where and how to hit somebody to do them serious damage, but that proves nothing. You are all physically capable of ploughing through a bus queue in your car, or holding a cushion over your granny's face, but that doesn't mean you'd actually go through with it.'

There was another twitch of amusement from the others and I grinned at them. I hoped nobody would notice I was side-stepping the question, because I didn't really know the answer.

In the relatively short period I spent in the British army I was never required to get close enough to the enemy to actually shoot at them. I learned to fire handguns, rifles and light submachine guns simply as part of the training. I often wondered when I was out on the ranges how I would feel about squeezing the trigger if that cut-out board thirty metres away was a living, breathing person.

When you went to paste the little squares of paper over the holes left by the high velocity rounds in your target, all you found were sets of splintered holes. No blood, no shattered bone or ripped intestines, no screams of the wounded. I avoided finding an answer. That was OK, because the occasion never arose.

And afterwards, when my blood should have been up, when I should have been out looking for violent retribution, I folded like a coward. I tried to comfort myself with the knowledge that it was the only sensible course of action. It took me a long time to come to terms with the fact that I'd run away.

Donalson, Hackett, Morton, and Clay. They'd threatened me with death, and I'd believed them. Believed them enough not to fight too hard to save myself. I'd always wondered what would have happened if I'd had the skills I now possessed. How far I would have gone to survive.

I shook myself out of it as Joy looked vaguely dissatisfied and I tried a different tack. 'The law says you're allowed to use the minimum amount of force necessary,' I said. 'Gauging exactly what constitutes minimum force is not an easy one. You just have to use common sense.'

I picked up one of the fake daggers again. 'Look at what we've just been learning today,' I said. 'When you've got the knife away from your attacker, use it to skewer his hand to the ground—just remember if you're on concrete that doesn't work so well, so take the knife with you.'

More laughs, short, nervous, fading quickly. I waited a beat, then went on. 'Do not sink the knife hilt-deep into his jugular vein. I'm afraid that doesn't really constitute minimum force in the eyes of the law, whatever satisfaction it might give you at the time.'

But if it was me—now, today—I considered privately, I might just be tempted. I thought again of the list of dreadful injuries inflicted on Susie Hollins. Oh yes, I'd be tempted to go for it and to hell with the consequences. I looked into Joy's eyes, and saw the same thoughts reflected there.

'OK,' I said, 'let's go through that again. Change partners this time so—'

I broke off suddenly. I'd turned as I'd started to speak and a movement at one of the French windows had arrested my eye. The curtains were rarely drawn at Shelseley. I think the faded velvet drapes in the ballroom would have disintegrated if you'd try to release them from their tie-backs, in any case.

As my eye passed over the window I'd just caught the flash of a moving shadow on the other side of the glass. It's amazing the way the human eye works. It only needs a fraction to fill in the missing pieces and put together a complete image.

A man, watching.

I knew I shouldn't have jumped to that conclusion over gender, because I didn't see his face. Not even a pale suggestion, which implied a mask of some sort, but I was working on instinct.

He ducked back out of sight instantly, and I felt a corresponding crunch of fear. Nobody goes lurking round windows with their face covered unless they're up to no good. I remembered the figure Nina claimed to have seen, and I just knew it was the same man.

A few of the others had seen him, too. There was a ripple of fright, anger, at this furtive observer. The first instinct of some of the women was to retreat. Others went straight on the attack.

'Come on!' cried Joy, heading for the door. 'If we're quick we can catch him!'

I ran, too. I told myself it was to see that she didn't get herself into trouble, but I was lying. I wanted the bastard who was playing games with Nina, and now with me. I wanted him badly.

We pelted along the hallway and took the front steps in a flying leap, neck and neck. I vaguely remembered that Joy ran half marathons and tried not to disgrace myself. A couple of the others soon fell back.

With the gravel slick under our feet we slithered round the corner of the house, heading for the back garden. There were no exterior lights, and we slowed from necessity, unable to see a clear way forward. I wished I'd stopped to grab a torch. Ailsa kept a couple in their sitting room, in case of power cuts, but I hadn't wanted to let Joy race on ahead. Not alone, at any rate.

The back garden at Shelseley consisted of a large lawn area leading down to trees and shrubbery at the bottom end. Nearest to the house was a mossy terrace, now criss-crossed with washing lines, which flew rows of brightly-coloured children's clothes like a regatta.

The far end of the garden, down past where the ballroom jutted out from the main body of the house, was a place of shadows and imagination. I didn't want to go poking about down there in the dark, but Joy started forwards again, and I had little choice but to press on.

The air was grainy with early evening mist. When we stopped near the line of laurel bushes at the edge of the lawn, we could see our breath in clouds against the cold night air.

'He's gone,' I said, trying not to pant. 'There's no chance of finding him out here. I don't even want to try looking.'

'Who on earth do you think it was?' Joy asked. She didn't seem to be out of breath at all. God, I needed to do a better cardiovascular work-out. My stamina levels were lousy.

I shook my head. 'Who knows?' I said. 'Maybe it was just some guy who gets his kicks looking at a bunch of girls wrestling with each other.'

'Jeez, some people!' Joy said, pulling a face. 'Doesn't he have satellite TV?'

Noise from up the garden behind us made us turn. Ailsa appeared from the back door, carrying a flashlight. There was a big group of Lodge residents with her, spilling out onto the terrace. Everyone seemed to be talking at once.

'Charlie?' Ailsa called, her voice high with alarm. 'Are you all right, love?'

I shouted back that we were fine, and we started trudging back up the grass to where she was standing. Ailsa had pulled on a huge knitted shawl against the cold. Tris was beside her, huddled into his old parka.

'That does it,' Ailsa said tightly when we were closer. 'I've called the police. They've said they'll send somebody out right now.'

Not wanting to just sit around twiddling my thumbs until the cops arrived, I took my students back into the ballroom and continued the class. For all the good it did me. They were nervous and distracted, and I admit that I taught the rest of the lesson with half my attention on the row of French windows, just in case our mysterious observer was stupid enough to put in a reappearance. Needless to say, he wasn't.

The police, in the form of a small Asian WPC in a Fiesta panda car, turned up about half an hour after I'd finished. By that time my students, including Joy and any other potential witnesses, had all gone home.

She had a noisy poke round the back garden, came and made a few desultory notes, and left again. It didn't do much to inspire confidence in anyone, least of all me. I gathered from Ailsa that Nina had locked herself into her room and was refusing to answer the door. I couldn't really say I blamed her.

I told myself that finding out the details about Susie had made me jumpy, that was all, but that didn't have much of a calming influence, somehow. When I left the Lodge later and started up the Suzuki I was aware of a sudden overwhelming vulnerability that I didn't like.

I didn't like it at all.

Eight

BY THE TIME I started my stint at the New Adelphi Club that Saturday night, the police had made little progress in tracking down Susie Hollins' killer. According to Clare's contact on the crime desk, at any rate.

I asked her to keep me informed, and she promised to give me an update when I went over to eat lunch with them on the Sunday. I think it was Clare's not-so-subtle way of reminding me to turn up.

I was still smiling to myself at her heavy hints when I pulled into the car park of the New Adelphi Club. I left the bike in a corner. Out of the way, but still covered by the cameras, of course, and ambled round to the back door.

Deciding what I was going to wear had been a difficult one. Marc eventually relented on the black jeans front. Considering my limited wardrobe, he didn't have much choice.

Some discussion had taken place about the rest of me, apparently. The best compromise they could come up with was one of the badged polo shirts worn by the bar staff. It was the only thing they'd got that was something like the right size.

Marc said if it worked out on a longer-term basis, he'd see about getting me something more suitable. He didn't specify what. I had visions of the mini-skirt and stiletto outfits worn by the girls waiting on the tables at the club. My acid comment that putting me in high heels would reduce my agility to that of a kipper had been received in noncommittal silence. Ah well.

I hammered on the back door until it swung open. I was expecting Gary, but it was Len who admitted me, dressed in his usual dinner suit uniform. I could imagine him going to ASDA, or down the launderette in it.

He looked me up and down insultingly, making it clear he didn't think he was looking at much. I kept my expression bland while he played his little game. I've dealt with the Lens of this world before, and this time I didn't want to join in. So I didn't challenge, didn't show fear or irritation. I just stood and waited until he decided I'd had enough.

'Let's just get this straight from the start,' he said at last, bolshy, jabbing a sausage-like finger a millimetre from my nose. I resisted the urge to bite at it. 'The boss may have hired you, but I'm in charge of security in this place, see? You got a problem, you come to me. You don't go running to Mr Quinn. Clear?'

'Crystal,' I said, making my voice drawl just because I knew it would wind him up.

He grunted, but said nothing, turning and stamping off down the corridor and leaving me to follow on in his wake.

I sighed. It was going to be a fun evening.

Len eventually led me to one of the bars where the rest of his team were gathering. He didn't bother to introduce me while we waited until the last of them turned up. There were six of us altogether, including me, which proved me right in my own mind about Marc's problems. For a place the size of the New Adelphi, a dozen working security wouldn't have been overdoing it.

They were uniformly big men, who walked with their arms pushed out from their sides because of the amount of time they spent working on their back and chest muscles. It must be a qualification for the job that you have to have your neck shortened. I made an educated guess that their combined police records would make long and interesting reading.

They obviously all knew each other, judging from the friendly jokes and comments that were being tossed back and forth. I was carefully excluded from this display of macho camaraderie.

As opening up time approached, the walkie-talkies came out. Some of the team looked mildly taken aback when Len handed one to me.

'This is never the new lass is it, Len?' one of them asked. 'Sorry, love, I thought you were bar staff,' he said to me. 'The way Dave described you, I thought you'd be bigger.'

'Has nobody ever told you that size is not important?' I asked dryly. 'You do surprise me.'

There were a few jeers at that. Even Len grinned, but he didn't ease up enough to show me how the walkie-talkie worked. He left me to work out the tangle of wires by myself.

Eventually I got it sorted. The main device, about the size of a mobile phone, hooked onto my belt, with a separate earpiece and a clip-on mic. The mic had its own remote transmit button. By leaning over someone's shoulder I gathered the channel we were operating on.

Len's only advice was short and sweet. 'Unless it's a real emergency, stay off the air,' he told me, then turned to the others. 'We're still spread thin, so you all know your areas. If you get a problem, give us your location first, then what's happening, otherwise we don't know where to come and get you out of the shit, do we?'

'So what's my brief?' I asked as the rest of the team each headed off to their own pitch.

'You can stick with me for tonight, I suppose,' he said grudgingly. 'You can make regular checks on all the ladies' loos, and if Angelo needs you to search anyone on the door he'll send for you. He's not allowed to search the birds.'

At risk of appearing stupid, I chanced a question. 'What am I looking for?'

He shrugged. 'Nobody gets in if they're carrying a weapon,' he said. 'If they've got drugs on them, it depends how much. If it's for their own use, we take it off them and let them in. If it's enough to deal, they're banned.'

'Sounds reasonable,' I said, nodding.

He swung round and glared at me unsuccessfully for signs of insubordination. That meaty finger prodded at me again. 'They might offer you something to turn a blind eye. Don't take it—and if you do, don't think I won't find out about it,' he advised grimly. 'Nothing—but *nothing*—goes on in this club that I don't know about. Clear?'

THE EVENING STARTED slowly enough. I shadowed Len for the first couple of hours or so as he made his rounds. It was interesting to take note of the reaction he received from the punters in the club.

Most people dived out of his way as he strutted past, anxious not to attract his beady eye.

'So, how long have you been in this game, Len?' I asked when we reached a bit of a lull. He'd stopped pacing and we were leaning on a balcony overlooking one of the dance floors. His eyes never stopped moving over the growing crowd below us.

'Ten years, on and off,' he said shortly.

I waited, but he wasn't going to elaborate without further encouragement. 'You must have seen quite a bit of trouble,' I ventured.

He glanced at me sharply, then nodded. 'Goes with the territory.' I'd seen people give up teeth with less reluctance, but I thought I detected the faintest loosening.

'How does the New Adelphi compare?'

He shrugged. 'No better, no worse,' he said. Just when I thought that was going to be the end of it, he decided to expand on the theme, turning towards me. 'You'll always get the Friday night heroes when you open a new place. Want to prove how big a man they are by having a go at the doormen, right? Happens everywhere. That's why Mr Quinn brings his own people in, like me.'

He jabbed a thumb at his own chest. 'Me and Angelo, we've been working for him in Manchester for years. He knows we'll stamp out the trouble before it starts. We've had to crack a few heads up here to begin with, but it doesn't take long before your reputation is enough to keep 'em out. You take on local guys and you don't know who they've pissed off and who they've given in to. You just run the risk of long-running feuds being brought into the club.'

It was the longest speech I'd heard him make. I opened my mouth to ask more, but my earpiece crackled. 'Len, it's Angelo. Go to seven, mate.'

Len straightened up. 'Keep checking for trouble in the loos, then stay round this area,' he ordered, striding away fiddling with the settings on his walkie-talkie and muttering into the mic.

I did much as I was told for the next hour. Nothing untoward appeared to be going on under my nose on the dance floor. I was quite surprised who I saw at the club, though.

I recognised one face, but took a few moments to put the right name to it. Joy, the brave one from my last class at the Lodge. She looked different away from her baggy track suit and serious expression.

Tonight she was thrashing around on the dance floor with a group of other girls, laughing and joking, with her arms draped round their shoulders. She didn't see me and I was suddenly wary about calling too much attention to myself.

At regular intervals I patrolled the ladies' on each floor. I nodded to Gary who was busy serving drinks in one of the upper bars. He flashed me a quick grin, harassed and sweating.

The loos didn't yield anything much to report. I wandered in, but nobody was actually shooting up over the washbasins. The most I found to complain about was the ladylike way some of the girls stubbed out their dog ends on lipstick-coated bits of sodden tissue in the sinks.

I discovered one couple in a passionate clinch in one of the cubicles and was about to throw one of them out for being in the wrong toilets when I realised they were both female. I made a mental note to ask the club policy on lesbian behaviour and left them to it.

I hardly saw Len again for quite some time. When I did he seemed to spend most of his time checking out the gents'. It was an interesting way to make a living, I supposed.

When I got back to the lower dance floor, Dave was well into his second set of the evening, lording it over his decks. He was biting his bottom lip in concentration, body jerking to the pulse beat of the music.

He had headphones, worn half on so they only covered one ear. More form than function. He looked up and caught sight of me, pulling his mic down to his lips with a wolfish grin. 'Hey, it's the Foxy lady!'

I rolled my eyes, ignoring the smirking glances thrown in my direction. 'Up yours,' I mouthed, heading for the stairs. I went back up to the next level, and resorted to watching the goings on from the balcony again.

'Don't worry about Dave, he tries to wind everyone up,' said a voice next to me. I turned to see one of the girls from the bar, carrying two fistfuls of empty glasses. She was tiny, not much over five foot, with dramatically spiked white blonde hair. The plastic badge pinned to her boyish chest told me her name was Victoria.

'I can handle him,' I said.

'Oh I don't think you'll have any problems,' she said. She broke into a big grin, the action dimpling her cheeks. She had a silver ring circling into one side of her nose, and two diamond-studded pegs through her eyebrow. 'He's like a dog chasing cars, if you know what I mean—wouldn't know what to do with one if he got hold of it. And I should know.'

'He's tried it on with you, has he?' I asked.

She laughed. 'Tried being the operative word. Trust me, the only place Dave can keep anything up is on a dance floor! Now Angelo on the other hand . . .' She winked at me, and darted away, somehow managing to pick up another glass as she weaved a careful path through the crush.

I turned back to the floor. Dave was just coming to the end of his shift. He handed over to another DJ and jumped down off the stage. It took him a while to get across the dance floor. Everyone, it seemed, wanted to stop him and give him a thumbs up, or pat him on the back. Anyone would think he'd just picked up a medal.

He jogged up the stairs and spotted me, grinning as he came over. He leaned on the balcony next to me. Sweat was dripping off him, his tight-fitting T-shirt streaked with dark stains.

'Well, Charlie, what did you think of the set?' he asked, although clearly he was already well aware of his own brilliance. He wiped a hand across his face, but he was sweating too much to make a difference.

'It seemed to go down very well,' I said cautiously.

'*Very well?*' he repeated, his voice almost scathing. 'They love me out there. That's real power, that is. And there's nothing like it.' He looked down at himself. 'I gotta go change before I go on again,' he said, straightening up.

He saw my sceptical look and fixed me with an intense gaze. 'Believe me, Charlie, out there, knowing I've got this whole place in the palm of my hand—well, it's the best feeling I've ever had!'

He swung away. Victoria's scornful words came back to me. 'Yeah, Dave,' I muttered under my breath, 'for you, I bet it is.'

I was just about to go and make another dutiful tour of the toilets when my earpiece crackled again.

'Charlie? Front door,' came Angelo's distorted voice. 'I need you for a search.'

I obligingly made my way to the entrance. Angelo and one of the other doormen were involved in a stand-off with a group of three blokes and their dates. They all looked pretty useful, and the body language when I arrived made it clear a confrontation was almost inevitable, if not already in progress.

'Listen, dickhead,' Angelo was growling at one of them, nose to nose. 'The last time you tried to come in here, you had some stuff on you. Either you *all* get searched, or you *all* piss off. Now, which is it to be?'

'You lay one finger on my girlfriend and I'll fucking take you apart,' snarled the other bloke.

'I'm not going to lay a finger on her,' Angelo said, managing to imply that the girl was somehow unclean. He smiled his crocodile smile and gestured to me. 'She is.'

The bloke looked like he was going to make a fuss, then realised he'd been backed into a corner. His girlfriend came forwards with a dare-you look on her face, her arms spread. I could have told Angelo I was wasting my time before I began by the gleeful look on her face, but I kept my mouth shut.

The last time anyone did a search on me it was a bored-looking policewoman on the way into one of the big indoor bike shows. I think they'd had a bomb scare. She seemed very keen to feel carefully along my arms. I remember wondering at the time if people really carried plastic explosive stuffed up their sleeves.

I racked my brains to recall the procedure and gave the girl what I hoped was a pro-looking pat-down search. I checked her pockets, then ran my hands along her arms and legs, waistband and back. I stepped back and shook my head at Angelo. He just smiled and held his hand out to her.

'Handbag,' he demanded, beckoning.

I saw the alarm flash across her face then. 'You've no right to go through my things!' she blustered. Angelo beckoned again, making it clear his patience was wearing pretty thin.

I don't know what the girl had in her bag, but as she handed it over her boyfriend took advantage of Angelo's distracted hands to throw a fairly hefty punch at him.

He was obviously an amateur fighter, hoping to end it quickly with a heavy right. He wasn't prepared for Angelo's snake-like reactions. Wasn't ready for a swift and merciless counter-attack.

The fight that ensued should have been a one-sided affair. Three blokes and three women against two and one. It should have been, but it wasn't. The other doorman waded in to one of the men with a cheerful brutality. Word games were not his forte, but when it came to violence he was a poet.

Angelo was something one step removed. When I'd first seen him with Len, I'd thought he was the milder of the two, but I was wrong.

Now I had a chance to watch him in action as he head-butted the first bloke, then punched low into another's stomach, using more than enough force to put him down. When one of the girls jumped onto his back and tried to claw at his face, he dealt her a savage back-hand blow that knocked her sideways, without hesitation.

He spun round in a half-crouch, hands clenched, just waiting for the next chance to strike. His lips were drawn back from his teeth in a soundless snarl. The blood vessels under the shaven skin of his head were pronounced and pulsing.

I recognised the blood lust in him, saw it in the wide, exultant eyes. Where Dave got his high from mixing music and controlling the crowd, Angelo's kick came from sinking his fists into another's face. No drink or drug could equal the buzz.

The girl's friends joined the battle with a shriek at that point. Angelo shrugged them off like he was batting away flies.

The man he'd head-butted was back fighting by then, blinking away the blood from a cut across his eyebrow. He took advantage of the girls' attack to launch a counter-offensive on Angelo's blind side. I reluctantly supposed it was time to put my two-penny-worth in.

I stepped round his flying fists without much difficulty, getting a good grip on his shirt front. I twisted my body into him and he flew straight over my hip, landing heavily. Before he had time to catch his breath I punted him over onto his face, yanking his arm up behind him and angling a pretty effective lock onto it. It was enough to keep him where he was and out of the action until it was all done.

Angelo and the other doorman looked disappointed that the clash was over so quickly. The opposition retreated, apart from the one I'd still got on the floor. I was about to ask what to do with him when Angelo ambled up.

Before I could react, he'd kicked the man viciously in the kidneys.

I couldn't keep the shock out of my face. My feet took me forwards on a knee-jerk reaction, not to assist Angelo this time, but to obstruct him. I seriously contemplated taking him down.

Angelo looked all set to go after the guy again, but he caught my intention and stiffened, neck banded with gorged muscle, hands clenched. We stood each other off, my eyes meeting his steadily. I don't know what Angelo thought he saw there, but for some reason he changed his mind about the pursuit.

He exchanged a nasty grin with his colleague. 'You gotta deal with trouble hard and fast, Charlie,' he said when his victim had crawled to his feet and staggered away, helped by his mates. 'You show any sign of weakness, and they'll rip you to pieces.'

He gave me the once-over, as if making up his mind about something. 'You'll probably do,' he decided, his patronising tone putting my back up. 'Your reflexes aren't bad. You just don't have the killer instinct.'

He turned away then, clapping the other doorman on the shoulder. They straightened their jackets, looking pleased with themselves. Angelo inspected his knuckles, which were slightly skinned. I could see the fresh wounds alongside the scabs from some previous engagement with the enemy.

He was trying to act calm, but he was still wired, jittery, couldn't keep his hands still.

Len arrived at this point. 'You!' he said, glaring at me. 'Get back to the lower floor.'

'Suit yourself,' I said as I moved past him. 'Angelo called me up here.'

'Trouble?' Len asked him.

Angelo gave him a big smile. He flickered a glance over to me before replying.

'Nothing I couldn't handle,' he said.

When I got back to the lower dance floor things looked pretty quiet down there, if quiet's the word to use for music belted out of a massive sound system at full whack. Still, at least Marc seemed to have fitted decent equipment, and had it set up to perfection. Distortion is very wearing to listen to. At the New Adelphi, there wasn't any.

I made another round of the loos, still without finding anything startling to report. I noticed Len coming out of the gents' again on one of the upper floors. Either the guy was paranoid about the punters getting up to mischief in there, or he needed a good dose of Imodium.

I worked my way back down through the different levels again. If nothing else, climbing all these stairs was going to get me fit.

The club was starting to really fill up now. Getting from floor to floor was more of a push and struggle. My eyes were beginning to ache from constantly scanning the crowd in the smoky gloom. From trying to spot the furtive movement, the sly gesture. The first hint that something was wrong.

In the end I didn't see the trouble going down.

I heard it.

Nine

I WAS ON the stairs down to the lower dance floor when I first heard the screaming. I took a moment to focus on the direction, then started sprinting.

I took the last three stair treads in one stride and tunnelled through the press of bodies on the floor itself. Once I got closer I didn't need to ask exactly where the problem was. The way everyone was scrambling out of the way told me the answer to that one. The more hurriedly they were moving, the closer I was getting to the epicentre.

Finally, I broke through the edge of the dispersing crowd and found the tableau.

There were three players. The girl was doing the screaming, the action revealing her pierced tongue. She was dark-haired and rather plump, in a skirt too short and a lycra top cut too low.

On the face of it, she was an unlikely inspiration for a jealous rage, but from the look of the battle going on around her, she was certainly the prize. She didn't look like an athlete, either, but there was nothing wrong with her lung capacity.

The lad I immediately pegged as the prospective boyfriend was on his hands and knees at her feet, dripping blood from his lacerated cheek onto Marc's polished flooring. The other—clearly the rejected suitor—was still standing, a few feet away.

He was rigid with fury, breathing fast through his nostrils like a hard-run racehorse. He still had the neck of the broken bottle clenched in his hand.

I thumbed the transmit on my walkie-talkie. 'Len, it's Charlie,' I said. 'Lower dance floor. There's a nasty one going on down here. I need some help. Now!'

The girl carried on screaming, at that high, intensely irritating frequency of small babies and hotel fire alarms. The boy with the bottle was momentarily distracted. As though he couldn't decide if his best next move was to continue the fight with the prospect, or hit the girl just to shut her up. He shook his head suddenly, as if to clear it.

While he was diverted, I took a deep breath, tried to centre myself, and stepped into the fray. At least with the noise she'd been making, Len and the rest shouldn't have any trouble finding us.

It was immediately clear that neither of the two lads really wanted any outside interference. The reject was desperate for the total humiliation of his rival. The prospect wanted the opportunity for revenge, served hot. It was like breaking up two fighting Pit Bulls. I was more likely to find them both turning on me than I was of stopping them ripping each other to shreds.

'Come on now son, put that down and let's finish this the easy way,' I said.

He twisted towards me, mad-eyed so the whites of them showed all round the irises. 'I'm not your fucking son,' he hissed. He brought the bottle up towards me, warning. The gleaming blood of his last victim still decorated its wicked edges. 'Stay out of it, bitch, or you'll get some, too.'

He was dangerously hyped up for it to be drink, or simple jealousy. It was in his voice, his eyes. The way he held his body, jerkily stiff, uncoordinated. There was a sheen of sweat pearling on his face, but he was shivering. Great! Where was bloody Len when I needed him?

The prospective boyfriend had used the break in the reject's attention to climb warily to his feet. I risked a glance at him. The bottle had been applied by someone who'd had practice. The thrust-and-screw technique had opened up the whole of the left-hand side of his face. The skin hung in ragged peels from the top corner of his lip to just below his eye. It was going to take a micro-surgeon with a special interest in jigsaw puzzles to piece him back together again so he looked anything like the picture on the box.

I flicked my eyes towards the girl. She'd stopped screaming by now, shoving both hands over her own mouth and gagging as though about to be sick. I turned back to the boy with the ruined face. I hoped whatever she'd been offering him had been worth it.

I didn't like the look in his eyes. He didn't need to touch a hand to his face to know what had been done to him. The evidence was splashing down the front of his shirt in a scarlet river.

He started to swear then. Softly at first, but growing in profanity and volume as he launched himself at his attacker, oblivious to the dangers of the slashing bottle.

I couldn't let them come together again. I knew that. I took the prospect first, sweeping his legs out from under him to send him crashing. I only just managed to jump back out of reach of the reject as he sliced the bottle at me, aiming for my stomach.

I caught him a fast blow to the face as I dodged away, bloodied his nose. There was no real weight to it, but a remarkable amount of nerve-endings meet in the nose. It should have been enough to put him down, should have slowed him down at any rate, but he was feeling no pain. He shook it off like a light tap and kept coming, weapon lifted now, like a dagger.

Christ! Now would be a good time, Len . . .

I swallowed hard. I was going to have to hurt him to stop him. My mind shied away from it, but the facts didn't change. I dithered and nearly lost it altogether.

I hadn't heard the prospective boyfriend get back on his feet until he grabbed me round the neck from behind. The rejected one was still coming, but now I was almost immobile and a much easier target.

I switched off my conscious mind and put a muzzle on my conscience. I needed fast, clinical action. The outlines of all the techniques I'd ever learned unrolled behind my eyes like computer graphics, clear and precise. There was no room for hesitation here. No time for compassion either.

I shifted my hips sideways and used a clenched backfist to hit the boy holding me hard in the groin. I didn't need to deal with the arm round my throat then. It simply melted away.

I shrugged him off as he crumpled backwards away from me, and moved forward to meet the charge of the crazy boy with the broken bottle held overhead. With deadly accuracy, he stabbed the glass down at my left eye. So directly that when I looked up I could see straight into the taper of the neck.

I blocked him high with my forearm, grunting at the jarring impact. I weaved my right arm quickly up through his to meet it, clasping my hands together round his wrist.

The movements were automatic, fluid, but I didn't want to do this! Oh I knew the moves, had *nearly* carried them to completion a hundred times, but I'd never had to take that final step. It was crossing the line. It was too far.

I looked up to see the stump of the bottle again, inches from my face. It was quivering from the sheer effort he was putting into trying to drive it downwards towards me. Into me. Oh shit . . .

Leverage is everything. They reckon it takes just eight pounds of pressure to break almost any bone in the human body. I must have applied quite a bit more than that now. I shut out the last lingering doubts and heaved, sideways and down.

The boy's shoulder dislocated with an ease that was mildly surprising. It made a soggy popping sound, like a spoon being pulled out of a bowl of set jelly.

I put my shoulder out once, falling off a horse when I was a kid. The pain is indescribable. You can't escape from it, can't move anywhere to make it hurt any less. It focuses you utterly and you'll do anything to make it stop.

The boy dropped slowly to his knees, the wild light in his eyes dulling as the biting pain of his injury finally took the edge off whatever was floating him. He let the bottle fall to the floor. I kicked it away.

There was the thump of heavy footsteps and I turned to see Len and Angelo had, at long last, deigned to put in an appearance. They skidded to a halt and took in the scene. One boy writhing on the floor, a trail of slimy vomit now mixing with the blood from his face.

The other was still on his knees, whimpering, his torso deformed into an unnatural shrug. Len stared between them, open-mouthed. Angelo just regarded me with those calculating eyes.

'What fucking kept you?' I demanded, stalking past them. I ignored Len's shouted order that I stay put. He was in charge, wasn't he? Well let him sort the mess out, then!

Behind me, the dark-haired girl had started screaming again.

*   *   *

I LEFT ANGELO and Len to deal with the aftermath. I went upstairs to one of the quieter bars and ordered coffee as an excuse to take in some sugar.

When it arrived, I found my hands were shaking too much to lift the cup.

I thought of Angelo's earlier treatment of the three couples outside the club. If you dealt with it every day, you became hardened to violence. If that was so, I didn't want to deal with it every day. Maybe Sam was right and this move was a mistake. Maybe I shouldn't have taken the job on.

Or maybe Angelo was right. I just didn't have the killer instinct.

'Are you OK?'

I hadn't heard Marc come up behind me. Without looking round I said tiredly, 'Yeah, just wonderful, thanks.'

He came and sat beside me, linking his well-manicured hands together on the table top. He was wearing another devastating suit over a collarless white shirt with no buttons visible except the pearl stud at the neck. I wondered how long it took him to choose his wardrobe in the mornings.

With a supreme effort, I managed to take a sip of coffee without slopping most of it down the sides of the cup. When I looked up at Marc it was with steady eyes.

He was watching me with a half-smile quirking his mouth. 'Once again it seems I have to say you've handled yourself pretty well,' he remarked.

'Once again without any back-up from your own security people,' I put in bitterly.

'So it might seem.'

It was the slight emphasis that tipped me off. My head came up and I stared at him. 'You told them,' I said, my voice a whisper as the realisation hit. 'You told them to leave me to it, didn't you?'

'I wanted to make certain you could cope on your own, take care of yourself,' he admitted without any visible signs of remorse, 'so, yes, I told them to let you handle the first incident that came up solo.' He allowed himself a rueful smile. 'I didn't realise it would be one quite so . . . serious.'

I felt a cold sweat break out between my shoulder-blades, prickling my skin. Would I have willingly gone into it knowing I had nobody behind me? I replayed the scene in my mind. Saw again the broken bottle, and the blood. I knew I couldn't have walked away and let those two slug it out until only one was left standing. 'And if I hadn't been able to cope?'

He left the question hanging for a few moments. 'I didn't doubt for a moment that you could,' he said calmly. His eyes shifted to focus behind me. 'Ah, Len, is everything sorted down there?'

'Yes sir.' Len took a chair alongside me, leaning back and scowling. 'Bad one. We had to get a meat wagon for the pair of them.' He glanced at me and said grudgingly, 'You did OK, but you should have gone in sooner. We're not the police. We don't have to give them a chance to surrender. You go in hard and fast so they don't know what's hit them.'

He demonstrated his point by smacking a fist against his palm. 'As soon as trouble starts, you stamp on it. Trying to talk them out of it is just a waste of time and it'll get you hurt.'

'Being reasonable is never a waste of time,' I said, trying not to grind my teeth. 'Most people will respond to reason, given the opportunity. Most people will respect reasonable force as well. Unlike back there at the door when Angelo kicked that guy when he was already down and out of the play. That's not being reasonable. That's just vindictive. That bloke'll remember that, and I wouldn't be surprised if he's back with a few more of his mates later. *That* is what will get you hurt!'

I watched with mild interest as the blue touch paper of Len's temper ignited. Marc's presence was probably the only thing that was keeping his hands clenched on the table top instead of round my windpipe. 'You don't know the first thing about this game, so keep your half-baked opinions to yourself,' he growled. 'We've seen it all. Done it all. And we know how to handle it!'

Irritated, he lifted himself back to his feet and stumped away.

I swivelled round in my chair and waited until he'd made two strides. 'If you're so all-seeing and all-knowing, perhaps you can tell me what the boy was on?'

Len stopped, revealing quite a bit by the way his head ducked at the question. He turned back slowly, eyes flicking nervously to his employer as he did so.

'On?' It was Marc who made the demand, his voice sharp.

'Yeah, Len here was only too keen to let me know earlier that nothing went on in this club that he didn't know about, so he should be able to tell me—what was he on?'

'What are you talking about?' Len asked. He didn't make it sound convincing.

'The kid with the bottle,' I said patiently. 'I hit him hard enough to put him down, but he stayed on his feet, and he kept coming. I don't know what shit he had in his system, but I'd lay money that you can't buy it over the counter at Boots.'

Marc sighed, as if talking to a child. 'Charlie, we don't ask people for a blood sample on the door before we let them in. If he *had* taken something, he probably did it before he came into the club.' He pinned me with those pale eyes. 'I can tell you now that nobody with any sense tries to bring anything in to my place. Not if they know what's good for them.'

Len vigorously voiced his agreement. Marc glared at him. He made a swift exit.

Marc stood, smoothing out his jacket, his face tightly controlled. Abruptly he leant forwards, resting his hands on the back of my chair and the table top. He spoke in a voice quiet with fury. 'I will not have *anyone* spreading rumours that the New Adelphi is open house for aspiring chemists. Is that understood?'

I had to force myself to hold his gaze, not to back away from him. Pure pig-headedness made me pause for a few moments, defying him, before I nodded.

Satisfied, he straightened up. 'Now,' he continued, his voice icy, 'if you're sure you're all right, I have a club to run.'

I FULLY EXPECTED that to be the last I saw of Marc all evening, but to my surprise he reappeared just as we were packing up, around two.

Most of the security lads had already said their goodnights, climbed into their cars and departed into the night.

It had started to drizzle around midnight, a fine spray which sat on people's clothing like dust when they came into the club. Now the rain had started in earnest. I wasn't looking forward to the ride home. What a night to forget my waterproofs.

I'd already pulled on my leather jacket and scarf when Marc caught up with me. 'Have you got a moment, Charlie?'

I paused, running quickly through a mental checklist to see what else I'd done to deserve another talking to. I couldn't think that the way I'd handled the brawl on the dance floor could have been dealt with any better. Angelo, of course, would have just kicked both their heads in. And probably the girl's as well.

Now, I just nodded and followed Marc upstairs. We went right the way up to the small dining area on the top floor. I was surprised to find one of the chefs waiting for us, still in his whites.

Marc turned. 'I was going to have a bite of supper. Will you join me?'

It was phrased as a polite request, but I wasn't sure of the reaction I'd get if I said I'd rather be on my way home to bed. I hesitated. Although I'd had a break at ten, I'd been too unsettled to do more than drink coffee. It had been good strong stuff and now it was doing its best to burn a way out through the front of my chest. Eating something might dampen it down a bit.

I smiled. 'Yes, please, that would be great.'

We made our way over to a centre table and two place settings were whisked in front of us. Marc ordered wine. Mindful of having my wits about me for the ride home, I stuck with water.

'You should smile more,' Marc said as he lifted his glass. 'It suits you.' His voice was strangely neutral. I looked hard for mockery, but couldn't find it in his impassive features.

I took a swig from my glass and avoided his eyes. When I next looked up it was to find him amused.

'What's so funny?'

'I was just thinking what a contradiction you are, Charlie,' he said. 'You field a right hook more easily than you take a compliment.'

'Maybe I'm just used to men seeing me more as a potential sparring partner,' I hedged. Or as a target.

The chef reappeared at that moment with two succulent Spanish omelettes that melted on your tongue. We both dived in like we were starving. There was a long pause before Marc took up the thread of the conversation again.

'I think it's only fair to tell you that a sparring partner is not how I think of you at all,' he murmured. His voice was rich with hidden meanings, most of which I didn't want to think about right now.

'Yeah, right,' I said, trying not to squirm.

'So cynical for one so young.'

I regarded him straight-faced. 'I'm forty-five really, but I've got this painting in the attic,' I said.

To my surprise, he frowned, shaking his head. 'I don't get you.'

'Oscar Wilde's *The Picture of Dorian Gray*,' I explained and dredged the abridged story line from a long-forgotten pigeonhole in my memory. 'He was an exceptionally beautiful young man who lived a life of total depravity, but he had a portrait of himself which he kept hidden away, and while he utterly escaped the ravages of time and the effects of his own immorality, his likeness in the picture grew more hideous and more ugly.' I shrugged diffidently. 'We studied him at school.'

Marc raised an eyebrow, and took another sip of his wine. 'They didn't go a bundle on Oscar Wilde where I went to school,' he said wryly. 'Didn't go much on education either, for that matter.'

'It doesn't seem to have done you much harm,' I commented.

He inclined his head slightly with a modest smile. I must remember that method of accepting praise. It was gracious without being smug.

'Ambition can overcome plenty of obstacles if you're determined enough,' he said quietly. He pulled out a packet of cigars and lit one, dunking the end directly into the flame until it caught. 'I grew up with plenty of ambition and not much else.'

He pushed his empty plate to one side and twirled the stem of his glass between his forefinger and thumb. He watched the pale golden liquid shimmer in the bowl for a few moments, lost in his thoughts. That single diamond on his little finger dazzled as it caught the light.

Finally he looked up, and met my eyes levelly. 'I was born in one of the grimmest tower blocks in the roughest areas of Manchester,' he said. 'My mother overdosed when I was seven.'

The bald statement hung in the air between us like it had suddenly grown a body. Stricken, I searched for the right thing to say, but had to admit defeat. There wasn't any right thing.

Marc suddenly seemed to realise what he'd said. He waved an elegant hand mockingly towards his expensive attire, as if only too aware of the contrast with his present-day situation. 'If you saw anybody round my old haunts wearing a suit it was usually because some time that day a judge was going to be referring to them as "the accused".'

I felt my shoulders relax a fraction. 'Sounds like one of those places where the ambulance crews have to go in wearing flak jackets.'

Marc half-smiled, little more than a derisive twist of his lips. 'Oh no,' he said, 'they never bothered sending ambulances.'

WHEN I FINALLY left the New Adelphi Club it was almost three-thirty. There are not normally two three o'clocks in my day and I was shattered. My eyes felt as though someone had emptied the contents of a seaside sandal into them. My hair and even my fingernails stank of cigarettes.

There was almost no traffic on the ride home, and I was able to give part of my brain over to thinking about the snippets of his past that Marc had handed to me during supper.

The contrast with my own upbringing was stark. While he'd been avoiding rats in pissy stairwells, and dodging the drunken fists of yet another temporary uncle, I'd been taking ballet classes and going to the Pony Club. There'd been a lot of distance travelled between then and now. For both of us.

The rain hadn't eased off on the way back to Lancaster, so I wasn't surprised when I hit the light switch at the bottom of the main staircase in the hallway below my flat and nothing happened.

I think the wiring in the whole of the building was rejected by Noah for the ark because it was past its best even then. Every time there's heavy rain with the wind in the north-east the water seeps in somewhere like a thief and the circuit breakers in the basement click out.

It took me ten minutes or so, swearing, to stumble down there with a torch and flip them back in line. I tripped over a pile of junk on the way and I just knew I was going to have a bruise on my shin the size of a beer mat.

Great! Still, the way things had gone at the club, it was probably the perfect end to a pretty shitty sort of a day.

I fell into bed and into sleep almost simultaneously, but it wasn't untroubled slumber. I woke abruptly in the early hours, before it was light, from a jumbled dream where my father was trying to inject my mother with rat poison through a huge syringe.

She kept screaming and struggling and my father was ordering me to hold her down. I tried to do as I was told, crying because I knew it was wrong. When I looked up at him and he'd changed into a giant rat with yellow eyes.

I looked back down at my mother, but she'd changed, too. It was Susie Hollins I was holding now, on the dance floor at the New Adelphi, while a shadowy madman with a razor-sharp knife reared over us both. He laughed as the blade came slashing down to cut her throat.

Ten

AFTER THE RAIN, Sunday morning showed up dry, lit by pale watery sunshine. The sort of crisp weather, close to warmth, that fools spring plants into making an early break for the surface, only to be decapitated by the next frost.

Not that I saw much of the morning. By the time I'd dragged myself out of bed it was past ten o'clock. I worked out to try and lift my energy reserves up from semi-dormant, but I'm not sure I managed to hoist them much over hibernating tortoise level.

I showered straight after, glad to finally wash the last of the smoky smell out of my hair. I dumped all the clothes I'd been wearing into the washing basket, wrinkling my nose.

I had grapefruit juice for breakfast, drinking a glassful with the shutters open, looking out across the Lune. The water level was high that morning. Sometimes the river seems no more than a stream, sandwiched between two rock-strewn, greyish mud banks. But during high springs, with an onshore wind giving it a step up, it can completely flood the stone quay.

At times like those the residents try, Canute-like to fend the water away from their front doors and cellar windows with sandbags. The unlucky ones discover just how good the anti-corrosion warranty is on their cars, parked outside.

I took the precaution of buying a set of tide tables just after I moved in. If the weather looks bad I shift the bike up the ramp they used to use for loading trucks at the back of the building. It leads to a solid brick platform, about four feet above pavement level, just outside the old boarded-up rear doorway. Then I watch the mopping up exercise from the safety of my first floor balcony.

OK, so maybe balcony makes it sound grander than it really is. In reality all I have is an old iron railing about three feet off the floor, embedded in the sandstone and misshapen with rust. I usually treat its protective qualities with caution. I've no desire to find out the hard way that the railing is only held in by the skin of its teeth and a bit of flaky mortar. There's a good twenty-foot drop to the flagged pavement below.

Now I stood leaning on the stonework enjoying the view. I checked my watch, looking forward to nothing more strenuous than a ride out to Jacob and Clare's for lunch.

Afterwards, I looked on the half an hour or so I spent then as a little oasis of calm before I was hit by a full-blown hurricane. Complete with monstrous winds and tidal waves.

Traffic on the other side of the river heading into Morecambe was reasonably light. There was just the soothing rumble of a train crossing the Carlisle Bridge to the west of me. The odd car moving past on the quay below.

Then the phone started ringing.

Reluctant to spoil the mood, I turned away from the window and went to answer it. I had no premonitions as to who was calling me, just a mild curiosity. My pupils tended to respect my weekends, and I'd never built up the kind of friendships with people who loved to chat from a distance.

'Hello?'

'Hello Charlotte.' A man's voice, authoritative, but quiet and self-contained. The sort of voice you could imagine imparting the news of terminal cancer with cool detachment. He had probably done so on more than one occasion.

My father.

I was momentarily stunned. In all the time since the rift between my family and I had first opened up, through all the attempts by my mother to heal the breach, he had never contacted me. Not once.

The last time I'd seen him was just before the court martial. He hadn't bothered to embroil himself in the civil action I'd then impulsively brought against my exonerated attackers. Not after I'd turned down the exclusive legal services of one of his golf club cronies. The guy was a full-blown silk and I couldn't afford those sort of rates. Not when, if I'm honest, the realistic chances of winning looked so slim.

My father had offered to pay, of course, but by then relations had deteriorated enough for me to haughtily refuse my parents' charity. Perhaps, if I hadn't been so proud, the outcome might have been very different.

'What do you want?' I demanded roughly now, shock making me ungracious, and resentful that he was the cause.

I could just picture him, sitting in his study at home, with his back to the high sash window. His rosewood desk would be in front of him, with the leather-cornered blotter sitting exactly centred. Besides the telephone, there would be nothing else on the desktop. Paperwork was ruthlessly dealt with the moment it arrived.

'Your mother is very upset,' he said, his tone eminently moderate.

'That makes two of us, then,' I shot back.

He sighed. 'At risk of stooping to cliché, two wrongs do not make a right, Charlotte,' he said.

'Is that so? Perhaps she should have thought of that before she betrayed me.'

'Don't be so emotive,' my father rapped, more like his old self. It made what he said next so much greater a surprise. 'Can't you simply accept that she made a mistake? An aberration in a weak moment. It's something that she bitterly regrets, and it's causing her untold grief that you can't find it in you to forgive her.'

Typical of my father, that. Giving with one hand and taking back with the other. An admission of guilt coupled with a pointed reminder of my own failings. He made my reaction sound like a character defect. Hardly surprising, when I thought about it.

'An aberration?' I snapped, unable to prevent my voice rising like a police siren. 'She refused to stand up and support me when I was on trial, and you call it an *aberration*?'

'The evidence against you was substantial, Charlotte. On principle, she had to believe that the judicial system came to the correct conclusion. You must understand that,' he said, more gently. 'She is a Justice of the Peace, after all. What else could she do?'

'What about me?' I cried, feeling like a child. 'What about her daughter? Surely that takes precedence over the damned system? Where were her principles then?'

'She is sorry, you know. She may not be able to admit it outright, but she is, all the same,' he went on, as though I hadn't spoken. 'For the damage she's done.'

I tried that out for size on the twisted corner of my psyche that had been feeding on my bitterness and hostility towards them for the last couple of years. It had been leaching acid into my mind like a perforated ulcer. His words should have acted like a balm, but all they did was make it burn more savagely. So she was sorry, was she? For the result, not for the cause.

It was much too little, and way too late.

'And what about you?' I demanded.

His pause, a fraction too long, spoke volumes. 'That's not the issue, here, Charlotte,' he said evasively. 'This was never about you and me.'

'No, it never was, was it?' I said woodenly. 'I don't think I've anything more to say to you.' And I'm not ready to forgive either of you, I added silently.

'In that case, I'm sorry to have disturbed your Sunday morning,' he said without inflection. 'Goodbye Charlotte.'

The phone clicked and went dead in my hand. I put it down like it weighed heavy, and moved slowly back to the open balcony, but where before the hum of cars across the river had been hypnotic and anodyne, now it grated.

I finished off the last tepid dregs of my coffee and was about to turn away from the view when I idly noticed the Vauxhall police car approaching along the quay. I felt the first stirrings of apprehension as it moved slowly into view, the occupants glancing up at the houses, obviously looking for an address. They stopped outside mine.

Two uniforms climbed out, adjusting their caps. It looked like the same pair who'd come looking for me the week before at Shelseley. I sighed, and went to spoon instant coffee into a couple of mugs. If being paid a visit by the local law was going to become a regular occurrence, I suppose I'd better at least be sociable.

I left the front door open and heard them stumping their way up the wooden staircase, having a minor argument about who'd done what in the staff canteen the night before. When they reached the landing they paused uncertainly.

'Come on in and take a seat,' I called through. 'The kettle's on.'

'Morning Miss Fox.' They did as instructed and made themselves at home on the sofa. As I appeared out of the kitchen, drying my hands on a tea towel, they'd taken their caps off and plonked them upside down on the coffee table. I almost expected them to put their feet up.

I left them to it while I ducked back into the kitchen, returning a few minutes later with two mugs of instant coffee. 'So, what can I do for you *this* time?' I asked, handing them out.

'Yeah, this is getting to be a bit of a habit, isn't it?' the older one said with a grin.

'I didn't realise this was going to happen every weekend or I'd have bought some cake,' I said waspishly, taking the chair across from them.

They looked disappointed, then exchanged glances and pulled on businesslike expressions.

The younger one, Tommy, pulled out his notebook. 'We're here because there's been a very serious allegation made against you,' he said, consulting it, 'of causing Grievous Bodily Harm during an incident at the New Adelphi Club in Morecambe last night.'

'What?' I realised I had my mouth open and shut it abruptly. 'You are joking?' I said, looking from one to the other. Actually, they were both looking faintly amused, as though the whole thing was some gigantic wind-up.

'I'm afraid not, Miss Fox,' Tommy said solemnly. 'At the moment no charges are being brought, but we've had an official complaint, backed up by a medical report, that shows one young lad with a forcibly dislocated shoulder, and another with severe facial lacerations and,' he looked pained, 'a ruptured testicle.'

'Nasty,' agreed the older one, straight-faced but only just. I wondered if they were practising a comedy double act.

'Hang on a minute,' I said, feeling my temper beginning to rise. 'Who exactly is it that's made this complaint?'

He read out a female name, which meant nothing to me.

'And who is *she*, for heaven's sake?'

'She claims to be the fiancée of one of the injured parties, whom you attacked, without provocation, on the dance floor at the club.' I remembered the dark-haired girl with the pierced tongue.

'OK,' I said, holding up my hands. 'I'll admit to the shoulder and I suppose to the testicle, but one of them had already glassed the other one in the face before I got there. That was nothing to do with me.'

'So you just waded in there, two against one, when you claim one of them was armed with an offensive weapon, and you inflicted major injuries on the pair of them?' the older one demanded incredulously. He caught sight of my punchbag on its hook in the corner of the living room. 'A bit of a boxer, are you?'

I ignored his last sarky remark. 'Yes, he still had the bottle on him when I got there,' I said. 'Look, I was employed as a member of the security staff to deal with trouble. I saw the fight and I went to break it up, but they both had a go at me. What was I supposed to do while one had his arm round my throat and the other was trying to disembowel me—reason with them?' Oh God, I sounded like Len.

'And you fought them off?' Tommy asked, a picture of dubiousness.

'That's right.'

'By yourself?'

'Yes!'

'Any ideas what started this fight in the first place?' the older one put in.

I shrugged. 'It looked like it was probably a classic case of "Oi, get your hands off my girlfriend" but it didn't help that he was definitely on something at the time.'

I thought of Marc's warning, delivered almost as a threat. *Nobody* spreads rumours that the New Adelphi is open house for aspiring chemists, he'd said. Don't worry, Marc, the only people I've mentioned it to are a couple of coppers. Oh well . . .

The pair opposite me exchanged pointed looks again, but to my surprise they didn't pursue it further. On cue they both got to their feet.

The older one screwed his hat into place and regarded me dubiously. 'That will be all, for the moment, Miss Fox,' he said. 'We'll let you know if any charges are being brought.'

I rose, too, stuffing my hands into my jeans pockets. 'Is that likely?'

'Who knows? But if I were you,' he said with a faint patronising tone, 'I'd try and stay out of trouble for a while.'

'Thanks a lot,' I muttered under my breath as they disappeared down the staircase. 'That's a great help.'

Their footsteps faded as they reached the street. It was only as I turned away from the door that I saw Tommy had left his hat lying upside-down on my coffee table. I crossed the room and picked it up. I was just debating whether I wanted to bother going after them to give it back when I heard a single set of footsteps on the stairs again and Tommy reappeared in the doorway.

I dangled the offending item from a finger. 'Forgotten something?' I asked, my voice acidic.

To my surprise, he gave me a level look as he retrieved his headgear. 'No, actually,' he said, 'I just wanted a chance to have a quiet word with you. On your own, like.'

I raised my eyebrows and said nothing.

Tommy hesitated, glancing uneasily over his shoulder as though his mate might somehow miraculously materialise on the landing behind him.

'I just wanted to give you a word to the wise,' he went on, hurriedly. 'On the face of it, you don't look a likely candidate for a Section Twenty assault, know what I mean? You haven't got a record, but quite a few of the guys Quinn's got working for him have. You're mixing in dangerous company if you want to keep your nose clean.'

'You mean you don't believe that's how it happened?' I demanded, feeling my temper rise like a prickle of hairs. 'You think that the kid was clean and I just went overboard?'

He flushed, looking uncomfortable. 'Quinn swears security's tight enough so that nobody manages to get into the place with anything on them,' he said.

When he saw my face he added hastily, 'Not that I take that as gospel, but by the time the boy was through with Casualty and our lads got to see him, he wasn't showing any signs of being on anything. On the other hand,' he went on, 'he didn't seem very happy with his girlfriend that she'd got us involved, which was good for you.'

'What do you mean?'

'Well, if he hadn't been so dead against pressing formal charges, we'd have been breaking your door down at five this morning and hauling you down the station instead of coming round now for a friendly chat, like.'

'But I was just doing my job,' I protested.

He shrugged. 'That's not the impression we got from Quinn's staff. They were dropping hints that you might have gone in too hard, like. You want to watch your back there, Charlie.'

'I will.' I managed to remember my manners enough to be slightly less ungracious. 'Thank you, anyway. I appreciate the warning.'

He looked embarrassed. 'Yeah, well, you do quite a bit of work up at the Lodge, don't you?' he said. 'I get called out to a lot of domestics. Mrs Shelseley's a nice lady.'

'Tom!' yelled a voice from the bottom of the stairs. 'Are you going to be all day? Get a shift on, will you.'

'OK,' Tommy called back. 'I'm on my way.'

He flashed me a quick smile, jammed his hat on, and trotted away to join his colleague.

I sighed, trying to roll away the tension that was cramping my shoulders. All in all, it wasn't quite the way I'd envisaged starting off my quiet Sunday morning.

BY THE TIME I'd changed into my leathers, got the bike fired up, and locked the flat, it was well past the eleven-thirty by which I'd promised to be at Jacob and Clare's. I knew Jacob, who timed the cooking of his meals like a covert military operation, was going to be spitting feathers, but I also knew it was going to be easier to explain my lateness face to face.

As I gunned away along the tree-lined quay towards town I should have been having a good time. The weather was just right, the sort of cold air the Suzuki really runs well in, but I would have felt better if it had been dark grey skies and raining buckets.

I was so angry it made my hands ache.

I slipped through into a gap in traffic on the main road going past the bus station and weaved smoothly across all three lanes to make the best progress. If I was going to ride like that, I really should have been giving it all my concentration, but half my mind was on other things.

How dare they not believe me! OK, so you tend to get pulled by the lads on Traffic more when you're on a bike than if you drive a car. Even so, that hardly made me a criminal, for heaven's sake. And anyway, it was clear they didn't have a clue about my past to damn me by.

I barrelled left round Sainsbury's and, by dint of dropping down two gears and caning it, managed to hit the temperamental lights on Parliament Street just as they were turning to amber.

I always used to think of myself as very law-abiding. Still do, I suppose—I even have a TV licence. But when I'd needed justice in the past, it had been spectacularly unforthcoming. Now I was suddenly on the receiving end of the boys in blue, when all I'd been doing was my job.

If this was the sort of treatment I could expect working for Marc, I made up my mind to tell him to stuff it!

I made it out to Jacob and Clare's place on the outskirts of Caton in record time for me. Clare came out to greet me as I pulled up. She had a couple of the dogs with her, a loopy wire-haired terrier called Beezer and a clumsy old half-blind black Labrador named Bonneville.

I wasn't surprised to see Clare waiting for me. Jacob not only deals in classic bikes, but all sorts of interesting antiques as well. He stores the stuff in the numerous barns and outbuildings dotted around the place and he doesn't like surprise visitors.

Somewhere along the drive are two hidden sensors, connected to warning buzzers inside the house. I've never been able to work out exactly where they are.

Now I cut the engine and toed the side-stand down, pulling off my helmet. Beezer greeted me by bouncing three feet into the air and yapping excitedly. Clare took one look at my face and swallowed the crack she'd undoubtedly been going to make about me being late.

'What's happened?' she demanded, leading the way in through the studded oak front door.

'Don't ask,' I said. My anger had dissipated, replaced by a weariness that went through to my bones. I told myself I was just tired, but I knew it went deeper than that.

We moved along the uneven stone flags of the hallway to the big cosy kitchen, where Jacob should have been slaving over a hot stove.

He was actually sitting at the scrubbed pine table. There was a glass of wine by his elbow and a pile of paperwork in front of him, and he was speaking in what appeared to be Klingon on the telephone. It turned out to be Japanese. Clare whispered to me that he was winding up the sale of a pair of restored Velocettes to a collector in Tokyo.

'On a Sunday?' I whispered back.

Jacob looked up and dazzled me with that slow grin of his, then went back to his unintelligible conversation.

Clare dragged me a cold beer out of the fridge and we went through to the snug back sitting room to leave Jacob to finish the call in peace. Despite the sun outside, a blazing fire was lit in the huge open hearth. I disappeared into the depths of their big squashy sofa when I sat down, quickly buried by the arrival of the terrier on my lap.

'So,' Clare said when I'd had my first mouthful of beer, 'are you going to tell me what's been going on?'

I told her the whole tale about my experiences at the nightclub since I'd rescued her from the clutches of Susie Hollins. Jacob came in just as I was telling her about my confrontation with Len. They both sat in silence until I'd gone through the events of the night before in full, and my subsequent encounter with the police that morning.

'The fascist little shits!' he said with feeling when I'd finished. 'Do they honestly think you're going to start a major fight on your first night? Unbelievable!'

'What are you going to do?' Clare asked. Bonneville came waddling into the lounge then, following the sound of our voices, and collided with a standard lamp. Clare caught it without taking her eyes off me, well used to the dog's blunders.

'There's not a lot I can do,' I said. 'I'm not sure I want to carry on working at the club, though. I rely on recommendations from the local police for some of my business. I can't afford to upset them.'

'What interests me,' Jacob put in slowly, 'is why they came round to see you at all.'

'What do you mean?'

'Well, why didn't this Len and Angelo back up your story? I thought you bouncer types were supposed to stick together,' he said with a bit of a grin. 'It doesn't sound like they've tried to help you at all. In fact, it sounds more like they're actively trying to drop you in it.'

I thought about it for a moment, then nodded. 'I know Marc said afterwards that he'd told them to let me handle something on my own, just to check me out, but I would have thought it should have been obvious to someone of their experience straight away that it was serious.'

'Exactly,' he said, downing the last of his wine as he stood up. 'Perhaps you should be asking yourself what you know that could be so important, Charlie. Or what you might find out when you're there. It might tell you why someone seems to want to get you out of the way.'

'That's ridiculous,' I argued. 'I didn't go after them for a job at the place. Marc made me an offer last Saturday night when Susie had a go at Clare. Why on earth would he do that one week, then try and get rid of me the next?'

'Maybe he didn't have a choice,' Clare put in. 'If I remember right it was actually that bar manager chap—Gary is it?—who first suggested they employ you. Maybe Marc couldn't say no without it appearing suspicious.'

'Suspicious to whom?' I asked, idly scratching the terrier's head. Beezer wriggled her muscular little body with delight. 'He could have shot Gary down in flames instantly and it wouldn't have looked anything out of the ordinary. No,' I shook my head, 'he seemed quite keen then.'

'So,' Jacob said, 'what happened between then and yesterday to make him change his mind about you?' He moved stiffly over to the door. 'Do you want to come through to the kitchen, by the way? I'll see if anything of my culinary masterpiece can be salvaged at this late hour.'

Clare grinned at me behind his back as I stood up, tipping the disgruntled terrier off my knees. We followed Jacob's halting steps back along the hallway. He walks with a permanent limp, his legs more steel than bone in places.

Jacob used to race bikes when he was younger, with more courage than was good for him. If he travels abroad he jokes that he has to take his X-rays with him to avoid being strip-searched going through the airport metal detectors.

Once we were settled round the kitchen table and Jacob had retrieved an absolutely perfect beef and baby onion stifado out of the oven in the Aga, he repeated his earlier question. 'So, come on— what's happened to warrant this man Quinn's sudden reversal of opinion of you?'

'Susie Hollins was murdered for a start,' Clare supplied, getting carried away with the idea. 'Hey, that could be it! She'd just been in his club, and we've only got his word for it that he actually threw her out.'

'Clare,' I said, tearing off a hunk of crusty bread to shamelessly sop up my gravy with. 'Marc was sitting down talking to us just after that. I hardly think he'd had time to do Susie in, change into an identical set of clothes so there'd be no bloodstains, and get back upstairs to chat, all within the space of about ten minutes, do you?'

She looked crestfallen. 'Oh. No, I suppose you're right.'

I recalled the incidents at the Lodge, but I didn't mention them to Jacob and Clare. I don't know why. I suppose I just didn't want to admit that since Susie's rape and murder someone had been taking rather too much of an interest in other vulnerable women. It was as if putting voice to my fears would make them more real.

Jacob got up to replenish our drinks, giving Clare's shoulder a reassuring squeeze as he went past. 'Anything else you can think of?'

'Well, Terry did come round last Sunday with a computer he said he'd picked up from someone at the club as part of a debt,' I said uneasily, remembering he'd been supposed to be collecting the lap-top this weekend, but he hadn't been in touch.

'Hang on a minute—who's Terry?' Jacob said, sitting down again.

'He's the local mobile video man,' Clare put in promptly. 'He comes round to the office every Friday. Or he usually does, but this week he didn't show up.'

'And he gave you a computer as part of a debt?'

'No, no,' I explained. 'He told me that someone at the club owed him money, and they'd given him a lap-top computer instead, but they'd password protected it, so Terry couldn't use it.' I forked a chunk of meat into my mouth and savoured it as it dissolved on my tongue. If I believed all the scare stories that I was going to get mad cow disease from eating British beef, I reckoned it was probably worth it.

'So why did he come to you?' Clare asked. 'You don't even own a computer.'

'No,' I agreed, 'but I have friends in low places. You remember Sam Pickering, with the Norton? He's a bit of a whizz with the things and he managed to get round it, no problem. The only thing was, when we got into the machine, there didn't seem to be anything on it, so I don't know if it was one stolen recently from the club itself, or if it just happened to belong to somebody who worked there.'

'How did Sam get round the password?' Clare wanted to know, elbowing Beezer who was trying to sneak onto her lap to beg food from her plate.

I shrugged. 'I've no idea.' Under the table, Bonneville decided I might be a softer touch and dumped her greying muzzle on my knee, sighing noisily. If she thought I was going to share Jacob's cooking with her, she had another think coming.

'More to the point, what *was* the password?' Jacob asked.

'Bacchus,' I said, spelling it.

'Bacchus,' he repeated, almost to himself. 'Hm. Someone's into Greek mythology with a twist.'

'You know what it means?' I asked, surprised. 'My dictionary didn't include it.'

'It's the Latin name for Dionysus, who was the son of Zeus and the god of wine,' Jacob said promptly, raising his glass and grinning at me. 'Your education is sadly lacking, Charlie.'

'That's a bit obscure, isn't it?' Clare demanded. 'And anyway, apart from the wine bit, what's the connection with the nightclub?'

Jacob held up a finger to silence our questions and left the table. After half a beat, both the dogs scrabbled after him. Bonneville cannoned off the door frame on the way out.

Jacob returned a few minutes later, carrying a book on Greek mythology. The dogs circled him expectantly. He sat down and pulled out a pair of delicate half-moon glasses. They should make him look like an old man, but they actually have a magnifying effect on his sex appeal.

'Ah, here we are. Bacchus. Also known as Bromius the Boisterous, which gives you some idea what he got up to in his spare time. Married Ariadne. He was also god of tillage, law-giving and intoxicating herbs like ivy and laurel. And,' he looked at me, 'he was worshipped at Delphi.'

I felt a shiver ripple across my back.

'But Delphi isn't the same as Adelphi,' Clare protested.

'True,' he allowed. 'Adelphi isn't mentioned by the ancient Greeks at all, but it would be an easy mistake to make.'

'Particularly,' I said slowly, meeting Jacob's dark gaze, 'if your education was sadly lacking.'

IN THE AFTERNOON we had a ride up to the local bikers' meeting spot at Devil's Bridge near Kirkby Lonsdale, stayed there until about three, then headed back towards Caton.

I was easily persuaded to stop off at Jacob and Clare's for another quick coffee, and we ended up slouched in the lounge watching the Superbike racing on Eurosport. It was past five o'clock and pitch dark outside by the time I dragged myself reluctantly away.

The lack of cloud cover meant the ground was crystallised with frost. I rode back into Lancaster very cautiously, taking corners strictly upright and feeding the brakes in gently. The Suzuki's pathetic headlight, even on high beam, would have made hurrying a reckless exercise, in any case.

Town was quiet as I stooged through and I was soon chaining the bike up outside the back of the flat. I pulled the cover over it and set the alarm, then ambled round to the front of the building.

I jogged up the wooden staircase without any thoughts of stealth, my bike boots clattering loudly on the treads. My mind was on nothing more than a bite of supper and trying to catch up on some of my lost sleep from the night before.

I was right up to the flat door before I noticed that it wasn't locked any more. Wasn't even shut, in fact. Before it dawned on my sluggish and outrageously slow brain that getting away from the place very quickly was possibly the best idea I'd had in a long time. Maybe I just wasn't having a logical day.

Of course, in that sort of situation the last thing you actually want to do is walk away. I was filled with anger that someone had broken in, gone poking through my things while I'd been away. Pawed all my belongings. I thought all too briefly of bringing in reinforcements, then pushed open my front door.

I only took a couple of steps inside the door of the flat when I froze. Almost literally. It was like an ice box in there. I realised I'd been so irritable when I'd left that morning, I'd forgotten to close the shutters to the balcony. Now the night air cast an arctic chill over the interior. Damn.

The second thing was the smell of cigarettes.

Zoë Sharp

Not only do I not smoke, but I don't let anyone else who does do so in my flat. My heart lurched in my chest. I turned to flick the overhead lights on and that's when they jumped me.

Something very hard, moving very fast, landed with a sickening crunch just over my right ear. I remember starting to fall, but there the recollection ends.

By the time my floorboards had rushed up to meet me, I was out of it.

Eleven

MY AWARENESS RETURNED slowly, and not without discomfort. It brought with it an irritating headache like pins and needles, as though from the release of a constricted limb.

I was still lying face down on the floor, presumably right where I'd fallen. There was an annoying tickle round my right eyebrow. It took me a moment before I vaguely registered it was probably blood. By the feel of the dull throbbing, there was a lump behind my ear the size of a closed fist.

I mentally retraced my steps. I remembered chaining the bike up, and walking up the stairs. Then what? Oh yeah, the busted lock and the smell of cigarettes.

I could smell them again now, stronger and fresher, if that's the right word to describe the sickly choking odour. Whoever had decided to lamp me over the head had obviously lit up shortly afterwards. A sort of debonair Neanderthal.

I could hear lowered voices, arguing somewhere in the middle distance. I struggled to orientate my thoughts. It all seemed unconnected with me, somehow. As bizarre as a dream.

Without opening my eyes I could tell that somebody had got round to completing my last manoeuvre and switched on the lights. No need for stealth now they'd got me right where they wanted me.

Footsteps approached, causing the floorboards to bounce under my cheekbone. I struggled not to wince at the vibration it set up through my head. I kept my eyes shut, trying to regulate my breathing so they didn't realise I was conscious.

'You shouldn't have hit her so fucking hard!' one voice said. It was harsh, raspy. I put him down as my smoker.

'Well he never told us it was a girl, did he?' complained a second voice, with a strong Liverpudlian accent. I hazily wondered if men's skulls were generally considered thicker than women's. 'Charlie's a feller's name, for Christ's sake!'

'If you've killed her, the shit's really going to hit the fan after last time,' the smoker warned.

'Look, she's not dead, all right? Let's finish what we came for and get the fuck out of here,' the Scouser said. 'Have you got it?'

'Yeah, for what use it is. We're going to have to bring her round, though, just to make sure.'

'OK, get her legs and we'll stick her over there.'

One pair of less-than-gentle hands grabbed my arms, while another got hold of my leather jeans. When they swung me off the floor and carried me across the room, it took more willpower than I thought I possessed not to go utterly berserk.

I gritted my teeth. I knew I had to stay quiet for as long as possible, but having their hands on me was almost too much. A wave of pure panic washed down over me. I fought to keep it under control, but long term I knew I was onto a losing battle.

Fortunately, after no more than a few yards, they stopped. I was dropped onto what felt like my own sofa, and rolled, half-sprawled onto my back. Still I kept my eyes shut, allowing my head to loll over to one side.

I heard one of the men move away. The other one went very quiet for a few moments. All I could hear was his breathing.

'Well, well,' he murmured, 'aren't you the pretty one?'

My skin crawled so hard it tried to turn inside out. That was it! I was going to have to make a move. I took in a last deep breath, preparing to tense my muscles before I struck.

Suddenly, all the air was ripped out of my lungs as freezing cold water landed across my face and chest. I must have inhaled half a cupful, because I instantly started heaving and coughing, doubled over. I opened my eyes then, but could see nothing for wet hair plastered over them.

Blinded and gasping, I spent what seemed like an interminable age fighting for breath, but it can only have been half a minute or so. When they deemed I'd had enough time to recover, a hand grabbed hold of my hair and yanked my head back.

The sight that faced me then was of two men. Big, thickset, purposeful-looking men, wearing gloves and ski masks. The one who had hold of me had a cigarette poking out through the mouth hole of the fabric covering his face. The other still clutched one of my saucepans, which was what he'd used to tip a couple of pints of cold water over me. Hadn't these guys ever heard of smelling salts?

The ski masks both terrified and reassured me. If whoever had sent these men wanted me dead, they wouldn't have bothered hiding their faces. If, on the other hand, whoever it was wanted me severely done over, I was going to be lucky to come out of this with my kneecaps intact.

This was not a situation where looking strong was going to have any benefits. I let my face crumple, let my fear show. It didn't take much acting ability on my part.

'Please!' I whimpered. 'Don't hurt me!' I reached up to clutch at the wrist of the hand that was still buried in my hair. My fingers located three useable pressure points, but I hesitated from drilling deep in to them. Not yet, Fox, not quite yet . . .

Even through the ski mask, I could see the twist of disgust on the smoker's face. He gripped harder and wrenched me off the sofa onto the floor. If I hadn't been taking my own weight by holding on to him, he would have torn my hair out by the roots. I gave a squeal of shock that I didn't really have to feign.

'Shut the fuck up!' he roared. He slapped me across the face, making my eyes water. I slumped at the base of the sofa, my left cheek on fire. I couldn't work out which side of my head hurt worse.

I don't know what they'd hit me with to start off with, but blood from the hole it had made was still running into my right eye, making me blink.

'What do you want?' I sobbed.

The Scouser moved in then. He grasped the back of my neck to jerk my head up, and pushed a flat square object under my nose, about the size of a telephone directory. I recognised the lap-top computer Terry had given me. Oh shit.

'See this?' he demanded.

I tried to nod, but the steely fingers digging into my neck gave me a very short range of movement. He shook me viciously. Like he was training a stupid dog that continually stayed when it should have sat, and rolled over when it should have come to heel.

'Wrong!' he snarled as he rattled me. 'You don't see it. In fact, you've never seen it. You don't even know it exists, right?'

'O-OK,' I mumbled. He threw me back on the floor with a grunt of contempt.

'She don't sound too sure,' the smoker observed dispassionately. He sucked on his cigarette until the end glowed red. 'She might do something stupid when we've gone, like call the filth. I think we might have to be a bit more *persuasive*, eh?'

A cold fear gripped me then. Unless I did something drastic, and real soon, I was going to get a pasting. Sadly, it seemed that my assailants had overcome their initial squeamishness over gender. Now I was afraid they were going to go overboard to compensate.

For the first time I noticed the state of the rest of the flat. It had been comprehensively and professionally trashed. My books had been pulled from the shelves and littered over the floor, my TV set had the tube put through. Even the sofa had its stuffing protruding from a dozen slashes in the fabric.

My heart-rate kicked up into overdrive. I hadn't seen a weapon, but one of them had to be carrying. Or possibly both of them. I had no way of telling. But if I went for one bloke and the other pulled a knife on me, I was going to be in more than deep trouble.

I was going to be dead.

I took a full breath. I told myself that I'd taught plenty of class scenarios covering attacks by two players. I wasn't kidding myself that it was easy, but I knew I could do it.

Don't think. Just act.

In the event, it was the smoker who acted first. He strolled over to me as though he was out for his Sunday constitutional and punched me hard in the sternum, putting his bodyweight behind the blow.

I rolled away, gulping for breath, ending up at the furthest edge of the sofa. He advanced, smirking, with his hands clenched by his sides, and making no attempt to keep his guard up.

Still making a play of looking terrified, I managed to slide onto my knees. We'd moved ten feet or so away from the Scouser, and there was an overturned chair between us. The odds were lousy, but they were probably as good as they were going to get. When the smoker was towering over me again, I went for it.

His kneecaps were about on eye-level. Blocking out the pain in my ribs, I drew back and hit the one nearest to me. The heel of my open hand landed just under the patella itself, slanting upwards. I closed my mind to the wet crunch his knee made, like a big dog chewing through chicken bones.

He staggered back, bellowing. I reinforced the damage by smashing the point of my elbow into his thigh, dead-legging him. He went down like a knackered lift.

Unfortunately, the Scouser's reactions were faster than I'd hoped. He leapt over the fallen chair like an Olympic hopeful. By the time he landed, a wicked-looking hunting knife with a six-inch blade had magicked into his hand. Sheer rage boiled out of the holes in his ski mask, fuelled by the smoker's screamed instructions that he should kill the bitch.

The Scouser did his best to comply, cornering me by the balcony. We were in full view of the opening, silhouetted against the lights.

A brief thought flashed into my head that if a bored passenger on a bus happened to glance across the river, they could suddenly find themselves in the middle of a Hitchcockian nightmare.

I had no time to expand on that theme, mentally or otherwise. The Scouser launched a blistering attack of swipes and slashes, but he'd let his anger contaminate his judgement. He was getting wild, leaving himself more and more open. I paused momentarily. Timing was everything.

Then he thrust the knife at me once more. I dodged and it slid past my side with inches to spare. I locked my fingers round the wrist of his knife hand. Control the weapon, and you're halfway to winning the fight.

Using my own forward momentum to tip him off balance, I swept his legs out from under him and dropped him heavily onto the floor. I went forwards onto one knee with him as he went down, keeping hold of the knife hand. I now had his elbow straightened out nicely over my bent leg and I levered it hard, clawing my fingers into his wrist. Drop the knife, damn it!

He was a big tough bloke, but it's difficult to keep your mind on stabbing somebody when your elbow feels ready to explode. For a bit of extra persuasion I jabbed a knuckle into the hollow just below his ear. The combination was enough. His fingers went suddenly nerveless and the knife clattered onto the floor.

'Good boy!' I said tightly, and hit him with my clenched fist on the side of his neck. I don't know why I chose that target. It was exposed, and I took the opportunity. Striking the muscles there makes the throat contract and can leave you fighting for breath. If nothing else it's painful and worrying, but I knew at best I'd gained only a few seconds of escape time.

By this time the smoker had crawled to his feet and was hobbling forwards, looking malevolent. He was between me and the front door. I just had time to scoop up the fallen knife and fling it out over the balcony, praying there were no passing pedestrians below at the time.

Despite clutching at his throat and squawking, the Scouser didn't stay on the floor for long. He was soon back in the play. He started for me as well, and there was death in his eyes.

The balcony suddenly seemed my best option. I turned and ran the last few strides towards the opening, aware all the time that the Scouser was only a heartbeat behind me.

It seemed ironic that only that morning I'd been wary of even leaning on the rusted balcony rail for fear that it would give way. Now I swung myself over it, double handed, with a certain amount of gusto bordering on abandon. I winced as I heard the dusty graunching noise of the rail's anchor points taking the strain.

For a moment I dangled there, suspended over a drop to the pavement below that looked horrendous from this angle. Oh great idea, Fox! What the hell are you going to do now?

The Scouser made it to the balcony and he decided my next move. Now he'd had his toy taken away from him he resorted to simply punching me in the ribs, through the railing. The air gushed out of my lungs and my hands simultaneously lost their strength.

I let go, half-falling, half-slithering down the crumbling sandstone front wall of the building, my fingers scrabbling at the masonry. I managed to find a tiny crevice on top of a window lintel, and gripped on to it by the weakening strength of three fingers.

I know it's possible to support your body weight by such slender means. I've seen them do it on the telly. Unfortunately, I'm not a whipcord-thin elastic free-form climbing expert. Maybe I just needed one of those little sacks of chalk on my belt. Or is that Sumo wrestlers? Whatever, inexorably, my fingers started slipping.

The Scouser decided to put his two penny-worth in by depth-charging me with what was left of an occasional table. I ducked instinctively, my grip slackening in panic, and I plunged the final ten feet towards the pavement.

In theory, a human body falls at thirty-two feet per second, per second. This probably explains why one moment I was suspended in mid-air, and the next I was thumping down onto the flagstones, with no discernable gap in between.

I landed on my feet, but my legs were forced up and I crashed straight onto one side. Never have I been so grateful for wearing leathers. The Kevlar reinforcement in key areas saved my hip and elbow from real damage, but I still hit the ground with enough violence to bash the air out of my battered lungs again.

I forced myself to my feet out of sheer bloody-mindedness. OK, so the smoker might be out of the play as far as a running chase was concerned, but the Scouser was only injured enough to make him mad. If I wanted to be able to stay moving, I had to start moving. Now.

Head thumping, I dragged myself upright, snivelling with the effort, and limped off along the frosted quay.

As a getaway it was pitifully slow. I was so numb that I didn't even register until I'd been going maybe fifty yards that I was heading the wrong way. Not towards the middle of town and the brightly lit, crowded bus station, but towards the industrial estates. Hardly likely to be Piccadilly Circus at this time on a Sunday evening.

I hesitated, nearly turned back, but then I heard the thunder of heavy feet rushing down the wooden staircase. The Scouser was coming after me. I put my head down and stumbled on.

Even in my leathers, the cold was biting. My breath was visible in clouds around me. It didn't help that the whole of the front of my shirt was soaked through. I was wheezing like a chronic consumptive on their last legs.

I ducked through the next alleyway which brought me out onto the waste ground behind the building. They'd pulled down most of the Victorian factory next door, but never really got round to finishing the job, never mind redeveloping the plot.

One piece of the building was still standing, a gable end wall, two storeys high, with part of the roof beams sticking out from it like a skeleton. The rafters hung down at a drunken angle, and there were huge cracks in the brickwork itself. I always expected to wake up one morning to find the whole thing had collapsed and saved the demolition team a job.

The ground was littered with broken bricks and debris. It made my progress far too slow. I turned and headed for the road again, only to spot the silhouette of the Scouser moving along the pavement, obviously searching.

I held my breath, but he was in the glare of the streetlights, and I was still in the shadows. As long as I stayed here I was hidden, but it was a temporary respite.

The Scouser turned inwards, away from the river, and started coming towards me. I edged back the way I'd come, aware all the time that I was fading.

The cold was scorching my lungs and leaching the feeling out of my fingers. I'd started to shake with delayed reaction. My head was banging so hard it was making me feel sick.

All the while, I cursed myself for not hitting the Scouser harder. I could have continued the lock I had on him to its logical conclusion, and cracked his elbow joint using my knee as a fulcrum. I could have hit him in the groin while he was down on the floor. I could have fractured his clavicle, one of the easiest bones to break, or thumped him in the throat to slow down his breathing. I could even have jabbed at his eyes, which would have required little strength and given me a much better chance of evading him now.

I knew, though, that part of me had revolted against what I'd done to stop the fight at the New Adelphi Club. I just hadn't been able to bring myself to do it again. I'm sure my reasoning must have been clear and sound at the time, but now it seemed a foolish, if not deadly mistake.

I tried to creep quietly over the rough ground, while the Scouser closed on my position in a less surreptitious manner. I could see the alleyway in front of me. Only a few yards more.

At that moment, I saw the headlights of a car approaching along the quay. The extra illumination bled into the alleyway. I heard a roar of triumph from behind me, and realised that it had given away my location to the Scouser.

I abandoned all attempts at secrecy and made a run for it. I burst onto the pavement just as the car was drawing level. With my attacker only a few feet behind me, I had no choice but to keep going.

I threw myself into a forward roll, hit the front wing in a dive and clattered over the bonnet. I even had time to realise that the vehicle was a big BMW as I spilled across the bodywork.

The Scouser didn't have quite the same incentive to practice his aerobatics. He skidded to a stop on the pavement, and judged in a second that the odds had tipped against him. He turned and pelted off along the quay on foot.

The BM driver's reactions were remarkably fast. He had already slammed on the brakes by the time I made contact with his paintwork. As I bounced off the other side and tumbled into the far gutter, he had already opened the driver's door and was halfway out.

'Charlie!' he yelled. 'Christ, are you all right?'

It was Marc Quinn.

Twelve

I TRIED TO climb to my feet, but my legs wouldn't obey the usual commands. I made two attempts, like a punch-drunk boxer with the count on him. I ended up on my knees both times. The referee would have had no choice but to stop the fight.

Marc saw the state I was in at first glance and his face closed in with fury. He looked longingly after the rapidly disappearing Scouser for a moment, then moved quickly to pick me out of the gutter.

His instinct was to grab me round my ribs to lift me. The pain it caused made me cry out, pushing back away from him and ending up back where I started.

He started to swear then, amazingly inventive oaths about what he was going to do to the people who'd worked me over, as and when he ever caught up with them. It was educational to listen to even if, afterwards, I couldn't remember a single piece of invective.

Eventually, using him as a crutch, I managed to haul myself upright more or less under my own steam.

'Can you make it to the car?' he asked, his voice terse. It was only ten feet or so away, but it seemed like half a mile to go round the bonnet to the passenger side.

I took a deep breath, regretting it as my ribs protested, and nodded.

'OK, come on, take your time.' He put a gentle arm round my shoulders, keeping it light. 'I'll be right here.'

I stopped suddenly and peered up at his face. 'Marc, what are you doing here?' I asked. My voice seemed awfully reedy and thin. I was still shivering from the cold, which was making my ribs hurt all the more.

He gazed down at me, reaching to move my hair away from my eyes. Most of it on the right-hand side was now glued to my scalp. I daren't even begin to imagine what I looked like.

'I came to see you,' he said, smiling that slow long-burning smile of his.

My heart flip-flopped over in my chest. I couldn't help it.

Maybe it was a ploy to take my mind off things, because the next thing I knew he was pulling open the passenger door of the BM. I stopped short when I saw it had a cream leather interior.

'I can't, Marc, I'll ruin it,' I protested. Not only was half my hair plastered with blood, but I'd picked up a good layer of masonry dust sliding down the front of the building, and a liberal coating of road dirt from the gutter.

'I'll have it valeted,' he dismissed impatiently. 'Now for Christ's sake lady, get in!'

I subsided into the soft upholstery without further demur. He slammed the door and moved round the bonnet to the driver's side, looking suddenly hard and dangerous. An unexpected fear needled me. Was I doing the right thing allowing myself to be put into his car so easily?

I quashed it as he climbed into the driving seat and glanced at me, the concern clear in those pale eyes.

'I think perhaps I should take you straight to Casualty,' he said.

'No!' It was a reflex. I hated the damned places. Besides, I had a good enough knowledge of my own body to recognise when an injury was serious. Those I'd sustained this evening were painful, but they were in no way life-threatening.

'Well, I need to do something with you,' he said, touching a hand to my cheek. His fingers felt so hot they almost burnt me. 'You're freezing and you're in shock.'

He took my hands between his and tried to rub some warmth into them, but I yelped again. Turning them over, I realised I'd torn and scraped my palms and fingers, but I couldn't for the life of me remember doing it.

He gave me a dark look, but said nothing. Instead, he settled for just turning the car's air con control round to maximum heat and putting the fan on full blast.

We set off sedately along the quay, turning left away from the river to weave through the back streets up towards the railway station, and the castle.

By holding my hands directly over an air vent in the dash for a few minutes, I managed to persuade some sensation to return. Unfortunately, with it came a pulsating pain in my fingers. I clamped them together in my lap and tried not to think about it too much.

As the heat permeated the interior of the car, I was aware of a grinding weariness soaking down over me. 'Aren't you going to ask me what that was all about?' I said tiredly.

Marc glanced sideways at me, his face lit by the eerie orange glow from the car's instruments. 'I assumed you'd tell me when you were ready,' he said, concentrating on the road ahead.

'Someone at your club doesn't want me there, Marc,' I said, feeling abruptly groggy, 'and I don't know why that is.'

I felt the BM react as his hands twitched on the wheel. He favoured me with a brief look. 'Do you have any idea who?' he asked sharply.

'Not a clue,' I said hazily. I let my head flop back against the padded rest.

'So why do you think someone doesn't want you there?' he demanded. 'Come on, Charlie, talk to me!'

I opened my leaden eyelids with an effort. 'Hm? Oh, I don't know,' I mumbled. 'And I don't know what I *do* know, either, which Jacob thinks is half the problem.'

'Charlie,' he said dryly, 'you're rambling.'

'Mm, sorry,' I muttered indistinctly. For some reason a picture of the man outside the French windows at the Lodge slid into my woolly mind. He'd worn a mask, too. 'Somebody's been watching me, and I've got a bad feeling about it,' I informed Marc with a sigh. 'A very bad feeling.'

The line between consciousness and oblivion was blurring. I felt it closing in on me.

I slept.

IT ONLY SEEMED a few seconds before I felt a hand on my shoulder, shaking gently.

'Charlie, come on, wake up.'

I came fully awake with a jerk, automatically tensing to strike before I recognised Marc. He backed off quickly. 'It's OK, don't panic.' His voice was calm, soothing.

I realised he'd stopped the BM, and slithered further upright in my seat. I recognised the front entrance to one of the most up-market hotels in the area. His hotel.

'Why are we here?' I felt dazed, disconnected. My mind seemed to be working at half speed.

His face was unreadable in the gloom inside the car. 'You were most insistent I shouldn't take you to a doctor, and I didn't think it was wise to take you home again,' he said. 'It was either here or drive you round in circles all night.' He put his hand under my chin and tipped my face up, studying. 'You're a mess,' he added. 'We need to get you cleaned up.'

'Thanks,' I said, 'you really know how to make a girl feel good about herself.'

He flashed me a quick smile as he opened the car door and climbed out, moving round swiftly to help me out of my side. I got out experimentally, and found my ribs seemed to grate protestingly when I moved. I stifled a gasp as I stood up.

Marc caught me. 'Are you OK?'

I shook my head. 'It's nothing. I'm fine. Nothing a hot bath and a stiff whisky wouldn't cure—and not necessarily in that order.'

Despite my denials, it seemed a long walk to the front door. Marc walked slowly alongside me, watching like a hawk for the first sign I was about to keel over. At one point I stumbled and his arm snaked round my shoulders instantly. His musky aftershave mingled interestingly with the smell of man.

'I can manage,' I said. Having him so close when I wasn't in full control of my senses to begin with was altogether too distracting.

The expression on the receptionist's face when we staggered in to the grand lobby area of the hotel spoke volumes about the state I was in. I suppose with my bloody face, dirty soaked shirt and scuffed leathers, I wasn't exactly representative of the target clientele. Marc silenced her protest with a single hard stare.

'Miss Fox has had an accident,' he said, his voice like stone, brooking no argument. 'She will be in my suite.' The woman probably thought he'd run me down in his car.

Somehow, I don't remember the ride in the lift, or how I got from there to Marc's room. The next memory I have is the crackling noise of an open grate. I opened my eyes to find I was on a deeply cushioned sofa, with a soft blanket thrown over me. Marc's face appeared.

'You had me worried for a moment there,' he said. 'Here's that whisky you wanted, and the bath's running.' I fumbled to a sitting position and he handed me a lead crystal glass of liquid the colour of old gold.

I stuck my nose into the glass, recognised single malt quality, then gulped two-thirds of it down like a rough blend anyway. The resultant fire lit my stomach and roared through my veins with a welcome blast.

Marc moved round in front of me. He'd taken off his jacket, and folded back the sleeves of his shirt, revealing muscled forearms, covered with a fine layer of dark hair. I was surprised to see he had tattoos on both arms, blurred with age. He was carrying a wet flannel and a towel with the hotel crest on it.

'Now,' he said, 'let's get the worst of that off and have a look at the damage.' He smoothed my hair back and dabbed efficiently at the blood on my forehead.

I sat with my eyes closed and let him get on with it, too weary to put up much of a fight. His hands were cool and careful, their touch firm but reassuring. The movement lulled me.

'It's only a small cut, and it's stopped bleeding,' he murmured at last. 'Scalp wounds always look worse than they are to begin with.'

He took my hands and turned them over, wiping the worst of the grit away gently.

'They're not too bad,' he decided. 'Where else do you hurt?'

I opened my eyes reluctantly and admitted that my ribs were still aching. Hardly stunning when I thought about it. I was lucky to be still walking.

Marc had pulled my shirt out of my leather jeans and started to unbutton it before I had the wit to object. 'Hey!' I tried to bat his hands away, but my depth perception was off, and he was determined. When he slid his hands over the skin of my ribcage my protests died in my throat as my heart leapt up and bounced there.

'You're going to have some cracking bruises, Charlie,' he said, and his voice suddenly seemed very deep. 'I don't think there's anything broken.' He seemed to be too close to me. I could see the individual pores in the skin of his face. The faint line of an old scar running through his eyebrow. Much too close. My breath hitched.

He looked straight into my eyes and smiled, then got to his feet. 'I think I'd better go and check on that bath,' he said, and strolled away.

The brief pause gave me chance to look round the suite for the first time. The sofa had a low mahogany table in front of it, and beyond that was the open fire I'd sensed, full of burning logs. It was so healthily ablaze that it could only have been one of those fake gas affairs, but it was pretty convincing.

There was a desk on the far side of the room, and doors leading off for the bathroom and bedroom. The decor was subdued, expensive. I didn't even begin to want to know how much a night it was costing him. I chucked back the remainder of my whisky and set the glass down on the polished wood without regard for watermarks.

Marc returned, drying his hands on a towel. 'You're all set,' he said. 'Do you need any help?'

I wavered for a moment, enticed, then shook my head. 'I can manage,' I said. It was becoming a mantra.

I got to my feet stiffly, trying to ignore the complaints from my body, and tottered across to the bathroom. Inside it was all white marble and mirrors clouded with steam from the bath. I almost groaned at the sight of it. Marc had dropped in a generous quantity of the foam bath furnished by the hotel, and hadn't stinted on the hot water. It was filled to the brim.

I shut the door and took a moment to study my reflection in the mirror. What I saw made me grimace. Marc had managed to mop away most of the blood from my face, but my hair still looked matted like a stray cat's. The flesh over my left cheekbone seemed swollen, closing my eye a little, but some ice would probably sort it.

I stripped off my shirt and prodded experimentally at my ribs. There was moderate blueing along them that was slightly alarming, but it was nothing I couldn't handle. More bruises came to light as I peeled off my leather jeans. Even with the Kevlar and the padding, the hip I'd landed on was turning a regal shade of purple.

I held my hands out in front of me and inspected the damage. A few cuts and scratches; a big graze on one palm. Nothing drastic. All in all, I was lucky to have got away so lightly.

Despite my aches and pains, I finished stripping off in record time, sliding chin-deep into the delicately scented water. For someone who doesn't own a bath—all the flat has is a shower—it was the apex of luxury. I lay back and let the heat seep into my bones. My eyes closed, and I drifted off.

It didn't seem like more than a minute or two before I was groggily awake again to find Marc perched on the side of the bath, staring down at me.

'Is there no peace?' I grouched, nerves jangling at the sight of him. It didn't help that he was still fully clothed and I was naked. The bubble bath, traitor that it was, had dispersed enough to leave little to his imagination.

'You've been in there nearly an hour,' he pointed out mildly. 'I was worried about you and besides, the water's cold.' He reached in to the far end and yanked the plug out. The admittedly tepid bath water started to slip away with disturbing speed. It hadn't provided much in the way of a modesty blanket, but it had been better than nothing.

Oh, what the hell. If he fancied me when I was doing my best impersonation of a human punchbag, the man needed help. I struggled to my feet, suddenly ponderous. He moved back to let me step dripping out of the bath, his face giving nothing away.

Marc engulfed me in a huge fluffy towel, warmed from the heated rail. I was happy to sag weakly against the strength of his body. I rested my head against his crisp shirt front, and let him rub me dry. My eyes closed again, but even I couldn't sleep standing up.

He sat me down on the edge of the bath while he dried my legs, then towelled my hair. I was so far gone I nearly nodded off while he was doing it.

'Oh Charlie,' he said ruefully, catching me as I rocked. 'You've no idea what a temptation you are, but if I take advantage of you now it will practically be necrophilia.'

I was too drowsy to make either comment or objection as he hoisted me up into his arms and carried me through to the bedroom. The bed was voluminous and gave invitingly when he tipped me gently onto it. He pulled the covers up round my chin and tucked my damp hair away from my face, as you would a child.

I think I was asleep before the mattress finished swaying.

* * *

I STARTED INTO wakefulness four hours later with a clear head and no idea where I was. I sat up abruptly, the bedclothes tangling round my legs so that when I tried to climb out of bed I ended up dropping in a knotted heap heavily onto the floor. The jar of it highlighted a myriad of bruises. Despite my efforts to stifle it, I cried out.

It was only then I realised I wasn't alone in the room. I could sense someone's movement, but it was too dark to see them. I tried to scramble away, get to my feet, but the bed covers were relentless in their grip.

There was a man looming over me. Instinctively, I lashed out with a strong right, connecting into unbraced muscle with enough force to leave him winded. Mind you, the effort didn't do my own ribs any good, either.

'Charlie, for God's sake, it's me!'

I recognised Marc's voice over the thundering of my heart, and dropped back, sweating and breathless, clutching at the bedclothes. I heard him move away and the next thing the bedside lamp had been clicked on.

When I'd finished blinking in the glare, I saw Marc by the switch, rubbing at his stomach. One of the large armchairs had a rumpled pillow and quilt on the floor next to it. He'd evidently been keeping his eye on me.

Marc was wearing the thick towelling robe the hotel provided, and pretty obviously nothing else. I felt a furious colour flaming my face. Never a good idea to blush when you've got my hair colouring. It clashes horribly.

Marc looked at me sardonically. 'You're feeling better,' he said, and it wasn't a question.

'I'm sorry,' I said, shakily, climbing hastily back onto the bed and pulling the covers back with me. Marc came and settled on the edge, looking dangerous again, but for a different reason. I swallowed nervously as he traced a finger round my face, my eyes fixed on him.

'Oh Charlie, you're such a puzzle,' he said, almost to himself. 'So strong, but so vulnerable. Such a temper to go with that red hair.' He picked up a few strands, let them slip through his fingers, murmuring half to himself, 'Not that it's really red; all those different shades of

125

copper, and honey, and gold. And who'd have thought there'd be such a glorious body under all that denim and those heavy leathers you wear, hm?'

Looking back afterwards, I can't think what made me do it, but at the time it seemed the most natural thing in the world. To reach up for the back of his neck, and pull those tantalising lips down to meet mine. Maybe it was just the best way of stopping a flow of compliments I still didn't know how to cope with.

He kissed me slowly, with great precision, pulling back after a few moments to look deep into my eyes as if asking a question. If I wanted to turn back, now was the time. I didn't want to. I closed my eyes and kissed him again, feeling little feathers of reaction stir through my body. I wanted him. It was as simple as that.

There had not been many times over the period since my attack when I'd felt the urge to go to bed with a man, I admit, but that didn't mean I'd been celibate, either. I'd learned, almost to my surprise, that the horrors of rape had not made me shy away from all physical contact. Instead, they had served to detach it in my mind from the emotional involvement that seems to be so much a part of the female psyche.

I didn't know if my reaction was normal for victims of sexual assault. I'd been offered the usual counselling, but the thought of discussing what I'd been through with anyone, however well-qualified and sympathetic, had sickened me. I'd turned them down, turned in on myself for a time, and followed my own direction instead.

I suppose what made it worse, in some ways, was that I'd believed myself to be in love at the time. Sean Meyer had seemed so perfect, so right, and I'd been crazy about him. He'd gone overseas just weeks before the night when Donalson, Hackett, Morton, and Clay had buoyed themselves up with a malignant mix of alcohol and bravado, and my nightmare had begun.

I'd discovered afterwards, to my utter disillusionment, that Sean was nothing like the hero I'd always imagined he would turn out to be. It had taken me a long time to forget him. I wasn't in any hurry to expose myself again by replacing him with anyone else in my affections.

I'd developed my own code of conduct instead. One that said if it feels good, and doesn't hurt anyone, then do it, and to hell with the hearts and flowers.

Besides, I was willing to bet that anyone with Marc's magnetism was either going to be a striking success, or a spectacular disaster in bed.

And I was intrigued to find out which was right.

Marc proved himself an experienced and sophisticated lover. Somewhere along the line some farsighted woman had taken the time to develop his natural ability. He must have been a Grade A student.

Some men appear to take it for granted that the knowledge of how to make love is instinctive, something they're born with. It isn't. It's a skill that has to be worked at and acquired like any other, although some do seem to have more aptitude than others.

I was neither surprised nor insulted when Marc pulled open one of the bedside drawers and produced the sort of protection you can't afford to be without these days.

I wasn't under any illusions that this was a sudden out-of-character burst of passion on his part, just as it wasn't going to turn into a great romance on mine. Sex was obviously just something he enjoyed, and was good at. I couldn't really see him being unprepared for it.

Men, I've always thought, find it difficult to hide aspects of their true character when they're in bed. Marc was no exception. He was unselfish, yet at the same time utterly ruthless, and his control was absolute.

If the way he reduced me to bonelessness, then rolled me gasping over the final precipice was masterly, it was perhaps because he wouldn't have tolerated the failure of anything less.

Thirteen

THE NEXT MORNING Marc took me back to the flat. It wasn't something I was looking forward to and, if I'm honest, I was relieved to have him with me.

He drove back into Lancaster as he did everything, with a kind of restlessness bordering on restrained anger. His mobile phone rang almost from the moment he switched it on and he spent most of the journey with the lump of plastic stuck to the side of his head, steering with one hand. I was glad the BMW was an automatic.

I took advantage of my enforced silence to turn over thoughts about last night. We hadn't talked much afterwards, not of anything that mattered, at any rate. Taken purely as a physical experience, though, it had been quite something. I couldn't honestly say I regretted it.

He'd ordered a late supper—very late, actually—from room service. The elderly waiter had taken in my discoloured face as I sat huddled in a bathrobe on the sofa in front of the fire, and favoured Marc with a scandalised look.

When Marc offered a folded banknote as a tip on the way out, the man had glared accusingly at him and point-blank refused. I managed to hold on until the door had firmly closed behind the waiter's back before I collapsed in a fit of giggles.

Marc, who'd missed the man's glances, looked bewildered at his behavior, and mine. 'What the hell is the matter with everybody?' he demanded.

'He thinks you've been indulging in a bit of S&M and been beating me up,' I said when I'd calmed down.

Marc's head reared up, shocked. I took one look at him and burst out laughing again.

* * *

WHEN WE'D EATEN we'd gone back to bed, together. I was used to sleeping alone, but tonight it was nice to have the warmth of a male body curled round me. My eyes closed straight away and didn't open again until the grey streaks of morning came slinking through the arrow-slit between the drawn curtains.

In the cold light of day we'd edged round each other carefully, being too polite about who got first crack at the bathroom, dressing coyly behind closed doors. Two breakfasts arrived, kept warm under silver domes on a spotless trolley. I realised, as I poured from the silver pot, that I'd been to bed with the man and I wasn't even entirely sure how he took his coffee.

We left about half an hour later making a very odd couple. Heads turned as this flawlessly dressed businessman, and a beat-up scruffy little biker ambled out side by side. Hell, I'd managed to sponge the worst of the blood off my leathers.

Such was Marc's pull with the hotel, they'd even arranged for someone to clean the interior of the BM while we slept. The cream interior was immaculate again, as though last night's events had never happened.

Although I was nervous about returning to the scene of the crime, I was glad of the breathing space it gave me. I was going to have to get my head around what had happened. Both with my masked attackers, and with Marc. I needed some time alone.

Eventually, we pulled up on the quay outside the flat. While Marc finished his last call I sat for a few moments, staring out of the window. My eye rested briefly on the wreckage of the small table the Scouser had thrown over the balcony at me, still lying in a splintered heap on the pavement. I wondered vaguely what had become of the knife I'd sent spinning out of reach into the night.

Marc switched his mobile off and tucked it into the inside pocket of his jacket. I started fumbling with the release for my seatbelt when he reached across and undid it, along with his own. I glanced up at him in surprise.

'What are you doing?'

'What does it look like?' he quizzed with a touch of impatience. 'You don't think I'm going to let you go up there alone, do you?'

'I hardly think they'll still be hanging around,' I pointed out. Mind you, after what I'd done to his kneecap, the smoker would have probably needed assistance to make it down the stairs. I was disconcerted to find the thought cheered me immensely.

'I've seen half of what they've done,' Marc said, his glance flickering down my body. 'Now I want to see the rest.' He spoke in a quiet tone, but I knew that arguing would have been futile.

I shrugged and heaved myself out onto the pavement. I was feeling the after effects good and proper. There didn't seem to be a part of me that didn't ache, and I never realised bruises drew from such an inventive palette of colours.

A sudden thought struck me, and before we went in I tottered round to check on the bike. I admit I breathed a bit of a sigh of relief when I saw it, still chained and covered. Whatever else they'd done, at least the Suzuki had escaped unmolested.

By chance, I'd still got my keys in my leathers, but I wasn't too surprised, when I finally managed to stagger to the top of the wooden staircase, to find my front door standing wide open.

In daylight, the mess looked a lot worse. I stood in the living room, staring round me, feeling detached. Marc prowled through the rooms, head down, jaw clenched, simmering.

Finally, he came back into the living room. 'Bastards,' he said tightly. 'Pointless bastards! What the fuck did they think they were doing?'

I glanced at him, a half-smile twisting my lips. 'You need a reason to be a psycho?' I asked.

He came and put his arms round me, but I stepped out of his embrace and moved away from him, uneasy. I knew I didn't want his comfort, nor his pity, but I wasn't sure what I did expect from him.

We seemed to have bypassed the first few stages of normal courtship, moved too fast into intimacy. We'd become lovers when we hadn't even had time to become friends.

I wandered through into my bedroom. It hadn't escaped their attentions, either. The Scouser had sliced his way through my mattress, the curtains, and even taken the knife to every pillow. One of them was from my mother's, a feather one. The stuffing was now scattered all over the room like confetti at a full church wedding.

The ingredients of my drawers had been turned into a novelty carpet. He'd taken particular care to rip his way through what seemed to be my entire stock of underwear. It was symbolic, somehow, too personal, and it sent a prickle of apprehension through me.

Marc had followed me through. Now he gripped my shoulders and turned me to face him. This time I didn't pull away.

'Charlie, listen to me,' he said urgently. 'Whatever it is you've been doing, stop it. Let it go. Whoever these people are, they're obviously deadly serious. Don't take any risks.'

I broke eye contact and let my gaze slide across my ransacked home. 'But there's a connection to your club,' I argued.

He cut me short, curtly. 'If there's anything going on at the New Adelphi, *I'll* take care of it,' he said grimly. 'I don't want to see anything like this happening to you again. Understand?'

I bristled under his glare, wavered for a moment, then gave in. I let my shoulders slump.

'Yes,' I said at last, wearily, 'I understand.'

WHEN HE'D GONE, promising to call me, I sat on the remnants of my sofa for a long time without doing anything other than thinking. I hadn't recognised the two men who were responsible for my new line in interior decor. It certainly wasn't anyone who I'd met, or they would have known that in this case Charlie wasn't a man's name. So who were they and, more importantly, who had sent them?

I thought, briefly, about calling the police, but decided against it, for a number of reasons. I tried to tell myself that my reluctance to involve the authorities had nothing to do with the men's threats, but I'm not entirely sure I believed me.

In any case, what did I tell them about Terry's computer? I was pretty sure it had been nicked from the New Adelphi, which meant I'd been handling stolen goods. And the last time our paths had crossed they'd as good as accused me of beating up the two boys at the club. Somehow, I couldn't see my current predicament interesting them greatly, especially after the desultory response they'd made to Ailsa's call from the Lodge.

Shelseley. The name almost made me start. I'd just assumed the prowler there had some link with the residents. An ex-husband or boyfriend maybe. That it was just coincidence he'd first appeared right after Terry had given me the lap-top. Was there a connection there?

I turned this idea over a few times, then dismissed it. The men who'd come after me were too professional to go in for such half-hearted scare tactics. They knew what they wanted, and they'd gone straight for it.

I'd had time to conduct a quick search, and discovered the lap-top had definitely gone. Either the Scouser had come back for it, or the smoker had hopped away with it under his arm.

If that was the case, if my manic burglars were solely connected with Terry's damned computer, and they hadn't been trailing me round to Shelseley, then how the hell had they known where to look for it?

'If you've killed her, the shit's going to really hit the fan after last time.'

I remembered the smoker's words. What last time? I thought of Susie, and shivered, trying to push the sudden irrational fear out of my mind.

It wasn't the same man, I told myself. It couldn't be the same man. I closed my eyes with the effort of forcing a return to calm, and order. I would not let myself be terrified by what had happened.

People lock themselves away, turn their homes into fortresses when the possible risk simply doesn't demand such precautions. Their own sense of panic imprisons them. Marks them out to be victims. If I let myself become incapacitated with fright, I was halfway lost before I began.

I dredged up enough energy to stir myself off the sofa, climbing stiffly to my feet. Despite my resolution not to be scared into retreat, my first action was to sort out the busted lock on the front door. I rang a local firm who said they were stacked out, but promised to be round at four that afternoon.

I tried Terry's mobile number again, but it was still switched off, and his home number rang out without reply. I couldn't face starting on the clearing up, and I didn't want to sit around and mope all day. Besides, I needed to do something about my mobility. I stuffed some surviving clean clothes into my tank bag and headed out.

I pulled the front door closed behind me and left it at that. Everything of value I owned appeared to have been trashed anyway. I didn't think any opportunist burglar could do anything more than had been done already. Maybe they'd even tidy things up a bit.

The Suzuki was reassuringly familiar as I cruised out along the quay, even if riding it made me wince. My back and shoulders felt as though they were wired tight, and every pothole and undulation in the road surface jerked the breath from my lungs.

I needed time to think, and some mindless activity to keep the rest of me occupied while I was doing it. I rode round the one-way system and up to the gym I use. It was once a dubious auto salvage yard, but that went by the wayside years ago. The graffiti-decorated corrugated iron fencing that used to keep the guard dogs in is still up, though. It tends to discourage the posers, but the hard-core of people who go there to train don't do it for the image.

I sometimes do a bit of work for the owner, a strapping German whose real name had been lost in the mists of time. For as long as I'd known him, I'd never heard anyone call him anything but Attila.

He was into body building of serious proportions, and was constantly being offered doorman jobs. This was despite the fact he was as soft as they came. He confided to me once in a reflective moment that he actually fainted at the sight of blood.

I hadn't been in to the gym for ages, and was feeling guilty about it. Right now, it was the nearest place I could think of that had a decent steam room.

I spent the next two hours sweating. The first hour it was caused by trying painfully to force some flexibility back into my screaming muscles. The second it was brought on by the eucalyptus-scented wet heat from the sauna.

As I sat, wrapped in a towel and dripping, I had time to consider what had occurred with Marc. I've always been attracted to bad boys, and he definitely had that air about him. Physically, we were certainly compatible.

The only thing that bothered me was that I'd thought he would be more aloof with his one-night stands. The last response I'd expected from him was to cling. He was good company, but that didn't mean I wanted commitment from him. Did it?

I shook my head, feeling the sweat drop from my hair. There was no way I was going to open up on an emotional level. Not to Marc. Not to anyone. Not again.

I comforted myself with the thought that his base of operations was Manchester. He'd soon be itching to get back there. I was never going to be more than a mildly interesting diversion for him.

Which was OK, because that's all he was to me.

Afterwards, I stood in the shower, letting the water run as hot as I could stand it. I didn't think I was kidding myself by claiming I definitely felt easier. I dressed again and walked—OK, hobbled—out to say goodbye to Attila.

'You want to go and get yourself a decent massage,' he told me, eyeing my stiff movements critically, like a vet watching a horse trot up that's severely lame all round.

A picture of Tris and his array of soothing essential oils popped into my mind so suddenly I'm amazed a lightbulb didn't blink on over the top of my head.

I borrowed Attila's phone and called Shelseley. Tris, bless him, said he could slot me into his schedule right away, if I could get there inside a quarter of an hour.

'No problem,' I said gratefully. As I put the phone down I silently blessed the bike's ability to slide through town traffic.

IN FACT, IT took me less than ten minutes to get to the Lodge. Tris was already in the drawing room, sitting reading a faded little book. When I stuck my head round the door he closed its fragile covers with great care and went to return it to its place on the shelves.

The ceilings are high in all the downstairs rooms at Shelseley, and two huge bookcases in the alcoves on either side of the fireplace took full advantage of the fact. Tris even had one of those short wheeled ladders so he could reach the ones at the top.

'What were you reading?' I asked, unwinding my scarf and dumping my helmet and gloves on the rattan sofa.

'W.H. Auden,' he said, eyes still roaming the shelves with the affection of any collector. 'It was my father's. A first edition. He—'

Whatever else he was going to say was lost as the door burst open and three small boys came tussling into the room. They were bound up in some violent game of tag, the rules of which seemed to demand the forcible removal of a quantity of the taggee's hair.

Whatever, the two taggers had the smaller of the trio in a pretty effective headlock and were attempting to comply with enthusiasm.

They danced further into the room, clanging off items of furniture as they went. Tris only reacted when they came perilously close to his collection of essential oils.

'Now, now lads,' he said nervously, trying to intercept them. 'Calm it down a bit, hey?'

One of the taggers raised his head enough to give him a single stare that said clearly, 'You have to be kidding.' Then they carried on with their game as if he hadn't spoken.

Tris jumped in front of his oils with his hands out, jigging from one foot to the other like the smallest school team goalkeeper, faced with the other side's biggest striker. Eventually, inevitably, the ball was going to come smashing into the back of the net. It was just a matter of time.

I sighed, moving over to the boys. It only took a moment to visually unravel them enough to identify the taggers. I dived into the scrimmage, and came out with a hard grip on the back of a pair of grubby necks.

The two boys wriggled briefly, then went limp in my hands like cats. The taggee took the opportunity to bolt, letting the door swing wide on his way out.

I bent down enough to be able to look straight into two sullen faces. They must have been about eight. 'That's a great game you're playing,' I said conversationally. 'Now go and play it somewhere else.'

I let go and watched them disappear rapidly into the hallway with the heavy footsteps of someone twice their size. It would have been too much to expect them to close the door behind them. Tris did it instead, taking a key out of his pocket and locking it firmly behind them.

'Thanks,' he said, relief in his voice. 'I wish I could deal with them so easily.'

'They just need a firm hand,' I said. 'Well, strong fingers, anyway.'

'I have to be so careful, you see,' he explained, anxiety underwritten by just a thread of annoyance. 'With half this lot you only have to raise your voice and they threaten legal action.'

I briefly considered telling Tris he ought to call their bluff, but thought of Ailsa's reaction, and re-considered again.

He turned as I shrugged my way out of my jacket. 'Now then, what have you been up to?' He looked at me properly, and frowned. 'What happened to your face?'

'I lost an argument,' I said.

He looked about to push it further, but changed his mind. 'Do I take it that's why you're here?' he said instead.

I grimaced. 'I've felt better,' I agreed.

He asked where the problem areas were, and I listed them. It would probably have been quicker to tell him which bits didn't hurt.

He nodded a couple of times, moved over to the shelves, and took down several of his little bottles without seeming to hesitate over the choice. It was strange to see the normally abstracted Tris so focused.

'I'll just go behind there and mix these up for you,' he said, indicating the old-fashioned concertina screen that stood in front of the bay window. 'If you'd like to slip out of your things and lie face down on the couch. There are warm towels on the heater. Help yourself.'

In fact, the couch in the centre of the room was surrounded by four small free-standing electric radiators like a heated corral. I left my clothes draped over the arm of the sofa and struggled into a prone position as instructed.

Tris seemed to know when I was ready, and he popped out from behind the screen rubbing his hands together briskly to take the chill off them. He covered me in another couple of hot towels, then placed his hands quietly on my back for a few moments, rocking me gently.

I hadn't had a massage for years, but even so I could remember enough to tell that Tris had a real talent for it. After the first five minutes I felt my muscles begin to unlock themselves and I allowed myself to fully relax.

'I'm using frankincense for calming, and eucalyptus and rosemary for the aches and pains,' he said, sliding his hands long and slow up the nape of my neck and into my hairline.

He worked his way down my spine slowly, easing the loops out of my trapezius, sensitive to my nervous twitches when he went in too keenly. 'You've got good muscle bulk,' he told me, 'but you probably need to stretch more.'

He hesitated altogether when he reached the badly discoloured hip I'd landed on. 'Are you sure you want me to work on this?' he asked.

I gritted my teeth. 'Keep going. I'll let you know when I can't stand it any more.'

'Well, if you're sure,' he said doubtfully. I heard him lift another bottle down from the shelf and unscrew the lid. 'I'll add in some lemongrass, then. It should help with the bruising.'

He started in, tentatively at first, while I bit back the odd groan. I searched my mind for a subject to take my mind off it. 'Any more sign of your prowler?' I asked, almost on a gasp as Tris's fingers plunged unexpectedly deep into torn and knotted muscle.

'Sorry,' he murmured. 'You really should have seen a doctor for this, Charlie.' When I remained stubbornly silent, he went on, 'Anyway, no, we haven't had any more unexpected visits.'

'How's Nina?'

'She's still very upset,' he said, and I could hear the distress in his voice. 'Hardly comes out of her room, poor kid. Ailsa's worried about her, but she's got a lot on her plate anyway at the moment,' he added. 'Another of the girls has left, did you know?'

No, I didn't. I paused to catch my breath as he leant the heel of his hand into my gluteal muscles and put his weight behind it.

When I could speak again, I said, 'What will she do if they all go?'

'I don't know,' Tris said. 'I thought maybe we should start planning for the worst, though, you know? Look at the possibilities of changing direction a little. Ailsa did hypnotherapy when she trained as a counsellor, and I've done reflexology as well as aromatherapy.' I felt him shrug, before adding diffidently, as though wary of ridicule, 'I thought we could maybe look at becoming a sort of holistic healing centre.'

He straightened up, pausing to squeeze more oil onto his hands. Tris used to have his oils in delicate little bowls, hand-painted in rainbow colours. They had been a wedding present from a glass-blowing friend, but the decoration had proved too glittering, and the glass too fragile, to stand up to a house full of other people's careless, magpie children. Now he used a selection of lidded plastic bottles, like you'd find put out for ketchup in a cheap roadside café.

I considered the idea in silence for a few moments while he circled his thumbs down the back of my hamstring. Beyond trying the odd homeopathic cold remedy from one of the health food shops in town, I'd never given alternative medicine much thought. I certainly didn't know what sort of a local following it would generate. 'What does Ailsa think?' I asked cautiously.

He sighed, 'I haven't really talked to her much about it,' he admitted.

'Well, I suppose at least it would mean you could keep this place afloat,' I said. 'Save you having to sell up.'

Tris's fingers stilled momentarily. '*Sell?*' he said, in the same shocked tone of voice that he might have used if I'd suggested sacrificing small children. 'There've been Shelseleys on this site since the Wars of the Roses. We couldn't ever sell the Lodge.'

He ran his hands down my calf, and announced I was done. 'I'll leave you to get dressed in your own time,' he said, wiping his hands on a towel. 'Try not to bathe for a few hours. The oils will keep working as they're absorbed into your skin, but drink plenty of water.'

He unlocked the door and slipped out of the room quietly. I sat up, feeling strangely light-headed. But better. Definitely better.

Despite Tris's warning about the oils, I admit I wiped the most obvious excess away with a towel, otherwise I was going to need my leathers dry-cleaning before I could wear them again. As it was, the hair round the back of my neck felt slick with it.

When I went out into the hall, I was pleased to discover that the limp had almost gone. Tris was waiting for me by the front door.

'How does that feel?' he asked brightly.

'Much better, I think,' I said. 'What do I owe you?'

He shook his head. 'Compliments of the house,' he said. He looked at me seriously. 'I'm just sorry that I hurt you.'

I shrugged. 'I've had worse,' I said. 'Besides, there's a school of thought that says if it doesn't hurt, it's not working.'

'I'll take your word for it. You take care now, Charlie.' He flashed me a quick grin. Topped by that ragged haircut, it lent his face an urchin's charm. 'And maybe next time you have a massage, it'll be for pleasure, rather than because you've been arguing with someone bigger and uglier than you.'

I smiled back. 'Let's hope so,' I said fervently.

*   *   *

I STOPPED IN at the indoor market on the way back round town, picking up what fresh fruit and vegetables I could fit in my tank bag. By the time I reached the flat again, it was early afternoon.

Making it up the stairs still took noticeable effort, but at least the single flight no longer seemed like the difficult way up K2. I was three treads from the top when I realised I wasn't alone.

The hairs prickled on the back of my neck. I dumped my tank bag down slowly on the top step, moving up onto the landing with my back to the wall. I ran through a mental checklist of options and actions. Movement, when it came, was sudden enough to be shocking.

A figure reared out of the shadows on the other side of the landing, making me spin round fast. I had an instant flashback to the night before.

I went straight into a half-crouch, with my heart pounding, eyes frantically straining to catch the first glimpse of the angle of attack.

'Bloody hell, Foxy, you don't mess about, do you?'

I recognised the voice and unwound gradually, coming upright. I took a couple of deep breaths to try and slow my body systems down. My hands were clenched so tight into fists I could feel my fingernails digging in to my palms.

The fear had made me suddenly cold, and now I shivered. 'Christ, Dave,' I said, annoyed to hear my voice shake. 'You frightened the *shit* out of me.'

Dave grinned. 'Better than you *beating* the shit out of me,' he said. As he came forwards into the light I saw he was dressed in zip-up orange nylon jacket that I thought went out of fashion twenty years ago. If you were into the club scene it was probably right back in now, which shows how much attention I pay.

I picked up my bag again, still feeling ruffled. 'What are you doing here?'

'Waiting for you,' he said. The grin died and he was suddenly pensive. 'Look, Charlie, I need your help.' His voice grew sober. 'There's some serious shit going on at the New Adelphi and I think I could be in danger.'

Fourteen

I CONSIDERED HIM for a few moments, trying to gauge if he was serious or just winding me up. I couldn't help but be intrigued. It was worth the trouble of finding out, I suppose.

I pushed the front door open. 'Come on in, it isn't locked,' I said.

He looked disgusted. 'You mean I've been hanging around on your draughty landing all this time when I could have been lounging around on your—' He saw the state of the living room and stopped short.

'I should point out that this is not my normal idea of good housekeeping,' I told him dryly.

'Fuck me,' Dave murmured in wonder, looking round wide-eyed.

I thought his reaction was a bit over the top. Irritated, I dumped my tank bag down on the table. If I carried on like this, most of the fruit I'd bought was going to be so mashed I was going to have to purée it.

'OK Dave,' I said with a touch of impatience, 'what's the script? As you can see, I've got rather a lot on my plate at the moment.'

He swallowed and dragged his eyes away from the slashed furniture. 'What *happened?*'

I sighed, not really wanting to have to explain. 'Just cut to the chase, will you?' I said tiredly.

'Sorry.' He finally managed to get his thoughts back on track. 'This is just so—' His voice petered out and he shrugged, lost for words.

I glared at him. He took the hint.

'OK, OK. It's just that there's something spooky going on at the club right now. Len and Angelo have been in foul moods since last week, and so's Mr Quinn, but it's been worse the last couple of days. At first I thought it was the fuss over those lads you laid out on

Saturday, and having the police round. The way you did that was brilliant, by the way,' he added, flashing me an engaging grin.

I refused to warm to his charm. Disconcerted, Dave ploughed on. 'Well, then yesterday I was in the club sorting out some new material. I'm normally there on a Sunday. Anyway, when they came in—Len and Angelo—that is, they didn't know I was there.'

He eased his shoulders nervously, almost a twitch. I didn't interrupt him, waiting for him to carry on. After a pause, he did.

'Len was furious about something, really crazy with it. He was practically screaming at Angelo that he'd gone too far this time, and he—Len—didn't think he could cover up for him. Angelo was just really on edge, not far away from exploding. I thought they were going to start killing each other at any moment. It was scary stuff.'

'So what had Angelo done?'

'I don't know. Len was yelling like a madman, when the boss man walks in.'

'Marc?' I said, startled.

'Yeah,' Dave grinned again at my reaction, more slyly this time. 'He broke them up and they all went into the office. They were only there about five minutes before there was all this crashing and shouting going on and they came bursting out of there. Of course, I stuck my head up to see what was happening.'

'And?' I prompted.

'Well, it looked like Mr Quinn had clouted Angelo good style, split his lip and everything. The boss was white with anger. You know how some people go kind of deadly quiet with it? He told Angelo he'd broken the rules and he wasn't going to stand for it, no way. Len looked like he didn't know whose side to go for. I mean, Angelo's his mate, right? But it's pretty obvious he thinks Mr Quinn's the dog's bollocks.'

'But why on earth did Marc hit Angelo?' I wondered.

Dave shrugged. 'Search me. Old Angelo's obviously been up to something he shouldn't and got found out for it. Maybe Mr Quinn found out that the kids in the club are not just getting their kicks from the music, if you get my drift?'

He shivered suddenly and when he next looked up at me, there was fear in his eyes. 'They saw that I was there, then, and Mr Quinn really lost his rag. He got me up against the wall and told me to keep my nose out of things that didn't concern me. Look.'

Dave unzipped the top of his nylon jacket. It crackled with static as the material folded. If he walked across a man-made fibre carpet and then went out in the rain, he'd probably electrocute himself. Underneath the jacket he wore a T-shirt. The round neck revealed a band of livid bruises circling his throat.

I eyed the yellow and bluish marks with a certain amount of sympathy. After all, I had more or less a matching set of my own. My body seemed to be covered with them. Big blotches like spilt ink on tissue paper. There were so many smaller dabs I'd lost count. 'So why are you telling me all this?' I asked, keeping my voice neutral.

Dave tried another grin, but it didn't quite come off. 'I'm scared, Charlie,' he admitted. He fastened the jacket right up to the top again and gave me a level stare.

'I need your help,' he said baldly. 'I need to know how to look after myself because, I tell you, whatever's going on at the New Adelphi, it's starting to get real nasty.'

'What do you mean, Dave, it's getting nasty at the club?' I asked. I tried to shake off an uneasy sense of misgiving. If this was true, what was Marc's real part in it?

Dave looked indignant. 'Isn't this enough?' he demanded, gesturing to his neck.

I gave him a pointed stare. 'All that proves is they don't like eavesdroppers,' I told him.

'Oh come on, Charlie! Think about it!' Dave jumped up, agitated, and paced around. The floor was too cluttered in debris for him to make a proper job of it. After a few moments he sat down again, leaning forwards with his muscular forearms resting on his knees, intent. 'Look, I've seen quite a few of the kiddies on the dance floor high as kites, even though Mr Quinn swears nobody brings anything into the club, right?'

Reluctantly, I nodded.

'So, they must be getting it from somewhere, yes?'

I nodded again.

'And if they're not bringing it in, they must be getting hold of it *after* they're inside. If Angelo's been indulging in a bit of private enterprise, and Mr Quinn's found out, he'll be for the chop—one way or another.' He shivered again. 'If Mr Quinn's going to get serious about it, well,' he swallowed, 'he won't want any witnesses, will he?'

'I suppose not,' I agreed slowly. Something wasn't right with Dave's argument. Something didn't gel, but right now I couldn't put my finger on just what it was.

I knew Marc worked by his own code. The lines he drew might not have matched legal ones very closely. If you stepped over them, his retribution would be swift and without mercy. I could almost feel sorry for Dave. His fear seemed genuine, even if I wasn't sure about the cause.

'So what help do you want from me?'

'Well, like I said, I want you to teach me some self-defence.' He regarded me hopefully, looking anxious when I didn't immediately respond. 'That *is* what you do, isn't it?'

'Yeah,' I agreed tiredly, 'but it's not as simple as that, Dave. You can't just have a quick lesson and turn into Jackie Chan overnight.'

Without persistent training, knowledge was irrelevant. In fact, it was probably more dangerous than not knowing anything at all. Understanding the right moves for taking the knife away from the Scouser last night would have been useless without an instinctive reflex speed and sense of timing. That only came with constant practice. It seemed I'd been getting plenty of that lately.

'No, no, I want you to teach me regularly,' he said. 'I'll pay.'

I was about to refuse. When I glanced at him he was so tense you could have tuned a guitar by banging his head on a chair and listening to the resonance.

I sighed. 'OK, Dave,' I said.

He jumped up again, unable to contain his bounce. He made me feel dog tired by comparison.

'That's great!' he said. 'When can we start?'

'Soon,' I promised. I got to my feet with an effort, my muscles protesting from the brief period of inactivity. The flexibility from Tris's ministrations earlier seemed to have evaporated. I flicked him a pained look. 'Just not right now, OK?'

AFTER DAVE HAD gone I made a half-hearted attempt at clearing up a little. At least I managed, with sweat and swear words in almost equal amounts, to turn my shredded mattress over so I had something solid to sleep on.

The locksmith turned up with commendable promptness, only shortly after four o'clock. He was a skinny old bloke with a sorrowful expression, and a foul-smelling cigarette permanently drooping from his bottom lip. For once I was too wearied to protest.

He came in, clucking at the state of the place, and barely concealing his disgust at the lack of security provided by my existing lock.

'Can't beat a good old five-lever mortice,' he said, wriggling his eyebrows. It was only when he asked if the police thought they'd catch the little buggers who'd done it that I realised I still hadn't called them.

It didn't take me long to work out that I wasn't going to.

When he was finished, I thanked the locksmith and secured the door behind him. A locked door might not have proved much of a barrier last time, but I admit it made me feel better.

I ate a thrown-together tea in silence. Mainly because everything I owned that made noise had been comprehensively destroyed. It was eerie and uncomfortable.

Then I dragged myself back out to teach my usual class at Shelseley, rearranging the curriculum so I did as little physical stuff as I could get away with. One or two of my pupils looked curiously at the more visible bruises, but they didn't ask too many questions. I was grateful for their reserve.

I made it home again by early evening, and the time seemed to stretch away in front of me. I tried ringing Jacob and Clare, but there was no reply. Even Sam's answering machine was on. I put the phone down without leaving him a message.

Instead, I managed to uncover the local phone directory, and looked up Terry Rothwell's address. It wasn't too far away, one of the new estates, and the weather was uncharacteristically dry. I had quite a few questions for Terry, not least of which was to find out from whom, exactly, he acquired that damn lap-top in the first place.

My next question would probably have concerned the fact that he chose to drop my name into it, when all I'd been doing was a favour for a friend. As I gathered up my leather jacket and helmet, I was in the mood to get stroppy with someone who wasn't in a position to shout back.

I FOUND MY way to the collection of streets where Terry lived easily enough, but finding his house was another matter. The planners in their infinite wisdom had used the same name for a Street, an Avenue and a Way, all right on top of one another.

The light was gone by the time I got there. I had to park up and dig out the piece of paper I'd scribbled his address down on before I could discover which one Terry actually lived on. By that time it wasn't worth moving again and I left the bike where it was. I didn't chain it up, just set the alarm, and took my helmet with me.

Wilmington Avenue consisted of a featureless sprawl of brick boxes. They were detached, but only just, with an alleyway between each that was so narrow you could have reached out and touched both walls without stretching.

At first I couldn't work out what looked wrong about the way they were laid out, but then I realised there were no pavements along each side of the road. The pocket handkerchief-sized front lawns ran straight down into the gutter with only a line of edging bricks between the two.

I didn't know how long the estate had been built, but little attempt had been made by the occupants to individualise the houses. A few little stunted shrubs in the gardens, the odd neat planting of small clumps of unidentifiable greenery. In the driveways stood two- or three-year-old sensible saloon cars.

As I rounded a curve in the road I spotted Terry's house. There was nothing very different about the exterior, except for the fact it had his damn great green Merc van parked smack outside. I'd bet the residents' association—and there had to be one—loved that.

I toddled up by the side of the van to the front door, wondering how he put up with keeping it next to the house. It must block out half the light from the downstairs area. It was pretty dark down there as I rang the bell. The door was made up of wooden slats, with long thin frosted glass panes between. I peered through the glass and could see a light on, somewhere in the back.

I rang the bell again, listening carefully for the chime indoors to make sure it was working. I tapped on the glass with my keys as well, just to be certain, but there was no movement inside.

I carefully made my way round the side of the house, squeezing through the narrow alleyway between house and garage. There was a window into the garage and, instinctively nosy, I peered in through that as well. I could just make out the front wing of the Merc coupé in the gloom. If the car and the van were here, Terry surely must be, mustn't he?

Bolder now, I carried on round to the back, looking warily round the darkened fence bordering the garden. There were no lights on in the houses overlooking the rear of the property, which made me feel slightly better. If Terry *wasn't* in, the last thing I wanted to do was get wrestled to the ground by some rabid Neighbourhood Watch brigade as a suspected burglar.

The back garden was as featureless as the front, with a flat slabbed patio and a couple of steps leading up to a big sliding door. There was a bit of light sliding out down the steps from between partly drawn curtains and I cautiously edged my way over to it.

The first thing I saw, when I looked through, was a picture on the far wall oddly tilted to about a forty-five degree angle. The wallpaper was a horrible mixture of red, grey and silver diagonal stripes. Hm, very eighties, Terry. I moved round slightly to get a different view, and saw a small table tipped over, with the clock and ashtray that had obviously been on its surface strewn across the carpet.

A kind of fear jerked in me then. Even for someone who was as much of a slob as Terry, this didn't look like normal living conditions. I moved further, jigging from side to side like some obscure exotic dancer to try and get a full picture through the narrow gap in the curtains.

A lampshade was awry, throwing strange long oval shadows up one wall. I caught a glimpse of a sofa, in grey velour, which had a hole in the backrest, the yellow foam puffing out of it like a dirty cloud.

I peered more intently. The place was a mess. There were dark patchy stains all over the carpet. Right at the extreme edge of my vision was the doorway leading, I assumed, out into the hall. On the wall by the door frame was a handprint. It looked as though whoever had made it had dipped their hand liberally in brown paint, there were drips running down the wallpaper. Perhaps Terry went in for finger painting. Or perhaps . . .

I shook myself, suddenly feeling cold with an unease that gripped me tightly, making it hard to breathe. Without really knowing why, I reached for the handle of the patio doors. Partly to my surprise, they moved.

I should have turned round then. I should have walked away down the side of the house and not looked back, but I didn't. And it probably wouldn't have made any difference to the final outcome, anyway. The train was already rolling down this line, and the brakes had failed.

With my heart pounding against my ribs, and my mouth dry, I slid the door open a foot and slipped through the gap into Terry's lounge.

From inside, the room looked even worse than it did from the garden. The sofa had been comprehensively slashed, the stuffing bursting out from a dozen slits in the fabric. Books, papers and a broken glass vase were scattered across the floor.

I crouched and looked more closely at one of the rusty brown stains. Was it blood? Frankly, I'd no idea. It was dried in, just a dull mark. Where the water from the vase had run across one patch, it seemed paler, but it could have been anything, including beer, or wine.

Who was I kidding? I just knew it was blood. You don't spill alcohol round the place in such a way that it sprays across a room, up the sides of the sofa, on the coffee table, even across the face of the TV.

I moved carefully over to the door and checked out that handprint. It was so detailed that the hand which made it must have been covered in blood. The lounge door, the usual flimsy internal plywood job, had a splintered fist-shaped hole at about shoulder height.

I moved cautiously through into the hallway, looking very carefully each way before I did so, like a kid on a kerb who's just had the Green Cross Code hammered into them. I felt like a character in one of those films where you sit there clenched on the sofa watching, shouting, 'No, don't go in there! Get out of the house!' because you know full well the madman with the axe is lurking behind a curtain in the next room.

Damn it, why do I have to go thinking thoughts like that? I shook myself, annoyed. *Just get on with it, Fox.* On the other hand, technically I was breaking and entering. Legally, I didn't have a leg to stand on when it came to a right to be there. I knew I should just turn round and high-tail it out of there. I should, but I didn't.

Just plain nosy, I guess.

I edged forwards into the hallway, pausing just inside to let my eyes accustom to the gloom. Right ahead of me was the slant of the stairs. There was another brown stain round one of the bannister rails, which had dripped down onto the wallpaper beneath. A small, three-legged, triangular table was upturned against the skirting board. It was black and modern-looking, like some cast-off from a progressive milkmaid.

I crept further on towards the front door. I could focus more easily now, could see the tangle of jackets half-pulled from the hooks on one wall. There seemed to be debris scattered all over the floor, coats, a strange trilby-type hat, pairs of battered slippers and a single training shoe.

It slowly dawned on me as my eyes scanned the objects that there was something different about that trainer. It seemed to take an awfully long time for me to realise what was wrong.

There was a foot in it.

Not just a disconnected foot, but an ankle as well, leading into a leg. I could see about to mid-calf, before the rest disappeared round the bottom of the staircase. It had to be Terry's foot. He usually wore designer trainers, but he walked with his feet turned in, pigeon-toed, and he always seemed to wear his shoes down at an extraordinary and uneven rate. After a month on his feet a pair of top of the line sports shoes looked like something he'd bought from a market trader.

For a few moments I just stood and stared at the foot, as though expecting it to move. It didn't. Then I realised I could see his other leg. It was stretched out along the bottom of the front door, like a rather ineffective draught-stop. A tumble of mail from the letterbox had fallen on top of it.

I think it was only then I started to realise that this was looking very, very bad. The letters meant he'd been there all day, at least. It could only mean he was badly injured. Or dead.

My heart had the right idea. It was doing its best to make a break for it through the front of my ribcage. I only recognised I was holding my breath when I started going dizzy. I forced myself to relax enough to gulp in some air.

As soon as I began breathing again, the smell hit me. The same smell as a piece of meat that's fallen out of the rubbish bag and been lurking in the bottom of the kitchen bin for a week or so, right next to a radiator.

My feet were taking me forward, but the rest of my mind and body didn't really want to go. I shuffled on until the rest of Terry's body came into view. I was moving a millimetre at a time like someone balanced on the edge of a cliff. This was going to be bad news, I just knew it.

Even so, it was worse than I was expecting.

I never thought of myself as being a particularly hairy person. As soon as I saw Terry, all the hairs on my arms and neck stood bolt upright. I almost jumped backwards away from the sight of him, going, 'Oh shit, oh shit.' My voice was a subdued wail.

Terry had always been sensitive about his appearance, but he wasn't in any state to be offended. He wasn't in any state to be anything, come to that, apart from very, very dead.

Unless you go in for the particularly gory sort of horror films, which I don't, most portrayals of dead bodies are pretty tidy, really. They might be liberally sprinkled with fake blood. They might have wide open, staring eyes, but they're usually all together, in one piece.

Terry was only just together, only just in one piece. The same knife that had made light work of his sofa had made light work of Terry as well. He had been wearing a pale T-shirt, but this was almost totally soaked through with blood. His hands were across his stomach, the arms drenched up to the elbows. His forearms were covered with slits and minor wounds. One thumb had been sliced through to the point where it was nearly completely severed.

At first I thought he had something on top of his stomach, a weird blueish, greyish mass of bundled twisted cloth, smeared with blood. It took a few horrible, horrifying moments for me to realise that it probably was Terry's stomach.

He'd been split open right across his gut and the contents had spilled out in a tumbled heap. He must have tried to fight off his attacker in the lounge, then staggered through here in search of help. The telephone sat unmarked on the window ledge above his head.

I glanced at his face. He'd been cut there as well, the skin peeling back raggedly to reveal the white-ish gristle of his nose. His dull, flattened eyes seemed to be looking straight at me, accusingly.

I couldn't hold it any longer. My stomach revolted. I turned away, stumbling, and retched in long, convulsive heaves on the hall carpet until there was nothing left in my system to chuck. What a hell of a way to diet.

For a minute or so afterwards I stayed clinging weakly to the bannisters. Then I pushed myself away and started to think. Did I call the police from here? In which case they were going to ask an awful lot of questions I didn't want to have to cope with. Like why did I call round to see him? And what about this computer which I'd accepted from him, in the full knowledge that it might be stolen? Oh yeah, I'm sure everyone says they were just trying to return it to its rightful owner . . .

Or I could do what I should have done as soon as I saw that handprint on the wall. I could make a fast exit and ring the police from a call box as far away from home as possible. I looked at the disgusting calling card I'd just left on Terry's floor. That couldn't be helped. I was just thankful I'd kept my gloves on.

Turning my back on Terry was one of the most frightening things. As though he was suddenly going to sit up and reach for me. Too many films, too much imagination. I don't know why, but I wasn't afraid that whoever had rearranged Terry's features was still going to be in the house. He'd obviously been dead too long for that.

I retraced my steps through into the lounge and out into the garden, sliding the patio doors shut behind me. They seemed to close with a terrifyingly loud thunk. I ducked into the shadows by the garage and waited, heart thudding, listening for the sounds of alarm, pursuit.

None came.

I moved down past the side of the garage and along the path, walking back along the street as quickly as possible, trying hard not to break into a run. My back was tense. I expected any minute a voice to shout, 'Oi you, stop—*murderer!*'

It never happened, of course, but I was never so glad as to see the bike sitting waiting for me, like the hero's faithful steed in an old black and white western. Shame I couldn't whistle and have the Suzuki start up and meet me halfway. I dare say if there was the demand the manufacturers would work on it.

I couldn't decide if it would look more suspicious to push the bike quietly out of the road or start it up there as normal. I plumped for the latter, but made sure my helmet was on before I kicked the two-stroke motor into life. It sounded raucously loud. I didn't look, but I could just feel all the curtains twitching in the surrounding houses.

Without waiting for the bike to warm up, I did a wobbly U-turn in the road, abandoning my dignity and paddling it round, feet down. I felt an awful lot better once I was on the move. The solidity of the bike was comforting. I leaned down and patted the bulge of its tank. A ridiculous action, but it made me feel more secure.

Part of the road leading away from Terry's place wasn't streetlit. The cone of illumination thrown out by the bike's dipped headlight seemed pitiably feeble. My eyes were constantly at its outer limit, waiting for the mad-eyed murderer with the bloodied knife, or the accusing policeman, to suddenly step into my path.

The streets of Lancaster were quiet, which was probably a good thing, because I was riding like a first-day learner, fluffing my gear changes and over-revving the engine, riding corners jerkily upright, too tense to be anything like smooth. The Suzuki's gearbox had never sounded so clunky, nor the motor so harsh.

I reached home in only a few minutes and left the bike parked up in the road outside. I ran up the steps, ignoring the dissent from half a dozen different muscle groups. I was panting as though I'd run a marathon.

I let myself into the flat like it was some sort of sanctuary. Well, they say an Englishman's home is his castle. Yeah, said a little voice in my head, tell that to Terry, lying slaughtered behind his own front door . . .

Fifteen

I SLAMMED THE door behind me and spent a few moments leaning back against it, eyes closed. It was only then that the full force of reaction hit me. I made a dash for the bathroom and spent the next few minutes heaving fruitlessly into the toilet bowl.

I needn't have bothered. I'd completely emptied my stomach in Terry's hallway. All I succeeded in doing was make my eyes and nose stream, and leave a vile taste in my mouth. My ribs felt as though the Scouser had been back for a rematch.

Suddenly I remembered again the words I'd half-overheard while I was lying on my lounge floor. The smoker had said, *'If you've killed her the shit's really going to hit the fan after last time . . .'* I'd initially thought they somehow referred to Susie's death. Now they made chilling sense.

I sat down on the toilet floor, resting my head on the seat. My skin felt cold and clammy and my hands were shaking. I knew I had to pull myself together, but it was a real case of easier said than done.

Finally, I staggered to my feet, blowing my nose on reams of loo paper. I splashed cold water on to my face, and cleaned my teeth. After that I felt almost human again.

I was going to have to call the police, but I made up my mind to do it from the anonymity of a public call box. I know you can dial 141 to stop your telephone number being registered by the person you're calling, but I'd never tried it. I didn't think this was the time to find out the police could override the system anyway.

I searched round for my voice changer device, but I hadn't yet found it among the flotsam that covered the lounge floor. I dithered over searching for it, then decided no. A good old-fashioned scarf would have to do the job of disguising my voice.

I had a complete brain dump about where the nearest phone box was. The marketplace. There were three or four phone boxes in the marketplace, near to the fountain. No, they were too public.

I racked my brains before I remembered the one on Caton Road. Not perfect, but it would do. At least you weren't likely to get loads of people hanging round it while you were trying to cryptically explain the discovery of a dead body to the desk sergeant.

By the time I'd ridden the short distance and parked up at the kerb next to the phone box, I was annoyed to find my hands were shaking again, so much I could hardly get my helmet off. I spent a few minutes just sitting there, trying to relax enough to work out exactly what I was going to say.

Finally, I couldn't put it off any longer. I left my gloves on just in case and fumbled dialling the Lancaster cop-shop, wrapping my scarf firmly round the receiver as I did so. A rather bored-sounding woman answered the phone.

'Listen up,' I said, my voice echoing gruffly in my ear. 'You got a pen? Then write this down.'

'Hang on—yep, go ahead,' the woman said. She sounded suddenly more interested.

'There's a body of a guy in a house on Wilmington Avenue, the one with the big van outside.'

'A body? What do you mean?'

I didn't think I could have been much clearer. 'What do you mean, "What do I mean?"? A dead guy, he's been knifed. Just get there.'

'OK son, don't worry, we're on our way. What's your name?'

On cue, I put the phone down. I hurried outside, cracked the bike up and struggled into my helmet. I expected a squad car to come screeching up at any minute and haul me inside, but there were only the usual few cars and trucks ambling past. I waited for a gap in the traffic and did another of my wobbly U-turns, then rode sedately back towards the middle of town.

In my mind I was going over it, trying to work out if there was any way I could be linked to Terry's place. It was only then that I remembered Terry's business partner, Paul. Shit. I didn't know if he was aware that Terry had given me the lap-top, but he was certainly the first person the police were likely to contact. If he mentioned me, and if any of the neighbours remembered seeing the bike . . .

With rather more urgency than before I dived through the traffic round the town centre and headed out towards Abraham Heights. On my way I passed the police station, lit up like late-night shopping.

There were no signs of undue activity and I wondered briefly if they'd taken my message seriously. I don't know what I expected to see—dozens of cars screaming out with lights and sirens blazing, I expect.

I got lucky with the traffic lights, and it was only a few minutes later that I pulled up on the pavement outside the video shop owned by Terry's partner. Or should that be ex-partner.

When I walked in Paul was lounging on the counter reading a sci-fi novel with an infeasibly well-endowed blonde in a sprayed-on jumpsuit on the cover. It must have been captivating, because he looked up with that slightly irritated expression of someone who really didn't want to be disturbed right at that moment.

Still, when he saw it was me he broke into a smile which did nothing to improve his looks. He and Terry had always made an odd couple. Where Terry had been fat, Paul was thin to the point of gauntness, his hunched shoulders emphasised by the bagginess of his jumper. Where Terry's features were spread across his face like he'd had a hard impact with a fast-moving object, Paul was sharp-looking, almost feral.

He had a small compressed line of a mouth, and a long narrow pointed nose. His chin was a good match for his nose, with a cleft. That would have been all right on Michael Douglas, but regrettably on Paul it looked like he had a small pair of buttocks hanging off the bottom of his face. I'd vaguely wondered once if the two men had been initially drawn together because each thought the other made him look more attractive.

'Er, hi Charlie,' he said. 'What's up? You look like you've seen a ghost.'

I made sure the shop was empty before I launched straight in. 'I've just been round to Terry's place.'

'Oh, right. I've been meaning to go round there myself. He's been off the last couple of days and I've had people from his normal round phoning up because he hasn't shown up. Did you find him?'

'Yeah,' I said grimly, 'I found him all right.' I paused awkwardly. 'Look, there isn't an easy way to say this, but Terry's dead.'

Paul took the shock well, but his skin actually turned slightly grey. In that moment I believed completely that he had nothing to do with his partner's death. Not that I had Paul pinned as much of a suspect, in any case. I don't know anyone who can change colour at will without the aid of a bottle. It had to be a genuine reaction.

'Poor bastard, what happened? Did he have a heart attack? I mean, is he in hospital? Are you sure he's dead?'

I nodded to the last bit. 'I saw him and I'm quite sure,' I said. 'And he didn't have a heart attack, he was stabbed.'

His head snapped up at that. 'Shitfire, when did this happen?'

I shrugged, leaning on the counter and suddenly feeling unutterably tired. 'I don't know,' I said wearily. 'It must have been at least a day or so ago.'

He blanched at the implications. 'Hang on.' He moved round the counter towards the door, turning the open sign to closed and flicking the catch. 'Come on,' he said. 'You look as though you could do with a drink.'

He led me through to the back of the shop where they had a small, untidy kitchen. There was an odd assortment of cracked but neatly washed up mugs on the scarred stainless steel draining board next to the sink. Paul cleared a load of scrap posters off a rickety, paint-splattered chair and motioned me into it.

He mentioned that he still had a bottle of leftover Christmas brandy about somewhere, and set about making coffee with generous slugs of the spirit in it for us both.

'So,' he said when we were sipping the steaming, biting liquid, 'you want to tell me exactly what happened?'

I went through the whole tale of going round to Terry's and finding the body, not skimping on the details. Paul made me feel better about my own weakness of stomach by turning quite green when I described the state Terry was in.

'I don't suppose there's a chance that it was suicide, is there?' he asked, almost hopefully.

I shook my head. 'Disembowelment's not a common method of suicide these days, unless you're a Samurai, I suppose, but in that case he wouldn't have had cuts all over his forearms from trying to fight the guy off, and there was no knife next to the body. Whoever did it came and went with his own equipment.'

'Shitfire. Poor bastard,' Paul repeated, nose in his cup. He looked up at me. 'How can you be so calm?' he demanded. 'I'm gibbering and all I'm doing is hearing about it.'

'Swan syndrome,' I said, taking another swig of coffee and trying not to chip my chattering teeth on the enamel of the mug. 'Unruffled on top and paddling like hell underneath.'

He gave a half smile, which disappeared as a sudden thought overtook him. 'Did you call the police? I mean, they'll have to be involved, won't they? If Terry's been murdered, there's no way they won't be.'

'I rang them before I came here, from a call box.'

'Shitfire,' he said again. 'I could be in big trouble.' He saw my raised eyebrow and went on, 'I suppose you know Terry runs—was running—a little sideline in videos that are, well, for a slightly more specialised taste.'

'Hard porn,' I supplied helpfully, amused at his discomfort.

'Well, yes, but the thing is, if the police start nosing around, they're going to find out about it and I could end up in prison. Terry was the one behind it, not me.' His voice sounded aggrieved.

'So claim you didn't know anything about it,' I said. 'Did he keep anything here, or was it all on the van?'

'Most of it was on the van, or I think Terry kept some stuff at home. His client book's here, though. He left it on the counter the last time he called in . . .' His voice faded away as though suddenly realising that Terry was truly dead and gone, and the last time he had been into the shop was actually the very last time.

My own last conversation with Terry came to mind, when he'd said none of his mucky video customers were written down in the usual book. 'Paul, could Terry's death have had anything to do with those videos?'

'What do you mean?'

'Well, they *are* highly illegal, the people who make them must be a pretty nasty bunch to cross.'

'Exactly, so he never crossed them, cash with order, no questions asked. He wasn't a fool.'

I felt my shoulders slump. Somehow I'd been hoping that there might be an explanation other than the one that was forming in my mind. I didn't like the sound of the one I'd come up with. It was too close to home.

'Paul,' I said, 'did you know anything about a lap-top computer Terry accepted as part of a debt for his porn videos?'

Paul shrugged. 'Terry ran that side of the business his way. I didn't really want anything to do with it. He'd quite often work on a barter system as far as payment went.' He gave a half-smile at the memory. 'He'd accept more or less anything, from servicing on his central heating system to booze and fags.'

'What about drugs?' I don't know why I asked it. The question just arrived on my lips without passing selection by the brain first.

Paul didn't need to think about that one. He shook his head emphatically. 'No way. Terry may have been into some dodgy stuff, but he was dead against drugs,' he said, without apparently hearing the irony of his own words. 'All you had to do was mention that you thought the government ought to legalise cannabis and he used to practically go up in flames. We used to have quite a laugh winding him up about it,' he finished sadly.

But, Terry's computer had come from the New Adelphi Club, and from what Dave had hinted at, there could be something going on there that was tied up to illegal substances. I recalled Terry's words when I told him what Sam had managed to get off the computer. *That's terrific!* he'd said, sounding tricky. *That should be enough to worry the bastard!*

'So if someone offered him drugs in payment for his porn videos, what do you think Terry would have done about it?' I asked slowly. There was a theory forming, but right now it was so fluid any slight imbalance might make it disappear.

Paul looked evasive, shuffling in his seat and taking a swallow of his coffee before he answered. 'Well, he might have tried to use that information to, well, put a bit of pressure on them, in one way or another,' he said, eyes not quite meeting mine.

'Blackmail, you mean,' I put in.

Paul dipped his long nose back into his mug and gave a faint nod. 'Yeah, something like that,' he muttered.

'Is that what happened this time?'

Paul didn't answer, looking more shifty than before.

'Paul, come on!' I said, losing patience. 'Last night I think the same people who knifed Terry came after me. They took back the computer I was looking after for him and damned near killed me, too.' His head came up at that, shock blanking his expression. 'I need to find out who it is, Paul.'

'God, Charlie, Terry would never have willingly got you into trouble, you should know that.' He hesitated for a while, then put down his coffee mug, standing and walking back into the shop. He was back a few seconds later, carrying a small blue book, which he handed to me.

'That's Terry's client book,' he said, 'but the truth is, I don't know who he got that computer from,' he admitted. 'He rang me just after he'd got it, told me it had come from someone at that club in Morecambe, but he didn't say who and I didn't ask. Like I said, I don't really get involved. When he didn't show up for work this week I had a look through the book, but he only kept a note of initials, and none of them mean anything to me . . .'

A sudden banging on the shop door made us both jump. Paul peered out through a gap in the stud partition wall between the kitchen and the shop.

'Oh shitfire, it's the police,' he said. He snatched the book I was still holding, grabbed an empty video case and shoved it inside. 'Look, take this with you, see if you can unravel any of it,' he said hurriedly. 'Don't worry, I won't mention anything to them about you. Go on, get out of here!'

I didn't argue as we both moved back through to the shop, trying to look nonchalant. There were a pair of uniforms standing with their faces pressed up against the door glass. One gave his mate a nudge and a leer when he saw us emerge together.

I have to give Paul credit, he did make a reasonably convincing display of surprise and concern at seeing two officers of the law on his doorstep. He unlocked the door and let them in. 'Er, can I help you?'

They asked him his name in serious voices and, feeling like a traitor, I kept walking. 'Cheers for this, Paul,' I said, motioning to the video case as I left. 'I'll drop it back later in the week.'

He nodded and gave me a distracted wave, but one of the policemen turned round. 'What's the film?' he asked.

I thought my heart was going to stop, or burst, or both. *'Psycho Cop,'* I said immediately. 'It's the English version. A group of deranged lads from Traffic go berserk on the M1 in unmarked Maestro vans.'

He gave me a twisted smile. 'Yeah, yeah, very funny,' he said, and they turned their attention back to Paul.

Once I was safely outside I shoved the video case down the front of my jacket, yanked on my helmet, and started up the Suzuki. I then made a complete fool of myself by trying to toe it into gear with the side-stand still down, which cuts the motor. Come on, Fox, get it together.

As I rode back towards the middle of Lancaster and home, I could feel the video case pressing against my ribcage. Did it hold the key to Terry's murderer? God only knew, and she definitely was keeping that kind of information to herself. What an unholy mess.

IT WAS TOO late by the time I got back to the flat to do more than glance at Terry's book that night, but the following morning I spent a couple of hours going through it.

He seemed to have a good system, keeping careful track of dates the porn videos had been borrowed and returned, by whom, and when the monies were collected. I say seemed because it told me just about nothing.

I managed to work out that the videos themselves weren't named, just numbered. They were expensive enough for one night's hire to make my eyebrows lift. And some people seemed to get anything up to half a dozen of them out at a time. It was hardly surprising that those paying on a weekly or monthly basis suddenly found themselves with a hefty bill.

As for the people, they were a mystery. Terry hadn't named anyone in full, relying on sets of initials. AC, AZ, BT, CA, DJ, EG, FA, GB. I stopped when I found PC, just in case it was connected to the lap-top, but the initials cropped up so rarely there was no way that PC—whoever he was—could have owed Terry enough to give him a computer.

As well as initials, there was a three-digit number preceding each one. A lot of people had the same number prefix. Eventually I cottoned on to the fact that the numbers probably related to an address. An office building, a private house—or a nightclub. I couldn't really find enough to identify there, either.

The only thing that was easy to understand was the day of the week when Terry called at each undisclosed location. He'd brought the computer round to see me on a Sunday morning, but that could mean anything. Did he usually call round at the club then, or had he just dropped in unexpectedly to do his debt collecting?

I tried again later that evening, when I got back from teaching my Tuesday evening class at the university leisure centre all about head-locks, but it made no more sense than it had done earlier.

With a sigh I shut the book and threw it down on the coffee table, rubbing at my aching eyes. Last week I was just an average person, living my life and paying my bills on time—mostly.

Now I was mixed up in porn videos, illegal drugs, rape and murder. I had a feeling things were going to get worse—and probably much worse—before they got better.

Sixteen

I TAUGHT MY usual class at Shelseley Lodge the next day. A couple of nights' sleep made my grisly discovery seem more distant. It was as though I was disturbed by having seen a violent film, rather than witnessing it in real life.

When Marc rang, asking how I was, it was difficult to recall that he was referring to my own attack, rather than simply my reaction to Terry's murder. I must have sounded vague and unfocused. He asked me three times if I was sure I was OK, and seemed dissatisfied with my woolly answers.

Despite another work-out and a couple of saunas at Attila's, I was still as stiff as an elderly Labrador with dodgy hips, so I abandoned my normal syllabus again and taught the class kicks and punches instead.

That didn't require much active participation on my side. I arranged the crashmats standing up, four-deep against the wall, and unrolled the targets over them. There was general giggling amongst my students as I set up. When I was done I grinned at them.

My targets were two long rolls of vinyl with life-size thugs printed on them. I'd chosen vinyl because they had to stand up to quite a bit of hammer. They were representations of big ugly fellers with bulging muscles and scowling faces. I found a long time ago that unless I gave my students something a bit more realistic to aim at, they were never going to be able to defend themselves against anything other than attacks by rabid gym mats.

'Meet Curly and Mo,' I said. 'I want you to divide into two groups and form an orderly queue to give these two a bit of stick. Basically, do what you like to them. Punch them, kick them, knee them in the knackers. Pretend they're your boss, your spouse, or whoever's been giving you grief lately.'

There was laughter at that. I showed them the basic line to aim for with a punch, from the temples down to the groin, taking in the nose, jaw, throat, and solar plexus on the way.

'OK,' I said. 'Anybody—where would be your first choice target?'

It was Joy who answered first. 'The goolies,' she said promptly. Several others concurred, with varying degrees of embarrassment.

'Go for his eyes,' said another. She was one of my older students, a middle-aged lady called Pauline, who'd only recently joined the class, but was taking to it with real enthusiasm.

When there were no further guesses I turned to the targets. 'Actually, you're all right,' I said. 'Any one of those areas can be very effective, as long as you practise it so it's second nature; so you don't have to think about it. If you have to nerve yourself up to hit someone, it'll show in your face, your body language, and they'll be ready for you. Given a choice, I'd go for the nose.'

I demonstrated with several different techniques. An open-handed chop with the edge of my hand, a swinging elbow, and a hammer fist, as well as a straightforward punch. I knew where the nose area of my targets was without having to sight on it first. I kept my eyes on my students instead, gauging their reaction.

'The nose will be unprotected by heavy clothing or glasses and a blow there will stop most attackers in their stride,' I told them. 'It's difficult for someone to keep fighting while their eyes are streaming.'

My own favourite was a sweeping chop upwards just underneath the nose, right on the sensitive septum between the nostrils. Get the angle right and even the biggest, toughest of blokes will hit the dirt.

Of course, angle the blow too straight onto the top lip, and you run the risk of paralysing the respiratory system by damaging the cranial nerves. Angle it too high and you can splinter the nasal bones where they meet at the bridge of the nose, with the inherent danger of then driving the fractured ends onwards, into the brain.

To do that you had to deliver an accurate and powerful punch. I glanced briefly round the group in front of me and considered that none of them were potential heavyweight boxers in the making. Their strength was limited to the point where telling them about the dangers would inhibit them too much. None of them were street-fighters by nature. In an attack situation, I wanted them to hit out as hard as they could, not worry about exactly where they placed the blow.

I showed them a few other locations, for good measure. 'Most areas of the face are pretty vulnerable to attack, like the hollow in the cheeks, the skin just under the eye, and then there's always the throat,' I went on. 'The throat is always a good one to go for, as is the side of the jaw. On the down-side, you are just as vulnerable to attack in that area, so be careful. That's why boxers keep their chins tucked in.'

'I always thought it was because they had glass jaws,' Joy commented.

I shook my head. 'If you keep your jaw shut it's more difficult to do it damage. You're much more vulnerable when you've got your mouth open.'

'My ex-husband would agree with you there,' muttered Pauline. There was laughter again.

I showed them how to form a fist without danger of dislocating their thumbs the first time they hit anything solid, and explained how you had to imagine punching straight through the object you were hitting, rather than pulling back when you made contact.

Then I let them get on with it. It never ceased to amaze me how much built-up anger and aggression came out during this particular lesson. People always claimed to feel surprisingly better afterwards. I know I usually did. I could recommend having a punchbag in the corner of the living room for stress relief and relaxation to anyone.

My mind drifted as I watched a group of normally sober and well-behaved women beat Curly and Mo to a pulp. I wondered how things might have turned out with the Scouser if I'd taken my own advice and hit him, hard, with no mercy and no hesitation.

Maybe my own doctrine that the law of self-defence was to use the minimum amount of force necessary had taken over. But maybe, if I'd known that he'd already got Terry's scalp on his belt, I would have been a lot less squeamish. I reflected, with some bitterness, that the Scouser and his mate certainly overcame their initial reluctance to beat up a woman with remarkable speed.

The thought jarred with me and I struggled to work out why. I backtracked. Somebody at the club gave Terry a computer as part of a debt. OK, I was clear on that. Then he'd tried to worry them by hinting that he knew what information had been stored on the machine. I was guessing for this part, but it seemed feasible.

He must have succeeded in worrying whoever it was. To the point where they had come round to retrieve the computer, with violence. Terry must have told them that I'd got it, and having seen what they'd done to him, I couldn't honestly say I blamed him for giving me away.

OK, so having failed to get the computer from Terry, why had they then waited a day or so before coming round to see me? Why hadn't they turned my place over on the Saturday night, when I was safely out of the way at the New Adelphi? And why, if they were connected to the club themselves, hadn't they known that Charlie was a female name . . . ?

The pieces of the puzzle just didn't fit together. Without them I was never going to see the picture clearly.

'Charlie, are you OK?' Joy broke into my thoughts, peering anxiously at me.

I shook them loose and smiled at her. 'Yeah, sure. What's up?'

She asked a question about elbow strikes and I stirred myself to demonstrate the technique. Joy wasn't a bad student, quick and smart, even if she did tend to forget some of the moves from one lesson to the next.

I kept stressing practice, practice, practice, but everybody was there by their own choice. I couldn't exactly put them in detention if they didn't do their homework.

She stayed behind to help me clear away after the rest of the class had gone, which was another point in her favour, considering my current state of health.

'So,' I said, stifling a groan as I bent to pick up the final mat, 'I saw you at the New Adelphi at the weekend. Have fun?'

I glanced up at her as I said it, and was surprised to see a strange mixture of expressions frozen on her face. Guilt warred with defiance, mingling into embarrassment.

In a heartbeat, I knew.

'Fun?' she repeated, her voice pitched slightly too high. She swallowed and lowered the frequency. 'Er, yeah, it was great. I didn't know you were into clubbing, Charlie.'

'I'm not,' I said as I straightened up. I fixed her with a grim smile, turning the screw. 'I work security there.' I paused just long enough to let the implications sink in, then spelt them out for her anyway. 'I keep the druggies out.'

She jumped as though I'd dropped ice down her neck. A strong suspicion became a dead certainty.

'Oh, really?' she said nervously.

'Yeah,' I said. 'So, purely as a matter of interest, what did you take on Saturday night?'

She opened her mouth to deny it, saw the expression on my face, and shut it again.

'T-take?' she tried, circling her head as though by doing so she could evade the line of questioning.

I sighed, dropping the mat back onto the pile and turning to face her. 'Joy,' I said. 'I have no interest what shit you want to shovel into your system in your own time, but I do have an interest in finding out where you got something at the New Adelphi, when I'm supposed to be doing a job there.'

She wavered for a moment, then sat down on one of the row of chairs that were pushed back along one wall, not quite meeting my eyes. I waited for her to form the right words.

She began with justification. 'I'm not into anything heavy,' she protested. 'A few tabs of Ecstasy at the clubs; a couple of joints to chill out again afterwards. Sometimes I'll go months without anything, then some stuff will come my way again.' She flickered her eyes up to mine, then slid them away, suddenly fascinated by a hangnail on her thumb. 'It's less addictive than alcohol and—'

I held up my hand, cutting her off. 'Joy, I've already said I don't care what you take, just tell me where you got it. Did you already have it before you got into the club?'

She gave me a slightly scornful look. 'Do restaurants let you take your own food in?' she challenged. 'You don't get to carry anything into that place. They want to make damned sure you've got to buy fresh on the inside.'

I was startled and tried not to show it. I thought of Marc's adamant statement that nobody brought anything into his club, and of Len's that nothing went on that he didn't know about. Were they naive, or just very clever? Mind you, if they suddenly found out that Angelo had been running a nice little sideline in disco biscuits, it would explain Marc's explosion of anger . . .

I turned back to Joy. 'So who did you go to for yours?' I demanded.

I viewed a first flash of temper. 'What the hell business is it of yours, Charlie?'

'You have no idea,' I put in quietly, although my own irritation was rising fast.

After a few moments Joy's eyes dropped from mine again. She shrugged. 'I don't know,' she said, almost sullen. 'I was with a group of friends. One of them went away and he just came back with some gear.'

'And you didn't see where he'd got it?'

She shook her head, then remembered something. 'The only thing was, I told him I was worried about taking anything so openly on the dance floor, in case we got thrown out by one of the bouncers. He just laughed and said where did I think the stuff had come from in the first place?'

'But you didn't see which one?'

She shook her head with such certainty I realised I was getting the truth.

I took a deep breath. 'Look, Joy,' I said. 'I really need to know who's dealing drugs at the club. Next Saturday, can you get your mate to identify who sold him the stuff last time for me?'

I knew I was going out on a limb on the grounds of a tenuous friendship, and it didn't quite come off the way I'd hoped. Her face flushed and she jumped to her feet. 'No way!' she cried. 'Oh sure, I do a bit of blow every now and again, and you want me to tell you everyone who's ever passed me a joint. You teach me self-defence, Charlie, not morality. If I want my soul saving, I'll go find a priest! Don't be so fucking high and mighty!'

She started for the door. I moved after her. 'Joy, wait, let me explain—' I was going to have to tell her about Terry, about the connection with the New Adelphi, about my own attack, but she had already reached the door out of the ballroom.

She rounded on me, eyes bright with tears. 'Just go to hell, Charlie!' and she rammed the door open, disappearing through it with an air of absolute finality.

I started after her, but as I reached the door myself, stretching a hand out, it opened inward towards me and a girl stepped through.

We both stopped with a little exclamation of shock. My mind registered the short frame and spiky hair of Victoria, the waitress from the New Adelphi, even as my mouth was saying, 'Sorry, excuse me a moment, would you?'

I dived out into the corridor, but Joy had already disappeared along the hallway, heading for the front door. I caught a final glimpse of her stiff back as she hurried down the front steps. I called her name again, but she was gone.

With a sigh I went back to deal with my new visitor.

'Have I come at a bad time?' Victoria asked with a hesitant smile.

'Oh no,' I sighed. 'I've just opened my mouth and only succeeded in changing feet. Don't worry about it. Now then, what can I do for—?'

I'd glanced up as I'd spoken and my voice died in my throat as I looked at her.

'Christ, Victoria, what the hell happened to you?'

The left-hand side of her face was one huge contusion, the bruising starting dark purple round her swollen eye and fading out to a sickly yellow at chin and hairline. Steri-strip dressings closed the edges of cuts to her cheekbone and eyebrow. Through the slit of distended lids, the white of the eye itself was speckled with blood. She looked like shit.

Victoria couldn't fail to take in my reaction. She gave a bravado half-smile that made her mouth tremble, suddenly in danger of losing the last thread of her slender self-control.

I put my arm round her shoulder and led her to the chair Joy had so recently vacated. Victoria sank onto it as though her legs wouldn't support her any more, twisting her hands together in her lap.

I perched alongside, keeping my arm round her and digging in the pocket of my jogging pants for a respectable handkerchief to offer. She threw me a brief smile of thanks and we sat in silence for a while as she searched for a logical entrance to her story.

I didn't try and hurry her into it. Whatever had happened to Victoria, although obviously not really fresh, was still close enough to be traumatic. By the way her hands where shaking, she was probably still in shock.

The shock always gets you. It certainly did with me.

The bright lights and the warmth of the Lodge receded, to be replaced with the memory of another time, and another place. It had been dark then, frosty, and cold enough for snow.

Donalson, Hackett, Morton, and Clay.

I'd been younger then, in some ways more self-assured, in others more vulnerable. We'd been learning some hand-to-hand stuff as part of the course, but my attackers knew exactly the same techniques as I did, and I was outnumbered four to one.

In reality, I didn't really know any more about self-defence than to try and knee my attackers in the groin, or punch them in the stomach. Now I can put my mind to over fifty sensitive areas on the face and neck alone.

I was strong and a bit of a fitness freak back then, but even so it was no match for superior male muscle. Under pressure I've always been able to think fast. So I didn't cower. I fought and kicked out instantly, tried to yell blue murder.

I suppose it was about then that the four of them realised they were going to have to kill me to keep me quiet about what they'd done. The memory that has stayed with me longest is of lying half-insensible on the frigid earth, listening to them discussing in panicked undertones how best to dispose of my body.

The emotional aftershocks had taken a long time to die down. I doubted I'd ever be without the ripples left behind. When I was able to view the events with the clarity of distance, I was just left with the anger of my own helplessness.

I felt a burst of that same anger looking at Victoria's battered face, and knowing that had she come to my classes I probably could have taught her how to avoid the worst of it.

Now, she made a determined effort to get herself together. I smiled encouragingly.

'D'you want to talk about it?' I ventured at last.

She sniffed and nodded. 'God, sorry, look at me, falling apart on you,' she muttered, blowing her nose loudly, which started it off bleeding. I made a quick decision that she could keep the handkerchief.

'Who did this to you, Victoria?' I asked gently, although I think I already knew the answer.

She sniffed again, dabbing at the fresh blood. 'Angelo,' she admitted, her voice breaking. 'We've only been going out for a few months, and at first he was great, but lately . . .' She tailed off, glancing at me, and I realised that the blood from her nose had been caused by the ring she usually wore there being half ripped out through the skin . . .

I was trying so hard not to let Victoria see my distaste at this piece of mutilation that I almost missed what she was saying next.

'He seems to really hate you, Charlie. It scares me.'

'Angelo hates me?' I stared at her blankly. 'Why on earth does he hate me?'

'Because you're not afraid of him,' she said, as though stating the obvious. 'He expects everybody to be afraid of him—especially women. He likes his women passive—submissive, even. When you'd been to the club for your interview he was dead scathing about you because you wouldn't take Len on. He thought it was because you couldn't do it. Then you took care of that fight last Saturday and now he thinks you were taking the piss out of them both.'

I made no response to that. There didn't seem to be much I could say. Victoria took my silence to be scepticism. She peered at me again. 'I think he hates the control you've got,' she went on, hesitantly. 'Angelo's driven by his anger, it takes him over. You're different. You get mad, but you use it. You don't let it dominate the way you behave. Angelo doesn't understand that, and it infuriates him.'

'So he takes it out on you?' I demanded.

She shrugged her thin shoulders. Some big man Angelo was, turning his fists onto a girl a third of his size and weight. It made me burn with the sheer injustice of it.

'What do you need from me, Victoria?' If there was anything I could do, I'd do it.

She looked surprised. 'I don't need anything from you,' she said. 'I just thought I ought to warn you, that's all—about the way Angelo feels.'

'Does he know you're here?'

A furtive flicker crossed her face. 'God, no! He'd go mental if he found out,' she said, unable to keep the trace of fear out of her voice entirely.

I turned to her, gripped her arm. 'Victoria, get away from him,' I warned. 'If he did this to you, get out now, while you still can!'

She slid her gaze away. 'I'm OK,' she protested. 'He'd had a bit to drink. He didn't know what he was doing and he was really sorry afterwards.' She got to her feet, tried a bigger, braver smile. 'He's promised it won't happen again.' I couldn't work out if it was me she was trying to convince, or herself.

I walked with her along the corridor to the hallway, and out into the gloomy evening. The air was biting, enveloping me in its bitter embrace as soon as I left the warmth of the house. I shivered and dug my hands deep into the pockets of my jogging pants. Victoria was only wearing a light denim jacket, but she seemed not to notice the cold.

Her car, a grubby-looking Mini with a different coloured front wing and a reshaped coathanger for an aerial, was parked with two wheels into the bushes, down near the bottom of the drive. A streetlamp outside the gate threw a sodium yellow glow onto it.

For a few moments I watched her walking away towards the Mini, head down as though trudging into rain. She made a diminutive figure, vulnerable, exposed. Despite her assurances, I worried for her.

I shook my head and turned away, intending to go and have a quick brew with Tris and Ailsa before I changed for the ride home. I must have managed about three strides.

Then all hell broke loose.

Seventeen

VICTORIA DIDN'T SO much start screaming, as let out a single high-pitched yowl of terror. It lacerated the night air, and gave me instant goose bumps. I spun round so fast I skidded and nearly tripped over my own feet on the lichen-covered slabs.

I had time to see a darkened figure grab Victoria's shoulders to shove her out of the way, thrusting past her. She crumpled by the side of the Mini as the figure made off down the drive and out into the road.

Something about the way it moved told me the flying outline was a man. Not only that, but the same man who'd fled from outside the ballroom window. He had his covered head down and was fleeing with a purpose, already thirty yards away. For a moment I was torn over direction. Did I give chase, or go to Victoria's aid?

Rescue won out over capture. I ran over to her, heart thundering far more than it should have been from such a short burst of exercise. To my relief, she was already starting to regain her feet, clinging onto the door handle of her car for support, her back half-towards me.

As she heard my footsteps she gave another stark cry, cowering back. It took me a couple of attempts—speaking loudly and calmly, and not trying to touch her—before her brain registered my voice. She quietened with a sob.

Then, she let me reach out to her, to help her up. I let go once she was on her feet and propped against the side of the Mini. My hands came away wet, and sticky.

Under the gloomy lighting it was difficult to distinguish the colour, but I knew.

'Victoria,' I said, 'where are you hurt?'

She looked at me blankly, then saw the blood on my fingers, and her legs gave out again. She slid down the bodywork, ending up back on the ground.

I checked her over quickly, searching for the wound, but I couldn't find one. There was blood on both her upper arms, quite a lot of it, but it didn't seem to have come from Victoria herself.

A little slow-motion action replay rolled through my mind. I saw again the black-clad figure swinging Victoria roughly aside. Saw his gloved hands grasping her shoulders . . .

I straightened up. Victoria's assailant could only have come out of the darkened foliage that bordered the drive. I didn't want to go in there, among the dark whisperings of the leaves, but I wasn't sure I had a choice. The man hadn't moved like he was injured. What did that leave?

As I started to move round the front of the Mini, I felt Victoria grab at the bottom of my sweatshirt, trying to prevent me from going. I had to prise her hand away from my clothes. 'It's OK,' I said. 'I need to check.'

Brave words. Shame I didn't quite have the brave heart to go with them.

It was dark in front of the Mini, the car casting its own shadow onto the gravel from the lighting in the road behind it. I edged forwards until my toes bumped against the terracotta coping that marked the border between drive and shrubbery.

But coping stones aren't soft, and they don't flinch when you kick them . . .

I spun round, told Victoria to turn her headlights on so I could see what I was doing, but didn't get a response.

When I glanced at her I found the blonde-haired girl had one hand clamped over her mouth as though to either prevent a rising tide of nausea, or bite back on her screams. Above her blenched fingers her eyes were stretched wide, the white gleaming clearly all around the iris. She kept moaning, over and over, 'Oh God, oh God.'

I went through her pockets until I found her car keys, opened the door, and fumbled with every knob and switch I could find on the Mini's dashboard until the headlights blinked on.

What I saw in their feeble glow made me wish I hadn't bothered.

The figure of a woman was lying in an almost perfect recovery position, with her feet disappearing into the shrubbery, and her upper body onto the gravel. She was on her left side, but nearly rolled onto her face, with her back to the Mini's front bumper. One arm was out behind her, the other crooked up in front.

It briefly crossed my mind that she might have fallen and hit her head. Blood had haloed round her face, soaked into her clothing. The palm and fingertips of her forward hand rested in the growing pool that covered the stones around her.

Victoria whimpered behind me. I turned back to her. Her ashen face made perfect sense to me now. I squatted alongside her.

'Victoria, listen to me,' I said gently, holding her head so she had to look straight into my eyes. 'I need you to go back into the house and get them to phone for the police, and an ambulance. I'll stay here and see what I can do for her. Go and find Ailsa and tell her what's happened. Can you do that for me?'

She clutched briefly at my hand, her fingers almost unnaturally cold, then gave a hesitant nod. She was shaking as she climbed to her feet. I watched her as she stumbled numbly back towards the lights of the hallway, like someone sleepwalking.

I hung back just until she was close enough to the front steps for me to be sure she was going to make it without collapsing, then turned back to the woman.

I got the same crunch of fear in my gut that I'd felt when I'd first seen Terry's body. I wondered how many corpses you had to see before you got blasé about them.

I pushed the memory of the fleeing man from my mind, and trod carefully round the prone form on the ground. The girl's legs were bare and one shoe was missing. Her hair had fallen partly over her face, and her coat collar had rucked up. I'd already crouched and put a hand out to smooth them away when I stilled, recognition as jarring as an unexpected thorn in a bunch of roses.

It was Joy.

Fearing the worst, I pushed her hair back, intending to check her airway was clear. She started under my fingers, making me jump back with a muffled curse. Her eyes opened, smoky with pain. She seemed to gaze at me, but unfocused, and began to struggle in panic.

'Joy, it's OK, it's me. It's Charlie,' I told her, trying to keep her steady. Christ, I needed to keep her still. I'd no idea what her injuries were. 'Don't worry, help's on the way. Where are you hurt?'

She was still thrashing around, hands fluttering at my wrists, making unintelligible noises like a wounded animal. I just couldn't understand what she was trying to tell me. Later, it was the sounds she made that haunted me.

She lifted her head, eyes wide. A spurt of blood oozed from between her parted lips, staining her teeth like a heavy smoker. It joined the steadily expanding puddle, which was pooling round my feet. Joy was losing it at an alarming rate. I knew I needed to stem the flow if there was going to be any chance of saving her.

The fight went out of her abruptly and she sagged back. It seemed like even that short spasm of energy had drained her. I took advantage to open her coat, searching for the cause of all that bleeding.

It didn't take me long to find it.

As I pulled back her collar I couldn't suppress a gasp of revulsion. Joy's throat had been slashed straight across from one side to the other.

Her windpipe, a tangle of sinews, and disconnected blood vessels were all clearly visible through the gaping wound. Blood was pumping out at a speed which dismayed me. I yanked my sweatshirt off over my head, balling it up into a pad to hold over the gash. I dredged through my memory and recalled that pressure was the only way to stop bleeding. Trouble was, how did I press on her windpipe without hastening her death?

I squeezed as tightly as I dared, but all that seemed to happen was that my sweatshirt turned steadily dark with blood.

Joy was lying quietly now, her skin taking on a clammy pallor. Her breathing was so shallow I could hardly tell if she was still alive or not. Come on, for God's sake! How long does it take to get an ambulance up here? They always seem to be in a damned hurry whenever I've hustled the Suzuki out of their flightpath.

'Come on, Joy, don't give in!' I think I knew in my heart that she was fighting a losing battle.

I felt tears begin to slide down my cheeks. I didn't notice the cold, even though I was down to a thin T-shirt. I knelt beside her, not caring that her blood soaked into the knees of my jogging pants.

I ran our last conversation round and round like a loop tape. I couldn't get it out of my head. If I hadn't confronted her, we would probably have walked out together. Her attacker might have backed off. If he had got brave then maybe, together, we would have been able to take him down.

Right now we should have been laughing and congratulating each other, boosted by the adrenaline thrill of success. We should have been waiting for the cops to show up and cart off a very surprised and down-trodden mugger. One who wasn't expecting his victims to fight back.

Instead I was waiting for the paramedics to come and tell me with their serious eyes and their sober stance that there was nothing they could do . . .

The sound of running footsteps shook my foggy mind aware. I glanced up and saw Ailsa and one of the other residents hurrying down the drive towards us. The other woman took one look at the scene illuminated in the Mini's headlights, then reeled away and threw up onto the edge of the lawn.

Fortunately, Ailsa had a slightly stronger stomach. She edged forwards like someone approaching the loose edge of a chalky cliff, her hand squeezing my shoulder in silent support.

More footsteps made us both turn. Tris came jogging out of the house, pulling on his old parka jacket and carrying a couple of blankets. 'Help's on the way,' he said in a hushed voice when he reached us. 'Is she . . . ?'

I grimaced up at him and shrugged.

Joy's eyes snapped open again at that moment, making the pair of them jerk backwards, cursing. With a sharp movement she gripped tight onto my wrist, desperation lending unearthly strength. She tried to mouth words her destroyed voice box couldn't begin to form.

Blood bubbled between her lips, speckled with saliva, then she went limp. I swear in that moment I watched the light dim in her eyes, like the last flicker of a torch with an exhausted battery.

In the distance, came the faint wail of sirens.

* * *

IT WAS WELL after midnight when I wearily climbed the stairs to the flat and let myself in. The half-cleared debris of the interior seemed even more depressing as I flicked on the lights.

I put the kettle on for coffee as a reflex rather than out of any real desire for caffeine. I was too wired to sleep, too tired to do much else. My mind couldn't stop turning things uselessly over and over.

I stripped out of my ruined jogging pants and threw the sweatshirt straight into the rubbish, pulling on fresh clothes. I suppose I could have soaked the blood out of them in a bucket of cold water, but I didn't have much of an inclination to try.

The pants had been pale grey and looked worse than the shirt, which was green. Blood goes black on a green background. I remember my father telling me that was why surgeons wore it. Saves making the relatives faint when they came straight out of the operating theatre splattered with the stuff.

I checked the answering machine for messages. There were a couple of pupils letting me know about classes they couldn't make, and one from Sam, asking me to get in touch. The last message was from Marc.

'Just calling to check you're OK,' said that rich voice, perfectly at ease talking to a machine. 'You sounded slightly off-line the other day. Call me, Charlie. Any time—I mean it.'

I half-smiled. People who say things like that on answerphone messages so often don't really expect you to take them up on it. Like the ones who say, 'you're always welcome' or 'see you soon'. They'd be horrified if you actually turned up on their doorstep at two the following morning.

On an impulse, I picked up the phone and dialled Marc's mobile number. I nearly changed my mind in the time it took to connect, but once it had started ringing out I held my nerve.

'Yeah?' His laconic greeting wasn't quite what I expected. For a moment I couldn't think what to say that didn't sound foolish, or inconsequential. 'If that's you, Zachary, you better have a good excuse for ducking out of work tonight! Hello? Talk to me.'

I rushed into speech. 'Hi Marc, it's me. You said call any time, so—I'm calling.'

A fractional pause. 'Charlie! How lovely.' There was genuine warmth in his voice. 'It's late. Are you all right?'

'Er, yes—no. I don't know,' I faltered. There was the heavy beat of music in the background at his end of the line. He must still be at the club. Busy.

'Want to tell me about it?' he suggested without impatience. The gentleness in his voice was nearly my undoing. I'd been fine all through the impersonal information-gathering of the police who'd turned up at the Lodge. Now I was in danger of losing it big time.

Victoria had gone to pieces so badly that a woman constable had driven her home in the battered Mini, after the medics had given her a sedative. It was the only effective thing they'd been able to do. By the time they arrived Joy was past even their best-trained ministrations.

'A friend of mine has just died,' I said. It sounded so lame, such an inadequate way of describing the events of the past few hours.

'Oh Charlie, I'm sorry,' he said politely. 'Was it sudden?'

'You could say that. She had her throat cut. I was with her.' The surface tension broke and the tears spilled over. 'I watched her die, Marc, and there was nothing I could do.'

There was another pause, longer this time, tense. 'Would you like me to come over?'

I pulled myself together. 'N-no,' I said. 'I'll be OK.' I caught sight of the hand that gripped the phone receiver and stretched the other one out in front of me. They were both ingrained with dried blood, sunk deep into my pores and laced under my nails. I grimaced at the sight of it. 'Besides,' I added with the semblance of a smile, 'I look a mess.'

He laughed softly. 'How very female,' he murmured, then, 'Hold on a moment, would you?' I heard him take the phone away from his mouth. There was the mutter of voices in the background.

I took advantage of his absence to sniff loudly and tell myself to get it together. I suppose I should have been grateful that I hadn't gone off the rails quite as badly as Victoria. Maybe I was just getting used to bloodied corpses . . .

'I'm sorry,' I apologised when he came back on the line. 'You're obviously busy and the last thing you want is me blubbering at you.'

'Don't be stupid. You're hardly blubbering,' he said. 'It's been a relatively quiet night, but Len's just been having fun and games with a couple of rowdy punters. We're a bit short-handed.'

'I would have thought all you'd have to do is let Angelo off his leash and stand by with a mop and bucket to clear up the aftermath.'

'We probably would have done, but he wasn't in tonight,' Marc said with a hint of annoyance. 'He called in sick. In fact, that's who I thought was calling me now. I tried him earlier and couldn't get a reply. He's either too sick to answer the phone, or he's not sick enough and he's gone out somewhere.'

'He's probably too busy beating up his girlfriend,' I muttered, recalling suddenly the way Victoria's eyebrow rings had been torn out of her face. It made me wince to think about it. I didn't even have my ears pierced. Still, that was nothing compared to the level of violence that had been shown towards Joy . . .

'Sorry, Charlie the line just crackled. What did you say?' Marc asked.

'Oh, nothing,' I said, shaking my head to clear it. 'Look, I'm sorry Marc, I'm still all mixed up and my brain just seems to be going off at a tangent half the time.'

'Are you sure you don't want me to come round? I can be there in less than twenty minutes.'

'Yes I'm quite sure,' I said more firmly. 'Thanks anyway Marc. Maybe I'll see you tomorrow.'

'OK. I'll call you,' he promised. 'And if there's anything I can do, Charlie, you know you only have to say.' I heard the sincerity in his voice, knew he meant it.

'Thank you,' I said, grateful for his understanding, 'but I think I'll be OK. I'll talk to you tomorrow.'

As he rang off he told me to get some sleep. His tone suggestive enough to almost make me offer him a place in my bed to help me try.

MAYBE, IF I'D gone to bed then, I would have managed more sleep than I did. I sat for a long time on the most solid part of my leaking sofa—I really must finish clearing up the stuffing—cradling another cup of coffee and trying to blank the vision of Joy's desperate struggle to cling to life.

Would I have been able to fight any harder? Would I have held out any longer than she had? I looked down again and saw my bloodstained hands.

With a grimace I set down my cup and went to scrub the traces away. Soap struggled to shift the blood now it was dry. I ended up using washing up liquid, with some gritty brown sugar thrown in as an improvised scouring agent. By the time I'd finished my skin was pink and raw, but at least it was clean.

I had just walked back into the lounge again when the phone rang. I picked it up with a smile on my face, thinking that at this hour it could only be Marc, with some just-remembered remark.

'That was a close one, wasn't it, Charlie? Next time, it could be you.'

I lurched. It wasn't Marc. Instead, I heard a quiet sexless voice with a faint mechanical twang to it that took me a moment to place. Then I realised it was the way you sounded when you were using a voice-changer device, like mine. Correction—like the one I used to have, but hadn't been able to find since the flat had been turned over . . .

'Charlie? I know you can hear me,' the voice went on nastily. Oh shit. I jerked away from the receiver as though it had burned me. 'I know you're listening. Not so brave now, are you? Your friend wasn't brave. She hardly even struggled. No sport there, Charlie. Not like you.'

'Try me!' I threw at him. Oh Christ, where had that burst of bravado come from? The fear rippled down me, making my spine twitch. I wanted to run away screaming with my hands over my ears, but I was caught, dazzled, like a rabbit in the headlights of the car that was just about to run it over.

The voice gave a delicate laugh. 'Maybe next time, Charlie,' it said. 'Maybe I will.'

'There won't be a next time,' I said, amazed at how level my own voice sounded.

'Oh there'll definitely be a next time,' repeated the metallic voice. 'You won't know where, and you won't know when, but it'll happen. You can count on it.'

I didn't have the capacity to breathe enough to answer that one, but I didn't have to. There was a click and the monotone whirr of an empty line. I let the receiver drop back onto its cradle slowly, stunned.

My legs suddenly opted out of supporting me. I wasn't close enough to the sofa to make it, and I ended up on the floor. My vision started to tunnel out, the blood thundering in my ears. I didn't know if I was going to pass out, or throw up, or both.

I sat there for some time, eyes staring without seeing. He's coming after me! I couldn't get it out of my head. I wanted to panic, or run, but common sense told me that wasn't the answer. If I didn't stand and fight this, I was never going to be able to stop running.

I shook myself out of my stupor long enough to dial 1471 to retrieve the last caller. The frosty automated female voice told me I had been called today and gave me the precise time, then added unsurprisingly that the caller had withheld their number.

'Thanks,' I told her. 'That's a great help,' but she didn't respond to the jibe.

I DIDN'T MOVE far that night. I dozed fitfully, shivering, wrapped up in what was left of my quilt and still wearing the clothes I'd changed into when I got home. The thought of facing a would-be murderer naked was too much to bear. It was a long cold night, and I'm not just talking about time and temperature.

I kept the light on, and stayed away from the windows. The phone rang another couple of times in the early hours, but I'd put the answering machine back on by then. Both times the caller rang off without waiting for the beep as instructed, and the numbers were withheld.

I could only guess it was my friendly neighbourhood psycho again. It seemed only too likely.

By seven I gave up any idea of sleep and got up, pacing round the flat restlessly, unable to settle to anything. Eventually I gave in and admitted defeat. I picked up the phone, dialling Lancaster police station quickly, before I'd chance to chicken out.

When they answered I asked to be put through to whoever was dealing with Joy's death.

A detective inspector came onto the line and I explained to him who I was. 'I don't wish to sound alarmist,' I said carefully, 'but I think whoever killed Joy might have decided that it's my turn next.'

Eighteen

BY THE TIME the doorbell rang just after nine-thirty, I had managed to keep myself occupied by clearing up more of the rubbish. There was now a row of eight or so plastic bags near the door and I was just tackling the stuffing from the sofa.

I straightened up slowly, my vision narrowing sharply as I did so. Jesus, I was going to have to eat something soon. I hadn't been able to face food when I got in last night, and I'd missed breakfast.

Over-cautious, I checked through the Judas glass to see who my visitor was. A man was holding up an open wallet towards the outside of the glass. Even through the fish-eye lens I could recognise the police insignia. I unlocked the door and opened it warily.

'Miss Fox, is it?' he asked politely and I agreed that I was indeed she.

The man was smartly dressed, a good dark blue suit, well cut, with a startlingly white shirt and a conservative tie. At first I'd thought him in his late thirties, but looking closer I realised he was probably ten years older at least, wearing well. His eyes were an indistinct green colour, and they looked straight at me without blinking.

'I'm Detective Superintendent MacMillan,' he said, his voice was well-spoken, with a purposeful clip to the words. 'I thought it was time we had a little chat.'

He handed me the wallet. I've always thought warrant cards look more like a bus pass, encased in clear plastic with an unflattering photo on the front. I studied it for a while before handing it back and stepping to one side.

'Come in,' I said, adding wryly. 'Excuse the mess, won't you, but I've had visitors.'

The Superintendent favoured me with a moment of brief stillness, hovering between amusement and censure, then he walked into the flat and looked around him with detached professionalism. He didn't make the expected comments about how shocking the abrupt viciousness of Joy's departure from this life had been, or shake his head in disbelief at the whole sorry business.

There was a weariness about him that told me clearly he'd seen far too much to be shocked by anything anymore, and I could guess there was very little he wouldn't believe when it came to the lower reaches of human nature.

'Do you mind if I carry on sorting this out while we talk?' I said, gesturing to the half-filled bags. 'Only it's taken me ages to work up the energy to make a start and I don't want to stop now.'

He gave me a shrug of assent. 'Would it be pointless to ask what happened here?'

'I should have thought it was pretty obvious,' I said. 'I was burgled.'

'But you didn't report it,' he pointed out with a hint of reproof, and it was a statement, not a question.

'I was here at the time,' I said, opting for a half-truth. 'The men who did this made it absolutely clear what they'd do to me if I involved the police.' I bent to shovel more debris into the bag. 'Things can be replaced.'

The Superintendent didn't reply immediately, just favoured me with a long cool stare. He moved round the perimeter of the lounge with measured precision, ducking his nose into all the rooms with deceptive speed. He paused momentarily in front of the punchbag, still suspended from its hook in the corner.

He never seemed to be in a hurry, but by the time I'd thought to object to his inspection, it was too late, he'd already done it. I left him to it and carried on scraping more of the sofa stuffing into another bag.

By the time I'd finished he was back in the lounge, staring with a touch of wistfulness out of the window at the quay and the river below.

I straightened up and regarded him bleakly. The Superintendent reminded me of some of the best martial arts experts I'd come across. There was a deadly kind of calm about him. He was the sort who could walk into a pub where there was a full scale brawl going on and practically quieten the room with a half-dozen carefully chosen words.

He had an authority that doesn't just come with rank. And he was perceptive. I got the impression that very little escaped those muddy green eyes. He rattled me, and I was trying hard not to let it show.

I tied the top of the bag with string and chucked it onto the growing pile. He watched me in silence until my patience gave out. He'd probably intended that it should. 'So, what's the script?'

'You tell me, Miss Fox,' he said, turning away from the window with reluctance. 'You told my inspector that you'd had a threatening phone call last night. What did this man say? I assume it was a man, by the way?'

'I think so,' I told him. 'It was difficult to tell, but the speech rhythms were more male.'

He frowned. 'Difficult to tell—how?'

'I think he was using a voice changer. They're popular with women who live alone. It makes you sound more masculine, but there's a slight artificial note when you're using it.'

'You sound very well informed.'

I shrugged. 'I teach self-defence to women,' I said, adding with remarkable composure, 'and I used to have one myself.'

Used to, being the operative way of putting it. I'd spent a couple of fruitless hours searching the flat before he got there, but I'd singularly failed to turn up my voice changer box. I had to admit it— it was gone.

That was a nasty coincidence I didn't really want to believe in, but I didn't have much of a choice. For the moment, however, I pushed it to the back of my mind and tried to make like it wasn't there.

I repeated what my mystery caller had said to me as closely as I could remember. It wasn't difficult. The words were acid-etched into my brain.

When I finished the Superintendent looked pensive. He came and perched on my sofa, rubbing his chin absently. I noticed he was old-fashioned enough to be wearing neat gold cuff-links.

'You do realise, of course,' he said, 'that we have reason to believe the incident last night is linked to the serious assault on another young woman a few weeks ago, and a more recent rape and murder?'

My heart over-revved so hard it bumped painfully in my chest. My mouth was suddenly dry. 'It's the same man who killed Susie Hollins?' I said faintly. 'But she was raped, and so was the other girl. Does that mean—Joy—did he—?'

MacMillan's face was shuttered, giving absolutely nothing away. It wasn't difficult to imagine him sitting quietly behind a table in a darkened interview room somewhere, watching some villain sweat as he twisted on the hook of a confession. People would talk just to fill the silence in him.

I opened my mouth to ask, 'If it's the same bloke, how does Terry fit in?', but then I remembered I wasn't supposed to know about that. There hadn't been much in the press about his death yet. Not enough for me to have a viable reason to believe they were linked, at any rate.

I glanced up and found MacMillan studying me, as though he'd been eavesdropping on my thoughts. Instead of my question about Terry, I swallowed and said, 'So, what happens now?'

'Well, we could put a tap your phone and trace all your calls, intercept your mail, and put a watch on the place—if you really want us to go to those lengths, of course,' he said, his voice casual, even as he studying me with a sudden intensity. 'If someone really is threatening you, we can probably get them by one of those means.'

'What d'you mean, *if*!' I could feel my voice rising, and made an effort to control it. 'You mean you don't believe me?'

He cocked his head on one side. 'Well, let's look at the facts for a moment shall we, Miss Fox? We've got a rapist and murderer on the loose. A very dangerous man, but at the same time one who's shown himself to be both clever, and careful. So far, he's been selecting his victims apparently at random, probably because he knows how difficult that makes it for us to catch him.'

MacMillan started to pace again, measured steps, light on his feet. 'But now,' he continued in an almost silky tone, 'now, miraculously, he's made the seemingly ludicrous mistake of telegraphing his next move to us by ringing *you* up and nicely telling you that you're to be his next target.'

I felt the knife twist in my side. I'd been faced with this kind of suspicion before, and it had damned near finished me.

'Why would I lie?'

'Well now, Miss Fox,' he said quietly, 'it wouldn't be the first time you've cried this particular brand of wolf, would it?'

I wanted to speak, but my tongue seemed to have stuck itself to the roof of my mouth.

'I have to ask,' he went on remorselessly, 'why you think that claiming people have threatened to kill you would work any better in civilian life than it did four years ago when you were facing being thrown out of the armed forces? What do you hope to gain this time, Miss Fox?' There was something about the stress he put on my surname that alerted me to the dangers of this soft-spoken man. Much more than the actual words.

I met his eyes, and realised with a cold clutch of dread that he knew. He knew everything.

'I suppose I shouldn't really call you Miss Fox at all, should I?' MacMillan said, with the slow inevitability of a steam traction engine. 'Seeing as it was only when you moved to Lancaster that you changed your name, wasn't it? To Fox from Foxcroft. Now, why was that, exactly?'

There was no point in prevarication, or lying. 'You've obviously done your digging,' I said instead, feeling my face curling up like a salted slug. 'Why don't you tell me?'

My words were empty bravado. I didn't need the Superintendent to remind me what had happened.

My case at the court martial had rested mainly on the testimony of another soldier, Kirk Salter. A man I barely knew, but one who'd saved my life.

Kirk had scraped onto the course mainly because of his physical prowess. His head might have been little more than a life support system for a beret, but he could carry a GPMG and two hundred rounds of belted ammunition over an assault course without breaking sweat. And his heart was firmly in the right place.

If he hadn't stumbled on my attackers before they'd put their cover-up plan into action, I'd have ended up as another tragic crime statistic. If my body had ever been found.

Donalson, Hackett, Morton, and Clay.

They'd been fully intending to snap my neck like a winged pheasant and bury me in shallow grave somewhere in the nearest woods. Kirk had stopped them going through with it, and I'd always be grateful to him for that.

Then he'd been pressured—bullied, cajoled—into denying, under oath, that such a plot had ever existed. I reckoned that just about cancelled out the debt.

'Was changing your name your idea, or your parents'?' MacMillan asked now. 'It caused quite a scandal at the time, didn't it? First the court martial, then when you tried to pursue the matter in the civil courts.' He looked at me briefly and I thought I saw the pity in his face before he lowered his gaze to concentrate on adjusting his cuff-link. 'The tabloids had a high old time of it with you, didn't they, Charlie?'

I swallowed. Oh yes, they had indeed.

There hadn't been anything in the papers to start with, of course. The army don't tend to wash their dirty linen in public if they can help it. Once I'd made the foolish mistake of bringing a civil action, though, then they really let rip.

To begin with, the headlines had just been sensational. *Girl soldier gang-raped by fellow squaddies.* As if the ordeal itself hadn't been enough to live through, I'd then had to face the vindictive clutches of the media. At first they'd overflowed with fake sympathy. My story should be told, they said. Make it a lesson that others could learn from. Stop it happening to some other poor girl.

Then, God knows how, some particular ferreting had brought out my relationship with Sean. Oh, he wasn't married, or anything like that. That would have been too straightforward. Instead, he was one of my training instructors, and that was a complete no-no as far as the top brass were concerned. Relieved to have so easy a get-out presented to them on a plate, the full might of the army had swung against me. I never stood a chance.

As for the press, in the space of a print-run I was transformed from an innocent victim into an immoral slut. If I was prepared to screw one soldier, why not a whole bunch of them? Maybe, they reasoned, the men's claims that I'd been a willing participant weren't so far-fetched?

My parents' house had been besieged. We had reporters and photographers creeping through the garden for weeks. By the time of the civil case, the twisted facts and outrageous stories they'd printed had hopelessly biased any chance of my getting a fair hearing. The media went into a frenzy over the Not Guilty verdict against my attackers. By the time they'd finished with it, it was me who was as guilty as hell.

'It must have been quite a shock that your mother refused to support your appeal,' MacMillan said now. 'Especially with her being a magistrate herself.'

'She's a great believer in the criminal justice system in this country,' I said through gritted teeth. So great a believer that she'd refused to acknowledge the possibility that there might have been a miscarriage of justice. She'd shut her mind to it. And shut me out. It had been the final nail in my coffin.

The Superintendent made no comment as he came to his feet. He'd obviously gone over the reports from the time, and the scepticism was plain on his face. I'd been pilloried as a cold-blooded liar in a court of law. Why on earth should he take my word as gospel now?

'I don't suppose,' he said, although clearly not holding out much hope, 'that you *do* have any idea of who might be behind these attacks?'

I wasn't sure whether to be surprised that he'd bothered to ask my opinion, or insulted, but I remembered Joy, and gave it thought. 'There's always Angelo—one of the door-men from the New Adelphi,' I suggested. 'The girl who found Joy yesterday, Victoria, she's his girlfriend. He'd beaten her up pretty badly, and I'd say he probably enjoyed doing it.' When MacMillan didn't respond, I added, 'And he could have picked both Susie and Joy when they were at the club.'

'That would be Angelo Zachary, would it?'

I nodded.

'We've already interviewed Mr Zachary after the death of Miss Hollins,' he said. 'He had an alibi from the bar manager, Gary Bignold from the time Miss Hollins was ejected from the club, to well past the time we believe she was killed.'

If it had been Len who'd vouched for Angelo, I would have suspected it, but Gary had no special allegiances as far as I could tell. I shrugged. 'I can't help you, then.'

He moved to the front door, paused on the threshold. 'Not very loyal to your colleagues are you, Charlie?'

I just glared at him, and he sighed, reaching into an inside pocket of his jacket. He produced a rather plain-looking business card, enlivened only by the colouring of the Lancashire Police crest. 'If you do have any further contact with this man,' he instructed, 'call me.'

I took the card. It gave me a good reason to unclench my hands. 'Will you let me know—if you make any progress?' I asked.

He nodded. 'Of course.' There was a pause, then he said, 'You're not quite what I was expecting, Charlie.' He cocked his head on one side.

'Maybe I just don't scare easily,' I said. But I was more scared than I would like to admit. Not to the Superintendent, and not to myself, either.

It was a nasty, insidious kind of fear, that eats away at you from the inside out, twists your guts into knots, beads sweat on your upper lip.

You only have to relax your guard for a second and it's away and running, like a bolting horse. I concentrated on keeping a tight rein on mine.

MacMillan showed himself out, and I watched from the window as he climbed into a big dull-coloured Rover saloon parked next to the far kerb. Just before he drove away he glanced up and looked directly at me. It was too late to pull back without making it appear more suspicious, but the whole encounter left me feeling restless and uneasy.

AFTER THE SUPERINTENDENT had gone I hadn't the will to go back to my clearing up. Instead I dug out Terry's code book and leafed through it again, half-heartedly. The sets of initials swam past my eyes.

I tried to remember people's surnames from the club. Gary's was Bignold, but there were several different GBs listed. Dave's was Clemmens. Hm, not so many DCs.

'Oh this is hopeless!' I muttered, throwing the book down on the sofa. It landed open and something caught my eye. I stopped dead.

Angelo. Angelo Zachary. AZ. I grabbed the book again. Those initials were only listed with one number prefix, 168. I'd found the New Adelphi.

All I had to do now was find out which of the people listed in Terry's book had owed him big sums of money. That should lead me to his killer. A man who'd started getting his kicks out of raping and murdering women.

And now, it seemed, he was hoping to get a real thrill out of planning to kill me . . .

I jumped up. I had so many disconnected theories forming and I needed someone to bounce some ideas off. To see if I was way off base. Most of all, I needed to get away from the possibility that the phone was going to ring at any moment and scare me to death again.

I thought all too briefly of calling the number on the card the Superintendent had given me, but I had no desire to get back into the ring for another round. He didn't trust me, and I suppose I couldn't really blame him for that.

I went over to the phone and snatched up the receiver, dialling Jacob and Clare's number. To my surprise Clare answered. I'd expected her to be at work, and I'd planned to run a few things past Jacob's cool, logical mind.

'No, I've got a day off,' she said. 'Why, what's up, Charlie?'

'I can't really explain over the phone,' I hedged. 'Look, are you in all morning? Can I come round?'

'Of course,' Clare said promptly. 'I'll put the coffee on now. You sound very mysterious. I can't wait!'

I climbed into my gear, aware that I was still feeling stiff and inflexible as I struggled into my leather jeans. It was raining when I got outside. Miserable great grey blobs that made me blink when they splashed into my hair. By the looks of the darkened sky, this was as good as it was going to get all day. I was glad I'd put my waterproofs on.

The Suzuki, bless it, fired up first kick and it didn't take more than ten minutes before I was bumping down the drive to Jacob and Clare's place.

This time, with one eye on the downpour, the dogs made do with greeting me by way of excited barks from the shelter of the porch. Sensible animals. Clare came out, though, with Jacob's giant waxed cotton stockman's coat draped over her head.

'Come in and dry off by the Aga,' she instructed, grinning at me with button-bright eyes. 'Jacob's all agog to know what you're being so secretive about!'

It didn't take long, once I'd got into my story, for the smile to leave Clare's face. We sat round the kitchen table to talk, warming our hands on mugs of hot cappuccino, sprinkled with real chocolate.

Having made sure there was no food on offer, Bonneville had retreated to her blanket pressed up against the front of the Aga. The room was soon permeated by the vague smell of hot dog. Beezer had made straight for Jacob's lap. She was now sprawled on her back there, delighting in his preoccupied scratching of her tummy.

I brought them up to speed on recent events, including the break-in at my flat, Terry's murder, and now Joy's death. They both listened in horrified fascination, and it took a while to satisfy them that I really was OK. I suppose it helped convince me at the same time.

'It sounds like this Angelo bloke is a complete psycho,' Jacob commented. 'From what you've said he has a remarkable capacity for violence.'

I nodded. 'And he's got a rotten temper to go with it. So, maybe if Terry had found out that Angelo was dealing drugs, and then been suddenly presented with something that he thought might give him leverage against Angelo, Terry might well have decided to indulge in a little extortion.'

'If that's the case, he certainly picked the wrong man to blackmail,' Jacob put in grimly.

'So Angelo goes round to see him. Maybe he was intending to pay him off. Maybe he was intending to do him over. Who knows?' I went on. 'But that wasn't how it happened. Terry didn't have the computer to give back to Angelo, because he'd already given it to me. So Angelo pulls a knife and guts the poor bastard.'

Clare pulled a squeamish face and got up to refill our coffee mugs. Jacob just nodded at my logic.

'It would be a real *1984*-type Room 101 scenario,' he mused. '"Don't do it to me; do it to Charlie! She's the one you want!" That sort of thing.'

George Orwell's classic had made enough of an impression on me as a schoolkid for me to know what he was on about. 'Exactly,' I said. 'So, in the meantime, Len—and then Marc—find out about the drugs

Angelo's been dealing in. Marc would never go to the police in a thousand years. But he'd take action of his own.'

'But you said it wasn't Angelo who beat you up, so who were those two men?' Clare queried as she sat down again.

'I've no idea,' I shrugged, frustrated, running a hand through my hair, 'though there's no reason why Angelo would need to turn out in person. He must know plenty of hired muscle in his line of work. The trouble is, when I got that phone call last night I was convinced that whoever killed Joy—and Susie—was connected to whoever had come looking for that damned lap-top.'

Clare's mouth opened, and stayed that way for a while. 'You mean you think Angelo killed them *all*? But why?'

'The voice changer,' Jacob said slowly, as it came to him. 'They must have taken it when they ransacked your flat.'

'Exactly,' I said. 'And if the same man murdered both the women—which was certainly the impression I got from MacMillan—then it can't be Angelo. He's got an alibi for the night of Susie's death.'

'What did the police say about Terry?' Clare asked, but Jacob answered her before I could.

'Come on, love, Charlie's not supposed to even know he's dead. She couldn't very well start giving the old Superintendent the third degree without admitting she was the one who discovered the body, now could she?'

Clare was frowning. 'But, if it wasn't Angelo, who does that leave?'

I drained the last of my coffee. 'I wish I knew,' I said. 'I'm going over to see Ailsa this afternoon to see if there's anyone she can think of that they've had trouble with at the Lodge. A husband or boyfriend maybe. After all, it seems that our murderer was hanging round there on a couple of occasions before he got Joy.'

Besides, I'd promised Dave his first self-defence lesson, and the Lodge was as good a place as any to teach him.

They stood silent as I climbed back into my waterproofs. Clare had hung them in the inglenook near the Aga, and they were not only bone dry, but the plastic material was almost too hot to touch.

'I could be way off base about it all, in any case,' I said as I made my way, rustling, to the front door. 'Just because Angelo beats up his

191

girlfriend doesn't mean he's a murderer. It could be someone else at the club who's involved with the drugs, and gave the computer to Terry. I don't have a shred of proof. I just wish I knew if there was any forensic link. That would really clinch it.'

'I'll try my contact on the crime desk again, but she's going to get very suspicious if I suggest something the police haven't already come up with by themselves,' Clare said. 'I'll come round on the bike on Sunday morning and let you know what she says. We can have a blast up to Devil's Bridge together.'

I nodded, aware that when Clare said a blast, she meant it. I usually struggled to keep up.

Now though, she was still frowning in thought as she came to the door to see me off, hugging herself against the cold. 'There must be some other way to find out, isn't there?'

'I'm sure there is,' I said. I pictured myself calling up MacMillan and asking to pick his brains. It would be a cold day in hell, I predicted, before that happened. I gave her a wry smile. 'I just haven't thought of it yet.'

Jacob came up behind her, put his hands on her shoulders, smiling. 'What you need is a tame doctor,' he said to me. 'Don't you know anyone you could sweet-talk?'

It wasn't until I'd said my goodbyes, coaxed the Suzuki into life, and was halfway back to Lancaster that Jacob's words sparked a thought. A thought that was so ridiculous it made me snort with suppressed laughter inside my helmet.

Yes, I did know a doctor. Was very well-acquainted with him, as a matter of fact, but whether I could sweet-talk him into anything was another thing altogether.

My father.

WHEN I GOT back to the flat, I went straight upstairs to the phone, without even stopping to take off my waterproofs. I knew my parents' phone number off by heart and I dialled it without having to think about it. Maybe if I had, I would have hesitated.

Fortunately, or unfortunately, it was my father who answered the call.

'Good evening,' he said, giving his number clearly and precisely. I knew I should tell him it was bad practice to do that, but at the same time I knew I wouldn't bother.

'Hi, it's me,' I said.

There was the fraction of a pause. This really was a very bad idea. 'Charlotte,' he said neutrally. 'It's nice to hear from you. Are you keeping well?'

'I'm fine. No, that's not true, I'm not *fine*,' I said crossly. The gulf between us seemed suddenly wider than the Grand Canyon. I had no idea how to begin going about crossing it.

'I'm sorry to hear that,' he said. 'What seems to be the matter?'

I sighed. I hoped he showed more warmth to his patients, but I wouldn't bet on it.

I swallowed. 'I need your help,' I said. God, it was difficult to say.

There was a longer pause this time. 'In what way?' he asked cautiously. Not, yes of course. Not, anything I can do. Not, you only have to ask, darling . . .

'There've been three murders in Lancaster over the last few weeks,' I said, forcing myself to speak quickly in case I changed my mind. 'Two of them are rape murders of women that are definitely connected, but the third was a stabbing of a man. I think there's a link between all three. The police don't. I need to know if there's any forensic evidence that relates them.'

I rushed on, listing the names before he had a chance to refuse. When I'd finished I held my breath, tense, waiting. It seemed to take him a long time to speak again.

'May I ask what makes you think I might be able to help?' His voice sounded cold over the phone line. It wasn't quite the response I'd been hoping for.

The tension snapped. 'Of course you could help—if you wanted to!' I cried. 'How long were you a consultant at Lancaster hospital for heaven's sake—ten years? You should know everyone there, or didn't you ever speak to the pathology department?'

He chose not to answer that one, asking instead, 'Don't you think the police are perfectly capable of handling something like this without your somewhat amateur interference?'

'Probably,' I snapped. 'In the meantime someone's beaten me up, trashed my flat, and threatened to cut my throat. I'm sorry if that doesn't mean anything to you!' I gave a laugh, more of a half-hysterical yelp. 'Of course, how silly of me, I was probably asking for it, wasn't I?'

I slammed the phone down, staring at the pattern of the fabric on the sofa for a few moments, determined not to cry.

He'd never been like other fathers, but I should be used to that by now. As a teenager I'd always been quite proud of the fact that he hadn't embarrassed me with public shows of emotion like the other kids' dads. That he hadn't tried dancing at the school disco. Hadn't make a fool of himself on sports day.

I shook my head to clear my vision of the tears that had been threatening dangerously to spill over. I grabbed my helmet again and moved to the door. I didn't care about the filthy weather. I just needed to get out there and ride. To give the bike some pain, get it out of my system.

Most of all, I needed to get away from the silent telephone. To escape from the fact that I'd just dropped an emotional bombshell on my father. And it didn't seem to have gone off.

Nineteen

DAVE WAS STANDING in front of me with both his hands clasped round my throat and, in my opinion, he was putting a bit too much gusto into pretending to strangle me.

'I can only show you roughly the sort of things I normally teach,' I told him. 'Most of my students won't be as physically strong as their opponent. They have to be a bit more scientific because half the time brute force just won't cut it. See?'

I demonstrated by tugging at his wrists. All I succeeded in doing was making him tighten his grip round my windpipe. Throwing him a sideways glance I said, 'This will be the shortest set of lessons in history if you choke me to death on the first day.'

He slackened off slightly with an apologetic half-smile, but was obviously happy that he'd proved his point. That the only reason I wasn't getting hurt was because he was being gentle, not through any level of skill on my part. Typical macho bullshit.

We were alone in the ballroom at Shelseley Lodge. I hadn't particularly wanted to teach Dave at the flat, and he claimed his own place was so small that swung cats left with a blinding headache.

The Lodge had seemed a logical compromise, and Ailsa had put forward no objections. The police had finished combing their way through the gardens, she told me, although the area where Joy had fallen was still fenced off with fluttering yellow incident tape.

I'd spent a little time with Ailsa before Dave had shown up, seeing if she could think of any possible suspects. There were plenty of women who'd passed through Ailsa's care with violent and unpredictable men in their lives, but no one specific sprang to mind.

'Besides, the police already asked me all this, love,' she said, giving me a tired smile. 'I had some hawk-like Superintendent round yesterday, asking endless questions.'

I didn't like to press her further. She had enough problems of her own to worry about. When I'd arrived there were a couple of cars in the driveway being loaded with possessions, as more of the Lodge's residents moved out.

The day had been lit by thin pale sunshine and now the light level was falling fast. I had to flick on the overhead lights before Dave and I could continue.

Now, I re-focused with an effort. 'OK,' I told him, 'your priority here is to get away very quickly. It takes remarkably little time to be strangled. You can't afford to waste it.'

I suppose I cheated a bit, really. I'd left my hands on his wrists and as I spoke I went for two pressure points on the back of his right hand. A quick twist and I'd not only broken his grip, but I'd put a solid lock onto his wrist and started taking him down with it.

Dave could have stayed upright, if he'd been really determined, but it would have hurt him to do so. The only way to escape the pain was to roll with it. When I let go he favoured me with a rueful smile and climbed to his feet again.

'Nice one,' he allowed grudgingly. 'Can I try that on you this time?'

I nodded and put my hands round his throat. He was wearing another of those dreadful nylon jackets, but today it was over a lime green polo-necked jumper with a designer label stitched into the collar. I remembered the bruising from his altercation with Marc and tried not to clutch him too tightly.

I'd found Marc's hands much more careful when they were touching my body. And dextrous.

I brought myself back on track with some difficulty and explained the technique to Dave. Finding the right pressure points isn't easy. Most people require practice to get it right, but Dave picked them up more or less straight away.

Next thing I knew I was hitting the crashmat in a half-roll. As I came back to my feet, I found him watching me with a crafty grin on his face.

'You've done this before,' I said accusingly.

He looked suddenly innocent. 'I've just always been a quick learner.'

Before I could answer there was a tentative knock on the already open door to the ballroom. I turned to see Nina hovering from one foot to the other on the threshold.

'Hi,' I said, giving her an encouraging smile. 'Come on in.'

'Oh.' After some hesitation, she advanced further. She was wearing a long knitted skirt and ugly shoes that seemed to be the zenith of current fashion. I would have broken both my ankles the first time I tried to walk down a flight of stairs in them. 'I don't want to disturb you,' she said. 'I just came to say goodbye, that's all.'

'You're leaving?' I tried to sound surprised, but I don't think I could really raise it.

She nodded, not quite meeting my eyes. She flicked a nervous glance in Dave's direction. He caught it, and casually wandered off to one of the French windows in apparent contemplation of the rapidly darkening garden. I watched some of the tension seep out of Nina's body as he moved away, and was grateful for his unexpected sensitivity.

'I wanted to say thank you as well,' she said.

'What for?'

'Well, for the other night.' Edgy, she checked that Dave was far enough away not to be obviously listening in. 'You went out to see if you could find him—you know, th-the man I saw.' She was wearing a Celtic design silver ring on one hand, and was twisting it round and round until I thought she'd screw the end of her finger off.

'I didn't know, you see, not until Ailsa told me—what h-happened to you,' she said quickly, when I still looked nonplussed. 'But you went out anyway, into the dark. I-I don't know how you could bear to do it.' She shrugged, almost helplessly. 'I hope one day I'll be able to do that, too.'

'You will,' I said, and meant it. 'If you want to, you will.'

She seemed about to say more, but a middle-aged couple appeared in the entrance to the ballroom and made throat-clearing noises. They were too well-dressed, too well-fed, to ever look comfortable in their present surroundings, and by the looks of it they hadn't tried too hard.

'Nina,' the woman said, 'we need to go, darling, if we're going to miss the worst of the traffic.' There was a trace of strain in her voice, like the owner of a runaway dog forced to pick out their prized pedigree hound from among the mongrels and strays of the city pound.

'OK, Mummy,' Nina said over her shoulder. She turned back, gave me a smile that hinted at the sunny teenager she used to be, and impulsively hugged me. Her thin arms were fleetingly tight around my shoulders. 'Thank you,' she said, breathless, then she was scurrying away across the wooden floor.

Her parents both put a protective arm around their daughter as she reached them, and their brief stare in my direction was cold to the point of hostile. I ignored them.

'Take care of yourself, Nina,' I said, giving her a final wave.

When they'd gone, I turned to find Dave watching me with curious and calculating eyes.

'What happened to her?' he asked, nodding towards the empty doorway.

'She trusted someone who wasn't to be trusted,' I said shortly. 'Now, are you here to talk, or fight?'

I spent the next half an hour or so running through various moves with Dave that should get him out of a few potentially nasty situations. By the time we'd finished both Dave and I were sweating and breathless. I was down to a T-shirt and Dave had lost the jacket, but he must have been regretting the choice of jumper, bruises or no bruises.

To finish, we did a brief recap. I quickly ran through each of the moves again, but there was really no need. He'd got the hang of them.

Afterwards, he helped me drag the crashmats back over to their corner and stand them up against the wall. I pulled my sweatshirt on again, and Dave shrugged back into his jacket. He dug into a pocket and handed over the amount of cash we'd agreed on for the first of his lessons. I accepted without demur. I think I'd earned my money.

It wasn't until we'd moved out of the ballroom and along into the hallway that Dave voiced the question that had probably been on his mind for a while.

'D'you really believe that the stuff you teach these young lasses can actually save them?' he said. He clearly had Nina in mind, but I immediately thought of Joy. It took me a moment to answer.

We'd covered knife attacks in the classes Joy had attended. She knew the theory. She should have been more than capable of fending off her attacker, disarming and disabling him.

Should have been.

But wasn't.

And now she was dead. Just thinking about it twisted a knife in my own side. Joy had paid a mammoth price for not doing her homework. Still, I couldn't help wondering about it. Were her reflexes against a surprise attack really so poor that she'd let a stranger, whoever he was, get close enough to her to pull out a knife and slash her with it? Surely not.

I hedged. 'If I didn't believe it, I wouldn't be doing it.'

'Don't you think, though, that people misjudge you at the outset, like those two kids at the club last week, and you rely on that element of surprise too much?' he asked. 'OK, so you're fine against someone with comparatively little skill, who's not expecting a counter-attack, but against a stronger opponent, one who knows what he's doing, no way.' He shook his head, grinned at me. 'I mean, come on, Foxy. No woman could ever hope to beat a man when their abilities are well matched.'

By woman he meant a smaller, lighter, weaker adversary. I thought of all the martial arts gurus whose work I'd studied. Hardly any were six-foot blokes. They were mostly short in stature, quick and nimble. I'd seen them wipe out bigger, heavier challengers without raising their pulse rate enough to register on an electrocardiogram.

'I'd have to disagree,' I said.

Dave just grinned again as he zipped up his jacket, dug in the pocket for his car keys. 'Well, you would say that, wouldn't you?'

I was just about to argue, when the door to Tris and Ailsa's sitting room was flung open, and the lady of the house came galloping out. Grasped in her upraised right hand was a heavy rolling pin with wooden handles and a white marble centre.

'Quick, quick!' she yelled. 'I've just seen him, from the kitchen window. He's heading for the front!'

I didn't stop and ask who she meant. I didn't need to.

Before Ailsa had even reached us, I'd spun round and was already running for the open front door. I took the entire flight of steps in one reckless bound, then skidded and nearly lost my footing on the mossy flags at the bottom as a result.

As I fought to regain my balance, cursing, a figure came bolting along the side of the house. Even with the loose gravel underfoot, he was running like an Olympic sprinter, arms working furiously to propel him forwards in a desperate rush.

He came level with the front steps, passing within about twenty feet of me, and moving fast. He must have caught the flurry of movement, though, because he turned his head and looked straight into my eyes.

It almost seemed like everything moved forwards into slow motion. I had time to create a mental record of the dark trousers and ribbed sweater, the black ski mask covering his features. Only the eyes stood out, whites gleaming.

The sudden, stark memory of the two masked men who'd broken into the flat materialised like a phantom, and almost sent me reeling. It was only the thundering approach of Ailsa, with Dave following on, that jarred me into action.

I set off like a hare across the lawn on a diagonal intercept course. The grass was easier to run on. Anger gave me speed. I didn't care that the man was most likely carrying a knife big enough and sharp enough to cut my throat. I didn't care that he'd already proved beyond any shred of doubt how prepared and how capable he was of using it. Stupid, really.

The man almost made it out of the gateway, but at the bottom of the drive the gravel was at its most rutted. Two deep troughs had been gouged out by the constant wheel tracks of the cars turning between the gateposts.

He caught his foot on the crest of one, stumbled with his arms outstretched, and nearly went headlong. The streetlight from the road outside was shining down onto him. In the yellowed glow I saw the fingers of his gloved hands splay outwards. Open.

Empty.

That was all it took. In the next moment I'd taken a final stride forwards, and leapt.

I hit him with the point of my right shoulder just an inch or so below the small of his back, and grabbed. He went down with a violent whumph, like he'd been hit by a fridge.

The force of the impact drove us skittering along the drive for another ten feet or so after we'd hit on the ground. The man was face-down in the gravel, floundering. Of the two of us, I reckon I probably had the easier ride.

We were half out onto the pavement itself by the time we slithered to a messy halt. The man brought his elbow back sharply, more wild than scientific, but it was enough to throw me off his back.

I landed hard, but scrambled up instantly, screwing round into a crouch. The man was on his knees, taking longer to rise. His mask and the front of his jumper were torn and bloody. Frantic, I checked his hands again, and readied myself to strike.

Then, a whirling figure entered stage right at a dead run and unfurled a sweeping upward blow with the rolling pin that snapped the man's head sideways, blood spraying. It would have made an easy six over the boundary, had the head not been still firmly attached at the neck. If the England cricket team selectors had been there, Ailsa would have been capped on the spot.

The man's arms flapped as his body twisted, then he slowly collapsed backwards onto the pavement behind him. I had to grab Ailsa's arm to stop her going in for the kill. She was trembling violently all over, and screaming abuse so tangled it was almost totally incoherent.

The noise had brought out most of the remaining residents from the Lodge. They filed down the drive and approached cautiously across the lawn, but they had the grumbling air of a lynch mob about them. It would only take one brave one to throw the first stone, and things were going to get very nasty.

I thrust the still-quivering Ailsa onto Dave, having first carefully prised the bloodied rolling pin from her fingers. Robbed of the adrenaline that had fired her, she more or less fell into his arms. He took her weight with obvious strain.

Over the top of her head he demanded, 'What the hell is going on?'

'Remember Susie Hollins?' I nudged the inert form on the ground with my boot, none too gently. 'I think this is the bastard who killed her.'

Surprise and awareness leapt in his eyes.

I dropped down by the side of the man and reached for the edge of the balaclava.

'Now then, shithead, let's have a look at you,' I muttered. I yanked off the mask, to reveal a face that was horribly familiar. The silence that followed screamed at all of us.

Before I could move to block her, Ailsa had peered down over my shoulder. She let out a single wailing cry, then collapsed totally. Dave tried manfully to keep her on her feet, but he was fighting a losing battle from the outset. In the end, the best he could manage was a kind of controlled descent.

Looking back at the figure on the ground, lying bleeding and unconscious, I could understand Ailsa's reaction completely.

After all, it's not every day that you take on a terrifying masked intruder, armed with little more than a marble rolling pin, and discover that the man you've just knocked halfway into next week is your own husband . . .

THIS TIME, THE police arrived at the Lodge much quicker than they had when Ailsa had summoned them before because we'd spotted a prowler in the garden. In fact, Tris was only just starting to come round when they rolled up with lights and sirens blazing.

We didn't get much out of him before he was bundled into the back of a police Transit, other than a single quiet apology to Ailsa.

Somehow, that made it worse.

Right up until then, I suppose I'd still been hoping that he might deny it, that there might conceivably be another reason for him to be running through his own garden, heavily disguised in a manner designed to spark panic, and confusion. In the end, I had to face it, there wasn't.

The idea was taking me some getting used to. OK, so I hadn't known Tris for more than a couple of years, but he was the last man I would have had down as a sadistic rapist and murderer.

My mind re-ran recent scenes like a video that was stuck on 'play'. Memories that made my scalp break out into a sweat, and my stomach churn. It was as much as I could do to stay on my feet and functioning until the police took over.

I remembered Tris's soothing hands gliding over the skin of my back. Had he spent all the time he'd been giving me a massage wondering what it would be like to run a knife blade across my throat?

The concealed voice on the other end of the telephone the night Joy had died. I tried to match up Tris's gentle tones with the malicious spite that had hummed clearly along the wires. How could it be one of my friends who had done this?

I tried hard not to let it get to me. Not until the police had carted Tris away, and Ailsa had been given a sedative by her doctor. Dave had ducked out as soon as the emergency services had reached the scene, relieved to hand Ailsa over to the professionals. The Shelseley girls banded together to offer comfort in such a way that I felt like an outsider among them. It wasn't hard to make my own excuses, and slip away.

I rode home slowly, and with great care. It's difficult to watch where you're going when your eyes are burnt with tears.

I stopped on the way to stick another few gallons of juice into the Suzuki. The tank on the RGV is pretty small, and if you're giving it some serious beans you go onto reserve after less than a hundred miles.

I was just squeezing the last few drops into the filler when there was the roar of a Norton pulling in alongside. I looked up to see Sam's big brown eyes crinkling at me through his open visor.

'Hi, Charlie. I thought it was you,' he said, pulling off his helmet and stuffing his scarf into it. 'Didn't you get my message?'

'Yeah.' I vaguely remembered Sam's voice on the answering machine. It seemed like years ago. I hung the nozzle back into the pump and locked the filler cap back down. 'Sorry, I've had a bit on my plate.'

'What could be more important than talking to me?' he demanded with an irritatingly cheeky grin.

'A friend of mine was murdered,' I dropped on him, just to watch his smile fade. I knew I wasn't being fair, but what the hell? Life's like that, and I wasn't feeling very fair right now.

He made all the usual noises of shock and commiseration, but his eyes had that twitchy look of someone searching wildly for a suitable change of subject. He opened his mouth, but only succeeded in changing feet. 'So, what happened to that lap-top, then?'

As he spoke it suddenly occurred to me that it was probably only Terry's ignorance of Sam's full name and home location that had prevented my unwanted visitors from paying *him* a nocturnal visit as well. No doubt they would have got round to forcibly extracting that information from me, if I'd given them the chance. 'The computer was nicked when my place was turned over at the weekend.' I said flatly.

He looked stricken. I was almost beginning to feel sorry for him. 'Jeez, Charlie, I'm sorry. And about your friend. What happened?'

I gave him a brief précis of how Joy had met her death as he filled up the Norton's tank. He took it in pale silence, and we went in to pay together. There were a couple of people in front of us, dithering with chequebooks. The girl behind the counter looked hard-faced and bored.

As I stood there in the queue, I knew I still hadn't really taken it in that Tris, my friend, was a cold-blooded murderer. That he was responsible for three vicious crimes. I couldn't begin to understand what had driven him to do it.

I idly watched another car pull up to the pumps, catching the monochrome echo of it on the security monitor behind the cashier's head. Sam must have been following my gaze.

'It's a shame there weren't any closed circuit cameras at that Shelseley place where you teach,' he said. 'They might have spotted who did it.'

'Oh, we know who did it, and they've got him,' I said automatically as I stepped forwards to pay.

I waited while Sam handed over the money for his own fill-up, then we walked back to the bikes.

When I'd said the words, it all sounded so cut and dried, but somewhere in the dark recesses of my brain there was a stirring of unease, of apprehension.

There was still a connection with the lap-top Terry had given me that I hadn't figured out yet. Otherwise, how had my voice changer got from the flat on the night of the burglary, and into Tris's hands? And where did Angelo fit in to all this?

Something wasn't finished, wasn't over, but I was damned if I could put my finger on exactly what it was.

* * *

I POTTERED THE rest of the way through the dark and busy city streets and down onto the quay. I was surprised when I got back to the flat to find Marc's sleek BMW waiting outside. I don't know how long he'd been there, but he was still sitting in the driver's seat when I arrived.

As I parked the bike up, he climbed out, leisurely, pulling on a superb long wool overcoat against the bitter wind.

'Hi,' he said. 'Are you OK?'

I found myself smiling as I took off my helmet. 'Yeah,' I replied, unsettled to find how pleased I was to see him. He was slipping under my skin. I wasn't sure if that was really where I wanted him.

Heedless of the dirty weather, he stood waiting for me to pull the cover over the Suzuki, then followed me up the stairs.

I bunged the coffee machine on, and went to change into some dry clothes. Waterproofs over the top of leathers make you look like the Michelin man and rustle so alarmingly when you walk that you have to resist the tendency to raise your voice to be heard over the noise.

When I came back, having hastily thrown on some clean jeans and a shirt, Marc was standing by one of the windows, staring out across the river. Everyone seems to be fascinated by the view. I must admit it was one of the things I most liked about the flat when I moved in.

He offered to take me out for dinner, but I passed on that one. I didn't feel much like eating out. In the end I rang one of the local Indian takeaways and they brought round chunky lamb tikka and chicken dupiaza with sweet moist peshwari naan bread and crisp poppadums.

I'd only seen Marc on his terms, as lord of the New Adelphi, and in his up-market hotel suite. It was a nice surprise to find that he could still slum it. He lost the overcoat and his suit jacket in short order and we sat on cushions on the floor to demolish the food, mopping up with bits of naan bread and fingers.

'I like watching you eat,' he said at last. 'You don't order the most expensive thing on the menu and then make a pretence of picking at it.'

I eyed him over the last piece of poppadum. He didn't get to it fast enough. 'You've been going out with the wrong women,' I said, grinning as I used it to scoop up the last of the mint raita.

He smiled at me for a moment, then his expression sobered. 'You're looking better than I expected,' he remarked, leaning back against the arm of the sofa with his head tilted to one side, considering. 'It's not every girl who could go through what you've had to over the last few days and come out of it looking so unruffled.'

I shrugged. 'You either cope or you give in. I don't like to lose.'

'I don't see you as the losing type,' he said, smiling wryly. 'You're quite a fighter, Charlie Fox.'

'I wasn't always,' I said suddenly, needing to tell him. 'I was a victim once. I swore nobody would ever make me feel that way again.'

He frowned. 'But you were still attacked.'

I gave him a level stare, told him, 'It's a state of mind.'

I left him to ponder that one while I fetched us both a coffee. When I came back he'd cleared the debris of the meal into the cardboard box they'd delivered it in, and put it by the door to take out. Not bad—house-trained as well.

He smiled lazily at me from the sofa and motioned for me to sit in front of him, with my back to his legs. When I complied he began to knead the knots out of my shoulders. Those long, agile fingers were merciless, but the results felt wonderful. I was aware of the tension slowly loosening up, like ice defrosting from a long-neglected freezer.

Then, in the midst of it, I had a vision of Tris again, rubbing scented oil into my skin with hands that had robbed two women of their lives, and raped and beaten a third.

I smelled Joy's blood again, snapping upright and jerking away from Marc's hands.

'Calm down, Charlie,' he said. 'What do you think I'm going to do to you?'

I gave him an apologetic smile as I twisted to face him. 'Sorry. I'm still a bit jumpy.'

He smiled also. 'Well, at least you didn't punch me this time.' He smoothed a strand of my hair away from my face. 'You need to relax more.'

'I can't afford to,' I said. I couldn't afford to let my guard down, even for a moment. It seemed that I'd dipped out of getting my father's medical assistance, but I still needed to find that link between Terry's murder and the attacks on the women. And then between those and the New Adelphi Club . . .

'Would it help to talk about it?' Marc's voice broke into my thoughts.

I took a deep breath, then launched straight in. Once I'd started, it was difficult to stop. It all just came tumbling out like I'd opened the door on a precariously over-stuffed cupboard.

I told him the story right from the start, all about Terry coming round with the lap-top, and how I'd agreed to help him get into it so I could find out if it was the one Marc had mentioned. I only left out my suspicion that Terry had known about drugs at the club. Whenever I'd brought that subject up in the past, Marc had really gone off at the deep end. I carefully skirted round Sam's role in the proceedings too, unwilling to expose him to any further danger.

As it was, Marc listened with a face that might as well have been cut from stone. When I got as far as relating the fact that my voice changer had seemingly disappeared from the flat during the robbery, then apparently turned up again in the hands of Joy's killer, he jumped up and moved over to the window.

'Are you sure it's the same device as the one that was taken from here?' he demanded.

'Not absolutely,' I admitted, 'but they aren't exactly commonplace, and mine has definitely gone. Apart from the lap-top, it was the only thing those two jokers took.' I spread my hands, indicating the debris around us that I'd only partly finished clearing. 'They simply smashed up everything else.'

'And who did Terry say he got that computer from?'

I shrugged. 'He just said he'd been debt collecting at the club, but he didn't mention any names.'

Marc looked thoughtful. 'The only lap-top of that type that's gone missing went weeks ago, and I've already sacked the culprits, or *thought* I had, at any rate,' he said, letting out an annoyed breath. 'I don't suppose you got any inklings from this Terry character who it might have been?'

I thought of Terry's coded client book, but I wasn't quite ready to turn that over to Marc. Not just yet.

'Terry had quite a few video customers among the staff at the New Adelphi who weren't exactly hiring out *The Little Mermaid*,' I said, and saw from his face that I didn't need to explain any further than that. 'I think one of the people who owed him a bucket of money was Angelo.'

For a moment Marc stared out into the darkness with no expression on his face, but the way he held his body stiff spoke volumes about the anger, bubbling away just beneath the surface.

'Angelo!' he said at last, and his voice was quiet, as though he was speaking to himself more than to me. 'He was the one who pointed the finger at the lads I sacked. If I'd known *he* was the one I would have . . .'

He broke off, glanced in my direction, made a visible effort to control his temper.

'Of course, there is a way we might be able to find out what Angelo's been up to,' I said, almost diffidently.

Marc turned back in to the room. 'How?'

I hesitated, although I knew what I was going to suggest. Had known it ever since I'd filled up with petrol earlier.

'You have security cameras all over the inside of the club, don't you?'

Surprise crossed his face at the question. 'Yes, of course, covering most of the main areas, anyway.'

'After Susie Hollins was killed, did the police take the tapes from the internal cameras?'

'Yes, they did,' he said slowly. 'But there was some sort of glitch in the recording. They didn't get anything out of them beyond blurs and static. They gave me a hard time about that, as I recall. They seemed to think the interference was caused deliberately. But why? What does Susie's death have to do with the lap-top? I thought you said they'd got the man who killed her.'

'Well yes,' I said, still unable to think of Tris without a shudder. 'But supposing those tapes also showed Terry being given that computer the following day. What then?'

I saw the relevance strike him, then he sighed, and made a frustrated gesture. 'It's all immaterial,' he said. 'There's nothing on those tapes to see.'

'Yes,' I said again, 'but what if it was put about round the club that you were getting in some computer techie whizz who reckoned he could clean up the image enough to get an ID?'

'Is that possible?'

I shrugged. 'I've no idea, but then, neither would anyone else. If it was you, would you want to risk it?'

He frowned, thinking hard. 'If that rumour was put about, whoever tampered with those tapes might start feeling pretty insecure. He might be tempted to come and destroy or even completely remove them, just to make sure.'

I nodded. 'Where are the tapes kept?'

He smiled again. It would have been sinister if it hadn't been following my own train of thought so closely. 'Locked away in my private office. No one has a key except Len, and he knows it's more than his life's worth to let people go wandering about in there when I'm not around.'

'So all you have to do is spread the word, then pretend to be out for the evening, and see who comes a'burgling.'

Marc's head came up. 'I'll see to it,' he said, and the cold tone in his voice was unforgiving.

'I want to be there when the trap's sprung,' I warned.

He nodded shortly, crossing the distance between us on long legs. 'If it is Angelo, we'll get him,' he promised. 'And I'll deal with him in my own way. No police. Agreed?'

After a moment, I nodded. I didn't know what Marc had in store for Angelo, if he was guilty, and I didn't really want to know.

'I don't want you doing any more digging on your own, Charlie,' he said. He gripped my shoulders and I couldn't help but stare up into those compelling pale-coloured eyes. 'I don't want you taking any more risks alone, OK?'

'OK.' I just had time to murmur my agreement as his mouth came down onto mine. Hard, fast, demanding.

I let go of everything and drowned in the sensation.

MARC LEFT AT around three the following morning, slipping into his clothes and out of the flat quietly, leaving me dazed and exhausted.

As I slid into sleep, I realised that I felt safer than I had done in days. Safer for the knowledge that I wasn't fighting this battle single-handed any more.

Twenty

WHEN I WENT in to the New Adelphi Club that Friday evening, ostensibly to pick up my pay packet for the Saturday before, I'd been racking my brains for a way to get the subject of the security tapes into casual conversation. In the end, I needn't have bothered trying to be so devious.

As I walked in through the back door, the capture and subsequent arrest of Tris Shelseley was the main topic under discussion. I knew there was something up the moment I arrived by the way most of the security team stopped talking and turned to stare at me.

'What?' I demanded. I paused, hands on hips. 'Do I have something in my teeth?'

'Most of that Shelseley bloke's knackers, by all accounts,' one of them said with a grin. 'Proper little terrier, aren't you, Charlie.'

I pulled a face, dumping my helmet and gloves down on the bar top where Gary was sorting bottles into the appropriate return crates. I should have taught a class at the Lodge earlier that day, but it hadn't seemed right, in the circumstances, so I'd rung round as many of my regular students as I could and cried off. I couldn't help wondering, once the news about Tris got out, whether any of them would want to go back there, in any case.

Dave, I noticed, was eyeing me now with that sly smile. He was sitting in the midst of the group, relishing his role as storyteller, and I wondered what embellishments he'd added to the tale. In particular, about his own role in the proceedings.

'So, they reckon it's the same bloke as got that girl who was here as well, eh?' another of the doormen commented. 'He must have been here that night, then. We might all have seen him.'

'Well, they'll know better in a few days, won't they?' I said casually. 'When they've had chance to look at the tapes properly.'

It was Len, bless him, who bit. 'What tapes?' he growled.

'The ones from the internal security cameras,' I supplied helpfully. I was watching Angelo while I said it, but he just bent his head to light a cigarette with calm deliberation. Then he looked at me through the smoke, slowly, almost in challenge.

His lip was inflamed, I noticed, and remembered what Dave had said about Marc hitting him. There was also a nasty cut just below his right eye, just scabbing over, which Dave hadn't mentioned. Was that work, I wondered, or pleasure?

'But they said there wasn't anything on those tapes,' Dave objected.

I remembered Terry's client book. There wasn't a DC for Dave Clemmens listed under the number for the New Adelphi, which surely meant that, if Dave wasn't hiring out blue movies from Terry, he was in the clear. There was a GB, on the other hand. Gary Bignold, possibly? There was no L either, although I didn't know Len's surname. I made a mental note to ask Marc later, just to be sure.

For now, I shrugged as though the whole thing was of minor importance. 'Don't look at me,' I said. 'All I know is, they're bringing in some spotty computer nerd tomorrow to look at that weekend's tapes, and he reckons he can get something out of them. Why don't you ask the boss about it, if you're so worried?'

'He's not in tonight,' Len said, grumpy. He pointedly checked his watch. 'And that doesn't mean you lot can slack off. Get your kit and let's get this place opened up on time, right?'

I hung around while everyone collected their walkie-talkies, then moved up one of the spiral staircases and made my way surreptitiously to the manager's office on the second floor.

I tapped on the locked door. Marc came to let me in, then went back to his desk to complete a phone call. He waved me into one of the leather chairs opposite, and I took it to wait until he'd finished.

Behind him was a bank of half a dozen television monitors, showing black-and-white pictures from the security cameras around the club. The outside ones covered bits of the car park, including the main entrance, and round the back where I'd tucked the Suzuki away.

I looked round the office as Marc talked on. It was furnished in a fairly spartan, modern style, limed oak cupboards and minimalist light fittings over abstract paintings. Through a partially open doorway I could see a private toilet and washbasin. Just so the manager didn't have to mix with the proles, not for any reason.

Marc's desk was large, with curvy sides and a fashionably modern matt-finish surface. The chair behind it was a high-backed leather swivel job, in the best James Bond villain tradition. There was a low suede sofa against one wall that looked like it had been designed purely for its stylish appearance, with no regard to comfort.

Over on the cupboards was a stainless steel coffee machine, with half a pot of coal-black liquid gently steaming. The smell of it was enough to set my mouth watering. I looked at it longingly and Marc caught my gaze.

He cupped his hand over the mouthpiece. 'Help yourself,' he murmured, smiling. 'Two sugars in mine.'

I poured for us both, discovering a small built-in fridge containing the milk behind one of the cupboard doors, like a hotel mini-bar. All mod cons.

Marc finished his call and sipped his coffee. 'So,' he said, 'Are we all primed up and ready?'

'I think so,' I replied. 'None of them seem to have cottoned on to the fact that you're here, and Len took the bait beautifully.'

Marc nodded.

'D'you think—if it is Angelo—he'll bite?' I asked, frowning. My nerves were jittering and I was so taut it was making my head ache.

'I don't see how he can't,' he said confidently. 'If he's been responsible, and he's got away with it so far, how can he fail to be burnt up by the fact that there might be some evidence he's overlooked?'

He put down his cup and moved smoothly round the desk, perching on it in front of me. His black suit and dark hair made him suddenly look like Lucifer. His fingers were cool on my face, making me jump. 'Don't worry, Charlie. If it's him—he'll come,' he promised solemnly. 'And if he does, we'll get him.'

I didn't reply to that, just drained my cup and put it back by the coffee machine. Marc went to check the office door was secured, removing the key from the mortice lock.

'Are you sure that's a good idea?' I queried as he dropped the key onto the desktop. 'What if he comes and tries the door, finds it's locked, and simply goes away again.'

'The office door is usually locked when I'm not here,' he said. 'It would be more suspicious for it not to be. Besides, Len leaves his keys in his locker. It wouldn't be that difficult for someone to get hold of them, if they really wanted to.'

I nodded, appreciating the logic. 'So, what do we do now?' I asked, on edge.

Marc turned off all the lights except a small desk lamp. 'Now,' he said, smiling whitely in the semi-darkness, 'we wait.'

WE WAITED FOR three hours.

Three hours during which time the clock slowed to half-speed, while my heartrate alternately over-revved or stopped altogether, in line with every unexpected noise from outside the door.

We heard the club opening up, the music getting under way. The melody was indistinct through the various walls and floors between us and the source. Only the beat of the bass came through.

It was enough covering noise for us to be able to speak in whispers to each other. We talked of something and nothing, nervously passing the time.

The security monitors showed groups of people arriving at the club doorway, being admitted. It wasn't difficult to recognise Angelo's shaven head and swaggering stance, even through the grainy distortion of the lens.

Peering closely, I could even see the marks on his face. I glanced at Marc's hands, relaxed on the arms of his chair, and wondered how much further he'd go to punish Angelo if he thought the man had crossed him.

I wondered again about that cut under Angelo's eye. I didn't think Victoria had managed to land a punch on him, more's the pity. I thought of the petite waitress and my thoughts hardened. Christ, the bloke was a complete bastard.

'He really isn't right for working the door,' I muttered.

Marc glanced sideways at me. 'He's a good man in a scrap,' was all he said, voice neutral.

'Yeah, I'm sure he is,' I agreed dryly. 'The trouble is, he probably started the fight in the first place.'

Marc opened his mouth to reply, but before he could speak something made me reach out and grip his arm, bringing a finger to my lips to caution silence.

He frowned at me, was about to question my action, when the noise came again, louder this time.

The unmistakable sound of a key being fumblingly slotted into the lock.

Marc's eyes narrowed and he was on his feet in a moment, moving stealthily to the shelter of the hinge side of the door. It looked strange to see him dressed like a city slicker, but behaving like a commando.

I joined him, trying to stay flat to the shelving unit.

Marc cupped a hand round my ear and whispered. 'You get the door—I'll take care of our friend.'

With only a fraction of hesitation, I nodded. I remembered the professional way he'd grabbed hold of Susie Hollins that night when I first met him. God, it seemed so long ago. I knew I'd feel happier tackling Angelo myself, if it was him, but now wasn't the time or the place to argue about it.

The door opened with agonising slowness. I felt Marc half-crouch alongside me, instinctively tensing his body without realising he was doing it. I knew I was probably doing the same. My blood was pounding so hard in my head I could hardly hear anything over the roar of it.

The door inched further open and a figure started to appear round the leading edge.

'Now!' Marc yelled.

I hit the door with my shoulder, slamming it shut. Marc went straight for the man who'd entered, body-slamming him low, taking him down hard and fast. I had a moment to admire the precise economy of his movements, then all three of us were on the floor.

The man didn't even get a chance to lash out. We had him face down in a flash, rearranging his nose into the pile of the carpet. Marc rammed the bloke's arm up behind his back so forcibly his joints cracked. I'm amazed he didn't fracture the bone.

As I got shakily to my feet, the adrenaline still pumping, one overwhelming realisation hit me.

It wasn't Angelo.

For a start, he had far too much hair. And the build was wrong. He was much too slight. Marc must have come to the same conclusion because he let go of his arm lock and punted the man over onto his back so we could get a better look at him.

'Bloody hell,' I swore. 'Gary?'

Marc's face closed in with an anger that was more frightening because of its apparent calm. He hauled his hapless bar manager to his feet and almost threw him onto the hard sofa. Gary cringed away from the pair of us, cradling his arm as though it didn't work any more. His colour was high and he looked close to tears.

'I don't suppose you'd care to tell us exactly what you were up to?' Marc enquired silkily.

'Nothing!' Gary protested, his voice high and whingey. 'I haven't done anything!'

Marc didn't bother with threats. He crossed the distance between them with deceptive speed and hit Gary with a considered and quite clinical blow to the face. I tried not to wince at the squelchy tear of cartilage.

Gary squawked and clamped his hands to his nose. Blood immediately started dripping out between his fingers. He automatically leaned forwards so it didn't ruin his evening suit.

I went into the bathroom and brought out a roll of toilet tissue. Gary didn't acknowledge me when I handed it over, just ripped off a dozen sheets and held them to his face. He was rocking slightly backwards and forwards, distressed and shocky.

Marc was sitting on the edge of the desk, watching him like a Rottweiler eyeing up a baby. He took advantage of Gary's distraction to wink at me, but I was too shocked to return the gesture, even though I tried not to show it. Marc had slipped so easily into the role of interrogator. Too easily for comfort, perhaps?

'Cut the crap, Gary,' he said coldly now. 'You're not entitled to keys for this office, and you know it. So what were you doing sneaking in here?'

For a heartbeat Gary gave thought to another lie. Marc only had to shift his weight towards getting off the desk for the other man's nerve to fail him. The menace he projected in that room was oppressive.

'OK, OK!' he cried, voice nasal and muffled. 'I came for the damned tapes! From the bloody security cameras.'

The words sent a chill washing down over me. I hadn't even considered Gary as a player in all this.

'And why would you want those?' Marc demanded softly.

'I, well, I—' He glanced from one of us to the other, but obviously didn't see a way out written in either of our faces. He swallowed convulsively, grimacing like someone trying to take a pill without water. The bleeding seemed to have slowed and he pulled the makeshift handkerchief away from his nose, heedless of the bits of fluffy tissue left adhered to the light stubble of his chin.

Marc sighed. 'Don't make me hurt you again,' he warned, sounding tired.

Suddenly, I remembered about all those not-quite-empty bottles Gary removed from the club bars, his uneasiness, and I put it all together.

'Why don't I help you out, Gary?' I suggested. 'Why don't I tell your boss about your little scam?'

His eyes widened, flickering apprehensively to Marc, then back to me. 'S-scam?' he tried. 'What scam?'

Marc's second blow landed deep into his solar plexus. Gary spent a couple of minutes doubled up on the chair, gasping and moaning. I twitched with the memory of the smoker's fist landing on my own body and scowled at Marc over Gary's wheezing head, but he just met my gaze levelly.

He didn't enjoy this sort of thing, I realised, not in the way Angelo would have done. It didn't please or excite him. It was just a job to be done, ruthlessly, efficiently, and he had no qualms about doing it.

And it worked. When Gary could speak again he didn't bother with any further denials. He launched straight into a full confession.

'All right, all right, I'll tell you all about it,' he said sullenly. 'When I've been bottling up the bars I've b-been—' his voice wavered, but he swallowed again, less awkwardly this time, and went on, 'I've been changing the bottles in the optics a bit early.' The last piece came out in a rush, as though saying it quickly would make it easier.

'A bit early,' Marc repeated. Something in his voice made me turn towards him. 'Every bottle, in every optic, on every change, throughout the club?' he queried.

After a moment's hesitation, Gary nodded. When Marc put it like that it started to sound like a major fraud. I had no idea about the price of spirits. With the exception of the occasional whisky, I was more of a beer drinker myself. I liked the odd glass of wine, but hated the pretension that went with it.

I suddenly remembered the price of drinks in the club, when I'd been that first time with Clare. It wasn't so much that Gary was robbing Marc of vast amounts, but he must surely have been curtailing his profits by quite a chunk.

Marc slid off the desk, dismissing with a contemptuous glance the way Gary shrank back away from him. He moved over to the coffee machine, pouring two cups and handing one to me. When he spoke again his voice was deadly quiet.

'And did you really believe, with computerised tills which record every drink, that I wouldn't notice?' he asked. 'That I wouldn't begin to wonder why the bar costs were higher here at the New Adelphi than at any other club I own? Why, miraculously, you didn't seem to be able to squeeze the standard twenty-eight shots out of a bottle that they manage everywhere else.'

The dismay flared in Gary's eyes. He had that trapped look, that look of someone who's slipped and slithered their way into deep trouble, rather than taking a calculated gamble. He knew that he was in way over his head, but there was still something that might drag him out of the slime again.

'He made me give him an alibi,' he said quickly. 'Angelo, I mean. The night that girl was killed—Susie. Angelo knew what I was up to and he said if I didn't cover for him, he'd drop me in the shit.'

He looked from one of our faces to the other, opened his mouth to speak, then wisely realised that anything he said would probably make things worse. He shut it again.

Marc sat down in his leather chair behind the desk. With his dark colouring and clothing he looked like a Mafia don. 'Just get out,' he said grimly. It sounded like as soon as Gary turned his back Marc was going to shoot him in it.

Gary got painfully to his feet. 'A-am I sacked?'

Marc tilted his head on one side and considered him, like something he'd picked up on his shoe. 'I don't think so,' he said, surprising both of us. 'Not this time.' He stood abruptly. 'But if you ever try stealing from me again, I'll finish you,' he said, his voice chillingly pleasant. 'You won't work again.'

He could have just meant 'in the licensing trade', but the way he said it made it sound like Gary's lack of employment would be caused by his sudden inability to eat solid food.

Gary stumbled out of the office, pulling the door shut behind him. For a moment there was silence.

Without looking at Marc I asked, 'So, how long have you known about Gary's little scheme?'

He smiled at me. 'Right from the start,' he admitted.

'So why did you let him keep doing it—keep robbing you?'

'I've found staff are notorious for it,' he said, as though it was obvious, 'but if they're putting their energies into comparatively small-time stuff, like Gary was doing, at least they're not ripping me off in any bigger way. I look upon it as an acceptable level of loss.'

'And what about this business of him giving Angelo an alibi for the night of Susie's death. What on earth is that all about?'

I was about to ask more, but suddenly Marc's body stiffened and he came out from behind the desk at a half-run, his eyes fixed on the other side of the room.

I snapped my gaze in that direction, just in time to see the door swinging ajar.

Marc reached it first, wrenched the door open wide, and we hit the corridor outside almost together.

It was empty.

'Shit!' Marc snarled. 'There was somebody there!'

We charged down the short corridor, turned the corner and kept running. The noise of the music was getting louder with every step as we made the main body of the club.

The corridor brought us out onto the gallery area near the entrance, overlooking the lower dance floor. The place was already crammed. It was impossible to tell who had been lurking outside the office door.

Marc swore, slamming his clenched fist down onto the rail in frustration.

I scanned the room again. My eye was caught by a still figure among the swaying of the clubbers and I froze.

Angelo.

Over on the other side of the gallery, near the entrance, he was standing looking directly across at me. The swollen lip was distorting his mouth into a scornful Elvis-type sneer.

Or maybe that was just Angelo's intended expression. That he knew I'd tried to trap him. And had failed.

With a final, arrogant glare, he turned away, disappearing into the crowd.

I realised I was grasping the railing so hard my knuckles were showing white through the skin. When I unclenched them, I was annoyed to find my hands were wavering.

I'd made my move and, with a shiver of foreboding, I knew the next one was probably down to Angelo.

All I could do was wait for it to happen.

I LEFT SOON after that. There wasn't much point in staying, and neither Marc nor I had the stomach for going on with it.

I rode the bike home through the gloomy streets, feeling as though I was permanently living my life in semi-darkness. I hate the winter, with its slow mornings and quickened afternoons. It doesn't matter how much they fiddle with the clocks, there just isn't enough light to fill a day.

I pulled the bike off the road onto its usual slab of concrete and killed the motor. I was bone tired, and not really concentrating, which was pretty dumb, when I come to think about it now.

I pulled my helmet off, set the bike securely on its side-stand, and climbed off trying to ignore the protesting of my muscles. It wasn't until I was crouched by the rear wheel, and was halfway through threading the roller-chain round the swinging arm that I heard it.

Slowly—too slowly—it seemed, I realised that I could hear someone breathing. And it wasn't me.

I got to my feet gradually, tense, started to turn. There was movement in the shadows, close to the wall of the building. My heartrate stepped up, but I wasn't prepared for the sheer intensity of the emotion that rose up when the figure of a man emerged fully into the light.

'Hello Charlie,' Tristram said.

Twenty-one

A SENSE OF pure panic assaulted me, ripping and tearing. *Oh God, I couldn't see his hands. What did he have in his hands?* I stumbled back against the bike, nearly rocking it off its stand. *Where was the knife?*

With something like a moan, I reached down and grabbed one end of the unfastened roller-chain, yanking it out of the spokes of the rear wheel like a whip. It wasn't the most wieldy weapon, but it was hard and heavy, and it was all I'd got. It would have to do.

For a moment, Tris stood and watched me in a kind of suspended hush. It was cold enough to be able to see his breath. Then he did the most extraordinary thing. Possibly the last thing I was expecting him to do.

His face crumpled, his shoulders began to shake, and he burst into helpless, racking floods of tears.

My first instinct was to offer comfort, but it didn't last long enough to translate into movement. I hardly needed to remind myself that Tris had stalked, and raped, and murdered. He was not the gentle man I thought I knew. He was a stranger. A monster. Maybe this was the ploy he'd used to get Joy to drop her guard. How he'd lured Susie to her death.

'Tris,' I said carefully, loud enough to be heard over his wretched sobbing. 'What are you doing here?'

He looked up at me for a second, too distressed to speak. He cut a desolate figure, with his ragged haircut and old-fashioned parka. Slowly, his tears subsided into a soft gulping. He lifted his hands to wipe his nose and eyes. Hands, I noted with relief, that were empty.

'I came to s-say I'm s-sorry,' he said at last. 'The police released me. You can call them if you like,' he added, reading my mind. 'I'm not on the run or anything stupid like that.'

'Why did they let you go?'

'Because I didn't do it,' he said simply. He shrugged at my doubtful silence, as if he hadn't really expected me to believe him, and I was surprised to find how much that hurt. 'They have a certain amount of forensic evidence, so I understand. I gave them sample of everything they could possibly wish for,' he shuddered delicately at the memory, 'and it didn't match. So, they let me go.'

I took a little while to digest the information. Tris wasn't the rapist. A sense of utter relief washed over me, but was short-lived in its duration.

'So what on earth were you doing skulking around the grounds in a balaclava?' I demanded.

Tris gave me a sad smile, and stuffed his hands into the front pockets of his coat. 'Making the most stupid and ridiculous mistake of my entire life,' he said, heartfelt.

I recognised the truth of that, felt some of the tension unwinding out of my shoulders. 'You'd better come up and tell me about it,' I said.

He looked pathetically grateful to be invited in, but even so, as I finished securing the bike, I made sure I turned my back on him as little as I could get away with. He seemed to understand my circumspect behaviour, not following me too closely up the wooden staircase, and standing well to one side while I unlocked my front door.

In the flat, I switched on the lights, and noticed for the first time how pale he was, with the exception of his nose, which had bloomed in the sudden warmth. He made no move to take his coat off, and he was shivering.

'How long have you been waiting?'

'I don't know,' he said. 'They let me go late this afternoon, and I went straight to see Ailsa. Then I came here. Four, five hours. Something like that.'

He hadn't, I deduced, spent long with his wife. 'How has she taken all this?' I asked.

'Badly, as you'd expect. In fact, when I arrived she and the girls were busily throwing all my stuff onto a mammoth bonfire in the garden. My books mostly.' His voice was neutral, but he was struggling not to cry again.

I thought of all those poetry first editions, and my heart went out to him. Ailsa had a huge capacity for compassion, but I could also well believe that she had an equally elephantine memory when it came to being wronged. And Tris had wronged her, of that there was no doubt.

I made him coffee, sat him down on my sofa, and gradually, in fits and starts, he told me all about it.

'I was eight years old when my father died,' he began. 'He was a wonderful man, but he had very set ideas about the role of women. He would never have approved of my mother having a job, but charity work was all right. So, she got herself involved with battered wives, and when he died she turned her whole life over to the cause. My life, too.'

He stuck his nose into his coffee, took a slurp, then went back to thawing his hands out round the mug. 'I suppose I was spoilt as a child,' he went on. 'I was the only one, the centre of attention, but after my father died the house was suddenly constantly full of children who all needed my mother's attention much more urgently than I did. I grew up on the sidelines, ignored.'

It sounded almost petulant when he said it, but I could still appreciate the sense of desolation he must have felt. There are more ways to abandon your children than to leave them wrapped in a blanket on someone else's doorstep.

'There's never any peace in the house,' he said. He stopped, sighed, and searched for a better way to explain. 'You have a baby of your own, and for the first year or so you expect sleepless nights, and constant crying, but they grow out of it.' He looked at me, and I saw the pain in his face. 'There have been babies crying in that house for nearly thirty years. I just wanted a little peace.'

Understanding arrived slowly, like a murky sunrise. 'So you thought you'd frighten them away,' I said, taking a sip of my own coffee.

Tris ducked his head, and an ugly red stain crept up the side of his neck. 'When Susie Hollins was—killed, we realised that both she and that other girl had been at the Lodge at one point or another. Some of the girls made the obvious connection, and they started to get nervous. Two of them left that night, you know.'

I nodded, but I remembered Nina's paralysing fear and had to bite down on my anger. 'Didn't you know how much you'd terrify them, doing what you did?'

He shifted in his seat, awkward. 'I suppose so, but it just seemed the easiest way. I knew Ailsa would never be persuaded to just close the place down. She'd see it as betraying the girls, throwing them out on the streets. But, if they left of their own accord, and the house was empty, then she might think differently.' He gave me another forlorn smile. 'I never meant to hurt anyone.'

'But it was you we saw, running away that night Joy was murdered, wasn't it?' I said. I have a clear memory for shapes and faces. The way someone moves is as distinctive as a signature. The masked figure who had shoved Victoria aside that night had been the same we'd captured. I would have staked my life on it.

'I found her,' he admitted, swallowing back the tears again. 'I was trying to help her when that girl saw me and started screaming. I-I panicked. I knew I couldn't explain what I was doing there, so I just ran. I'm so sorry.'

I didn't say anything to that. Joy's injuries had not been survivable, no matter how quickly we'd sent for the paramedics. I didn't think Tris's actions—or lack of them—had contributed to her death, but I couldn't find it in me to offer words of consolation, even so.

'So it wasn't you who rang to threaten me that night?' I asked.

He shook his head straight away. 'No, of course not. I never meant anyone any harm, Charlie,' he said, trying not to plead. 'You have to believe that.'

I asked him if he had anywhere to spend the night, but I confess I was relieved when he said that a friend out in Quernmore had offered use of a sofabed.

I called Tris a taxi. He wouldn't stay inside until it arrived, saying he preferred to wait in the street. I let him out in silence, unable to condemn or condone.

At the top of the stairs he turned back, and his voice when he spoke held the plaintive note of the eight-year-old boy he'd once been. 'They took away my home, Charlie,' he said. 'I just wanted it back.'

After he'd gone, I sat for a long time on one of the flat slate window ledges, hugging my knees to my chin, and staring out through the darkened glass without seeing anything beyond my own reflection.

So, Tris wasn't the cruel murderer I'd been so quick to believe he was. The relief was tangible, like a taste in the back of my throat. I was just disappointed in myself that I hadn't wondered more, doubted more. It didn't matter that the evidence against him had seemed so overwhelming.

I'd spent some time sitting there, in silent contemplation, before it registered with a creeping chill that this hadn't solved any of my problems. Far from it.

If anything, it had made them worse.

THE NEXT MORNING I woke up instantly panicky, heart screaming into the red line like a two-stroke motor with its throttle jammed wide open. When I opened my eyes I found I was already tensed upright in bed, shivering from the chill of the cold air on my sweating skin.

For a moment I froze, uncertain whether I'd really heard the noise that roused me, or if it was part of some instantly forgotten dream. I scrambled out of bed on legs that weren't quite steady, pulling on a towelling robe, and padded through to the lounge.

There was an untidy sprawl of mail across the doormat. I thought I heard footsteps retreating down the stairs, and when I crossed quickly to the window I saw the postman emerge from the doorway below. The sudden surge of relief left me feeling limp.

I went to pick up the mail, but my hand stilled. For a moment I couldn't escape the memory of those tumbled letters in Terry's hallway. The way they'd spilled down over his corpse. They might even have been delivered by the same postman.

I took a deep breath and gathered the mail quickly, almost trying not to look at the mat for fear that I'd see an inert trainer-clad foot at the end of rumpled jeans. I didn't, of course, but what I did see turned out to be much more frightening.

A plain white envelope.

It had obviously been hand delivered, pushed furtively under the door rather than dropped through the letterbox, because one corner had slipped under the doormat itself. I'd already got it in my hand before it dawned on me what it might contain.

I carried the letter over to the coffee table very carefully, at arm's length, as if it might explode at any moment. Placing it down gently, I went and fetched a pair of the thin latex gloves I normally use for cleaning the bike.

I checked with my fingertips for lumps, bumps or wires, then opened the letter with great delicacy, as you would if you were handling some long-buried ancient parchment. If this was a begging letter from some local charity, or a note from my landlord, I was going to feel the biggest fool going.

Inside was a single sheet of A4 paper, good quality laid stuff, folded with origami precision. I eased it flat, trying not to touch more than the edges. In the centre were two brief lines of bold type.

YOU WANT TO PLAY?
GAME ON

I put the letter down onto the table slowly, my mind numb. I didn't realise I'd got my hands to my face until the rubbery smell of the gloves started making me feel sick. Maybe I would have felt that way in any case.

So, the killer possibly suspected that the police were keeping an eye on my phone. Maybe he'd been watching this place the day that Superintendent MacMillan called round. Maybe he just knew the score because he'd done this sort of thing before. So, he'd decided to pay me a visit.

The sudden thought that the man who'd viciously raped and murdered Susie Hollins and Joy had been right up to my front door while I slept was too much. I lurched for the loo, and spent some time there, not exactly engaged in thoughtful meditation.

When I straightened up and studied my reflection in the mirror over the sink, a haunted face met my gaze. My skin looked white and stretched tight over my bones, emphasising the last vestiges of the bruising round my cheekbone. My eyes seemed sunk back into their darkened sockets, like a heroin-chic model. There was no getting away from it. I looked like shit.

I peeled off the gloves, washed my hands, then scrubbed my teeth thoroughly. For someone who's not normally sick, I'd spent far too much time throwing up lately. I didn't want to end up needing expensive dental work because the acid from my stomach had rotted out my teeth like an anorexic.

As I staggered back through to the lounge I wondered long and hard about calling Superintendent MacMillan. I thought about it, dug out the card he'd given me with his phone number on it, turned it over in my hands.

Trouble was, I'd been pretty badly mauled during our last encounter. I'd no desire to be accused of fabricating the note myself in order to reinforce what MacMillan saw as a dubious claim that I was under threat.

I had a growing conviction that the man they were after was Angelo. It had to be. Who else was there? Unfortunately, I didn't see that the Superintendent was any more likely to take my word for it now than he had been the first time I'd mentioned Angelo's name.

Besides, the police had already dismissed him as a suspect on the strength of an alibi I now knew to be bogus. The trouble was, Gary's admission had not been extracted without a certain amount of coercion that would probably make it totally inadmissible in any court in the land. And MacMillan was certainly not likely to take my word for it.

Then I remembered. Tris had told me that the police had enough forensic evidence to eliminate him from the suspect list as soon as they'd run the right tests. If I could get Angelo taken into custody, for whatever reason, they'd have their chance. I was sure MacMillan's finely-honed instincts would do the rest.

The only thing I could think of straight off was the possibility that Angelo was involved with supplying drugs at the New Adelphi. Trouble was, if I just made an anonymous tip-off about chemical activity at the club, it was likely to get raided, and that meant all the staff would probably be arrested. *All* of them. Including me.

I knew Marc had sworn to deal with Angelo in his own way over that matter, but the stakes had risen since then. Way risen. And besides, if Angelo was also guilty of rape and murder, I wanted more than the beating Marc was likely to arrange for him. I wanted justice.

And I wanted it quickly.

I looked again at the sheet of paper on the table. I couldn't do nothing. Couldn't let him stalk me, torture me with threats and promises. I had to act. Had to! If I wanted to stay sane.

If I wanted to stay alive.

And if I wasn't prepared to place my trust in Superintendent MacMillan and simply tell him the whole story, right from the beginning, I had to do it some other way.

I picked the phone up, dialled a number, listened to it ringing out. On the tenth ring, just as I was about to give up, it was answered by a voice thick with sleep.

'Hello?'

I ignored a pang of guilt when I realised it was only just past eight-thirty, and on a Saturday morning at that.

'Hi, it's Charlie,' I said. 'Yeah, I know what time it is, sorry, but listen, I need to ask you the most enormous favour. Are you into clubbing?'

WHEN I WENT in to work at the New Adelphi Club that evening, my nerves were racked so tight I could hardly breathe evenly.

Burning a hole in the back pocket of my jeans, wrapped in a plastic bag, was the threatening note I'd received that morning, together with MacMillan's card. I thought I might need both before the night was out.

We went through much the same ritual I'd been through the Saturday before. The security team all clipped on their walkie-talkies, straightened up their bow ties, and disappeared into their own areas of responsibility.

Len came stamping in, glowering at everybody, but particularly at me, it seemed. I wondered if I was just being paranoid, or if Angelo had told him about my failed attempt at entrapment. If he had, I wasn't sure if that meant things had just got safer, or twice as deadly.

I had plenty of time to think about it. The evening started painfully slowly, but put on speed and weight with an air of overwhelming menace, like gathering storm clouds in the tornado belt.

I went through the motions of my job, patrolling the ladies' washrooms, breaking up a cat-fight between two girls who'd just found out they'd both arranged to go home with the same bloke. I thought they should have been tearing lumps out of him, not each other, but I kept that opinion to myself.

I tried taking the quieter of the two out of the fray, but that didn't quell things. I ended up propelling the more aggressive of the pair towards the door. She was making an almighty racket, and grunting with the effort of trying to embed a four-inch spiked heel into my shin along the way. It probably made me not quite as gentle with her as I could have been.

We waltzed our way to the main entrance, and I gave her a bit of a push-start into the car park. She reeled away, dishevelled, screeching her thoughts on my parentage and sexual preferences to the world at maximum volume.

I listened with polite disinterest. When I'd had enough I turned away from her, catching Angelo and Len studying me with an intensity that jarred my already edgy nerves.

'What?' I demanded, my voice harsher than I'd intended.

Len shook his head and stalked away. Angelo flipped his cigarette end spinning into the darkness with a deliberation that was almost an insult.

'Getting a taste for this, aren't you?' he said. 'Thought you would. Hasn't taken you long, though.'

I was saved having to think of a suitably cutting reply by the arrival of a new group of punters. Among them was a bearded man with baby seal brown eyes. He looked nervous and fidgety, eyes dancing everywhere, fingers never still.

Angelo took one look at him and wanted to see the contents of his pockets. In the top one of his shirt was a twist of paper containing a couple of elongated yellow capsules.

'Oh yeah, and what's this then, sonny?' Angelo sneered.

'They're for me sinuses!' the man protested, none too convincingly.

Angelo just smiled and confiscated the pills, but waved the bearded man into the club.

Just then, my walkie-talkie crackled. 'Charlie, it's Len. The ladies' on the upper floor need checking. See to it.'

I thumbed the transmit button and murmured my agreement.

Angelo's leer was still in place as I made my way back inside. I gave him a stony glare, which he ignored. I was halfway along the entrance passage when I heard him on the radio to Len, with the obscure instruction for him to go to seven.

I'd heard Angelo and Len trade the same message the week before, and hadn't thought any more about it. Now it gnawed at me like a starving rat.

I made my way through the growing throng and caught up with the bearded man in the general press by the top of the stairwell on the first floor.

'So,' I asked him quietly, checking round for signs that any of the security staff were watching our exchange. 'What were those pills?'

Sam gave me his most innocent smile. 'They really are for my sinuses,' he said, 'but with the name scratched off. It's not my fault if King Kong back there didn't believe me.'

'I'd be careful who you say that to,' I told him. 'I know he's just a big ape, but if the real King Kong gets to hear about it, he might well be insulted enough by the comparison to sue for defamation of character.'

Sam just grinned. I'd warned him about the dress code, and he looked surprisingly smart in black trousers and a reasonably stylish shirt. It made a change to see him out of leathers.

I told him to keep his eyes peeled and to make out like he was a man in need of replacement chemicals, then climbed another few flights of stairs to find out what Len was after. Not a lot, as it turned out. I got the distinct impression I was just being given the runaround.

By ten-thirty my head was starting to ache with frustration. My eyes were twitchy from constantly scanning for some clandestine movement in the crowd. No one seemed to be very interested in selling anything to Sam other than over-priced drinks.

I dropped in past one of the bars, seeing Gary in his usual frantic guise. He looked up and caught sight of me, a mixture of fear and loathing on his face. The savagery of it took me aback. Christ, I didn't make him steal from his boss. I just helped catch him at it.

Dave was in his usual position, nodding so hard to the beat of the music that it moved his whole body, like the tail of a dog who's really happy to see you. He was wearing skin-tight trousers and another high-necked jumper, stained dark with sweat.

He also gave me a cooler glance than was his norm. I tried to work out what I'd done to offend him. Maybe he'd been told about my part in Gary's disgrace. I'd stepped over the line from being one of the gang to teacher's pet. It was like being in No Man's Land.

I kept my eye on Angelo as much as I could, but he barely shifted from the door, apart from a couple of short breaks. Well, I suppose you can't crack heads all night without a rest.

Just when I was starting to think I was utterly wasting my time, that I'd dragged Sam out on a wild goose chase, he brushed past me deliberately in the crowd.

'Bingo,' he muttered out of the side of his mouth.

I fought hard not to show any reaction to the news, just followed him casually into a quiet corner.

'What?' I demanded. 'What's happened?'

He looked around, then fished a couple of tablets out of his top pocket. Small round, white pills, slightly bulbous on the sides, without sharp edges. There was an impression stamped into them, but the meaning wasn't clear. It didn't take a genius to recognise Ecstasy.

'Where the hell did you get those?'

He smiled at me. 'I have to admit it's a slick operation,' he said smugly, basking in the fact he'd got my full and undivided.

I rolled my eyes. 'You're the one who's going to need an operation unless you tell me who dealt you those,' I growled.

Sam, however, wasn't to be deflected from his moment of glory. 'You see, they take anything you try and bring in with one hand,' he said, 'and sell you something else with the other hand. Very neat.'

'Sam—' I warned.

He must have seen the glint in my eye, because this time he cut to the important bit. 'The bald-headed bloke on the door took my own stuff off me, then one of the other penguins sidled up to me and offered me something for the weekend,' he explained.

'Just like that?' I asked, my face blank with something approaching disbelief. 'He offered you drugs right there in the middle of the dance floor?'

Sam gave me an old-fashioned look. 'No, not just like that,' he said. 'He made some casual remark about me looking like the type of bloke who wanted more than a quick drink in a place like this.' He laughed. 'To start with I thought he was offering me a woman.' He flashed me a quick grin and I realised that to Sam, this was all an adventure. A game. He hadn't seen first-hand what the penalties were for losing.

Terry had, though. Seen and suffered them. I came down hard on that line of thought. It was too dangerous to my resolve.

'And?' I prompted now, sharply.

'Well, we went up to the gents' on the upper dance floor, and by this time I was thinking, no he isn't going to offer me a woman, he's going to offer me a rent boy.'

He paused for me to make the appropriate response to his mind-bendingly funny joke. I glared at him in the sort of silence that has rocks in it.

He swallowed and went on. 'Anyway, once we're inside he asks me what I want, tells me how much it's going to cost me, and shoves me in to one of the empty cubicles. He tells me to stay put for a minute—and it was only a minute—and when he comes back and opens the door, there they are. Cost me a packet—about twenty percent over market value, I reckon, but then I suppose they have got a bit of a captive audience.'

'How come you're such an expert on Ecstasy prices all of a sudden?' I challenged.

He grinned at me again. 'Come on, Charlie, I work at the university. The place is crawling with students. You work it out.'

'So who was it?'

'Well, we didn't exactly swop names and addresses so we could send each other Christmas cards,' he said with a sarky tone to his voice.

I wanted to scream at him, but settled for grinding my teeth instead. 'OK,' I said with remarkable calm, 'tell me what he looked like!'

Sam shrugged. 'Like a bouncer. I don't know—a big bloke in a dinner suit.'

Terrific. That description fitted most of the lads working security. 'But not the same one who was on the door?'

He shook his head emphatically. 'Oh no, definitely not.'

Not Angelo then. Christ, just how many of them were in it with him?

'Can you point him out to me?'

Sam grinned again, said no problem, and we moved back towards the main body of the club. I'd already got a sneaking suspicion about who he was going to tag, but I needed to have it confirmed.

It didn't take us long to find him. We were moving along one of the galleries when Sam nudged my arm and pointed down to the next level where one of the security men was leaning on the rail, watching the milling clubbers below him.

'There you go,' Sam said. 'That's the feller.'

'Are you sure?' I asked, not really doubting him, but wanting to be dead certain.

'Absolutely,' Sam verified. 'Why—who is he?'

'That,' I said grimly, 'is Len, who's head of security. He's the one who's supposed to be in charge of keeping the drugs *out* of this place.'

I suppose, really, I should have known. Only the previous week Len had told me of his involvement in a roundabout sort of a way. 'Nothing—*but nothing*—goes on in this club that I don't know about!' he'd said. 'Clear?'

Oh yes, it was clear now. He and Angelo were in it together. In it up to their necks. In it plenty deep enough to resort to murder to keep Terry from exposing their activities. And to have me worked over as well.

So where did Susie and the rest fit in? Maybe they were just a diversion—a little side-line that Angelo was running for his own amusement.

I couldn't prove any of that. Not without the forensic evidence that was out of my reach. For now, the drugs would have to do.

I pulled Sam away from the balcony rail, so we were out of Len's possible sight.

'Listen, Sam, I want you to get out of here—right now,' I said, trying to get urgency across to him without the fear. I fished Superintendent MacMillan's card out of my pocket and slipped it into his. 'Call MacMillan, tell him about the drugs. Tell him if he wants to catch the guy he's after for the murders he needs to come down here mob-handed. Tell him,' I added, taking a deep breath, 'that I'm going to go and try and find those drugs before Len or any of the others has a chance to destroy them.'

Sam took all this in open-mouthed, but wisely decided against long questions. 'OK,' he said. 'I've borrowed a mate's car tonight. It's only a shitty old Peugeot, but he's left his mobile phone in the glovebox. I'll call 'em from the car park.'

'Just make sure none of the security lads see you doing it then,' I cautioned.

He sobered when he realised there wasn't a hint of humour in my voice, then nodded, swallowing, and started to turn away.

'Oh, and Sam?'

He paused, turned back. 'Yeah?'

I mustered a smile that didn't reach my eyes. 'Tell MacMillan he'd better hurry.'

Twenty-two

I WATCHED SAM leave the club, feeling a certain sense of relief as he cleared the front door without any apparent attention from Angelo or the rest of the security crew. I wasn't aware until he'd disappeared from view that I'd been holding my breath.

I picked my way back upstairs, feeling as though I'd got a neon sign over my head announcing my intentions. I suddenly couldn't think how to act natural, relaxed. My movements felt jerky, lacking in coordination, and I'd begun to sweat.

My nerve almost failed me. I stopped climbing on the next floor, breaking off my ascent to needlessly check round the bar area and washrooms. I glanced at my watch. When had Sam left the club? I cursed the fact I hadn't made a note of the time. How long would it take MacMillan's men to get here? More to the point, would they come at all?

Either way, I had to find that proof.

Unable to put it off any longer, I hit the stairs, reached the top level. I paused there for a while, peering over the balcony down to the floor below. I caught a glimpse of Len marching through the crowd, but he didn't look like a man in pursuit.

Even so, I couldn't help but wish he was further behind me.

I observed the gents' washroom Sam had indicated for a few minutes, mentally counting people in and out. When I reckoned it was about empty, I pushed myself upright away from the rail, and covered the distance to the door.

It was instinct to glance furtively round me before I went in, but I forced myself not to do it, not to look as if I was doing anything out of the ordinary. If you've got enough front, you can get away with anything.

Inside, the gents' was larger than the ladies' washroom on the same floor. The walls were completely covered with dark blue tiles, lit by low voltage spots sunk into the ceiling. I walked quietly past a row of uninhabited urinals to my left, with sinks beyond. Two big square pillars spaced along the centre line of the room helped support the roof. I checked carefully that there was no one lurking behind them.

There were no cupboards under the sinks, and no obvious breaks in the grouting round the tiles to suggest a hiding place. I thought of the ceiling, but when I looked up all I saw was solid textured plaster. No lift-out panels. Besides, there was no overall lock on the door to the gents', and I didn't think Len would want to be so exposed if anyone came in unexpectedly.

To my right was a row of numbered cubicles. They looked much more promising. I made my way along them, pushing the doors open carefully as I went. The cisterns were all enclosed in the tiled wall behind each toilet bowl. Just above, though, was an access hatch about eighteen inches square. I was sure I was getting warmer, but I could tell by the layers of undisturbed paint that this one probably hadn't been removed since the club was refurbished.

I tried the next, but that was the same. I was halfway along the row when the cubicle door nearest to me opened and a man walked out. I had to bite down hard on the startled shriek that nearly burst from my lips. To be fair, he looked as surprised as I did.

'Are you in the wrong place, or am I?' he asked.

I tried a casual smile. 'Just a security check,' I told him as cheerfully as I could. 'Wouldn't want you walking out of here with anything unsecured, now would we?'

He left quickly with a worried expression and I swore under my breath. If he went and complained to Len or any of the staff about them sending a woman in to check the gents' I was going to be in deep trouble.

I quickened my step. It wasn't until the last cubicle that I saw what I was looking for. I dodged into it quickly, shooting the bolt across behind me. The bolt was a flimsy-looking affair. A hefty shoulder to it would have popped the mounting screws from their chipboard holes like a fat man's shirt buttons, but it was better than nothing.

This time, in contrast to the bolt on the door, the panel on the back wall was held in place by a heavy duty lock. It didn't strike me as the type that could be picked easily, even if I was equipped or qualified to try. Without the right key I was going to be knackered before I began.

The smell from the toilet was making me feel vaguely sick, but maybe I would have felt that way in any case. I knew Marc had the cleaners round regularly, and wondered what it was about the male diet that could reek so badly at the other end. Perhaps, in prehistoric times, they'd used it to mark their territory, like tomcats.

I pulled my Swiss Army knife out of my pocket and pondered over which of its attachments would be best suited to the job of breaking and entering. Unfortunately, that was one purpose for which the Swiss Army didn't seem to have designed a specific tool.

There was a short, narrow blade on the back of the knife that I think is for cleaning mud out of the tracks of your hiking boots. It looked sharp and pointed enough for me to be able to use it to make an initial hole in the door just above one of the hinges. I hesitated a moment before digging it in, tapping the panel lightly with my knuckle. If it was made out of metal I wasn't going to be able to do more than scratch the surface. All that would do would be to alert Len that someone had cottoned on to his stash.

Oh, to hell with it! With a deep breath I carefully lined the blade up with the hinge and leaned my weight into it. It actually sank in much easier than I was expecting. Despite the valuable nature of the contents, the door was only made from bog standard eighth-inch plywood.

I quickly replaced the tread scraper with the shorter of the two knife blades, cursing the fact I hadn't bothered sharpening either of them for months. In the end, the slightly serrated edge of the nail file proved to be the most effective.

Even so, it was slow work. Every time someone came in to the washroom I had to stop, tensing myself into silence and praying that no-one would get inquisitive enough to peer over the top of the partition from the next stall. I wished I'd had the forethought to scribble 'Out of Order' on a sheet of paper and stick it to the outside of the cubicle door.

The earpiece of my radio crackled a few times, but fortunately it was other instructions for other members of the security brigade. Nobody, it seemed, needed my services for anything in particular. Good. As long as no one knew I was missing, they wouldn't be looking for me.

I worked on frantically, scuffing and scraping my hands on the rough edging I was opening up. My finger ends, still sore from my Spiderman impersonation down the wall of my flat, soon started to bleed. I mopped them up with loo roll from the dispenser and kept going.

I had made a hole nearly two inches long running down next to one hinge, but the panel was being surprisingly stubborn about giving way completely. It wasn't big enough to get my shoulder to, and the cubicle was too small and too awkward a space to kick at it with any degree of success.

I knew if I punched it, I was just going to break my knuckles. I couldn't afford to risk an injury. At the back of my mind was the knowledge that, if Len discovered me here, doing this, I was going to need to be very much intact to stand any chance of holding him off.

Although I was waiting for it, when the call came over the radio, it made me jump.

'It's the police! We're being fucking raided!' Angelo's voice, crackling with sheer rage. 'Len, go to seven, mate! Go to se—!' His transmission was abruptly chopped off. I could just imagine the reason for it.

I fumbled with the bolt on the door. The last thing I wanted now was to be trapped in an area too small to defend myself. The bolt stuck and as I tugged at it I was rocked by a moment of sheer panic.

I stopped, took a breath. Calm down, Fox! I couldn't let my fear incapacitate me. I let go of my anger, my fright, breathing out fully. If I wasn't calm and focused, I was nothing. I tried again. The bolt slid straight back without resistance.

As I stepped out of the cubicle into the empty washroom, I passed the number on the door almost at eye level. Number seven. I did a double-take.

Seven!

'*Go to seven, mate!*' Angelo had said. I'd always thought it was a preset channel on the walkie-talkies, but I was wrong. It was just

Angelo's way of telling Len that someone wanted to buy drugs from him.

In this case, I didn't think MacMillan's men were interested in a purchase, but Len would know he had to get rid of the stuff. Quickly. Oh shit.

I'd just time for the realisation to hit. Not enough to form a plan of attack, to decide a strategy. I'd just time to whirl round to face the outer washroom door as it burst open.

It flew back so hard on its hinges there was a sharp crack as the wood twanged against the frame and gave way. Len stood in the doorway, chest heaving from the exertion of getting here so fast. There was a sheen of sweat on his face, and his gaze when he caught sight of me was savage.

He advanced into the room, past me, slammed open the door to cubicle number seven. Saw, in an instant, the damage to the panel. Knew, just as rapidly, that it was down to me. He whipped back to face me. Fury and hatred began emanating from him in tangible waves, furring the air like a jet exhaust.

I knew we had a couple of minutes at the outside before MacMillan's boys reached the upper floor. No doubt that was why Len choose this particular place of concealment for his stash. Unless the drug squad had taken to helicopter assaults from the roof tops, any entry at ground level gave him more than enough time to flush the lot.

You don't have to take him out, I told myself as I dropped instinctively into a combat stance, you just have to slow him down until the cavalry gets here.

It wasn't much of a comfort.

It was crystal clear from the outset that there was going to be no chance for negotiation here. Len wasn't interested in any verbal attempt I might make to calm him down. He was too busy winding himself up to explode.

He started to swear. Spitting words bitter as poison, spilling over his teeth in a gush like blood from an arterial wound. If he could have struck me down just with the vitriolic force of them, I would have been dead already.

I wanted to recoil on a reflex, to cringe away from him, but to do that would have been disastrous. I stood my ground, faced him off, watched the chain reaction of his temper form until it was toxic in its intensity.

The stand-off didn't last long, a few seconds maybe. Then he snapped.

Len charged at me with a primeval roar. Two hundred and twenty-five pounds of solid muscle, shaped from years of cracking skulls, backed by a whole supermarket full of dirty tricks, fuelled by a vicious wrath.

I knew I couldn't retreat, knew I had to go forwards to meet his attack, but I daren't lose my control, or I'd lose even the sliver of a chance of winning.

The lessons I'd learned with the Scouser and the smoker in my flat still clung painfully. If I got the opportunity, this time I wouldn't hesitate.

I blocked his first punch as it sliced towards my face, jarring my forearm hard enough to feel the bruises forming instantly. Ignoring the discomfort I kept going forwards, moving in close and grabbing for his neck. Control the head and you control the point of balance. Where the point of balance goes, the body will follow.

The muscles in Len's neck were thick as a Pit Bull's, leading into massive shoulders, but I gouged a knuckle deep into the side of his chin and their resistance simply crumbled. I twisted his head round as though I wanted to rip it apart from his body and slammed him into the nearest pillar hard enough to burst the tiles.

The man's constitution must have been phenomenal. He rocked once, then straightened up, shook his head to clear it, and stormed me again. The blood dripping from the ceramic splinters in his forehead was a minor annoyance to him.

This time when I blocked Len's first swinging right, he didn't make the same mistake twice. He followed it up with a fast left to my ribs that ripped the air from my lungs in an explosive gust. I tried desperately to stay on my feet, allowing myself to reel backwards, absorb some of the impact.

Len sensed first blood. He came in like a dervish then, fists flying. I went down under the onslaught. I had no choice. I crashed backwards into the door frame, bumped past it, and went sprawling onto the floor of the club outside the washroom.

For the moment any attempt to re-group was impossible. I just rolled with the pounding, and tried not to let him hit me anywhere that was going to do me serious damage. The pain was coming from so many different directions it seemed to totally surround and immerse me.

As I fell back, Len pursued, lips drawn away from his teeth in a deadly grimace. His eyes had turned feral. His control was gone, shattered into fragments.

That was what defeated him.

He wasn't bothering to defend himself properly now, didn't feel the need to keep his guard up. As he leant over me, I lashed out for his throat. It was a lucky contact, and lighter than I'd hoped, but it halted his next assault. I twisted onto my side and swept his legs out from under him.

As soon as he was on the floor, I brought my heel down brutally into his exposed groin. Most men would have been out of the fight right there and then. Not Len. He howled like a scrapyard dog, starting to push himself off the ground with one hand, grasping for me.

I kicked his arm out from under him, aiming for the elbow joint, connecting with a dull crack. He folded. It sent a fierce and bitter spike of triumph lancing through me. I knew the feeling was wrong, knew I should feel nothing but a calm consideration of my leading options and next moves. But I couldn't help it.

I reverse scuttled out of range on my backside and was up on my feet in a flash. Len's jaw presented itself, just perfectly aligned and I pulled back my fist to strike, to finish this. It was a punch I knew would knock him cold.

I never got to land it.

With a shocking suddenness, my arms were banded to my sides by hands like mechanical steel clamps and I was hauled away from Len. I could hear someone baying in protest, a primitive shriek of sheer anger and frustration, the pack hunter with the fallen prey, denied the kill. At first I didn't recognise the source. Finally, it registered that it was me.

The policemen who had hold of me didn't so much put me down as throw me onto the floor. I quickly found myself face down without the opportunity to resist, my arms wrenched behind me. I felt cold circles of metal as the bracelets of the handcuffs were ratched tight onto my wrists.

If it took two of MacMillan's men to restrain me, it took four to control Len. They jumped on him with ruthless efficiency, not careful where they put their boots and fists to bring him down. He didn't go without a fight and, in the end, they were forced to settle for cuffing his hands in front of him, just to get him secured.

I let my eyes close briefly, weak with defeat. I was bone tired, my whole body felt pulpy from the beating I'd only been partly successful in dodging. One eye was swollen, my back was giving me hell where I'd hit the door frame and my left knee was on fire. I didn't even remember getting that thumped. Thank God it wasn't the right one or I'd never be able to kick-start the bike.

'Well, well Miss Fox,' said a man's voice from somewhere way above my head. 'When I asked you to call me if you had any more contact with him, I was talking about threatening phone calls,' he went on, annoyance making his voice more clipped than usual. 'This wasn't quite what I had in mind.'

I opened the eye that wasn't throbbing, leaving the other one to rest. All I could see at my level was a pair of good conservative black leather shoes. I watched them approach another couple of steps with mild interest, following the neatly creased trousers upwards past the suit jacket to the tilted head at the top. It seemed a long way away and much too small for the rest of his body, especially his feet.

'Hi Superintendent,' I mumbled, my throat raw. 'It's nice to see you, too.'

MacMillan jerked his head to someone out of my range of vision. The handcuffs were released and my arms, suddenly unsupported, flopped back to my sides. It seemed to take a long time before they'd obey the usual commands to lever my torso into an upright position.

One of the policemen who'd jumped me at least had the grace to offer me a hand up. It took my brain a moment or two to recognise him as Tommy, looking pale with excitement. I wondered briefly if he'd ever been on a drugs raid before.

'What the hell did you think you were doing, young lady?' MacMillan demanded quietly. When I looked at him fully, I could see the anger pinching his nostrils, flattening his mouth into a narrow, almost lipless line. He treated me to withering scrutiny.

'Finding you some proof,' I tossed back at him, trying not to sway on my feet.

'Did it not occur to you that we might have been in the middle of a highly sensitive investigation of our own,' he grated out carefully, as though speaking to someone of limited intelligence. 'That your interference could have put it in jeopardy, if not ruined it altogether.'

I'd had enough. I hadn't expected a commendation for stopping Len destroying the evidence of his own drug dealing, but I hadn't expected a damned lecture either.

'Up yours, MacMillan!' I snarled. 'While you were meandering along in your own sweet way, people were threatening to kill me. Excuse me if I didn't sit around twiddling my thumbs while I waited for it to happen.' I waved a hand towards the gents' washroom. 'You look in cubicle seven in there and you'll find a locked panel—Len should have the keys on him—behind which you'll find enough drugs to start a bloody dispensary, *if* you're interested!'

MacMillan paused, considered, then signalled two of his men to go and check. We all watched them go, and missed the fact that Len had also been listening to the conversation.

Now he seized the chance presented by the drop in numbers to swing his handcuffed hands, club-like, into the gut of the policeman next to him. The man didn't so much fall as plummet. He ended up on the ground, curled foetal and gasping.

Len nimbly hurdled his prostrate form and headed straight for my throat, hands clawed and reaching.

I elbowed the Superintendent out of the way and jumped forwards to take the offensive stand. This time I was going to make sure Len went down hard and fast. And that he stayed there!

Then MacMillan shouted, 'Gas him!' and my brilliant plan went all to shit.

In a practised instant Tommy brought his hand up easily from his belt, aiming a small aerosol. It was the smell of the propellant that was over-powering and horribly familiar. Reflex made me stop breathing, spinning my head away, squeezing my eyes tight shut. Len's fingers just brushed my throat as I tumbled past him. As for me, I missed my intended target completely, but at least I managed to avoid the spray.

Len wasn't so lucky. He got the full brunt, flat in the face. He made it worse for himself by having his eyes and mouth wide open, drawing in breath to yell a defiant battle cry as he went. The effect as the fine mist hit him was electrifying.

His eyes and nose began to stream instantly, like he'd been drenched with water. His face bloomed into redness. In half a second he was on his knees, hands over his face, contorted and screaming.

I ended up on my hands and knees almost alongside him, but he was too wrapped up in his own torment to care. He'd lost all interest in whatever nasty end he'd been planning for me, utterly compelled by the burning agony of his skin, the acid scorching of the delicate membranes.

The British police use CS gas in a six percent solution, stronger than the stuff they'd practised on us in the army. And that was more than enough to fell an ox, to turn grown men into cowering wrecks. I'd just caught a by-blow and I knew I'd got away lightly.

Tommy helped me to my feet for a second time, and told me not to rub my eyes. I fought hard against the swell of nausea that rolled through my body. I reckoned I was probably in enough trouble without adding 'vomiting on a police officer' to the list of charges.

The other men returned with a clear plastic bag filled with goodies from Len's store cupboard. MacMillan looked at them for a long moment, then turned back to me with something akin to respect in his muddy green eyes.

He put his hand on my arm, gave it the faintest squeeze. It was probably as near as I was going to get to thanks or apology. He let his hand drop and turned away from me. 'Right, bring the van round and let's get laughing boy here taken down to the nick before he really loses his temper and—'

'Would someone mind telling me what the fuck is going on in my club?'

Marc's voice cut through the assembly like a samurai sword through silk. He advanced smoothly and took in the scene. The numbers of police, MacMillan's unspoken authority, Len's incapacity, the damning bag of drugs.

Maybe I only saw the fractured moment of hesitation because I was looking for it, searching for it. Hoping against hope that I wouldn't see it.

Marc turned to me. Handsome, successful, sleek and charm-ing Marc, who'd rescued and bedded me. And I'd rolled over like the stupid gullible little fool that I was.

'Charlie! Christ, are you OK darling?'

I moved towards him. He held his arms out to me. There was relief in his eyes. I could see his mind beginning to whirl, searching for an escape, an excuse. In his mind, Len was already convicted, jettisoned, betrayed. He was clinging to the chance to move forwards, move on.

My eyes were locked on a point to the side of Marc's beautiful lean jawline. As my fist landed I must admit it made a very satisfactory smack. I connected plenty hard enough to make my already bruised hand sing.

Marc's head snapped round to the side and he staggered backwards, pupils dilating, glassy. Only shock kept him on his feet. One of the coppers had to grab his arms, steady him, or he would have ended up on the floor.

MacMillan rounded on me, pinned me with an astounded glare. 'What the—?'

'If you've got a van on the way, you may as well take him, too,' I said, my voice clear and cold as Christmas. I nodded to Marc, then to Len and the drugs. 'He told me once that nobody with any sense tried to bring anything in to his club, and he was right. They didn't need to, because he knew, better than anyone, that they could buy whatever drugs they wanted once they were here. He's the real one behind all this, not Len. Isn't that right, Marc?'

Twenty-three

'I THINK,' MACMILLAN said grimly, 'that you'd better start at the beginning and this time, tell me everything.'

We'd moved from the club proper to the manager's office where I'd set my abortive trap for Angelo. Len had been carted away, still yelling, but Marc had been handcuffed and brought with us. After recovering from the shock of being clouted so unexpectedly, his face was utterly unreadable.

Now MacMillan took the chair behind Marc's desk, subtly supplanting his authority. He leaned his elbows on the desk top and linked his fingers together with great precision.

'Well, Charlie, I think it's safe to say that you have our undivided attention.' He'd dropped the Miss Fox again, I noted wryly.

I swallowed, easing myself into one of the leather chairs opposite. They'd given me a cold cloth to hold over my swelling eye, but I had the mother of all headaches lurking just behind it. Everything hurt. I flexed my right hand warily. The knuckles had stiffened until I couldn't clench them without feeling as though my skin was going to split.

I glanced at the two men opposite. Both had their eyes fixed on me, expectant.

'It started with a man who wanted so desperately to escape his roots that he lost his sense of morality somewhere on the journey,' I began, staring Marc straight in the face.

He made a growl of protest, shifted his weight as if to stand, but MacMillan stilled him with a small movement of his hand. 'Sit down, Mr Quinn,' he warned softly. Marc subsided, looking disturbed with himself that he should have obeyed the Superintendent's quiet command.

'When you've no money, no qualifications and are given no quarter by anyone, drugs must seem a very attractive proposition,' I went on neutrally. 'Where better place to sell the more up-market stuff—Ecstasy, cocaine, speed—than in a nightclub? After all, the boys on the door will make damned sure nobody brings their own in, so they're a captive market, a ready audience. And it was all going swimmingly until Angelo Zachary stepped out of line.'

Marc's head came up. He was too proud to beg me to stop, but there was the fear in his eyes now, and maybe even a trace of hurt surprise, too. I closed my heart to the fact I held his future, his freedom in my hands, and pressed on.

'Angelo, you see,' I told MacMillan, 'has some nastily sadistic tendencies. When he's not playing SS man here, he likes to watch videos designed for a very specialised taste—that's when he's not beating up his girlfriend, of course.'

I glanced at the Superintendent, not entirely sure what I'd see, but both he and Marc were sitting impassive. MacMillan gestured silently for me to go on.

'Unfortunately, they don't come cheap, and Angelo hired out rather a lot of these videos, from a guy called Terry Rothwell.' The policeman tried not to show he had just snapped to attention, but I caught the betraying twitch of his hands.

'He had so many, built up such a tab, that when Terry eventually insisted he settle up, Angelo couldn't do it. So, he faked a robbery here at the club. He nicked a few expensive items of office equipment, like a lap-top computer, making sure others took the blame, and paid his debt that way.'

That was one thing Marc hadn't figured out. Not until I'd opened up to him that night in the flat. He'd agreed to set the trap for Angelo not because he wanted to see if he'd killed Terry. Oh no, he already knew all about that. He wanted to know if Angelo had committed the far more serious crime of lying to him.

'The only trouble was,' I continued, 'that I think the lap-top had been used to record information about the drugs being dealt here, and although Angelo wiped the data files, he thought he'd get cute and not tell Terry about the password. If he hadn't done that, Terry would probably never have looked any further into it. As it was, he just made it more suspicious. And Angelo wasn't to know that Terry would have a friend who had another friend who was good enough with computers to retrieve the files.'

'You.' MacMillan murmured the single word as a statement, not a question.

I nodded briefly, wanting to keep Sam out of this. 'I didn't know where he'd got the damned thing, but when I told him what data we'd managed to restore, Terry obviously decided to have a go at a little light blackmail.'

It was MacMillan who nodded now, understanding. 'And when he tried that, Angelo killed him,' he said, almost to himself. He moved quickly to his feet. 'I'll make sure we've got Zachary.' He frowned as he noted my more obvious injuries. 'Will you be all right on your own here with him for a moment?'

'I expect so,' I said. Even in this state I was fairly sure I could handle a handcuffed man on my own. It seemed so wrong to see Marc restrained in that way, as though all his self-confidence and polish was slipping away.

MacMillan nodded, as though he hadn't really doubted that I could, and hurried from the room.

As the door closed behind him I glanced at Marc, taking up the thread again for his benefit, and feeling I could speak more freely now. 'The problem was, when Angelo went round to see him, Terry didn't have the lap-top to give back to him, not with any persuasion. It could be that Angelo had meant to kill him anyway—he's certainly the type—or maybe he just lost his rag. Whichever way it happened, afterwards Angelo panicked, and he came back to tell his mate, Len what he'd done.'

I remembered Dave's report of the conversation he'd overheard. Len telling Angelo that he'd gone too far this time, that he didn't think he'd be able to cover up for him. At the time I'd thought Angelo was dealing drugs off his own bat. Now I knew different.

'Of course, the first thing Len did was turn to you.' I flickered my gaze towards his face, but was not rewarded with a response. 'Len thinks you walk on water,' I said. 'He would follow you to hell and back and not turn a hair.' I paused, then couldn't resist adding icily, 'It's a good job, because after this, he's probably going to have to.'

Marc's face twisted then. He must have known what was coming, but had still hoped against hope that I would veer off course at the last minute. I watched the realisation form for a few moments before I dug the knife in.

'He knew you would take care of the problem, and that problem was me. I suppose I should have known,' I murmured. 'The first time I met you, you gave me fair enough warning. If you work for me, you don't break the rules, you said. Not for anyone.' I shrugged. 'I didn't realise you meant *your* rules. I unwittingly stepped on your toes, so you sent the boys round. Nothing personal, that's just the way the game goes. Simple, really.'

He spread his hands to the limit of the handcuffs' chain, then let them drop back into his lap. 'I couldn't just let it go, Charlie, you must realise that.' I was surprised to hear a note of pleading in his voice. 'I never dreamed you'd get so involved, would take it so far. I told them to go easy on you. They didn't listen.'

I gave a short, harsh laugh. 'And I'm supposed to be thankful for that? Oh you told them to go easy on me all right, but not *so* easy. You didn't bother to tell them that Charlie wasn't a bloke's name, did you? What's the matter, Marc, afraid your boys wouldn't have the stomach for beating up a woman? Well, at least they didn't quite manage to stick a knife in my guts, like poor old Terry got from Angelo, now did they?'

He tried to run an exasperated hand quickly through his hair, nearly smacked himself in the face when the other one came along with it. Even his coordination seemed to have gone.

'That was a mistake. Angelo went too far.' He stopped, took a breath, started again. 'All I wanted to do was scare you off, stop you from following this course. I should have known that you wouldn't scare so easily.' He tried a half-hearted smile, rose and made as if to move towards me. 'Charlie, it doesn't need to end like this.'

'That's plenty far enough, Marc.' There must have been something in my face. He searched it for a long moment, then advanced no further.

'The really ironic thing is,' I went on, 'that Terry didn't have anything to threaten you with anyway. All we were able to get off that damned computer were a few file names and one list of dates. There was nothing that couldn't have been explained away or swept under the carpet.' Marc closed his eyes as if asking his God to help him.

'I don't know how Terry got to know about what was going on here. Maybe Angelo offered him something in the beginning as a trade. Terry wouldn't have accepted it. He was very anti-drugs.

'Whatever,' I continued, 'Terry had enough to drop a few of the right words onto Angelo. Did he ask for money? A charitable donation, maybe? That would have been like him. Striking a blow for freedom, he would have seen it as. A bit of private enterprise.'

'Charlie—' Marc protested.

'You took great pains to retrieve that computer, didn't you?' I ploughed on as though he hadn't spoken. 'That was why you sent your thugs after me. They obviously had orders not only to get the lap-top back, but to persuade me not to go to the police as well.'

I put a trace of emphasis on the word 'persuade', just as I could imagine Marc had done when he'd originally briefed his boys. I understood the reason for the delay coming to get me now. He'd had to bring them in from one of his other clubs specially. And he couldn't take them away from work on a Saturday night, now could he?

Marc didn't deny it. A part of me still hoped that he would, that I was wrong. He sat looking defeated, shoulders slumped, and didn't even meet my eyes. I hardened my heart along with my resolve, and kept going.

'What I really can't forgive, Marc,' I said acidly, mildly gratified by the fact that my voice didn't waver, 'is that after you'd let your boys work me over, you took me back to your hotel and gave me a working over of your own. Was that all part of the careful plan? The softly softly approach just in case they hadn't been able to beat enough out of me?'

His head came up at that, eyes haunted, face bloodless. 'Charlie, I swear I never meant for that to happen either.' His voice was a whisper, truth cutting through like daylight. Not that it mattered, I suppose, whether he was lying or not.

Not any more.

'Are you so cold,' he demanded, 'that what we had together— what we shared together—really meant nothing to you?'

I'd shied away from pursuing that subject too closely. The wound was still too raw. Instead I met his gaze levelly. 'Not when you saw it as nothing more than a means of control over me,' I said, 'no it didn't.'

251

The silence was still hanging between us when the door opened and MacMillan reappeared. His sharp eyes flicked between us, as though expecting to see fresh blood on one or the other.

'Well,' he said, 'you didn't hit him again, then.' I couldn't tell from his tone whether he was relieved or disappointed.

'Did you get Angelo?' I asked.

He shook his head. 'Not yet, I've got my men checking, but it's chaos out there, I'm afraid.' He peered at me closely, seemed to read my mind, and sighed. 'What else haven't you told me?'

I hesitated before I spoke. 'Yesterday we tried to lay a bit of a trap here for Angelo. Both Marc and I wanted to confront him about the lap-top, but not for the same reasons, it seems.'

MacMillan perked up again. 'What happened?'

'We didn't catch him, but we did discover that his alibi for the night Susie Hollins died was false,' I said. I took a deep breath. 'I think he might be your serial rapist.'

I explained about Gary's confession. 'Angelo must have thought it was a close call. This morning he left me this.' I peeled the anonymous note I'd received out of my back pocket and handed it to MacMillan. He looked at it without removing it from the clear plastic bag I'd put it in, his expression sober.

'You need to be very, very careful on this until we're sure we've got him in custody, Charlie,' he cautioned. 'He's a very dangerous man.'

'No shit, Einstein?' I bit back, unable to stop the rising sarcastic inflection. Careful? Right now I didn't even have the energy to go carefully down a flight of stairs.

MacMillan frowned at me and was about to speak when there was a knock on the door and one of his plainclothes men leant round the edge. 'Sorry to interrupt, sir,' he said respectfully, 'but there's no sign of Zachary. Apparently when we showed up he belted one of the bobbies good style and did a runner. I've got a car on the way to his last-known address now.'

'He was going out with one of the bar staff, a girl called Victoria,' I informed him. 'She might know where he'd have gone. You can't miss her—she's the one Angelo's been using for target practice.'

The man nodded without asking for further explanations, and ducked out again.

MacMillan nodded, satisfied, and got to his feet. 'I think you can leave things solely to us from now on, Charlie,' he said firmly. 'I'll have you escorted home and get a WPC to stay with you until we've got our hands on this Angelo character.'

'But can you at least tell me if that fits?' I demanded. 'If there's any evidence to link Terry's death with those of the two women?'

The Superintendent wasn't to be drawn. 'I'm sure you understand that I can't say anything that might prejudice ongoing investigations,' he said, falling back on that old fob-off line.

I sighed, resentful. A couple of uniforms arrived to conduct Marc to the waiting van, but as they took him away I stepped in front of him. There was one last question I had to ask.

'Why, Marc? Why did you do all this?'

He paused. 'Why?' he repeated, his voice vibrating with the same anger that suddenly lit his eyes. 'Like you've just so accurately reminded me—I was born in a slum, Charlie. Everything I have, everything I am, I created myself. I worked for it, fought for it, every step of the way.'

His carefully modulated accent was dissolving, the flat vocal tones of his long-suppressed Manchester beginnings seeping up through the cracks. 'Who are you to judge me when you were brought up in comfort, luxury even,' he jeered. 'You've never had to live day by day with hunger, fear, desperation.'

'That's true,' I admitted, 'but that doesn't excuse what you've done, Marc. Making other people desperate, and hungry and afraid doesn't make it right. Plenty of people have escaped from poverty without resorting to dealing in drugs to do it.'

'Oh yeah?' he flung at me. 'Name one!'

'That's enough,' MacMillan put in with that same measured quietness. He nodded sharply to the coppers and they resumed their escort duty. He put a hand on my arm. 'Are you sure you're OK? Would you like me to get one someone to give you a lift home?'

I thought of the Suzuki waiting in the car park and shook my head. The ride would do me good. I planned to take the long way back to Lancaster. I was weary to my bones, but I knew I needed to get the cobwebs out of my head before I stood a chance of sleep.

Besides, I realised as I watched the strange trio passing through the doorway, with Marc irrevocably lost to me the prospect of going to bed no longer held quite the same appeal.

SURPRISINGLY PERHAPS, I slept deep and untroubled that night. At around quarter to eight I woke with no nightmare sweats, just a vague sense of deep unease.

I climbed stiffly out of bed and pulled on my towelling robe, shuffling into the lounge. I registered without undue amazement that there was a small blonde policewoman dozing on my ripped sofa. I left her to sleep and headed for the shower.

I showered carefully, inspecting the new bruises that were mingling sociably with the fading old ones. My eye was puffy and tender and my back ached like I'd been doing twelve hours of manual labour. My hand had been so sore last night on the ride home that I could barely operate the front brake lever. I'd had to rely on the foot-operated rear brake to do all the work.

I dressed in jogging pants and an old T-shirt, then moved through to the kitchen, filling the filter machine. I think it was the smell of fresh coffee brewing that finally brought my companion round.

She sat up, doe-eyed with sleep, and looked round groggily. The change in attitude set off the sort of racking cough only committed smokers have first thing in the morning. When they haven't had the first cigarette of the day to bump-start their lungs. If she thought she was going to light up in here, though, she had another think coming.

MacMillan had introduced her last night only as WPC Wilks who, he declared somewhat cryptically, was going to look after me. She'd climbed into a panda car and patiently followed my meandering course along the seafront to Hest Bank before doubling back to Lancaster.

Once we'd arrived she hadn't tried to make our relationship any less formal, standing over me while I chained the bike down at the rear of the building. She took up station in the lounge when I went to bed, and now she was fully awake, she was sturdily back on duty again.

I had a sneaking suspicion Wilks was there to keep an eye on me as much as to protect me. She must have been two inches shorter, and weighed down with her Kevlar vest and bulky uniform. I tried not to let stereotyped prejudice colour my view of her. After all, clipped to her equipment belt she had the same aerosol spray of CS gas they'd used last night to such effect on Len. I dare say Angelo wouldn't prove any more immune.

It was clear, though, that the Superintendent didn't think Angelo would be stupid enough to come back for me. They were obviously expecting him to be halfway to the other end of the country by now, lying low.

I remembered the phone call, and the note, and I didn't share their confidence.

Wilks unbent enough to accept a cup of coffee, taking it Turkish—black with three sugars. She asked me if I minded her smoking, but took my solid refusal without offence.

I found her presence disconcerting, without really knowing why. I forced myself to go through some stretching exercises to try and loosen up my aching muscles. Wilks watched me with a polite expression on her face, as though I was performing some bizarre ritual.

'Did you know half your back's gone purple?' she remarked now.

I turned my head, surprised to see her staring slightly wide-eyed, and realised that my T-shirt had ridden up to expose some of the results of last night's activity.

'Yes,' I said curtly, pulling the cotton material down again.

She looked about to say more, but there was a robust knocking on the door. Wilks crossed to it, studying the visitor through the Judas glass for a few moments.

'It's an oldish-looking feller,' she said after a few moments, adding, businesslike, 'Would you come and see if you know who it is before I open the door?' I took her estimate of age with a pinch of salt. She didn't look like she'd yet escaped her teens, so anyone over thirty could well qualify for that description.

I took her place at the Judas glass. It only took a second to identify my caller. It was just the shock of recognition that delayed my response-time. The man knocked again, louder this time, with a hint of impatience.

'Well?' Wilks demanded. 'Do we let him in or not?'

'I suppose we should do,' I said slowly, reluctantly. 'Seeing as he's my father.'

I stepped back and left Wilks to admit him, looking all official. My father reacted well to having his daughter's door opened by an officer of the law. But then, we had been through something like this before.

'Charlotte,' he greeted me impassively. Eyes the same colour as my own studied the contusions on my face with professional detachment. I saw them shift downwards, as though calculating what other injuries lay beneath my clothing. I could almost hear his mind ticking over probable cause, course of treatment.

He looked the same as ever. Thinning grey hair cropped close to his scalp, skin tanned from three foreign holidays a year. He was wearing a good if rather funereal suit, topped by an impeccable raincoat, and carrying a leather dispatch case.

He could easily have been mistaken for a retired army officer. Major at least, but more like lieutenant-colonel. Matey enough with the lower ranks to earn loyalty rather than just expect it, I considered. And remote enough to order them to their deaths without a qualm.

Wilks broke in to our mutual visual assessment, cheerfully offering my father coffee, calling him sir.

He thanked her gravely, then returned his gaze to me. I waved to the sofa and, after a moment's hesitation at the prospect of placing himself on something with such a motheaten appearance, he removed his raincoat and sat.

'I take it,' he said, choosing his words with care as he checked the crease in his trousers, 'that there have been further developments since we last spoke.'

'You could say that,' I returned with equal caution.

Wilks reappeared with the coffee and then hovered, looking uncomfortable. 'I don't suppose you would be compromising your orders if you went to make a check on the stairs and left us to chat for a while, would you?' I asked her.

She smiled, looking suddenly human, and made for the door. I could see her brightening at the prospect of the day's first delayed fix of nicotine.

My father waited until she was gone before he slid the dispatch case onto his knees and unbuckled its leather straps. He pulled out three slim files and stood the case back on the floor.

'I didn't think it was wise to discuss these while your little friend was around,' he commented. 'Particularly as officially *I'm* not supposed to be in possession of them, let alone be showing them to you.'

He handed me the files. For a moment I stared at the stamp on the front that identified them as the property of a pathology lab in Preston. 'Are these what I think they are?'

He inclined his head in agreement, suddenly—painfully— reminding me of Marc. 'Results of the post mortem examinations on the three people you mentioned,' he supplied. 'It took me a little while to locate them. Suspicious deaths aren't dealt with at Lancaster. Those are the full reports,' he added. 'Would you like me to go through them and give you the layman's précis?'

I resisted the urge to bite at him and acknowledged that he wasn't being condescending. Left to my own devices I probably wouldn't be able to make out a single useful piece of information.

I gave in, not very gracefully, and he opened the first file. 'If we take the male victim first,' he said, his voice coolly unemotional, as though we were discussing the weather. 'This is a fairly straightforward case of disembowelment. Apart from numerous superficial defence wounds, there was a single large incision to the abdomen. Death was caused by massive trauma to just about all the major organs, blood loss, and shock.'

'Even I could spot that one,' I pointed out.

He stilled. 'You saw the body?'

I realised I'd just made a mistake, but covering it up now was going to be difficult. 'Yes,' I said shortly. 'What about the others?'

He continued to stare at me for a moment longer, then consulted his other files. 'The two girls were killed by the same man, without question,' he said. 'DNA evidence confirms it, not to mention the *modus operandi*. It seems he raped them both at knife-point, probably inflicted some of the injuries seen on the head and neck at the same time. Then he cut their throats. The first girl—Susie—was subjected to a longer, more sustained attack. Her facial injuries are more severe. The second victim was dealt with much more hurriedly, and she managed to scratch her attacker. Skin and hair samples were recovered from under her fingernails.'

I sat for a few moments digesting what he'd just said. I vividly remembered the marks on Angelo's face I'd seen the night we'd tried to trap him at the club.

Before, I'd assumed he'd either received that at the same time, or maybe Victoria had managed to land one on him during their bust-up. Instead, it must have been Joy who'd done him the damage . . .

'So Angelo did them all,' I murmured, almost to myself.

My father glanced at me. 'You think these three crimes were all the work of one man?' he asked. There was something in his voice that grabbed my attention.

Pulse jumping, I turned to him. 'Aren't they?'

He didn't answer outright, picking up the reports again. 'The knife wound to the man runs left to right, as you'd expect from an assailant who was right-handed,' he explained, 'but the two women were beaten on the right-hand side of their heads, and the initial wounds to the throat are also on the right side, indicating strongly that the rapist is a left-hander.'

He regarded me solemnly, and I didn't doubt for a moment that he was right. 'But if that's the case—' I began, my voice tailing off.

He nodded, following my line of thought. 'That's right. There are two very different men at work here, Charlotte. I'm afraid there's no doubt about it.'

Twenty-four

BY THE TIME WPC Wilks returned from her crafty cigarette, my father had gathered the post mortem reports back into their individual files, and discreetly returned them to his dispatch case.

There was more I wanted to ask him, but felt inhibited by the third set of ears. Wilks tried not to make it obvious that she was eavesdropping, but they were flapping, all the same.

My father left soon afterwards, giving me the sort of impersonal kiss on the cheek you would a maiden aunt. 'Take care of yourself, Charlotte,' he told me, his voice serious. 'And call your mother.'

'I will,' I promised, and realised that I probably meant it. 'Just don't tell her about—this,' I finished lamely. 'I don't want her to worry about me.' Or not to care, I added silently.

He nodded and agreed to keep my mother blissfully unaware of my troubles. I almost detected the faintest glint of a conspiratorial smile as he turned away down the stairs.

When he'd gone I sat on one of the window ledges, staring out across the river, lost in my thoughts. It was cold and windy, and by the look of the clouds sweeping across the sky, soon the rain would arrive to make it a hat-trick.

If Angelo had killed Terry, but not the women, then who *had* done it? And how had they got hold of my voice changer?

On the other hand, if Angelo *wasn't* Terry's murderer, then who was? I'd been so sure it was the same man that, suddenly faced with evidence to the contrary, I was utterly lost.

I tried to remember who at the club was left-handed, but even that fact escaped me. I couldn't recall ever having noticed Angelo writing anything down. He fought fairly evenly with both hands, and I'd never seen him pull a knife.

Somewhere, in the back of my mind, something rang a bell, but the harder I reached for it, the more elusive it became. Eventually, with a sigh, I gave up and climbed awkwardly off my perch. More coffee, that was what I needed.

I tottered through into the kitchen, my aching muscles protesting at the simple activity of refilling the filter machine. The rain started to fall, abrupt and heavy on the skylight over the sink. I had a sudden thought that there was no way I was going to ride up to Devil's Bridge with Clare if I didn't have to.

I moved back through to the lounge straight away, and picked up the phone, punching in Jacob and Clare's number.

Jacob answered, sounding slightly taken aback, but I jumped straight in with my excuses. 'Hi Jacob, it's me. Could you tell Clare that I'm not really feeling up to Devil's Bridge today? Would she mind if we called it off?' I paused expectantly. 'Jacob?'

'She's already set off,' Jacob said slowly, and I could hear the worry climb in his voice. 'She left a good hour ago. I thought the two of you would be up there by now.'

My mouth dried. 'Are you sure she was coming straight here?'

'Positive. Look, I'll have a run out in the Range Rover, just in case she's had a problem with the Ducati. You know what the electrics are like on these old Italian bikes. One drop of rain and they give up the ghost,' he said, trying not to sound as though he was panicking. 'If she turns up at your place in the meantime, let me know, would you?'

'OK,' I said, and rang off with my own anxiety rising to match. I had just started collecting my gear together when the phone rang again. Wilks looked up from her study of one of my fitness magazines, saw I was closer to it than she was, and went back to her reading.

I was half-expecting it to be Jacob again, to say everything was all right, but it was Clare herself on the line.

'Charlie?' To begin with I was too relieved to recognise her voice to realise that the pitch was slightly off and she sounded strained.

'Oh, hi, I was just about to come and look for you,' I babbled. 'Have you had problems with the bike? Have you rung Jacob?' I paused. Nothing. 'Clare?'

'Ye-yes, I'm still here,' she said jerkily. 'Listen, Charlie, there's someone here who wants to speak to you.'

'Clare, what's the matter?' I said, more warily now. 'You sound like you've been crying. Are you OK?'

But it wasn't Clare who spoke. Instead, I heard that metallic voice I'd come to dread.

'Your friend doesn't seem too happy to be here with me,' it said.

The fear laced down my spine, riffling the hairs, causing an involuntary spasm in my hands. 'What do you want?' I said sharply. Wilks looked up, but I ignored her inquiring glance.

'What do I want, Charlie? Now that's an interesting question,' purred the voice. 'I want vengeance. I want you naked and screaming under me. That's what I want.' The voice halted a moment, then delivered the death blow. 'But if I can't have you, I'm willing to take a substitute. Your friend Clare, for instance.'

'Go on,' I said tightly. There were bands round my chest. I couldn't breathe fully. I was gripping the phone so hard it made my hand pulse.

'The New Adelphi. Be here in ten minutes. If you're late, she dies,' the voice commanded, and even the voice changer couldn't disguise the swell of triumph. 'Oh, and Charlie, I know your place is crawling with filth at the moment, so make sure you wash before you come. Any sign of the boys in blue and she'll be dead before you make it through the door.'

'If you harm her . . .' I began, my own tone quiet but frozen. He didn't reply to that one. There was just a soft click, and he'd gone.

I put the phone down slowly, and turned to find Wilks at my shoulder, looking suspicious.

'That was him, wasn't it?' she demanded. When I nodded numbly, she turned up her lapel mic to her mouth and started to call her HQ.

It was enough to shake me out of my stupor. I grabbed her hand. 'What the hell are you doing?'

'Let go of me, Charlie. I've got to call it in,' she said.

'You don't understand. He'll kill her if your lot show up!'

She gave me a patronising look. 'We are trained for this sort of thing, you know,' she said. 'Did he tell you where he was?'

Anger star-burst behind my eyes. Without realising I'd done it, I'd shifted my feet into a stance, gauged the distances. 'Please,' I said. 'Let me handle it.'

She disregarded my final plea, so I hit her, just under her chin with my upswept elbow. Her teeth clacked together alarmingly, then her eyes rolled back in her head, and she started to crumple.

I half-carried, half-dragged the unconscious policewoman over to the sofa and left her lying on it. I suppose part of me was hoping she wouldn't hold it against me for ever, but part of me didn't care.

Within seconds I'd grabbed my jacket and helmet and pelted down the stairs to the street. The rain lashed down over my back, sliding under my collar. WPC Wilks's panda car was still parked three cars down, where she'd left it last night, but behind it, rear wheel slanted in towards the kerb, was Clare's Ducati.

When I looked, I found the bike's keys were still in the ignition.

Oh God, I'd never heard her arrive. He must have been waiting around outside the flat. Unwilling to come in and get me because of the obvious police presence. So he'd been waiting for me to come out. And he'd grabbed Clare instead.

Just for a second, I debated on taking the Ducati. It was far faster than the Suzuki, but an unknown quantity as far as handling went. I couldn't risk it.

I ran round to my own bike and slipped the chain. My only thought was that if I didn't get to the New Adelphi in time, Clare would be dead. And it would be all down to me.

I jammed my lid on, wincing as the side padding squeezed the swollen flesh round my eye, and kicked the Suzuki into life.

Usually I'm religious about letting the bike warm up, but this time it was in gear and moving the moment the motor caught and fired. I snapped the throttle wide open in the first three gears as I roared along the quay, short-shifting as the Suzuki squealed its outrage, the cold engine stuttering without revving freely to the red line.

There was hardly any traffic as I joined the main road and I gassed it again. As I hit the long tight left-hander over Greyhound Bridge on the river, I realised just how greasy the roads were.

The back end started to slide out. I daren't touch the brakes. I had to try and desperately control it on the power, feeding the throttle in evenly to compensate. By the time the road straightened out under the railway line, the speedo needle was wavering round ninety miles an hour.

By the college the cars were thicker, people on their way to the ferry terminal at Heysham, the supermarket or the Drive-Thru. I skimmed down the outside, slithering over the slick white lines, kicking up rooster-tails of spray like a water-skier.

I squinted through the rain blurring my visor, overtaking on the wrong side of a pedestrian refuge in the middle of the road when a truck blocked the left lane.

I braked hard for the first of the roundabouts, feeling the compression up through my arms, the pain in my hand. I ignored it, blanked it out. The Suzuki hit a trace of diesel on the second one, and shied sideways, damned near high-siding me into the back end of a lumbering Volvo saloon. It would have made an ironic change for a biker to have wiped out a Swedish tank, I suppose. I don't think the driver even noticed.

Come on, faster, faster! There's no clock on the bike, and the last thing I was going to do was take one hand off the bars to fumble for my watch. I had no idea how long it was since the phone call. It seemed like it had taken me hours to get this far.

I nearly didn't make it at all. A car on one of the side roads off Broadway misjudged the speed of my approach and pulled out in front of me. For once I didn't bother stabbing my thumb on the horn button, or gesturing rudely at him. I just swerved within a foot of the bumper and whacked the throttle against the stop, fighting to keep the front end in contact with the tarmac.

By the time I hit the car park at the New Adelphi, my heart was slamming like I'd just run a marathon and stinging beads of sweat were running into my eyes.

I kicked the side-stand down and jumped off the bike, yanking off my helmet. My left knee complained bitterly at the exercise as I ran for the main entrance on legs that trembled perilously.

When I reached it, the front door was firmly bolted and draped with 'police—do not cross' tape.

I stood back, wheezing, cursing, then jogged round to the back entrance. The tape had been pulled aside here, and the door was propped open with half a breeze block again, revealing a dark aperture beyond. The lion's den.

I took a deep breath, and stepped through the doorway, moving quietly along the corridor until it opened out into one of the main dance floors. My breath was coming in gasps now, my heart about to burst. I bent and deposited my helmet on the floor, putting it down without a sound.

As soon as I moved out onto the darkened floor, the big lights in front of the stage blazed on. I flinched back, couldn't help it, shielding my eyes with my hand.

The voice spoke from the other side of the lights, mocking. 'Ah, Charlie! Just in time. I do *so* love a woman who's punctual!'

The voice was undisguised and in a moment the tumblers of my mind turned, the lock shifted into perfect alignment, and the door swung open to reveal all the dark secrets that slithered inside.

'Hi Dave,' I said, admirably calm, coming further forwards. 'What have you done with Clare?'

'Oh she's here,' he said, disembodied in the shadows. 'I'm sure she'll be very relieved that you've come to give yourself up for her sake. Greater love hath no man—or no woman, in this case—than he will lay down his life for his friend. Isn't that the saying? Mind you, I thought there was something going on between you two the first time I saw you. I thought if I got lucky you might invite me to join in.'

I ignored the shudder of revulsion that twitched my shoulder blades. 'Dream on, Dave,' I said, my voice thick with contempt. 'That sort of thing only happens in the sick videos you used to hire out from Terry. Oh, I missed it at first. I was looking for DC, but he used to identify you by your job, not your initials, didn't he? Terry's client book was filled with references to DJ and I didn't spot it. I doubt the police will be so slow.'

He advanced then, jumped down off the stage with a supple agility that made the hairs rise on my arms. He had forsaken his polo-necked jumper in favour of a T-shirt. Where I expected to find the bruises round his neck from Marc's punishing grip, instead I saw two deep scratch marks, scabbing over. Oh Christ, Joy . . .

I'd missed that one, too.

He came towards me, menacing. I forced myself not to take a stance. I couldn't afford to provoke him without knowing where Clare was. What he'd done with her. To her.

Besides, gripped in his fist—his left fist, of course—was a survival knife with a metal-topped rubber handle, and a wicked eight-inch blade. I tried to avoid staring at it, but it pulled my gaze like a magnet.

'What's the fascination with me, Dave?'

'We're alike, you and me. Soul mates.' He circled me. 'I saw the way you dealt with Susie—so casual, so easy. And when I saw you fight those two lads that night in the club I knew, then,' he purred. 'I knew that you were just the same as me, Charlie. You had the power over them, and you revelled in it.'

I shook my head. 'I did what was necessary, Dave, and I didn't enjoy it,' I stated calmly. I turned to glance at him. At him, not the knife. 'You're forgetting a major difference between us. I didn't kill them. And I didn't rape them first.'

'You're a woman. Women are weak, stupid, vain,' he threw back at me. He paced then. Quick, short strides, agitated, speaking almost to himself. 'They promise everything with their come-to-bed eyes and their come-on bodies. Dressed up like whores, most of them. I see them!'

He spun back to me, his eyes fired. 'Every night, they come in here, flaunting themselves in front of me. Teasing. Look don't touch. They pretend they're going to come across, then they dance back out of reach. Make you beg for a touch, a taste. Well I wasn't going to let those little bitches taunt me any longer! I showed them who was in control!'

'So first you raped that young girl,' I said. 'Then you decided she didn't light your fire, so you raped and killed Susie. What made you pick her out, hm?'

He flushed, his cheekbones turning a dull red. 'She led me on, let me down, and then told that bastard boyfriend of hers all about it,' he complained. 'They were laughing at me!'

I remembered the insult Tony had thrown at Dave as Susie was dragged away. *You can shut up an' all, you dickless little shit!'* I wonder if he ever realised those careless words would be the cause of her horrific death.

'What's the matter, Dave, wasn't she very sympathetic when you couldn't get it up? Oh she probably promised you a quick one if you'd keep her winning the karaoke, but you couldn't do it without a fight, could you? So you waited until she'd been thrown out of the club and then you raped her instead. Nobody noticed you disappearing on your break, and you always changed clothes between sets anyway. It was the perfect opportunity. That was much more like it, wasn't it Dave?'

I allowed a sneer to creep in. 'Bit more of a thrill? Made you feel more of a man, did it?'

I saw his hand clench convulsively round the handle of the knife. Dare I push him any further? Oh, I dared!

'Joy put up more of a fight, didn't she, Dave? Caught you unawares, marked you, but even that wasn't enough was it? So then you came looking for me. Taking my voice changer threw me,' I admitted. 'I thought the thugs had lifted it, that it could only be Angelo threatening me. I didn't realise it was a little runt like you.'

Stupidly, I'd missed the fact that Dave had been inside the flat the morning after Marc's boys had turned it over. I remembered his exaggerated surprise at the damage. He was over-reacting because he'd already seen it . . .

'You think it can't happen to you? Your over-confidence is your weakness,' he hissed. 'I've watched you for a while, Charlie. You think you're equal to a man, but you never will be. Don't forget, I've had a private lesson. I know all about your feeble abilities. You're just like those other bitches, and you'll scream like them when I'm fucking you. You'll scream and you'll beg me to stop, just like the rest.'

'I wouldn't bet on it,' I said tautly.

'No? How about I just let you watch while I do your friend? She's a looker, all right. I bet she'll scream.'

I smothered my rising panic and shoved it viciously back down into the depths of my psyche. 'That's always the way with you, isn't it, Dave? Taking the easy way out,' I taunted. 'What challenge is Clare to you? She can't fight. There's nothing to stop you raping her, but I'm what you've really been after. Why waste time?'

'This—is—my—game!' Dave spelt out, face white with sudden fury. 'We play it *my* way!'

I knew I'd gone too far. I backed down. 'OK, Dave, whatever you say,' I murmured, holding my hands out, palms upwards, supplicant.

I didn't move while he stepped smoothly back into the shadows. He'd dropped all pretence now, and was moving like a pro, sure and economical. How could I have missed it before? I hadn't bothered to look beneath the surface veneer, to see past the mirage he'd created and I was kicking myself for it. How many times had people made that very same mistake with me? So often I'd almost come to rely on it as part of my camouflage.

When Dave reappeared, only moments later, it seemed, he was dragging Clare's weeping figure after him. I was horrified to see he'd bound her slim wrists together with one of the heavy duty plastic zip-ties he used to fasten his disco gear down. I knew that some police forces used them because the breaking point was phenomenal. It offered minimal chance of Clare being strong enough to force her way free.

Never let yourself be immobilised. It was one of the basic rules of self-defence.

When he reached the middle of the dance floor, Dave stopped and let Clare go. Without the support she collapsed, whimpering, cradling her wrists to her chest. The plastic had been snatched tight enough to dig cruelly through the skin. Now they left smears of blood on the front of her pale cream jumper.

Instinctively, my legs took me forwards. Dave stepped fluidly to the side, grabbed a handful of Clare's hair to yank her head up, and slid the blade of the knife under her delicate jaw. She went rigid, eyes wide with terror.

I froze, unable to take my eyes off the knife. Unable to move as Dave increased the pressure a fraction, so the razor-sharp edge just bit through the top layer of her skin and her blood began to weep down over the polished steel. I swallowed, my mouth abruptly arid, tongue swollen like a man too long in the desert.

Dave tutted, grinning. 'Oh no, Charlie, not so fast,' he warned. 'Your reflexes might be passable, but even you couldn't get over here before I'd given your friend a second mouth to feed. And you won't be able to save her afterwards, will you? Remember Joy?'

'So what happens now?' I asked, my voice a whisper.

'You strip,' Dave said. 'Get rid of that leather jacket, for a start.'

I did as I was told without protest, dropping the offending piece of clothing onto the floor next to me. Stared at him. Tried not to concentrate on Clare's shock-glazed face.

'And the boots. Take them off.'

I bent to unfasten them, but as I did so I had a chance sighting of Dave easing the knife slightly away from Clare's throat, changing his grip.

It was a chance, a slim hope, but it was there. There was nothing else I could do but grab it with both hands and pray.

Arms outstretched, yelling, I drove my body upright and onwards, and launched myself at Dave.

Twenty-five

DAVE KNEW ALL the rules of hand-to-hand. I found that out the hard way, but the surprise of my initial charge had the desired effect of making him move back, putting some distance between him and Clare. I hoped she'd take the opportunity to make a run for it, but catching a glimpse of her inert form slumped on the floor, it seemed unlikely.

Dave and I circled each other, half-crouched and intent. He held the knife like an expert, with the pommel of the hilt upwards and the blade slanted down, protecting his forearm. It stopped me being able to get a grip on his wrist, putting a lock onto him that would force him to his knees and disarm him.

I switched tactics. I blanked my mind of the knife, but at the same time was acutely aware of its position and direction. Instead I concentrated on the man behind it. He was focusing all his energies into the weapon he was carrying, relying on it to be both offence and defence. If I could just slip past his guard . . .

I tried it, feinting right, then dodging left and lashing out with my boot to his kneecap. Dave's reactions were faster than I'd hoped. I caught him a mild blow, enough to hurt but not disable, and received a thin slicing cut across my bicep for my trouble.

He only just nicked me. If I'd still been wearing my jacket, I doubt it would have pierced the skin, but the thin material of my T-shirt offered little armour.

I made a big play of clamping my fingers over the wound and grimacing, but in fact the pain was little more than a twinge. Knife wounds are clean and straight, and unless they're deep enough to be serious, they heal quickly. A punch on the nose would probably have done me more damage.

'You think you can defeat me,' Dave crowed now, 'but you've got no chance. You know what? I think I'm going to have you, then have your friend as well. She looks sweet enough to be dessert.'

'You better be into necrophilia then,' I growled, 'because you're going to have to kill me first, you sick bastard.'

Dave straightened for a moment, and the look in his eyes was quite insane. 'Oh by the end of this you're going to be dead, Charlie,' he said, his voice almost distant. 'Even if I don't manage it today, you'll always know that one day I'll catch up with you, and when I do, you'll die.'

He started to laugh, and as he did so, I shifted and sprang.

I managed to dive under his guard, get past the first layer of defence, but he swung his fist round sideways and hit me hard in the face, with the steel pommel of the knife. It landed just under my eye and the noise of my cheekbone fracturing sounded disgustingly loud inside my head.

Streaks of pain shot round my skull like cracks, stars exploded in my vision. That side of my face felt as though it had instantly swelled up to twice its normal size, half closing my eye.

I stumbled and fell onto the flooring. Once I was down Dave kicked me twice in the ribs, vigorously, just for good measure. Then he stood over me and checked my reaction like he was studying a lab rat. My body turned in on itself, fighting the pain. My ribs were on fire, every breath was agony.

'Where are all your supposed self-defence skills now, Charlie?' he demanded. 'You're never going to compare to a man with half your ability, never mind one who's your equal or master. You're nowhere near. Face it, you just don't have what it takes to stop me killing you. I think I'm going to enjoy it.'

'You can't hope to get away with it,' I said, my voice coming in gasps. It was an awful cliché, but right at that moment I didn't care. I just couldn't seem to fill my lungs with enough air. It was like I was drowning.

'Oh can't I?' he said softly. 'And who's going to stop me?'

'I am,' I said fiercely, pivoting onto my side and booting his legs out from under him.

The break-fall he did as he landed was practised and proficient. It took some of the shock out of it, but I'd hit the same leg as before, compounding the effect. It was enough to slow him down and for a moment he was down on his back, arms outstretched.

I scrambled onto my hands and knees and jumped for the knife, clamping onto his wrist, but I'd over-reached, was off-balance a fraction. He stuck his leg up and tipped me over, rolling his bodyweight crushingly on top of my tender ribs, with the knife still clutched firmly in his hand.

I could only watch in horror as it descended, as the blade disappeared from my field of vision and closed in on my throat. I felt the chill steel line of it, resting on my windpipe. The memory of Joy was stark and shocking. I looked up and saw death in his eyes, just as she must have done.

'Well, well, Charlie, looks like I've finally got you where I want you,' he panted, lips back from his teeth in a mirthless smile.

'Go fuck yourself!' I gasped. I desperately twisted my head sideways and back, bucking under him, clawing for his eyes.

He jerked. With a cold sense of finality I felt the sting of the knife going in, but there was little real pain. It was like being prodded with a stick. Just the sickly metallic smell of blood and the warm greasy wetness running down my skin.

Oh sweet Jesus, I thought. He's done it. He's cut my throat . . .

The cold logical side of my brain registered the probable depth of the injury. If I was lucky the main arteries into my brain would have been severed. I would quickly lose consciousness and bleed to death in minutes.

If I was unlucky the bleeding from the lacerated tissues would slowly weaken me. If it clogged my ruptured windpipe, I would quite simply drown in my own blood.

In the knowledge that I was most likely dead already, I went ballistic.

I had nothing to lose.

Ignoring the knife, I reached up, managing to grab hold of his ear, digging my nails in deep to the sensitive skin behind it. I used all my strength, ripping it sideways and down, and bringing his body with it. He tumbled to the side of me, bellowing, and the knife rattled to the floor.

I staggered to my knees. The blood was soaking down into the front of my T-shirt like a grotesque bib. I caught sight of the knife, clutched it, hurled it away into the shadows.

Dave lurched to his feet, his own blood sliding down the side of his face. He put a hand up to it. 'You *bitch*!' he howled. 'Look what you've done to me!'

Look what you've done to me, sunshine, my brain thought whimsically. I tried to get up, to match him. It was like wading through the surf on a loose shingle beach. I blinked to try and clear my vision, but it remained obstinately hazy.

The blast of adrenaline made me feel as though I'd been kicked in the chest. My heart was helpfully hammering my blood out of the hole in my neck as fast is it could muster. I was terrified I was going to pass out, lose by default.

Robbed of his weapon, Dave turned wildly to the stage, just behind us. He snatched up part of a mic stand, a thin metal rod about three feet long, and advanced, snarling.

I knew the end was coming, inevitable. It seemed important suddenly that I be on my feet to meet it. I lumbered upright, shaking uncontrollably, holding on to the edge of the stage to keep my balance as I turned to face him.

With an animal grunt, Dave swung his makeshift club double-handed at shoulder height like an American baseball player going for a home run. He put all his bodyweight behind it, the effort lifting him onto his toes, his face contorted with a burning passion.

I only saw him vaguely. My vision was tunnelling out, the edges blurred with smears of colour like spoilt film. I was going down, and I knew it.

The rod sizzled the air as it sliced through it. I did the best block I could manage considering I was fairly sure the floor was at ninety degrees to its real location. I took the full brunt of the blow diagonally across my left forearm and I swear I heard the radius and ulna let go with a sharp, staccato snap. The X-rays taken later showed a level, clean break line, as though the bones had been cut straight through.

The sound and the feel of the blow vibrated through my whole body. The impact spun me round and left me sprawled face-down over the stage, limp and nauseous.

Dave grabbed hold of my shoulder and yanked me over onto my back. 'Oh no, I want to see the look on your face, bitch,' he said quietly, his voice twisted and breathless.

I looked up numbly, my expression blank. It was his eyes that were the most frightening, wild with the excitement of what he was doing.

I struggled to a sitting position on the edge of the stage, using only my right arm to push myself upright, my broken left dangling uselessly by my side. I slowly pulled my feet back so they were under my knees to give me balance. Dave stood over me, breathing heavily, the rod lowered in front of him now he had me beaten.

Afterwards, I couldn't explain how I came to the decision. I didn't do it consciously, which scares me. The opportunity presented itself and I took it instinctively, that's all. I didn't hesitate for a second, didn't agonise over the moral rights and wrongs, didn't stop to consider the consequences. Dave had dropped his guard and I took advantage of it to hit him as hard as I could.

Yelling from the base of my screaming lungs, I burst suddenly upright, ramming my feet into the floor to lift my body off the stage as my arm straightened.

I hit Dave just under the tip of his nose with the heel of my open hand, but I was aiming for a spot about eight inches further on. It was a deadly punch to throw, and I was fully aware of the fact. I put everything I had left into it, every scrap and ounce of energy. The forfeit for failure was an ugly, prolonged, and vicious death.

It didn't fail. The force and the angle of the blow caused Dave's nasal bone to shatter just at the bridge of his nose, between his eyes, as I'd prayed it would. The sheered end was driven onwards and upwards, slicing deep into the frontal lobe of his brain.

According to the police pathologist, he was dead before his body finished falling.

He splayed backwards, landing hard on the dance floor, head cracking hollowly against the polished wooden surface. His body continued to jitter, trying to evade the creeping paralysis that slowly enveloped it as his heart finally gave up the fight.

It took a while for him to stop twitching. The lifeless fingers relaxed. The mic stand rolled out onto the floor, rocked a little, and lay still. It was only then I could bear to look.

There was a dribble of saliva stringing from the corner of his slack mouth. His eyes were still open in his flattened, distorted face, frozen with the momentary surprise that had been his final expression, right in the instant before I killed him.

For a while I was too exhausted to move. I don't know how long I sat there, shivering. It seemed an age. Finally, I dragged myself shakily to my feet, edging round Dave's sprawled corpse, and swayed drunkenly over to Clare.

At first I thought she was unconscious, but when I touched her shoulder she jolted like I'd stung her. She looked up, her pupils pin-point dots in her unfocused eyes.

'Charlie?' she murmured, her voice thready. 'You're all covered in blood.'

'I know,' I croaked. I reached up tentatively to my throbbing neck, suddenly realising that I could still breathe and talk. My fingers touched ragged ends of flesh and I dropped them away. If it wasn't that bad, I didn't need to worry about it, and if it was, I didn't want to know.

Besides, my left arm and my face were yelling at me through the central nervous system equivalent of a megaphone. I felt light-headed, and freezing cold. I couldn't stop my teeth clattering together like a flamenco dancers' convention. In a detached way I registered that my body was shutting down, going in to shock. I knew if I didn't do something soon, I was in big trouble.

One-handed, I couldn't manage to undo the zip-ties round Clare's wrists and had to give up trying. 'I'll get help,' I muttered.

It seemed a hell of a long way across the dance floor to the bar, where the nearest phone was, but I managed to get there by sheer bloody determination.

I had to dial the number of the police station three times before I got it right, and when they answered I asked them to put me straight through to MacMillan. There was only a short pause before he came on the line.

'Superintendent, it's Charlie Fox,' I said, my voice wavering.

'Charlie! What the hell do you think you're up to?' he demanded.

'Angelo didn't kill Susie and Joy,' I told him, launching straight in without preamble. 'It was Dave Clemmens and I missed it, all along. He raped and killed them, and he's just tried to kill me.'

'Charlie, listen to me. Stay right where you are.' His voice became terse, persuasive. 'I'll send a car to pick you up straight away. I give you my word that you'll be quite safe.'

'OK,' I said meekly, 'I'm at the New Adelphi Club.' He relayed the information to someone alongside him. I suddenly felt unutterably tired. I slid to the floor, cradling the phone with my good hand. When he spoke again I said, 'There's no need to rush—the bastard's dead.'

Epilogue

IN THE END I didn't go to trial for the murder of Dave Clemmens. They didn't even charge me with his manslaughter, which was a bit of a surprise really, considering the technique I'd used. I suppose if I'd waited until later and stabbed him to death with a pair of pinking shears, they would have sent me down for life.

Ironically perhaps, the only charges I did face were for assaulting a police officer. I think WPC Wilks's ego had been more bruised than her jaw. They let me off with a caution, though. MacMillan delivered my stern lecture himself, with only the barest hint of a smile.

The thing I regret most about this whole business is the effect it's had on my friends. Physically, Clare emerged from the encounter relatively unscathed, but the road back from the mental trauma she'd suffered looked like being a long and tortuous one.

Any attempts I made to offer comfort seemed to make things worse. Eventually I just had to leave her be and hope that, when she'd recovered enough to view things with a clearer perspective, she didn't hold me entirely responsible for what had happened.

It's bad enough that I blame myself.

Ailsa sent me a short little note telling me she didn't feel it was appropriate for me to continue my classes at the Lodge. She was divorcing Tris on the grounds of gross mental cruelty and, with the facts as they were, I doubted there was a judge this side of senility who wouldn't come down heavily in her favour. She had already announced her intention of selling the house to a local property developer and moving the refuge to somewhere on the north Wales coast.

I had a feeling Tris would mourn the loss of his family home more than the disintegration of his marriage, but I don't know for sure how he took the news. He never contacted me again.

The police picked up Angelo a couple of days after the raid on the New Adelphi. He'd gone to ground with an old mate of his from Liverpool. I couldn't ignore the possibility that the man was probably one of the pair who'd ransacked my flat, but there wasn't the evidence to pursue it. There was enough forensic to bind Angelo to Terry's killing, though, and that was the main thing.

When it came to Dave, after reviewing all the facts, the powers that be decided my claim of self-defence was justified. They judged that I didn't have a case to answer, and I walked away free. The police were able to lay the three recent attacks firmly at Dave's feet without question. It looked like I'd done everyone a favour.

But that doesn't make it any easier to forget.

The doctors at the hospital told me I'd been lucky, that wrenching my head away had caused the knife blade to slice into the side of my neck rather than across my throat, missing by fractions the trachea and vital arteries, which had slid back behind my neck muscles. They stitched me up again and set and plastered my arm. The ribs and the cheekbone, so they told me, were best left to sort themselves out, given time.

They sent me to see a community psychiatric nurse for counselling about coming to terms with what I'd done, but I have a feeling the bones will be mended long before my conscience.

Like I said, the worst part is knowing that, if I was ever in the same situation, I'd do exactly the same thing again. No doubt about it.

It doesn't sit well with me, that—the realisation that I have not only the knowledge, but the instinct to kill. It sets you apart from the other people you pass in the street, makes you feel alone, less human than they are.

I proved Dave wrong, though. Given a straight fight between a man and a woman, neither with any particular advantage in skill over the other, it isn't a foregone conclusion that the man will always win. I suppose then, right at the end, I could have said to him, 'I told you so.'

Just as long as I'd said it fast enough.

Afterword
by Zoë Sharp

When David Thompson, my publisher at Busted Flush Press, asked me to write an afterword for the new, American edition of *Killer Instinct*, it made me think afresh about this, the very first Charlie Fox book, and why I chose to join her story at this point.

This is not, after all, the beginning of Charlie's journey, but I look back on it as the major turning point in her life. The events covered during the course of the book change her forever from having been a victim, to not only fighting back on her own behalf, but as a protector for others. It sets her out, whether she is aware of it at the time, on the path she will subsequently follow into the world of close protection.

Ironically enough, it was Charlie's first official job as a bodyguard, in the events of book four in the series, *First Drop*, that brought her to U.S. shores for the first time in more ways than one. Setting *First Drop* in Daytona Beach, Florida over the Spring Break weekend caught the eye of a New York editor, who decided that's where the story should start for American readers, and the title mistakenly gave the impression there was no history to Charlie before then.

But there is, and *Killer Instinct* is the first installment.

I wrote this story at a time when I had just been the target of a number of death-threat letters through my work, and I probably identified with Charlie more closely during the course of this book than any other. Of course, those letters never escalated to anything like the level of threat that my protagonist faces here, but it planted the germ of the idea. And it did inspire me to go out and learn a lot of self-defense techniques, which have stood me in very good stead ever since.

I chose the northern English city of Lancaster for the setting because it was not only an area I knew well, but because I was intrigued by the dual-edged personality of the place. By day it's an attractive university town, filled with history and the kind of elegant Georgian architecture that has seen it called the Bath of the North.

But by night the number of pubs and clubs give the city an altogether darker feel. At one point it had one of the highest violent-crime rates per head of population in the country. And although one or two people asked if the events described in the book could really happen in a place like Lancaster, my answer is . . . they did, more or less.

In one of those weird twists of fate, shortly after *Killer Instinct* was published, one of the local nightclubs was shut down after a drug-dealing scandal, in which the owner and half the door staff were allegedly involved. (And if you're cheating, and reading this afterword before you've read the book itself, you better just forget that bit!)

So, how does it feel to finally have the beginning of Charlie's story out there again? Bloody marvelous, if you must know . . .

About the author

Zoë Sharp spent most of her formative years living on a catamaran on the northwest coast of England. She opted out of mainstream education at the age of twelve and became a freelance photo-journalist in 1988. She turned to crime writing after receiving death-threat letters in the course of her work, and this led to the creation of her no-nonsense ex-Special Forces heroine, Charlotte 'Charlie' Fox. She is now the author of eight Charlie Fox novels, including *First Drop*, which was nominated for the 2005 Barry Award for Best British Crime Novel, and *Fourth Day*, (due out in 2010). Sharp's heroine was featured in a story in Busted Flush Press's *A Hell of a Woman*, "Served Cold," which was nominated for the 2009 Crime Writers' Association Short Story Dagger. Sharp now lives on the edge of the English Lake District, where she and her husband, Andy, a non-fiction writer, have recently self-built their own house. Visit her online at www.zoesharp.com.

Look for Charlie Fox again in *Riot Act*.
Here's an excerpt . . .

PHONE CALLS THAT come out of nowhere, in the middle of the night, rarely herald good news as far as I'm concerned. This one arrived somewhere between midnight and one a.m. It yanked me forcibly out of the warm leisures of sleep, and proved no exception to the rule.

Right from the outset, in that fraction between dreaming and waking, I was overwhelmed by an instinctive dread.

By the second ring, I'd jerked upright in bed, fumbling for the bedside light and swinging my legs out from under the blankets before I'd really kicked my brain into gear.

It took a moment or two to work out that I wasn't safe in my own bed. Instead, I recognised a small, oppressively-wallpapered room, made smaller still by the pair of dark oak wardrobes that loomed over me from both sides.

Pauline's place.

I'd been house-sitting for Pauline Jamieson for three weeks at that point. Ever since she'd flown to Canada to visit her son. Waking up in her bed still brought a feeling of disorientation.

The phone noise ran on, shrill and imperious. I groped for the receiver and tried to rub the grittiness out of my eyes.

'Yeah, hello?' It was a relief to stop the damned phone ringing at last, but that feeling didn't hold.

'Oh, Charlie, please come quickly, and bring the dog!' A woman's voice, scratchy with alarm and close to weeping. 'They are in the garden and Fariman has gone out after them. I am afraid they will kill him!'

The last vestiges of sleep evaporated. 'Shahida?' I said, suddenly recognising one of Pauline's neighbours. One of *my* neighbours for the moment. 'Calm down. Now tell me who? Who has Fariman gone after in the garden?'

'The thieves!' she cried, as though it was obvious, the pitch of her voice rising like a banshee spirit. 'They are trying to steal his equipment. Please, come now.'

I started to ask if she'd called the police, but the phone was already dead in my hand.

With a muttered curse, I dialled the local cop shop myself, giving them the bare bones and demanding that they come at once. While I was speaking, I clambered into my clothes. By the time I hit the narrow staircase I was dressed and fully alert.

Well, almost alert. In the darkened hallway I nearly went sprawling over Pauline's Rhodesian Ridgeback, Friday. The dog had been sleeping with his back against the bottom riser, and he bounced up with a startled yelp.

I grabbed his lead from the hall table and snapped it onto the thick leather collar. Just for a second I hesitated over the wisdom of taking him with me, then dismissed my doubts. He might be a handful, but there were times when a big dog like Friday comes in very useful.

Now, he barely gave me time to lock the front door before he was towing me along the short driveway to the road. Fariman and Shahida's house was on the other side of Kirby Street from Pauline's, and further down the row of mainly dilapidated semis. I headed quickly in that direction.

I'd only met the elderly couple a few times, but I knew Fariman had been a cabinetmaker. Since he'd retired recently he'd kitted out the shed in his back garden with enough tools to keep his hand in. Trouble was, he'd turned it into your average burglar's car boot sale gold mine. By the sound of it, it hadn't taken them long to cotton on to the fact.

I was surprised now to see one or two other figures emerging from doorways, pulling on coats over their pyjamas. Some carried torches.

It startled me, the reaction. Lavender Gardens was a notoriously crime-ridden estate and I would have expected a far more apathetic response to any cry for help. Maybe there was hope for the area after all.

My sense of complacency lasted until I reached the far crumbling kerb and we threaded our way through the line of close-packed empty vehicles.

Friday lurched to a halt so abruptly that I ran into his rump and nearly stumbled. It only took a second before I realised the reason for his sudden check. For me to register a bulky figure rising behind a parked van.

Shock made me gasp, sent me reeling backwards. Fear convulsed my hands, so that I tightened my grip on Friday's lead.

A harsh laugh greeted my recoil, as though that was the effect its owner always hoped his appearance would have, and had yet to be disappointed. 'A tad late to be walking the dog, isn't it, Fox?'

The man swaggered forwards into the glow of a streetlight, sending a spent cigarette butt sizzling carelessly into the gloom. Three other shadows solidified behind him, keeping station. All of them were dressed in military surplus urban cam fatigues, and carrying an assortment of makeshift weaponry that would have been laughable if it hadn't been so deadly serious.

Friday settled for giving out a low growl. It was difficult to tell if his hackles were up, because Ridgebacks have a line of opposite-growing hair down their spines anyway, but the sight and sound of him was enough to stop the men in their tracks.

I unwound slowly, trying to steady my heartbeat. 'What are you doing here, Langford?' I asked sharply. 'Bit outside your territory, isn't it?'

With one eye on the dog, he treated me to a humourless smile, glancing round at the men behind him for back-up. 'We go where we're needed,' he said piously.

'Well, you're not needed here.'

'No?'

'No,' I snapped. 'These people have got enough problems with law and order without your bunch of bloody vigilantes joining in. Get back to Copthorne. There's plenty for you to do over there.'

'Oh, don't you worry,' he said, voice sly, 'we've got Copthorne all sewn up.'

'Well, that'll be a first,' I threw back at him, starting forwards again. The one nearest to Friday moved back quickly, but the other two made sure I had to shift course to step round them. The cheap little power play brought grins to their faces.

Langford, self-styled leader of the local vigilante group, shared the same basic mental genotype with playground bullies and third world secret policemen. I'd recognised it the first time I'd met him and his cronies, and I'd gone out of my way to avoid contact ever since.

Commotion broke out further up the street. I turned and started to run again, Friday loping alongside me, ignoring the heavy footsteps pounding along behind.

Shahida was standing in her nightdress in the middle of her driveway, wailing. She had nothing on her feet, and her normally neatly-plaited greying hair was a wild halo around her head.

Several of her neighbours clustered round, trying to soothe her. Their efforts only served to enrage her further. 'Of course everything is not *all right!*' she shrieked at them, half demented.

I skidded to a halt and pushed my way through. 'Shahida,' I said urgently. 'Where are they?'

'In the garden.' She waved towards a gate that led round to the side of the house. Then, having passed on the baton of responsibility, her face crumpled into tears. 'Please, Charlie, don't let him do anything stupid.'

Langford's men shoved past me, making it to the gloomy back garden first. Where the lawn had once been was now a square of gravel and artistically-placed rocks, leading down to the box hedge at the bottom.

The shed where Fariman kept his tools was a squat wooden building that stood over by the hedge on a raft of concrete slabs. It was a dingy corner, despite the orange glare of streetlights reflected by the low cloud overhead, and the light spilling out from the open kitchen doorway.

Even so, I could see that the lock that had once secured the shed had been ripped out, leaving a jagged scar, pale against the dark wood that surrounded it. It should have left the shed totally exposed, but the door was firmly closed, all the same.

Shahida's husband was thrusting his not inconsiderable bodyweight against the timber frame to wedge it shut as though his life depended on it. His bare feet were digging in to the edge of the gravel to give him extra purchase. Fariman wasn't a tall man, but what he lacked in height, he made up for in girth.

He looked up, proud and sweating, as the group of us burst into view round the corner of the house.

'I have them! I have them!' he shouted.

Something hit the inside of the door with tremendous force. It bucked outwards, opening by maybe three or four inches, before

Fariman's sheer bulk slammed it shut again. His thick, black-framed glasses bounced down his nose, and almost fell.

The fear leapt in my throat. 'Fariman, for God's sake come away from there,' I called. 'They can't take anything now. Let them go.'

Langford treated me to a look of utter disgust and strode forwards. On the way past, he swung a provocative fist at Friday's head.

The dog made a solid attempt at dislocating my shoulder as he leapt for the bait and the lead brought him up short. Goaded, he let out half a dozen rapid, raucous barks before I could quieten him. The deep-chested sound of a big dog with its blood up, raising the stakes for whoever was sweating inside the shed.

Langford flashed me an evilly triumphant grin. 'Keep the little bastards pinned down,' he bellowed, breaking into a run. 'We'll take care of them. Come on lads!'

The trapped thieves must have heard Langford's voice, and if they didn't know the man himself, they could recognise the violent intent. Behind the small barred shed window, I could see movement against torchlight. It grew more frantic, and the hammering on the door increased in ferocity.

'Don't worry, Charlie,' Fariman cried, the old man's voice squeaky with excitement. 'I have them. I ha–'

There was another assault on the shed door. This time, though, it wasn't the dull thud of a shoulder or boot hitting the inside of the panel. It was the ominous crack of metal slicing straight through the flimsy softwood.

Fariman's body seemed to give a giant juddering twitch. His eyes grew bulbous behind the lenses of his glasses, and he looked down towards his torso with a breathless giggle. Then his legs folded under him and he slowly toppled sideways onto the gravel.

Behind him, sticking out a full six inches through the shed door he'd been leaning into so heavily, were the four vicious stiletto prongs of a garden fork. Where the exposed steel should have glinted brightly under the glare of the lights, instead it gleamed dark with blood.

For a moment, the wicked tines paused there, then were withdrawn with a sharp tug, like a stiffly re-setting trap. Even Langford's brigade hesitated at the sight. The blood lust that had lit their initial charge faltering in the face of an enemy that hit back.

Before they had time to assimilate this new threat, the shed door was kicked open. Three figures emerged, furtive, moving fast. They were dressed in loose dark clothes, with woolly hats pulled down hard and scarves tied over the lower half of their faces like cattle rustlers from the Old West. Despite the disguises, it was clear at once that they were just boys.

Langford and his men had a renewed spasm of bravery. Then they wavered for a second time, coming to a full stop halfway across the back garden. When I realised what the boys were holding, I understood the vigilantes' sudden reluctance to continue the attack.

Fariman's shed was crammed with odds and ends, like any other. Old pop bottles that he'd never quite got round to returning; a bag of rags for cleaning brushes and mopping up; and plastic cans of stale fuel for some long-discarded petrol-driven mower.

All the ingredients, in fact, for the perfect Molotov cocktail.

The leader of the boys edged forwards. He was holding a disposable cigarette lighter ready under the wick. His hand shook perilously.

'Get back or I'll do it!' he screamed, voice muffled by the scarf. He sounded as though he was about to burst into tears. 'All of you, get right back!'

'Give it up,' Langford warned, teeth bared. 'This doesn't have to happen.' He held up both hands as though to placate, but he didn't retreat as ordered, wouldn't concede ground.

The two sides faced off, tension crackling between them like an overhead power line in the rain. They yelled the same words at each other, over and over, the pitch gradually rising to a frenzied level.

Behind the boys, close up to the shed doorway, Fariman's body lay still and bleeding on the ground.

Finally, Langford broke the cycle. 'Give it up,' he snarled, 'or I'll send the dog in.'

I knew I should have left Friday at home.

Before I could react to contradict this outrageous bluff, Shahida and a group of her neighbours appeared *en masse* round the corner of the house. They had the air of a mob, racking the boys' nerves another notch towards breaking point.

Then Shahida caught sight of Fariman's inert body and she started screaming. It was the kind of scream that nightmares are made of. A full-blooded howling roar with the sort of breath-control an opera singer would have killed for. It didn't do me much good, so it must have struck utter terror into her husband's attackers.

And, having accomplished that, Shahida broke free of her supporters, and bolted across the garden to avenge him.

'Shahida, no!' I'd failed Fariman, I couldn't let her down as well.

As she rushed past me I let go of Friday's straining leash and grabbed hold of her with both hands. Such was her momentum that she swung me round before I could stop her. She struggled briefly, then collapsed in my arms, weeping.

Suddenly unrestricted, Friday leapt forwards, eager to be in the thick of it. He bounded through the ranks of Langford's men and into plain view on the gravel, moving at speed. With the idea of an attack from the dog firmly planted in his mind, the boy with the cigarette lighter must have thought he could already feel the jaws around his throat.

He panicked.

The tiny flame expanded at an exponential rate as it raced up the rag wick towards the neck of the bottle. He threw the Molotov in a raging arc across the garden, onto the stony ground. The glass shattered on impact, and sent an explosive flare of burning petrol reaching for the night sky with a whoosh like a fast-approaching subway train.

Langford and his men ducked back, cursing. I dragged Shahida's incoherent form to safety, yelling for Friday as I did so.

He appeared almost at once through the smoke and confusion, ears and tail tucked down, looking sheepish.

Voices were shouting all around us. Langford's crew had skirted the flames and redoubled their efforts to get to the boys. Christ, would they never give up?

Another Molotov was lit, but it was thrown in the other direction. Away from the vigilantes.

And into the shed.

This time, there was more than the contents of the bottle to fuel the fire. With bitumen sheeting on the roof, and years of creosote on the walls, they couldn't have asked for a more promising point of ignition.

The flames caught immediately, sparkling behind the window, washing at the doorway. The speed with which they took hold, and the heat they generated, was astounding.

Fariman!

'Get the fire brigade,' I yelled, jerking one of the neighbours out of their stupor. 'And an ambulance.' Where the hell were the police when you needed them?

I shouted to the dog to stay with Shahida, but didn't wait around to find out if he obeyed me. I ran forwards, shielding my eyes with my hand against the intensity of the fire. The old man was still lying where he'd fallen by the shed door. The flames were already licking at the framework nearest to him. I grabbed hold of a handful of his paisley dressing gown and heaved.

For all the difference it made, I might as well have been trying to roll a whale back into the sea.

I shouted for help, but nobody heard in the brawl that was fast developing all around me. The smoke hit in gusts, roasting my lungs, making my eyes stream. I tugged at Fariman's stocky shoulders again, with little result.

In the mêlée, somebody tripped over my legs and went head-first onto the gravel, landing heavily. I lunged for the back of their jacket, keeping them on the ground.

'Wait,' I said sharply as they began to struggle. 'Help me get him out of here.'

The boy stared back at me with wide, terrified eyes over the scarf that had slipped down to his chin. He tried again to rise, but desperation lent me an iron grip.

Something exploded inside the shed, and shards of glass came bursting out of the doorway. I spun my head away, but still I kept hold of the boy. I turned back to him.

'If you don't help me, he'll burn to death,' I said, going for the emotional jugular. 'Is that what you want?'

There was a moment's hesitation, then he shook his head. Taking a leap of faith, I let go of his jacket and fisted my hands into Fariman's dressing gown again. To my utter relief, the boy did the same at the other shoulder.

He was little more than a kid, but between us, a few feet at a time, we managed to drag the old man clear.

We got him onto the crazy paving by the back door of the house. It wasn't as far away from the inferno as I would have liked, but it was better than nothing. The effort exhausted the pair of us.

I searched for the pulse at the base of Fariman's neck. It throbbed erratically under my fingers. I heaved him over onto his stomach and pulled up the dressing gown. Underneath, he wore pale blue pyjamas. The back of the jacket was now covered with blood, which was pumping jerkily out of the row of small holes in the cloth.

I glanced up at the boy, found him transfixed.

'Give me your scarf.' My words twitched him out of his trance. For a moment he looked ready to argue, then he unwound the scarf from his neck and handed it over without a word.

I balled the thin material and padded it against the back of Fariman's ribcage. 'Hold it there,' I ordered. When he didn't move I grabbed one of his hands and forced it to the substitute dressing.

The boy tried to pull back, didn't want to touch the old man. *If you didn't want his blood on your hands, sonny, you should have thought of that earlier.* With my forefinger and thumb I circled his skinny wrist, and dug cruelly deep into the pressure points on the inside of his arm, ignoring his yelp of pain. 'Press hard until I tell you to let go.' My voice was cold.

He did as he was ordered.

I checked down Fariman's body. When I got to his legs I found the skin on one shin bubbled and blistered where it had been against the burning shed door. It looked evil. I carefully peeled the charred pieces of his clothing away from the worst of it, and left it well alone.

Burns were nasty, but unless they were serious they were low on the priority list when it came to first aid. Besides, without even a basic field medical kit, there was little else I could do.

'Where the hell's that ambulance?' I growled.

Shahida reappeared at that point, with Friday trotting anxiously by her side. I braced myself for another bout of hysterics, but she seemed to have run out of steam. She slumped by her husband's side and clutched at his limp hand, with silent tears running down her face.

I put my hand on her shoulder and shot a hard glance to the boy, but he wouldn't meet my eyes.

The neighbours had swelled in number and organised themselves with buckets of water and a hosepipe. Where the first petrol bomb had landed there was now a soggy, blackened patch on the sandy-coloured stones.

Then the whole of the roof of the shed went up. A rejuvenated blast of flame kept the people back to a respectful distance. Burning embers came drifting down on the still night air like glitter, dying as they fell.

'Well, we lost the little bastards.' Langford's voice was thick with anger as he came stamping up. He lit a cigarette, cupping his hands round the match and dropping it on the paving. His cold gaze lingered briefly on Shahida, but he made no moves to try and help. The boy kept his head down.

The first wail of sirens started up in the distance. We all paused, trying to work out if the sound was growing louder.

When it became clear that it was, the boy's nerve finally broke. He jumped to his feet, abandoning his nursing duties, and ran like a rabbit. Langford suddenly realised that he'd had his prey right under his nose. He gave a bellow of outrage and took off after him.

The kid might have been built for lightness and speed, but gravel is murder to sprint on, and he didn't get the opportunity to open out much of a lead. Before they hit the hedge at the bottom of the garden, Langford had brought him down.

And once the boy was on the ground, the vigilante waded in with his feet and his fists. His methods were unrefined, but brutally effective, for all that.

I was up and running before I'd worked out quite what I intended to do. I only knew I had to stop Langford before he killed the kid. No matter what he'd done.

'Langford, for God's sake leave him alone,' I said. 'Let the police deal with him.'

Langford whirled round. In the light from the blazing shed, his eyes seemed to flash with excitement. This was what took him and his men out patrolling the streets night after night. Not some altruistic vision. It all came down to the age-old thrill of the chase, the heat of the kill.

'Get lost, Fox,' he snarled. 'I'm sick to death of all this passive resistance crap. Take a look around you. It doesn't work.' He held up a bloodied fist. 'This is all these bastards understand.'

'Leave him,' I said again, my voice quiet and flat.

He laughed derisively. 'Or what?' he said, turning his back on me. The boy had half-risen in the lull, and Langford punched him viciously in the ribs, watched with grim delight as he dropped again.

Though I tried to hold it back, I felt my temper rise up at me like a slap in the face. My eyes locked on to a target. I didn't need to concentrate on the mechanics. All the right moves unfurled automatically inside my head.

'Langford!' I called sharply.

And as he twisted to face me again, I hit him.

I'd like to think it was simply a clinically positioned and delivered blow, carefully weighted to disable, calculated to take him quickly and cleanly out of the fight.

The reality was dirtier than that. I hit him in a flash of pure anger, harder and faster than was strictly necessary, not caring for the consequences. It was stupid, and it could have been deadly.

For a moment I thought he was going to keep coming, then he swayed, and I realised that his legs had gone. He just didn't know it yet.

There was a mildly puzzled expression on his face as he struggled to focus on me. Then his knees gave out, his eyes rolled back, and he flopped gracelessly backwards onto the stony ground.

I started forwards on a reflex, but he didn't move. I stood there for a moment or two, breathing hard, my fists still clenched ready for a second blow I never had to launch. Then I slumped, defeated by my own anger. It slipped away quietly, leaving me with a fading madness, and a roaring in my ears.

I turned slowly, and found what seemed to be half the population of Kirby Street standing and watching me in shocked and silent condemnation.

Oh God, I thought, *not again . . .*

Somewhere beyond them, the first of the night's procession of police cars braked to a fast halt in the road outside.

Read more in Riot Act, available soon from Busted Flush Press!

Available in the U.S. for the first time, the early Charlie Fox thrillers by Zoë Sharp!

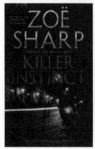   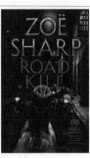

Killer Instinct (978-1-935415-13-8 / $15)
Riot Act (978-1-935415-15-2 / $15) *June 2010*
Hard Knocks (978-1-935415-10-7 / $15) *September 2010*
Road Kill (978-1-935415-41-1/ $15) *February 2011*

"Male and female crime fiction readers alike will find Sharp's writing style addictively readable—one of the very best crime fiction sagas out there."—Paul Goat Allen, *Chicago Tribune*

**www.bustedflushpress.com
bustedflushpress.blogspot.com
And look for us on Facebook & Twitter!**